Colorado Hope

THE FRONT RANGE SERIES, BOOK TWO

BY CHARLENE WHITMAN

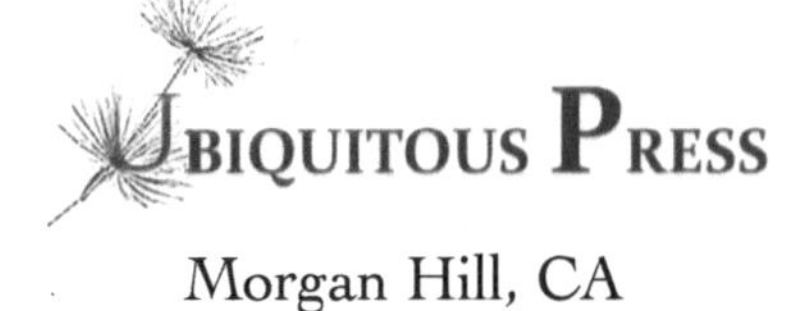

Morgan Hill, CA

by Charlene Whitman

The characters and events portrayed in this book, for the most part, are fictitious, although the author has tried to keep as historically accurate as possible. Some license was taken with names and settings of actual people and places but with honest intent. Any errors in this regard remain the fault of the author.

ISBN-13: 9780991389469
ISBN-10: 0991389468
LCCN: 2014957793

Cover and Interior designed by Ellie Searl, Publishista®

Morgan Hill, CA

Praise for *COLORADO PROMISE*

"A fresh new voice in Historical Romance, Charlene Whitman captured me from the beginning with characters I won't soon forget, a sizzling-sweet romance, a love triangle, spiteful villains, heart-throbbing heroes, and a plot full of intrigue that kept me guessing. Ms. Whitman's magnificent research transported me to the Colorado plains and left me longing to join the characters amidst the wildflower-dotted fields, rushing rivers, and panoramic Rocky Mountains. Fans of Historical Western Romance will not soon forget *Colorado Promise.*"

—MaryLu Tyndall, best-selling romance author

"An adequate writer of historical fiction will include minor bits and pieces about the setting of their story. A good writer will do a bit of research to make sure there are historical facts included in the pages of their novel. A superb writer will create characters that could have actually lived during the time in which the story takes place and allows them to act as people in that time period would have really acted. Charlene Whitman is a superb writer."

—Examiner.com

"Ms. Whitman's voice is honest and true to the times. Not only in the way her characters spoke but also in the narrative. I lost sleep because I wanted to know what happened next. It's one of those stories you become invested in the characters. Five stars and 3 'YEEHAWs' to Charlene Whitman and *Colorado Promise*!"

—author Su Barton

"The author has done a great job of telling the story about early Colorado and the settlers transplanted from the East. She drew the growing love between Emma and Lucas perfectly. I give it five stars."

—author Sheila Huntington

Chapter 1

May 16, 1875

A FIERCE WIND WHIPPED GRACE Ann Cunningham's hair, yanking at the long strands and pulling them free from their pins. She squinted through the haze of the blustery day and stroked her bulging belly, trying to comfort her baby, who seemed just as agitated by the sudden storm. Her back ached from sitting on the hard buckboard bench all these miles—much less comfortable than the plush sleeper car they'd enjoyed last week on the train from Illinois to Cheyenne.

She frowned at the dark roiling clouds that had moved in and quickly blotted out the sun. What had been a pleasant uneventful morning was now turning into an ominous and unsettling afternoon on the open prairie.

Grace sucked in a breath as the baby again kicked her ribs in protest. Her sweet husband's sun-browned face tightened in concern as he caught her gesture. He pulled on the reins of the two draft horses—sturdy ones they'd bought yesterday in Cheyenne. Surefooted, the seller had told them. And Monty knew his horses, so she trusted his purchase and assurance that they'd haul them without incident to Fort Collins. But looking at her husband's face now, seeing the subtle telltale signs indicating that he hadn't expected this squall nor felt at ease about it, gave her pause. And her normally talkative husband had been too quiet this last hour, eyeing the sky and listening to the roar of the nearby river, as if hearing their complaints and trying to suss out nature's intentions.

"The baby all right, darlin'?" He scooted over on the buckboard seat to look her over, then took her hands in his.

Warmth from his gentle grip comforted her, but not as much as the love streaming from his adoring gaze.

"I think so," she told him, then smiled as he laid his hand firmly on her belly.

Grace thanked the Lord in a silent prayer for this wonderful man who'd married her in a simple ceremony last September. All those years she'd lived with her doting aunt Eloisa in the boardinghouse back in Bloomington, she never imagined she'd be blessed with such happiness. When Montgomery Cunningham had first stepped into the parlor to take a room before starting college at Wesleyan University, she'd been a shy, giggling girl of ten. Neither of them foresaw the love that would spark six years later when he showed up again unexpectedly, about to head west to explore and survey lands unknown.

Monty closed his eyes, his hand still on the baby in her womb. She imagined him communing with their baby, speaking to it the way he spoke to rivers, to trees, to the land he traversed by boat and on horseback and on foot. Something had happened to him when he returned from the Hayden Yellowstone Expedition. He had changed from boy to man, yes—but it was more than that. He had fallen in love with the West, and with rivers in particular. Although he'd studied geology in college with John Powell, water captured his heart, and he sought out trips that had him navigating whitewater. Nothing made his eyes sparkle more than talking about the way water moved and sang as it cascaded and carved the face of mountains and spilled into waiting valleys. Well, except the way he looked at her.

Monty may have loved rivers, but Grace knew he loved her more. So much more, for he gladly gave up his exploring to settle down and marry and start a family. Although, Grace thought moving to the new town of Fort Collins, Colorado, was adventure enough. She hoped he'd come to see it that way as well and not be beset by a restless stirring to venture back out into the wild.

The West! Quite the change from her simple, comfortable life in Bloomington—if the lawless and untamed town of Cheyenne was any indication. She shuddered thinking of the seedy saloons and lecherous unwashed men they'd encountered as they sought purchase of their horses and wagon yesterday. If Monty hadn't assured her she'd live in the manner she'd been accustomed to—with the same stars twinkling overhead—she would never have considered moving west. Not that she fancied some ostentatious lifestyle; she'd lived in a modest home under her aunt's care. But she desired familiarity and the comfort of belonging to a community.

When he opened his eyes, she dared asked, "How much further?" They'd been traveling since dawn, making good time despite the roughness of the road and the boggy sections dotted with patches of melting snow. They'd been assured in Cheyenne that the fifty-mile road south through Colorado Territory was a bit rough but well traveled—but then, they'd also been given predictions of clear skies and gentle breezes the whole way to Fort Collins.

"Well," he said thoughtfully, glancing around as the unseasonably warm wind increased to a dull roar. "Not much further. The river is coming closer to the road now, and according to the map, that large bend in the road back there comes right before the northern ten-mile marker."

A finger of wind lifted the brim of his felt hat, showing eyes as stormy as the day, his one hazel eye catching a glint as a fork of lightning snapped out of the brooding clouds overhead. A second later the ground rattled with thunder.

Grace cried out as the horses reared and whinnied—then thumped down hard on hooves that pounded the ground in agitation.

Monty jumped down from the buckboard and calmed them, speaking words that the wind snatched from his mouth as he held fast the hat on his head. He took the closest horse's leather neck strap in hand and, cooing comforting sounds, got the frightened beast to take a step, then another. He shot Grace a look that set her heart racing. She could tell he was afraid, and that wasn't a look she'd often seen on Monty's face. He seemed to be searching for some shelter, but they were on wide-open land, with no trees in sight.

"We'd best turn back," he yelled to her over the snarling storm, leaning close to make sure she heard him. Dirt and debris swirled in the air around their heads, and Grace squinted as it pelted her cheeks. "Maybe head to that ranch we passed a couple o' hours ago."

Grace wrapped her shawl tighter around her body as the balmy air suddenly turned chilly and icy fingers of wind tickled her neck. Monty grumbled something under his breath as fat raindrops assaulted them.

Monty rushed back to the wagon and pulled out a canvas tarp from underneath their boxes and crates filled with their possessions.

Another flash of lightning streaked the angry sky, followed by an even louder thwack of thunder that sounded as if it had rent the earth.

Grace blurted out a cry and buried her face in her hands as she listened to Monty wrestle with the tarp. Presently, she felt it fling over her head, and the rain pelted the thick cloth sheltering her in dull thuds. Monty slipped in beside her and huffed, his body heat instantly warming the space.

He turned to her, and in the stuffy enclosure that ensconced them both, he planted a gentle kiss on her lips, then pulled her closer and deepened the kiss, as if to drink in every bit of her. As if the rain and the river were not moisture enough for his soul. Her heart thumped hard against his chest and the baby kicked again, making him chuckle as he reluctantly ended their intimate moment.

"He's a strong one," Monty said, his face gleaming. "And already making sure he's not left out of the fun."

"He?" Grace teased. For some reason Monty was sure she was carrying a son. But she knew he would just as gladly welcome a girl into his arms. He grinned and gave her a look that made her pulse race. That lopsided smile on his strong, square jaw never failed to stir her passion.

He lowered his voice and whispered hot words in her ears. "I'm looking forward to a bath and then a sweet night in your arms in a clean, warm bed—with a soft feather-tick mattress." He rubbed her bulging belly mindlessly as he peeked out at the storm that now howled like a sick wolf. Grace ran a hand through his hair as thick and brown as molasses, which inclined to curl around his ears.

"Maybe we should just wait a bit?" she said, thinking how Colorado weather was known to change suddenly. Just as this squall had come upon them unawares, perhaps it would clear up just as quickly. Or so she hoped.

He chewed on that idea a moment, then shook his head. "We're too exposed out here. The storm has stalled overhead, which means we're a likely target for lightning to strike. We need to get moving, get somewhere safe . . ." He blew out a frustrated breath as rain seeped in under the tarp and soaked his hair. His eyes grew stormier with the weather, and water dribbled down his rough-shaved cheeks and under his shirt collar. Grace felt the weight of her soggy skirt hem pulling on her, and noticed her stockings were wet and leaking water into her shoes. Her teeth started to chatter.

"It's bad and getting worse," Monty mumbled as the horses began dancing in place, just as eager to get out of the rain and the open prairie, as if they sensed danger coming their way. He jiggled the reins and yelled out, "Haw!" to get the animals moving. With a lurch they trotted forward, throwing their heads in protest.

Grace now heard the river as the wind momentarily calmed. It was close, and raging. They'd been skirting the Cache la Poudre for miles now, admiring the wild waters bouncing over boulders in the narrow sluices carved in the canyon. Most of what they'd glimpsed showed a swollen wide river moving at a fast clip, but as they neared Fort Collins, the banks had risen more steeply, with evergreens growing clear to the water's edge, and steep cliffs sweeping up into canyon walls that thundered with the echo of whitewater. Grace wondered if Monty would feel safer and more in control right now if he were at the bow of a canoe instead of holding the reins of two skittish horses he'd barely made the acquaintance of.

"The bridge can't be that far off," Monty said, pulling her attention back to the dirt road that was starting to resemble a pond before them. Grace shuddered. "Maybe we should try to cross, and seek shelter on the other side." His voice sounded unsure, which unsettled Grace even more.

"Can you make out the road?" What she really wondered was if the horses would mire in all the mud. They were less upset though, now that Monty had them moving again. Moving was better than sitting still, out in the open, she reasoned. Although, from what she could make out up ahead through the sheets of rain obscuring the horizon, there was nothing but more open, flat land. She hadn't been paying attention these last few miles. She'd been nodding off in the cool spring afternoon, the weak sun hardly warming her shoulders. How long would it take them to get to the bridge? Would it be safe to cross? A jolt of fear coursed up her back, and her baby kicked hard.

"Shh, little one," she said, more to herself than to her baby, "it'll be all right; just sleep . . ."

She fingered the silver chain around her neck and found the small round pendant, then gripped it tightly in her fist. Monty had given this trinket to her when he came back from his exploration of Yellowstone. An Indian guide had gifted it to him, after he helped rescue the man who had toppled overboard in some strong rapids. Etched into the flat silver disk was an eight-pointed star—an Indian symbol of hope, he was told.

She choked back tears as she huddled close to Monty, shivering and wet, listening to the rain beat on them, as if trying to drown out her dreams. She fussed with the tarp, trying to keep it draped overhead, as the wind grabbed at it, wrenching it from her grasp. Monty's full attention was on the road and the horses reluctantly pulling the wagon.

Would they make it to Fort Collins? She pushed down her panic as the wind attacked anew. The horses now fought Monty's attempt to urge them forward, and once more he jumped down and took hold of the long side strap and tried to coax them along the flooded road. Grace saw their hooves sink into mud with every step, which made them prance in agitation and throw their heads against the headstalls and blinders as if trying to get free.

Another crack of lightning exploded in the sky and set the horses into a near panic. Grace stiffened and clung to the side panel of the buckboard, shifting her feet but unable to get better purchase on the slippery wet wood.

Monty offered his hand. "You better come down, Gracie. I can't predict how these horses will behave. They seem right ready to bolt."

Grace nodded, and trying not to show her fear, gave him an encouraging smile, assuring him it was all right, that she'd brave this trial alongside him. She wanted him to see she was stalwart—despite her pregnancy—that she could handle the rugged West. They hadn't much further to go, she consoled herself, and now, through the haze of mist and wind and rain she could make out what looked like a sturdy wood bridge—unlike like others they had crossed, which had been constructed from old metal railroad cars—spanning the Poudre River just a ways ahead. The roar of the river gave her more shivers, for it sounded altogether monstrous.

But if anyone could assess a river and its dangers, Monty could. She trusted him to get them safely across to the other side. Although, even from here she could see the dark water roiling and churning and overflowing its banks, splashing the underside of the bridge with fury.

She gulped, let out a tense breath, then eased carefully down from the seat, Monty holding tightly to her hand and wrapping his other strong arm securely around her back to help lift her down and onto the saturated ground. Her nice new leather traveling shoes sank into sticky mud, but she would clean them later. Once they made it to the hotel in Fort Collins.

She steeled her nerves and took a deep breath. A surveying job was awaiting Monty's arrival—in their new western town. They'd head to the land office tomorrow and file a homestead claim. They had plenty of money from the sale of her aunt's property, plus the savings Monty had accumulated from his jobs as surveyor, cartographer, and river guide on the various expeditions he'd gone on over the last few years. They would spend the summer building a cabin and planting a garden and getting ready for the birth of their child—the first of many to come. They would make a home in the West, in the small but growing town of Fort Collins, presently to double in size with the advent of the railroad, assuring plenty of surveying work for Monty for years to come. The Indians no longer a threat, the West was becoming tamed, and towns like Fort Collins promised church, community, and hope for a bright future to those who dared to dream. Next year the nation would celebrate its centennial, and Colorado was slated to be admitted as the thirty-eighth state in the union. Yes, the country embraced hopeful prospects.

Grace consoled herself with these positive visions of her future, a way of fanning the flames of her hope against the attempts of the Front Range storm to snuff it out. With Monty's arm holding her close as he urged the horses forward, Grace settled into that hope and reminded herself she was safe. Monty would make sure they made it. He'd had many close calls on his wilderness expeditions, but he was careful and strong and knew how to keep calm and level-headed in danger—and he'd faced plenty of situations more dangerous than a little rain and lightning.

She managed a chuckle, thinking of how silly she was being. They weren't out in the wilderness. They were on an well-traveled road, and they'd passed not a few people riding north only two hours prior. She owed it to Monty to encourage him and show her trust in him.

But just as she turned to say something to him, the ground slipped out from under her feet. She screamed as a loud explosion erupted around her, and her world turned upside down.

Although the antique mirror was cracked and silver flecks of paint curled and distorted her image, Lenora Dutton could still see enough of her reflection in the glass to assess she was ready for the big day—a day she'd been long awaiting, yesiree. A quick glance out the window of the second-story room in the Drop Dead Saloon told her a nasty storm was brewing, but it only brought a pleased smirk to her face. God's judgment was about to descend upon the evil remnants of the Dutton Gang. Namely, her snake of a husband, Hank, and the last two beef-headed scalawags that had faithfully and blindly followed their boss everywhere he led them—which, much to her delight, included the last stop on their bank-robbing journey: the Denver City Jail.

The hanging had been scheduled for high noon, but due to the inclement weather—more likely the lazy men assigned to erect the gallows—it was now set for three p.m. Lenora figured it was approaching noon, but she had no timepiece. Her head was a little woozy after imbibing a bit too much whiskey last night. She craned her neck closer to the mirror and scrutinized the bags under her eyes, then reached for her powder puff and minimized the damage.

Last she remembered, she'd been sidling up to some such feisty card chisler whose name she couldn't recall—and didn't care to—and had no memory of being helped up the stairs and into her bed. Thankfully, when she awoke this morning, she still had her clothes on. Which made her wonder if the kindly but seedy saloon keeper had escorted her upstairs. The first thing she did upon waking was feel under the mattress for her leather satchel, then made sure all the contents were still there.

A little giggle bubbled up as she thought of Hank swinging on the end of that rope, his legs kicking frantically, a black hood over his ugly, squat face. Thank God she would never have to stare into that mug ever again or hear his grating laughter. Good riddance! She'd bided her time and paid enough dues all these miserable years, pasting her smiles on and playing sweet on his every word. But it had been worth it. Because after today, the gold would be hers. All hers for the taking. And then she could head to San Francisco and start her new life—buy herself a big fancy mansion in the heart of the city, overlooking the ocean. Far from the dirt and grime and all uncouth manner of folks on the Front Range. She'd be the lady she was meant to be.

Lenora grinned. Hank was as mean a rogue as ever was, but today he'd be dead. He'd rough-handled her plenty, and she'd had many a black eye and a few broken bones to show for her loyalty. *But it was worth it, all worth it.* Because she had watched him hide the gold in that cabin north of Fort Collins, up in the Poudre River Canyon. And it was a heap of gold.

As she dabbed at a bit of beeswax from the unlit candle on the dresser with a spent match, she puckered her lips and turned her head from side to side. She was still young and attractive. And she'd learned all the tricks to snagging a man's attention and heart, getting him to do her bidding. With her money and looks, she could live that high society life waiting for her in California.

She tapped her foot as she thickened her long lashes with the wax, then adjusted the combs in her ebony hair. The traveling skirt and neat wool jacket she wore would keep her warm should that storm edge in. But she didn't care if she arrived at the cabin soaked to the bone. She hadn't been there in months—not since the time she'd finally had the opportunity to ride up there and move the gold before Hank got back from his latest escapade in Nebraska. She'd sweet-talked Clayton into letting her go "visit her poor, ailing mother" for a few hours. He never could say no to her, and he was sour at Hank anyways, since Hank chose to assign Clayton the task of babysitting her while the gang held up a stage heading to the armory.

After plying that dunderhead with enough whiskey to choke a buffalo, she took his horse and rode north, returning the next day, Clayton nursing a pounding headache and none the wiser that she'd been gone a lot longer than promised. It gave her a thrill to know she alone knew where the gold was hidden, and it wouldn't be easy to find, nosiree.

But upon returning, she realized what would happen if Hank looked for his stash and found it gone. He'd question her, and she wasn't sure she'd be able to lie with enough convincing. Which made her go through with the plan she'd had all along. Her next opportunity, she used her feminine wiles—and another bottle of whiskey—to loosen Clayton's tongue to learn where that week's robbery would take place. And once the gang rode out of town, in the dark of night, Lenora slipped an itty-bitty note under the sheriff's office door.

Imagine her surprise when news spread through town the next day that there had been a confrontation at a bank in Colorado Springs, with a goodly number of outlaws shot—none other than members of the notorious Dutton Gang. Sadly, Hank hadn't been among the dead, but at least he'd been caught—along with Clayton "the Blade" Wymore and that simpering chucklehead Billy Hill Cloyd—who couldn't bear to hurt a flea, even though he was a better shot than Clayton and Hank combined.

Lenora checked her reflection one last time, figuring her wagon would be ready by now. She'd paid the boy triple the usual to make sure all her bags and boxes were neatly packed and ready for her departure. She'd be able to get as far as the turnoff to Coyote Gulch up the Poudre canyon, but from there she'd have to unhitch the horse and ride the last few miles to the cabin, which was situated up against a wall of rock above some of the biggest rapids on the river.

After pulling her satchel out from beneath the mattress, she stuffed her makeup and handkerchief in, then strode out of the room, her nose assaulted with the stale odor of cheap cigars and even cheaper perfume. Wind brushed branches against the cobwebbed windows that lined the walls near the long mahogany bar below the red plush-carpeted landing she marched across. She stepped over one drunk, who was lying facedown and blubbering something incoherent. She heard a loud snoring from the door on her right and lightly flounced down the staircase, eyeing the few patrons holing up inside the saloon on this stormy day. Most were nursing drinks and shuffling cards. Probably waiting to watch the hanging—along with everyone else in Denver City.

The varnish on the banister railing had been worn down by the thousands of grimy, greasy hands that had drunkenly gripped it over the years, which made Lenora look forward to gracing the proper, upstanding hotels of San Francisco. There she would pursue her dream to act on a stage—a real stage, not some rickety, termite-infested saloon platform. She was meant for the stage, and had talent. Oh, no one had told her such, but she'd fooled plenty of folks with the roles she'd played throughout her life. She had more acting experience than anyone on Broadway in New York City, she figured. She'd even chosen a stage name: Stella Twilight. Wasn't that just divine? It meant the stars in the sky—or something akin to that. She met a saloon gal once upon a time by that name and thought to use it someday. She would be that star on the stage, come hell or high water, yesiree.

A glance at the newspaper on a nearby poker table showed headlines announcing the hanging. Already a crowd was gathering outside, their excitement building just like the storm. She had chosen to stay the night in this saloon on Blake Street for its proximity to the square, the courthouse visible from the front door.

She positioned her shawl over her head, pulled on her long leather gloves, and ventured outside. Upon opening the saloon doors, she was hit with a blast of cold wind and a splatter of rain. Overhead, mean, thick black clouds hung, ready to dump their wrath upon the earth. A big smile lifted her cheeks. *Soon,* she told herself. *California, here I come!*

Suddenly, a loud explosion rocked the street. Rocks and rubble flew into the air the next block down—where the jail was. Shouting ensued, and then gunshots. Lenora ducked under the saloon's porch overhang, ready to bolt back inside, when she heard someone shouting and the rumble of horse hooves pounding down a nearby street.

"They've escaped!" a man yelled.

Lenora clutched her heart. Oh no! She prayed the man wasn't talking about Hank. How could they escape? She gritted her teeth. *Clayton's brother . . .* He wasn't a member of the gang, but he lived in Denver City, and he was a locksmith. He'd been useful when they needed to jimmy a lock. He owned some fast horses too. She hoped she was wrong and it was some other prisoner that had gotten out. She pursed her lips and grunted. Well, there was plenty of law around. Even if Hank got out, he wouldn't make it very far. He'd be caught before he hit the city limits.

At that moment, the boy from the livery rode up in her Schuttler & Studebaker spring wagon and jumped quickly down from the seat. He squatted alongside the wooden boardwalk, using the wagon for cover. More shots rang out in the air, and people screamed and ran as the bullets whined. Her horse reared up but didn't break from his harness. If only she could see what was happening. But no doubt she'd find out soon enough.

Lenora slipped behind a few of the men who'd run out from the saloon to see the commotion.

"What's happening?" one of them asked, his head darting from side to side, trying to make sense of the mayhem.

Lenora heard rather than saw more horses. This time they were racing down Blake Street, in front of the saloon. She counted the animals' legs—what she could make out through the crowd now huddled around her. Five or six horses, she figured. Then she caught a glimpse of the men riding like the Devil was on their tail.

She gasped. Hank! Followed by Clayton and Billy. She cursed under her breath. With clenched fists, she watched as more horses galloped past, kicking up dirt and grit that mixed in with the pellets of rain whirling in the air. She wiped her face and covered her eyes until the sound of hooves petered out, and the crowd erupted in animated talk.

The boy came up to her. "Miss, here's your wagon." His eyes caught hers, and she shook her head to sort what he was saying.

"Oh, yes. Here's somethin' for your trouble." She reached into her satchel and pressed a coin into his palm.

"Thank you, miss," he said, wide-eyed and craning to see down the street, where the outlaws had made a run for it. "I wonder if the sheriff will catch 'em."

She showed him a nervous smile. "I sure hope so. I'd hate to think of those horrid outlaws on the loose."

A nicely dressed man that oozed money next to her gave her a look-see and gazed approvingly. She saw the longing in his eyes and smiled demurely, a smile full of innocence and tinged with the appropriate amount of fear. "Perhaps you could find out . . . if it's safe for me to travel all alone . . . ?"

He gave a sweeping bow, removing his hat to reveal a large bald spot on the center of his head. Lenora hid a chuckle under her thick lashes. The moustache he sported must have borrowed all that hair from his scalp. "It would be my pleasure," he told her, giving his facial hair a twirl before walking purposefully down the street. She really didn't need his help, but she just couldn't resist watching another slobbering fool rush off to do her bidding.

Lenora climbed up with as much ladylike grace as possible onto the seat of her wagon and picked up the reins. Before she'd even said "giddap," she saw the sheriff and two deputies trotting back her way—with a man on horseback in tow.

She ducked her head under her shawl as Hank rode past, careful to not look up until they were long gone. She was glad she'd bought a new horse, for Hank would have surely recognized her piebald gelding. Not that he could do much about her being here.

She squelched the urge to ride over to the courthouse and watch the hanging—from the front row. Pictured giving Hank a sweet smile so he'd know just who put him in his predicament. But she didn't want to take the chance that someone, somehow, would recognize her and connect her to the Dutton Gang. She'd never joined in on any of their robberies, but she knew she could be considered an accessory of some kind. She'd been treated like one—that was for sure—Hank's accessory to wear on his arm and toss about when he lost interest. She knew he'd had other women on the side. He'd often come back to where they were laying low with his clothes reeking of another woman's perfume.

Through the shouting, running crowd, she'd determined they'd only caught him. And from what she could tell from the loud exchanges around her, two of the Dutton Gang had somehow given the sheriff the slip. A group of concerned citizens was gathering on the steps of the courthouse, but Hank was being hauled over to the gallows.

"They're not taking any more chances." The man she'd sent to suss out news ran up breathlessly to her, his eyes shining with longing. She knew he was more interested in her and what she could offer him than what fate awaited Hank Dutton, bank robber.

Lenora gave him a coy smile and demurely fluttered her lashes. "Whatever do you mean?" she asked.

He pointed. "Look, they're hanging him now, without any delay or last words."

"Oh my," she said breathlessly, imagining herself in the role of a helpless woman lost on the prairie. Her heart pounded hard, and she suppressed a cry of glee as she watched from the seat of her wagon as her husband, the long-sought-after brigand, was led up the pine-planked ramp to the gibbet sporting the waiting noose.

"But what about the others?" she asked innocently. "Weren't there more in the gang? Did they catch them?"

"They're assembling a posse. The men just . . . vanished." At her horrified look, he patted her hand reassuringly. "But don't you worry your pretty head about that, miss. I'm sure they won't get far. And then it's the noose for them."

A nervous tic attacked her gut, and she rubbed her gloved hands. She wouldn't be so quick to agree. Clayton had smarts when it came to disappearing. And there were plenty of places to hide in the bowels of the city. But she knew just where they were headed—of that she had no doubt. They'd beeline it to the cabin and look for the gold. Then, when they failed to find it, she knew exactly what they'd do next—look for her.

Perspiration broke out on her brow even though the day was cool. She pulled out a handkerchief from her jacket pocket and dabbed her forehead. She dared not take the chance of heading to the cabin. Not just yet. What she needed to do was find some place near it, where she could lay low and wait until word of their capture. And somehow not be anywhere obvious where they could find her. Surely not in Denver City.

She realized the man was speaking to her.

"Miss? I said, would you join me for lunch? I'm sure the events of the day have flustered you greatly. Let me help you down from that wagon—"

"Why, that's perfectly kind of you, sir," she said in a syrupy voice, using a gloved hand to gently push him back from the wagon, which he was leaning over to get close to her bulging bodice. "But, I'm afraid I have other plans. And I'm in a bit of a hurry."

More than a bit. If she didn't get far from Denver City quickly, she stood the chance of running into Clayton and Billy. And even though she had a Winchester rifle and a Colt pistol under her seat in a locked wooden box, she did not want to face "the Blade" anytime soon. If he had any inkling she was the reason for his recent appointment with the undertaker, she'd be carved like a side of beef. She'd seen some of his handiwork, and it wasn't pretty.

Without further ado, ignoring the rich suitor's protests, she swung her horse and wagon around to head north and slapped the reins to get the gelding trotting up the street. A bolt of lightning arced the sky, bright white against dark clouds, followed by a loud cheer erupting behind her, over by the jail. She didn't look to see her husband's fate, but she could see him in her mind's eye—swinging from the gallows. Relief washed through her as she smacked the reins harder and forced the horse into a run. The heavens opened up and dumped rain upon her, filling the streets with water and washing away her trail. There would be no trace of her now; she was leaving her loathsome life in Denver City—for good.

And one way or another, no matter how long it took, she would get the gold and head to San Francisco. The glamorous stage awaited her.

Chapter 2

"GRACE!"

Monty's heart lodged in his throat as he swiveled from the panicking horse to see his wife fall to the ground not three feet from stomping hooves. He muttered a curse under his breath, ruing his trust in the seller of these temperamental beasts. He should have looked harder for a team of mules, but he'd wanted to get Grace off the streets before dark. It didn't take a sackful of brains to see that Cheyenne wouldn't be safe past sundown. Monty chided himself for his impatience at wanting to get to Fort Collins and claim his quarter section. He'd waited so long, and he'd let his eagerness get the best of his smarts.

He threw aside the reins and lunged for his wife, using his body as a block from any blows that might be forthcoming from the powerful animals. He wrapped his arms around her and scooped her close, half crawling, half stumbling away from their rig.

The ground shifted. Monty froze. Grace moaned, then found his face and gave him a questioning look. But he didn't say a word; he was listening.

He had listened to rivers for the last twelve years of his life, and he knew every voice, every intonation. And this river was angry and crazed. Something caught in the corner of his eye, and his gaze locked on to a massive tree tumbling trunk over limbs in the churning water twenty feet away. He looked over at the bridge and watched the water chomp at its undersides, like a great beast hungering for anything to fill its belly. If they didn't cross now, they might never make it to Fort Collins. At least not today. But he felt the urgency to get Grace into a warm bath and feed her a hot meal. He never let on how much he worried over her and the baby.

He studied the muddy ground as he fisted his clammy hands at his sides. Clay, limestone, some sandstone. Practically no vegetation matting the sloshy mess underfoot. The thick gray color of the swollen river attested to lack of cohesion of the banks. This was desert, and the rivers here on the Front Range traversed mostly sand. Now that they'd passed the strong sedimentary rock of the mountain canyons, the riverbanks were being eaten away. He'd seen it countless times on his treks through the Great Plains and in Yellowstone. He'd seen it back when he was a youngster working the loading docks on the Missouri River and its tributaries.

He weighed all he knew with what he stood to lose. And he had much too much at stake to risk crossing the Cache la Poudre at flood stage.

"We're turning back," he told her over the bellowing wind whipping their faces. Grace looked down at her sodden, muddy clothes and mustered a weak smile—for his benefit, he surmised.

"I'm such a mess," she said apologetically. She tried to stand, but winced at the effort.

"What is it?" He studied her carefully, knowing she wasn't one to complain. She'd had a pretty easy pregnancy so far, and he had a mind to keep it that way. He grunted as he scooped her up in his arms and carried her—with some difficulty—away from the river, hoping to find ground a bit more solid and less slippery.

"Montgomery Cunningham! What do you think you are doing?" She added a playful swack with her protest. "I must weigh . . . two hundred pounds—"

He laughed as he gently set her down on the only patch of grass he could find amid all the mud. Rain squalled and squabbled like a flock of cantankerous birds overhead, and by now they were both thoroughly drenched.

"Well, maybe a hunnerd and eighty pounds . . . not two hundred—" He received another swat for his teasing, but at least Grace was smiling now—a genuine smile that heated his blood.

He could never tire of seeing the love burning in her eyes. He drank in her soft, sweet facial features: the small mouth and pouty lips, her high and prominent cheekbones and button nose. Sometimes when he looked at her he saw the feisty, outspoken ten-year-old he'd first met all those years ago sporting a patch of freckles galloping across her nose. But that little girl had grown into quite the lady—one still full of spirit, but mature and kind. And fully woman, her child's body given way to just the right curves in the right places. Curves he never tired over exploring.

What a shock it had been to check in at the boardinghouse years later, expecting to see Grace the tomboy. Instead, a stunning young woman with a radiant smile had opened the door, and for a long moment he hadn't recognized her. Not until she spoke his name. And on her lips, his name sounded angelic. Her dark amber hair that had tickled her ears six years prior now tumbled like a honey waterfall over her shoulders, unpinned and unbonneted, for she had just had her evening bath and hadn't had time to yet put it up properly. But at the sight of her, he had blushed, not she, for Grace made no apologies and welcomed him inside, as if long-lost family.

He shook his head, remembering how hard he'd fallen in love with her. How many hours they'd spent talking in the parlor, singing popular songs at the piano as her aunt pounded mercilessly on the keys, the notes coming from the ancient instrument as out of key as their voices. Sipping chocolate in the kitchen by the giant cast-iron stove while watching Grace roll out biscuits in the early hours of the morning, before all the boarders had awoken. He almost didn't leave to go on that first expedition with Ferdinand Hayden, but he had made a commitment, and the team was counting on him. But he knew he'd be back.

He didn't dare tell Grace how he really felt, for he nursed a certain trepidation, knowing what disasters often befell those who explored the wilds of the West. If he declared his love, she might fret all the more. And more to the point, he worried that she might not reciprocate the feelings he had, and he couldn't bear to head west to unknown parts for untold years knowing she wasn't duly fond of him. So he just gave her a kiss good-bye that he hoped she'd know was a promise, and if he made it back alive and in one piece and she was still unmarried, well then, he'd ask her to marry him. Which he did. And to which she agreed, much to his great relief and joy.

And here she now sat, a muddy mess, soaked to the bone, her belly round with their first child.

A frantic need to protect her welled up in his chest, unhinging his usual calm. Another blinding spear of lightning smacked the earth not thirty feet away, and Grace shrieked and covered her head with her hands.

The horses squealed and ripped at their harnesses, upending the wagon. A rush of helplessness swept through him as thunder ricocheted across the sky.

He wrapped soaked arms around her shivering body and nestled his mouth against her ear. He whispered, "Don't be afraid, Grace. We'll get through this. The Lord will make a way—He always does."

He felt her nod against his hammering heart. Oh, how he wished to stay with her, keep her safe in his arms. But he couldn't risk the animals suffering injury.

"Stay put," he told her, making sure she saw the seriousness in his eyes. She nodded, and then he raced back to the horses, who were tearing their breeching apart. When he saw they would not calm from any of his words, he threw up his hands, and with teeth gritted and steam snorting out his nostrils in the chill air, he fussed at the leather straps, his fingers numbing, even inside his thick gloves.

The ground shook again, and this time Monty felt his feet shift noticeably. He sought purchase and spread his legs for balance. The river roared at him like a vicious lion. He watched logs and railroad ties tumble in the raging waters, then felt a hard yank as one of the horses reared again, this time breaking away from the wagon. With straps flying and reins dragging, the horse ran pell-mell in frantic circles, causing the other horse to buck against its restraints.

Monty cursed again and lurched back, out of the mad animal's striking range. He thought quickly what he needed to salvage from the wagon. They would have to leave it, and the horses, and walk back along what was left of the road. How far behind them was that ranch? He'd seen the sign—Whitcomb—in an arch over a long, wide road west that wended into the hills. They'd passed it maybe two hours ago. But now, on foot, how long would it take them to get there? Three, maybe four hours, with Grace wobbling slow steps. Without being able to see the sun, he knew there were maybe two hours of daylight left.

He'd need a lantern, then. Fuel, matches. Rope, blankets. Everything warm he could wrap around them. He didn't have arms enough to carry all that they needed to make it to a safe shoal—one he hoped was out there. There just had to be someone at that ranch, and if not, surely they'd find shelter. He could make a fire anytime out of just about anything, so he wasn't concerned about getting Grace warm and dry once they got there—or even to a thick stand of trees. He doubted anyone would be coming down the road, not now, not anytime soon. They were on their own, but he'd survived worse. *Yeah, but not with a pregnant wife.*

Monty gritted his teeth and rubbed his stubbled jaw, watching the horses gallop back north along the road together, finally free, unconcerned about the fate of the two humans they'd been accompanying. The wagon sat listing in mud, the rain coming down in canted sheets from a black churning sky. The whole world was tumbling in turmoil around them. He slapped his fist into his palm. He was wasting precious time.

He checked on Grace; she was huddled where he'd left her. Good. First thing—his pack. That was the only thing that really mattered. In it were their important papers. Their marriage license. His letter offering employment with the Larimer County Land Improvement company in Fort Collins. Their personal letters and papers. His college diploma from Wesleyan University. And then, there were his surveying tools—the ones small enough to bring along and that he'd carried with him through all the hell and high water he'd encountered on his expeditions. His transit theodolite, his brass plane surveying compass that Hayden himself had given Monty, his circumferentor.

He looked over at the wet crates and thought about his reflecting telescope, and his books—especially Wollaston's *Catalogue of the Stars* and Mackelyne's *Observations and Tables*. They'd have to be left behind. He'd have to hope their things would still be here tomorrow—or whenever they'd be able to get back and fetch their wagon. He hoped no one would rob them, but he knew that was a lot to hope for. For now, all he really hoped was that he could get Grace and the baby to safety soon, unharmed. *Please, Lord, with your help.*

He grabbed the bulky leather pack from beneath the seat of the buckboard and slung it over one shoulder and across his chest. It also contained Grace's jewelry, and all their money, every last bit. They'd decided not to leave any in the bank in Bloomington, seeing as they had no plans to return—no one to return to, no family left, for either of them.

A quick sting of bitterness sliced his gut as he thought about his hateful father and drunk of a mother. He'd last seen them outside of ten years, surprised they were both still alive, living in that squalor and filth they called home. He'd run away when he was fifteen, as far from Chicago as he could get on the few dollars he had in his pocket. That's when he got jobs working the rivers, where he met the crusty but kindly Joseph Bartlett on the docks, who taught him about rivers and urged him to go to college and make something of himself. In those short months, Joseph had watched out for him and taught him what decency and honor were—something Monty had known in his heart but surely never learned in his home. And then the old man had died when a stack of logs broke their chains and crushed him.

No, he and Grace had left nothing behind that mattered. Their future was all they had. And each other. But that was all Monty needed. All he cared about in this world.

As the wind clawed in fury, Monty strained to grasp the edges of the thick tarp. He wrestled the tangled mess out of the metal struts of the bench and worked to lay it over some of the crates—the ones containing Grace's clothes and her keepsakes. Some had only sentimental value, but Grace treasured the items her aunt had left her, and Monty didn't want to see them ruined, especially the needlepoint that Grace loved. And her special dresses that she'd designed and sewn. Grace, taught by her aunt, was an expert seamstress and dressmaker, and hoped to one day open her own shop in Fort Collins. Monty was determined to make that dream a reality for Grace.

He'd tucked three corners over the front stack of crates, knowing the few trunks were mostly watertight. But when he worked to slip the tarp under the last large crate, he lost his footing.

He glanced down and watched the ground whisk his legs out in a torrent that raged beneath his feet. His hands flailed in surprise, finding nothing to grab on to. The road disappeared.

With the force of a tornado, he was pulled into water as thick as porridge. A gasp slipped out of his mouth. From of the corner of his eye, he watched the front end of the wagon slip down out of sight, as if the ground had sucked it in, and then the bench followed, with the wagon almost tilted vertically upright, its back end in the air.

Anger and frustration roiled like another river, inside him, filling him with fury and determination. He would not let this puny river best him.

The roar of water surged around his ears as it dragged him down, and freezing wet waves engulfed him, smacking in erratic abandon at his head as he struggled to stay afloat, his mouth filling with dirt-choked water. With effort, he managed to extricate his arms from his coat sleeves and shrug himself free of its weight. He did not panic.

But his aggravation and annoyance sought to undo him. And his worry for Grace—whom he was leaving behind and who he knew would try to run after him to save him. *No, Grace, don't,* he wished he could yell out to her. He knew if she came near the river, she would die. There was no question about it.

But he could not tell her, so he prayed. *Please, Lord, don't let her move an inch. Keep her safe in the storm, in the shelter of your arms.* His heart hurt. If only his own arms were now wrapped around the woman he loved.

Somewhere in the distance, as if miles away, he heard a scream. It was Grace's voice, and as the water yanked and pulled at him, thrusting him into an eddy and down a slipstream that spilled into the Poudre River, he realized he had never heard her scream before. The sound was a keening, mournful cry that rent his heart.

He took short, shallow breaths in the icy water, keeping his chin upraised. He'd tumbled in rivers before—many times. Some more fierce than this one. It took a moment to suss out the pulse of the water—its speed and force and turbulence. Rivers danced and jerked in a rhythm to the rocks and rain and temperament of the land. Thankfully, he knew this stretch of the river ran flat, then eventually widened and joined the South Platte at the confluence just north of Greeley. There would be no jagged rocks or cascading waterfalls. Nothing too dangerous. Nothing he couldn't handle.

With chattering teeth he rode the undulating waves that tossed and tumbled him, always righting himself, sucking air, going under. He was freezing in the rushing snowmelt. He could no longer feel his extremities as he tried uselessly to paddle toward the northern shore, but it ever eluded him. Fear pounded his temples. What if he couldn't get out in time to make it back to Grace before nightfall?

He doubled his efforts to reach the shore, but he was tiring quickly. Every time he clawed at the steep bank, a surge of water dragged him back to the center of the current, as if it had a mind to deny him his goal. He kicked hard at an angle against the current, playing with it the way he imagined a fish might as it spawned in desperation upstream, to its mating grounds. He was a salmon yearning for his mate, with only one goal in mind, a singular need pulling him. His arms stung with pain, and every sharp intake of breath was a knife in his chest.

He couldn't just roll onto his back and ride it out, knowing at some point the river would slow and spit him out like an unwanted fish miles downstream. He'd die of exposure soon if he didn't scramble out. And every mile the river carried him was a mile he would have to trudge his way back to Grace. He was already too far from her.

But the river had other intentions, and Monty had neither gills nor a strong tail to help him work his way upstream. The water fought him like a formidable foe, and Monty lost miles as he struggled, helpless and weak. He would have to relent and let the river carry him. He had no choice. He berated himself for his foolish decisions, for his bad choices this day. For endangering Grace and their baby.

As he rolled over resignedly onto his back, he gasped. He stared upriver, horrified.

Barreling toward him was another tree, bigger than the one he'd seen earlier. Branches of the massive pine thrust out from a dark rolling trunk as thick as a cow. Sharp, angular branches windmilled through the rapids, churning water as if it were soft butter.

Monty sucked in water. He coughed, spit, flipped over and swam downstream with all his might, to outrun it. But he knew it was to no avail. Within seconds he felt a heavy crash on his back and arms, felt bones snap. He screamed in pain, and reflexively rolled into a ball, hot throbbing engulfing his back. He went under as he saw black spots fill his vision.

Paddling with useless arms, he managed to get his head above water and sucked in a desperate breath, but more water filled his mouth, and his vision failed. As he slipped down beneath the turbulent surface of the Poudre River, something smashed the back of his head, and he reached out in one last, weak attempt to grab something, anything.

His frozen hand hit a hard surface. He curled fingers, latching on to a rough object. He found a way to wrap his arm around what he guessed was a branch, wedging himself into the wooden arms of the tree. Then the world drained away.

Chapter 3

LENORA SMACKED THE REINS TO get the horse to move faster, casting a grateful glance at the sky showing the tiny bit of blue breaking the clouds apart. She figured Clayton and Billy would have to hole up awhile somewhere. As masterful as Clayton was at sneaking and hiding, half of Denver City—and likely a good portion of Colorado Territory—would already be on the scout for the last two living members of the notorious Dutton Gang.

Lenora let out a little laugh as she wiggled her head from side to side and did what she could to re-tuck her errant strands of hair back under the combs. She regretted she hadn't stayed a few minutes longer to watch her dearly beloved husband choke and squirm under the noose. It wouldn't have delayed her much, and it would have given her a right nice feeling of satisfaction. But no matter. The deed was done, and dead was dead. She'd be mistreated by Hank Dutton no longer. And she had no doubt the posse would catch up with the two renegades before long.

The wagon she'd bought wasn't all that awful, but already she had been racing north on the road from Denver City to Evans for a few hours, through deep puddles and soggy ground, and she longed to stop and stretch her weary bones. Out here, on the open range speckled with prickly pear cactus and tumbleweeds, the wind wailed, singing a song—one Lenora liked to imagine was an Indian victory dance. Her heartbeat sped up thinking about all those bars of gold. All hers!

She'd studied the maps carefully. She knew the best spot to cross the Platte. Even with this storm, the river would have sand bars that weren't all that deep. She worried the wagon would get stuck, but she'd figure something out. She always did. She believed in serendipity.

A smile lifted her lips. That was a word her friend Dolly had taught her. It meant a kind of luck or good fortune in finding things. And she always found a way, by golly.

But right now, she wished she'd eaten something for breakfast. She was awfully hungry, and that meant a stop in Evans—the small town looming ahead of her a ways. She'd get some chow, maybe a whiskey—and one for the road. Then make it to Greeley and figure out how much time she had before she got to the Platte. If she could just get across and head east, she'd be in good shape. Wouldn't dare try to head to the cabin, but if she camped close to the foothills, she could start fresh in the morning, and the horse would be more agreeable. Maybe hole up in Fort Collins, since it was the closest town to the stash of gold. Then wait until word got out about Clayton's capture. How long could it take a posse to catch him and Billy?

Suddenly the wagon lurched to the side and wobbled violently. Lenora collected the reins and stopped the horse, letting out a string of curses and berating herself for not bringing an extra wheel with her. She jumped down, hoping it wasn't broken but only loose. Surely she could find someone in Evans who could help her. She'd didn't cotton the thought that she might have to spend the night there—she hadn't much money on her. A chuckle popped out of her mouth. Well, that never posed a problem. Money was no farther than a sweet smile, a wink, and a few sappy words away.

The culprit was the rear right wheel. The thimble cap was missing, and she noted the linchpin that held the wheel onto the axle had sheared clean off. She pulled out her handkerchief and dabbed her forehead and eyes, which were fairly caked with a sheen of red dust. The wheel was resting at an angle, partway off. She had to figure something out, and didn't want to try to elevate the wagon or get her hands and clothes full of tar from the lubricated joints.

Just my luck. She blew out a breath that lifted her bangs out of her eyes. If she had to walk into Evans looking this bedraggled, she'd only get pitiful looks. Although, maybe that would earn her some sympathy from a kindhearted cowboy.

A flash of movement caught her eye. Two horses, headed her way. She straightened and smoothed out her skirt and blouse, then tucked her hair back in place as best she could. If only she had a hand mirror. No matter. She would put on her "damsel in distress" act. That never failed to make them melt. Men just fell over themselves helping a helpless lady. And she figured whoever these two men were, racing down the road as if to beat the wind, they wouldn't try anything untoward with her—not in daylight on the main road the stage traveled. A Concord coach had passed her not an hour ago, heading to Denver City.

She waited until the two riders began to slow. Seasoned riders, not greenhorns. They rode like they'd been born on horses. They were young men—one appeared to be a half-breed. No, they both were. Brothers, she concluded—and plenty easy on the eyes, she mused appreciatively. One had fairer hair and eyes as warm as honey, but the resemblance was clear in their carriage and muscular build. The darker-haired one with the brooding eyes was older. He'd be the one for her to work.

They slid off their horses and left the reins loose over the saddle pommels. The horses stayed in place like obedient dogs, not even looking to munch the grass. *Horse trainers,* she thought. *Cheyenne, looks like.*

"Afternoon, miss," he said. The younger man merely nodded, then looked over her wagon. Lenora could tell they'd been raised with manners—her favorite kind of sucker. "C'n we offer some help here?"

"Why, I'm grateful! I fear I'm losing a wheel, and I don't have a spare."

She noticed the younger one give her a slight glare of disapproval. Maybe he felt she was a foolish, helpless woman with no sense, traveling alone in the frontier. The older brother showed only a polite, kind expression. Yes, both were plenty easy on the eyes, but they were a mite young for her. Still . . .

The two men eyed her wheel and talked quietly.

"We really don't have time for this, LeRoy," the younger told his brother. "We have to get to Burlington before dark."

LeRoy scolded his brother with his eyes. "Look, if you can find something to prop up the wagon with, I can fix this—enough so she can get to Evans. I've got some wire in my saddlebag. That'll work in place of the pin."

Lenora smiled demurely at the younger man. "And what's your name, Cowboy?" She resisted the urge to sweep the stray strands of unruly dark-gold hair from his face. He was sure a sweet one—a lot prettier than old, dead Hank. She would just love to run her long manicured nails through that mane.

"Name's Eli Banks, ma'am."

"Oh, please," she said with a pout, while watching LeRoy rummaged through his saddlebag. "*Ma'am* sounds so old! Call me . . ." She sucked in a breath, then coughed. She couldn't very well use her real name, now, could she? ". . . Stella."

The young man merely nodded, then wandered around looking at the rain-soaked ground—ugly, bleak desert potholed with prairie dog tunnels. Lenora enjoyed watching the way he moved, his strong back and well-toned arms evident under his cotton shirt. By the time LeRoy had returned to the wagon, Eli had found a broken plank of wood, something that looked to have been part of an old cabin or other building.

"Where are you two boys off to in such a hurry?" she asked as they worked to prop up the wagon so that the wheel hung loose.

LeRoy cast her a quick glance, then focused on wiring the wheel back on. He knelt beside the wagon. "We're joinin' a posse that's being organized in Burlington—that's just west of here a bit."

Lenora stiffened. "And . . . who are y'all going after?"

"Didn't you come from Denver City?" Eli asked, standing and facing her, his brows furrowed in suspicion. "You must've heard about the Dutton Gang, and the jailbreak."

"Jailbreak! No, I hadn't heard." She narrowed her eyes. "How did you know I came from Denver?"

Eli shrugged as if the answer was obvious. "C'n tell by your horse. How weary he is. And the color of the dirt caked on his ankles. You've been riding him pretty hard." A streak of ire crossed his features. "Seems you're in a hurry too. Need to get someplace before dark?"

LeRoy nudged his elbow into Eli's rib. Maybe he thought his brother was being rude. But Lenora only gave them both an innocent smile, admiring the Indian powers of observation the younger brother showed. He clearly had some worthy tracking skills. "Well, yes, I was in Denver City. Visitin' my sick sister. But she's better now. And I'm . . . headin' home now."

LeRoy turned his attention back to the wheel. Lenora stood in polite silence, making it clear she had nothing more to say. More mean clouds gathered overhead, and she longed to get out of her damp clothes and take a nice hot bath. But simple pleasures would have to wait.

Eli grunted and watched his brother. In a moment, LeRoy got to his feet and brushed his hands on his leather chaps.

"All set. I'd go easy until you get to Evans. The wheel's in good shape, but you'll need a new linchpin."

"And be sure to rub down that horse. And don't give him cold water to drink when you get there," Eli added in a lecturing tone.

Here's a man that loves horses more than women, that's for sure, Lenora realized. "Yes sir," she told him, like a soldier to his commander. "I'm mighty thankful for your help," she said, mostly to LeRoy, batting her lashes for good measure. She added with a bit of concern, "Those bad men you're after—"

"The Dutton Gang," Eli said. "Two of them were seen headin' north out of Denver City."

"They're very dangerous," LeRoy added in warning. "Best you stay on the main roads and travel only in daylight. I hope you don't have much further to go."

"Oh, I'll be fine," she said, distracted by the thought of Clayton and Billy still at large. And already north of Denver. How in the world had they eluded the sheriff and all his men searching for them? Those slippery eels. She just might run into them after all. The thought sent a shiver up her back.

"Well, I do hope a lot of brave men such as yourselves join that posse and catch those bad men. But take care and don't get shot at," she said, scrunching her face in worry.

"We'll do our best." LeRoy tipped his hat and swung up on his horse. Eli followed suit. "Afternoon, miss," they both said, then took off at a gallop down the wide dirt-packed road. A few sprinkles of rain lighted on Lenora's hair, and she clucked at the horse, putting him in a slow trot.

She mulled over her choices. She needed grub, and as prudent as it was for her to spend the night in a hotel in Evans, the thought of Clayton riding into that town made her uneasy. She had lucked out with those two half-breeds helping fix her wagon, and no doubt the way LeRoy wired the wheel, it would make it well past Evans. But she didn't want to push her serendipity nor her horse.

Wisest course would be to stop long enough to load up on supplies, maybe find a dry goods. Then keep heading north, to the river. She should make it well before nighttime, and once she got a good look at the water, she could decide whether to cross or wait it out somewhere—maybe find some abandoned shelter or cabin along the river. She just didn't cotton the thought of being in a town where people would notice her arrival. People in small towns talked. And every new face was grist for the gossip mill. She'd rather get in and out quickly without much ado, though sitting at a bar and drinking whiskey all night was a sore temptation.

With that decided, she covered her head with her woolen shawl and headed into Evans with a tired horse and a functional wagon, feeling a bit adventurous but aware of a sense of foreboding behind her, like a shadow following her. As if Hank's men were on her tail.

"Miss . . . miss?"

Grace tried to open her eyes, but they felt glued shut. Where was she? Who was speaking to her? She felt around with her fingers and grabbed mud, and the cold touch shot fear through her heart. Suddenly, memories rushed at her in a flood, as images of the raging water and Monty slipping into the river assailed her.

Her eyes opened and she cried out. "Monty!" She rubbed mud-encrusted fists across her face, and a stab of pain streaked her belly. *My baby!*

"Whoa, hold on there, miss."

A weak sun throbbed overhead. She turned to find the voice and felt arms helping her sit upright. She looked down at her dress, her waist bulging below her, no longer a pretty brown calico. Her clothes and shoes were covered in mud, and she shivered from the cold. With chattering teeth, she fumbled with words.

"Monty—where is my husband?" She swiveled her head, looking for him, but only found the unfamiliar but concerned rheumy eyes of an older cowboy with a grizzled face. His bony, weather-roughened hands helped her to stand, and she took shallow breaths, assessing her condition. As if in response, her baby kicked, and tears coursed down her cheeks.

"You all right, miss?" He held her arms firmly, as if she'd fall in a sodden heap should he let go.

"I . . . I think so." Panic raced through her cold limbs, setting her heart pounding in fear. "I don't see him. Where . . . where is our wagon . . . ?"

She looked around in astonishment as she got her balance, grateful for the man's assistance. Not far away the river squirmed in a tangled skein of muddied channels—the former raging waters now subsided. But where the wagon had floundered in the mud, she saw nothing. Nothing at all. Had everything she'd owned been washed away . . . along with her husband? She gulped back tears.

"Don't see any wagon, miss. Nor any man." His voice was quiet, apologetic. "But, don't go gettin' yerself upset, now. Best we get you somewhere warm and safe, where you can git a proper bath and into some dry clothes. You'll catch yer death 'fore too long."

She stared at the river, her mouth hanging open. How could the wagon just . . . vanish? She'd seen it sink partway into the mud.

"Oh no . . . oh no . . . Monty . . ."

Her head spun with horror, and brown spots dotted her vision.

"Here, miss." He gently tugged on her arm. "Can't have you swoonin'. Let's git you into my wagon. I just come from Fort Collins—crossed the river over yonder"—he pointed upstream a few dozen yards—"and it be best I take you back there."

She flailed at him with her arms. "No, I need to find my husband—"

"I unnerstand. But one thing at a time." He helped her take small steps, but her dress weighed her down, as did her petticoats, which were also caked with mud. The air was balmy, thick with moisture, but thankfully the wind had abated. Her whole body was racked with shivers, and her teeth chattered so hard her jaw ached. She prayed her baby was all right and put her hands protectively over her belly.

Surely Monty was alive. He understood rivers better than any man. He'd regaled her with many a story telling how he'd been thrown into raging waters in expeditions. How he knew to float on the waves and become part of the river. She didn't care about the loss of her belongings—those could be replaced, and although some held great sentimental value, they were just possessions, nothing more. All that mattered was finding Monty and making sure he was unhurt.

The thought of him lying along the riverbank, injured or dying, sent another rush of panic into her heart. She pulled away from the kindly cowboy who was trying to help her get to his small buckboard wagon situated on a soggy mound of grass.

"I have to look for him—"

"Please, miss. I promise I'll round up some help—to find your husband--once we git you to town. Night's a'comin', so we shouldn't dally. It's not far."

She stopped and looked at him, perplexed. "But . . . I have nothing. I've lost . . . everything. Lost . . . oh, Monty!"

Her knees buckled and she fell to the wet ground, shivering even harder, and sobbed in great heaves. She knew this couldn't be good for her baby, but she couldn't help it. How could she leave? What if he came back—stumbling and cold and hurt . . . ?

After a long moment, the man again reached for her arms. Like an invalid, she let him help her stumble to his wagon, then clumsily clambered up into the flat bed, where there lay a stack of buffalo pelts surrounded by filled burlap sacks. She smelled grain and dust and sneezed.

"Here," he said, taking one of the buffalo pelts and wrapping it around her as she sat on the wonderfully dry fur. The pelt around her shoulders warmed the chill from her bones, but her heart lay encrusted in ice and mud.

"Thank you," she muttered, willing her teeth to stop chattering. Finally, enough warmth permeated her skin to where she could draw in a deep shuddery breath without shaking uncontrollably. Suddenly she was tired, oh so tired. She couldn't keep her eyes open. Tears kept streaming down her face, and she moved a tentative hand to her neck and grasped the silver pendant tight in her fist.

I won't give up hope.

She knew more than anything else, the love they shared would buoy her, sustain her above the raging waters of fear. Monty loved her with all his heart. He would never let a river best him, rip him from the arms of his wife. He would come back to her. He was safe, somewhere. He knew how to survive in the wilderness.

She repeated these reassurances over and over as the wagon lurched forward and they forded the now-placid river engorged with silt. Off to the west, the snow-frosted Rocky Mountains towered, like sentinels watching her ambivalently. As the rocking of the wagon lulled her, she clutched the pelt tightly around her baby, the warmth making her drowsy.

I won't give up hope, Monty. I'll find you . . . no matter how long it takes. Oh please, Lord, help me . . . help Monty . . .

Chapter 4

EVENING STREAKED THE SKY A fiery pink as Lenora spotted the metal sheen of the river in the distance. She had made a quick stop in Evans, found a sap to fix her wagon, loaded up on some supplies, and headed north—all the while keeping an eye out for Clayton. No one in Evans seemed disturbed by the news of the jailbreak. But then again, she didn't hang around long enough to hear any gossip.

The wide dirt road was rutted so deeply, she had to take care not to mire the wheels. The thought of crossing the river gave her pause, but if the wagon sank into the mud, why, she'd just unhitch the horse and load as much as she could in her saddlebags. She could hide the rest of her belongings and come back for them later. In fact, that wasn't a bad idea—ditching the wagon and riding horseback the rest of the way to Fort Collins. She'd make better time that way. Maybe give her the advantage so that she'd disappear into that backwater town before Clayton could find her.

Then again, it might be more prudent for her to hole up somewhere farther away, awaiting word of their capture. *Don't be a fool, Lenora. You know what that cutthroat Clayton will do to you if he finds you.* She hated the thought that they might find the gold. Sure, she'd hidden it well, but in their desperation they would look hard—and take as long a time as needed—to tear that place apart, plank by plank. But she had buried it out in the meadow south of the woods. No way could they figure out where—not with a whole winter of snow dumped on the ground. No—they would not find the gold. And when they didn't . . .

Lenora thought back to when Hank had bought the cabin, when he first started his gang, figuring its location and difficulty of access made it the perfect hideaway. From time to time the gang met up there to plan their robberies, but since it was so far from Denver City, they'd rarely gone in recent years. She had sweet-talked him into taking her that last time—when he needed to hide all that gold. He didn't trust anyone in the gang to go with him. And he didn't trust her either. He made her stay with the horses down a ways from the cabin. But when she returned on her own just before he'd been arrested, neither the cabin nor the gold was hard to find. The fool had left a trail of muddy boot prints across the wood-planked floors, and he'd hid the gold underneath a loose floor plank. Hank wasn't much for neatness, and for that she was grateful.

She also knew he'd lied to his men, telling them the gold was in an old abandoned mine shaft near Boulder. But Clayton hadn't believed Hank; he told her so one night in his drunken stupor. No doubt Clayton had suspected all along that the gold was at the cabin—and that she knew where it was. So she'd better get to it before Clayton got to her.

Lenora huffed. *Patience, patience.* That was not her strong suit. She hated waiting for anything, and that gold was calling her. She wasn't getting any younger either, and her marriage to Hank Dutton had taken its toll on her youth and beauty. She hardly looked her twenty-five years. She could still pass as a young lady, innocent, untouched, untarnished. A dab of makeup here, a proper corset, and a few stiff petticoats could hide a multitude of shortcomings. She grunted. All this fretting wasn't helping. She would just have to trust serendipity.

As she got closer to the wide river, she noticed how the flat marshy land was reeling from a recent flood. Ugly gray water moved at a fast clip and tickled the tops of the banks. She huffed. Didn't appear she'd be crossing this anytime soon. A day, two days maybe?

She looked across the marshy land to the desert stretching before her. The Front Range went on for endless miles—a stark, drab, lonely place. Full of dust and cactus and tumbleweeds. Why anyone in their right mind would choose to live out here in this wasteland was beyond reckoning. All those stuffy rich people from back East, thinking to settle here and find their paradise . . . well, they were fools, every one of them. Putting up with blizzards and drought and tornados and locusts. Yep, truly fools to give up their creature comforts and heated houses for this. She had passed the temperance town of Greeley a few miles back—the "city of saints" it was called in Denver City. No drinking allowed—how fun was that?

She let her mind wander as she rode up to the river and watched the swirling, churning waters of the South Platte. To the northwest, the Cache la Poudre tumbled down canyons of rock and merged with the Platte. Only after traversing miles of flat desert did the river slow and widen enough for a safe crossing. Off to her right a ways sat a copse of willows and cottonwood, and she got a glimpse of a wooden structure. A cabin maybe. Aside from the ranch she'd passed fifteen minutes ago, there were no signs of habitation. And rightly so. Anything built close to the river would be in danger in a flood. She wondered how that little hideaway had weathered the many times the Platte overran its banks.

While she sat in the wagon, pondering her next move, toying with the idea of riding back to Greeley and getting a hotel room and then coming back at dawn to make the crossing, she caught something out of the corner of her eye. Upstream, a giant oak had speared itself into the riverbank, with dozens of branches like broken arms supplicating the heavens sticking every which way. But entangled in the branches was a shape that greatly resembled a man. A swath of brown fabric hung ripped in shreds from one branch.

She got down from the wagon bench and stepped carefully through the mud, her boots squishing as she walked. Upon closer inspection she noted that indeed it was a man—poor fool—and dead most likely. His mop of bark-brown hair hung down from his head as he lay facedown across the branch he was trapped in. Even from twenty feet away, she could tell he was young and strong. His body draped over another branch, his muscular legs in thick brown denim pants and feet in sturdy boots.

Not one to miss an opportunity, Lenora picked her way through the debris-littered riverbank—over broken timber and planks and mounds of upended grass that had been violently ripped from the earth and sent careening down the river. Her eye caught on light glinting off his finger. A gold ring!

Serendipity, she sang in her head, turning the word into a little ditty she began to sing as she pulled on the ring, twisting it this way and that, until she finally held the prize in her hands. It was a simple band of matrimony, not worth all that much—which made her wonder about the fate of this man's wife. Had he been traveling with her? She looked around and saw no other bodies. Then, she spotted what looked like a finely made leather satchel draped across the man's shoulder. She hadn't seen it at first, as it lay underneath the man. No doubt it contained his valuables.

She pocketed the ring, then grabbed the cold, lifeless body and flipped it over. She gave a little gasp of delight, which quickly turned to pity. What a handsome face! A chiseled jaw, strong nose, broad forehead, thick neck. The strong muscles his wet clothes hugged told her this was a man who had spent his life in physical labor, but the gentle features and lack of scars told her he was no scrapper. A man of means and education, she guessed. But one who reveled in work and using his body strength. She smiled as she ran a finger along his cheek, imagining such a man touching her. She wondered what color his eyes were, as he had them closed.

She sighed. Such a waste.

She pulled out the knife she kept strapped to her ankle and cut away the satchel. After some hard tugging, she freed it from the branch it was snagged on and walked back from the river a bit to look through her lucky loot. Would there be money? Gold? Her hands trembled in anticipation.

She found a somewhat dry patch of sand and dumped out the contents of the large satchel. A flutter of papers fell to the ground, along with some strange pieces of equipment. She picked up the two brass objects and studied them. They were heavy in her hand. Something to do with navigation maybe. Was he a sailor? What would a sailor be doing this far from the ocean? She craned closer and made out initials that had been etched into each piece—M.C. She doubted they were worth much, but she'd find out. She could sure use some extra cash.

Lenora set aside the objects, stuck her hand in the waterlogged pouch, and rummaged inside. Her fingers caught on a packet tied with string, and a folded silk scarf. And then a small box. She pulled them out and examined them. The packet she quickly unwrapped, for she could tell it held money. And lots of it. She giggled in delight and set the soggy bundle aside. The small box revealed the match to the ring that had been on the man's finger.

No doubt his wife had died—for why else would he be carrying her ring in his satchel? She concocted a sad story in her head and envisioned herself on the stage, under bright lanterns, playing the role of the dying wife, with this handsome hunk at her bedside, shedding tears of grief as his beloved wife crossed over into the great beyond.

Another search revealed nothing more in the pouch beside water and sludge, so she looked through the papers at her feet. Surprisingly, the papers were mostly dry, having been sandwiched atwixt the packet of money and the scarf. The first was a letter addressed to Montgomery Cunningham. M. C.—those were his initials on the brass objects. Lenora perused the letter and found it to be an offer of employment with the land office in Fort Collins. A surveyor job. That explained the brass objects. Poor fella. On his way . . . from somewhere . . . to start a new job, a new life. With his wife dead and still grieving over her, no doubt he'd been driven to leave his home—wherever that was—and find new hope in the West. She turned the letter over, but there was no indication of where it was from. The signature at the bottom was too garbled and the ink too smeared to read.

Another letter—this one a recommendation from someone named Hayden. Whoever he was. And another—one from a man called Powell. Lenora read with interest about this Montgomery Cunningham. Apparently he came highly regarded—had attended Wesleyan University in Bloomington, Illinois, and had gotten a degree in geology and then went on expeditions in the West.

That was the explanation for his manly figure. She sighed and fingered the man's ring. Such a sad, sad story. But the West was full of disappointment and death. Of dashed dreams and squashed hope. You had to be tough to survive—and lucky. But luck wasn't enough. You needed smarts, and she'd had to develop those quickly on the mean and dirty streets of Denver City, since her mother practically ignored her—so busy she was entertaining men.

The last slip of paper was not a letter but a certificate of marriage. Ah, the final sad piece to the puzzle. He'd married a woman named Grace Ann Wilcox, and the date showed they'd only been married about eight months.

She got to her feet, feeling stiff and sore and tired. She tossed the satchel into the river and watched it float away, leaving the pile of letters and papers on the wet sand, although she'd pocketed both rings. She would let the wind carry the useless papers away as it willed. None of them could benefit her, although she wondered if his surveying tools had value. With the tools and rings in hand, she turned to head back to the wagon, but then a noise startled her. She spun around.

The man groaned. He was alive! She hadn't thought to check if he was breathing—he was so cold and lifeless—go figure.

Before she could decide whether to hurry away and leave the man to his fate or stick around to see how he fared, his eyes opened and caught on hers. Inching closer to him, she noticed one eye was a deep mud brown, and the other was speckled with green. How odd, but somehow fascinating. She studied him passively, then realized if the man came to, he might realize she'd robbed him, and might apprehend her. Well, not likely in his condition. But he'd be able to identify her, and that could pose a problem. Better to leave him. He wasn't in danger of being dragged back into the water, and if he had any broken bones, no doubt someone would be along in the morning and would offer him assistance—if he survived the night. What if he had internal injuries?

He's not your problem, she told herself. Although, upon looking at his angelic face and the pitiable look of confusion he displayed, she thought what a nice problem he might prove to be. Here was a man mourning a dead wife, about to start a job in the booming new town of Fort Collins . . .

Her mind started plotting. Then, the man moaned again and tried to move. He made to pull out his arm, then screamed in pain. Her heartstrings were tugged. And she longed to touch him and feel those big, strong shoulders under her fingers. Why not just play this out and see where it led?

The man—Montgomery, she told herself—mumbled something incoherent. She drew close to his face, smelling the river and silt and sweet scent of his sweat.

He found her face, and his eyes opened wide as he looked into hers. His penetrating gaze sent a shudder through her. She found herself grasping for something to say.

"Where . . . what . . . ?"

"Shh, shh," she said in her best comforting voice. "You've been hurt. I think you may have broken your arm."

He ignored her admonition and wiggled on the tree until he could extricate his arms. Wincing in pain, he gingerly rubbed his right shoulder, his eyes filling with panic. She offered him her hand, which he took, and hesitantly, wobbling, he got to his feet, pulling his snagged shirt free from the branch.

He was a mess, but he was one handsome mess. He stood a good foot over her petite frame, with shoulders like a horse. He licked his dry lips, and Lenora couldn't pry her eyes from his delicious mouth.

"I have water," she said. "In the wagon."

When he dropped to the ground and sat with his head in his hands, moaning, she took the opportunity to scoop up the papers from the beach—just for leverage, if needed—then hurried to the wagon and hid them—along with the booty rattling around in her pocket—inside one of her boxes. She grabbed a bottle of water and a blanket and came alongside him, the darkening shroud of evening granting little light by which to see. Mountain air blew cold across the Front Range, and Montgomery shivered, cradling his arm.

She wrapped him in the blanket and watched as he guzzled the water down his throat. Her eyes lighted on his broad chest and slim waist. *An explorer, indeed. How I would like to explore his terrain . . .*

When he set the bottle down, he looked at her, a frantic expression searing his features. "I don't remember . . ."

"You don't remember what?" she urged gently.

He looked at her intensely, then scanned the river and the twilight-draped prairie. "I don't remember anything."

She stiffened, then her heart raced. Was this more good luck? "Your name?" she asked tentatively.

His brows furrowed as he thought, then he shook his head. "Where am I? And . . . who are you?"

She grabbed the opportunity for another challenging acting role. With a soft, worried look, she said, "Why . . . Malcolm—you don't know who I am?" She thought it best not to tell him his real name—at least not yet. More wheels turned in her head. *M.C.* She needed to give him a last name. Chambers, Chisholm . . . Connors! That sounded nice. *Malcolm Connors.* She smiled, then frowned when he shook his head with that sad hangdog look on his face.

She forced tears to spill down her cheeks—she was always able to turn on the waterworks with just a thought. It was one of her greatest talents, and had come in handy on many occasion. Men melted before a woman in tears. They were so frightened by such shows of emotion, they would do anything to stop the crying.

But, to Lenora's surprise, Montgom—*Malcolm*—took her hands in his and said, "How could I have forgotten you, your lovely face? I . . . I'm sorry." He bit his lip and used his good arm to wipe away her tears. "I . . . just don't remember."

My oh my! With that she fell into all-out weeping, while concocting a wonderful history in her head. "I'm . . . Stella." She looked back at the wagon and spotted the Childs & Co. name painted on its side, now softly illuminated by the rising moon's glow. She looked pleadingly at his face. "Stella Childs. Your fiancée. We were on our way to be married. We'd come . . . all this way from St. Louis. You'd hoped to find a surveying job in Fort Collins." She waited for any signs of recognition, but he only stared at her with grief and misgivings in his face. Oh, he was so endearing. And that deep, gravelly voice of his sent shivers up her back.

"And when we got to the river, you stopped our wagon and walked to the river's edge to see if we could cross. And then . . . then you slipped and hit your head on that tree coming downriver . . ." She sobbed anew, and, to her surprise, the man draped his arm across her shoulders and held her close.

He muttered into her hair. "Oh, Stella. I'm sorry, so sorry . . ."

Then, he let out another pained cry and doubled over. She tried to hold him up. He gritted his teeth.

"I'm sorely hurt," he said. "My arm's broken, but I think I . . . I . . . my stomach . . ."

He nearly passed out in her arms, but she did not have the strength to hold up so heavy a man. She felt his head—it was hot.

"Come, you must get in the wagon. I have to get you inside somewhere. Find a doctor."

He could barely nod, and stumbled along, trying to walk as she led him in the moonlight. She didn't dare ride into Greeley with him. What if Clayton was there? He could be anywhere. No, she had to lay low, someplace out of sight. That old abandoned cabin she'd passed would do the trick.

She could set his arm—she'd set bones enough with all the rough tumbling and fights the men in the Dutton Gang engaged in. But if he was bleeding internally, well then, there was nothing for him. Still, she was willing to help him. Who knew? He might just recover, and she'd have the perfect disguise. So long as his memory didn't return, she could nurse him back to health, help him "regain his memories" by weaving the stories of their romance and engagement. And then, once he was well enough, they'd marry and head to Fort Collins. What better way to hide out in plain sight than to be a married woman—a respectable member of the community. No chance Clayton would be able to find her then.

Mrs. Stella Connors. She smiled, liking the ring of the name. And—she looked over at Malcolm's handsome face—she liked the idea of holing up with this hunk, tending to his wounds, and getting him back on his feet through her loving ministrations.

With effort, she helped hoist him up into the wagon. He bravely stifled his cries of agony and nuzzled up to her, half incoherent, on the bench. Maybe he wouldn't even last the night. Though, she hoped he would. Regardless, she would do everything she could to make him comfortable, sidling her warm body next to his under woolen blankets. And maybe, in time, he would realize he was in love with her. Wouldn't that be dandy?

Chapter 5

GRACE WOKE UP IN A strange bed, with an urgent need to use the chamber pot. As she made to sit up, every muscle ached, and she was feverish all over. She laid a hand on her belly, but the baby was quiet, probably sleeping as it usually did in the morning. She could tell it was morning, for cool sunlight splintered through the frosted glass panes of this small, simply appointed bedroom. A patchwork counterpane lay over the bed, and gingham curtains adorned the two transom windows. The room reminded her of the neat little rooms her aunt used to rent out in her boardinghouse.

She jerked to her feet. Monty! The memory of arriving at this place in the dark was hazy. The man who had found her by the river woke her gently after she'd fallen into an exhausted sleep, saying they'd arrived in Fort Collins. All she remembered were hushed words exchanged between the man and an older couple—whose house she must now be in.

She looked down and saw she was wearing a long cotton dressing gown, a bit faded and threadbare, but clean. She could tell someone had made an attempt to clean her face and hands, but mud still left its smears along her legs and arms. Her head spun dizzily as she found her balance and wobbled to the door. She smelled bacon and perhaps hotcakes. Her stomach grumbled in hunger. When was the last time she'd eaten?

But how could she think about food when Monty was . . . somewhere out there, alone, hurt? Had he found his way to Fort Collins late in the night? Was he looking for her?

She found a thick white robe lying on the settee by the door and put it on. Fortunately it was large, and she could wrap it fully around her belly. She had to get help, to find Monty. Oh, how could she help him in this condition? She steadied her head with her hand. Every step she took sent shooting waves of pain through her limbs and back.

Hushed voices drifted toward her. She caught snatches of words as she leaned against the coolness of the bedroom door.

". . . said she had a wagon and a husband . . . no sign of it . . . no doubt traveling alone . . . lost her horse . . . foolish to travel pregnant . . . running away in shame, that's plain as day." The voices were a man's and a woman's, with the woman sounding irate and disbelieving. She heard the man say in a deep, calm voice, "For pity's sake, Charity, the Good Lord admonishes . . ." and then "the poor girl got herself in trouble, is what happened . . . must show mercy to those who need it . . ."

Grace shook all over. The man who'd brought her here had told this couple the account of her misfortune, but clearly they didn't give credence to her story. She couldn't bear the thought that they might not help her find Monty.

She opened the door, and the man and woman turned to her. They were an older couple, with gray hair and dressed in drab gray clothing, and they sat at a simple table with their breakfast before them. The heavy-set woman wore a snowy crape cap, and her shoulders were draped in a hand-woven shawl. The barrel of a man wore a strange black hat, and then Grace realized they must be Quakers. The woman, upon seeing Grace's face, leapt from the table and rushed over, waving her hands as if shooing her away.

"Dear, you're up. But you're feverish. You must get back to bed. I'll bring you some broth—"

"No, please," Grace begged. "You must help me find my husband. He was swept downriver—"

The woman laid a hand on Grace's shoulder and steered her firmly back into the bedroom. Grace's head felt about to explode. She made it to the bed and sank down into it. Before she could speak again, the woman held a finger to her narrow pale lips in admonition.

"The doctor will be by shortly to check on you and the wee one. You must rest—"

"Please, is there someone—a sheriff or a tracker . . . I need to talk to someone . . ." Her breath came out in shallow gasps, and she felt about to faint. The woman helped her lie back onto the goose-down-filled pillows.

As much as she tried to constrain herself, Grace let out a howl of grief, and tears exploded down her face. It hurt to cry, and her head pounded more fiercely than ever, but the pain of her loss was even greater. How she needed Monty and worried so over him! She didn't think her heart could bear the strain.

She began muttering, praying, pleading with heaven for help.

Somewhere on the edge of her awareness, she heard the woman leave the room. Words drifted in and out of her ears as her face burned and her stomach roiled in nausea. She hated how weak and helpless she was, and she worried these people—however kind they were to take her in—would not help her at all. Time was of the essence! Every minute that passed was another minute Monty could be lying along the river, dying of injury or thirst or exposure.

"She's delusional . . . thinks she had a husband . . . no ring on her finger . . ."

The woman's heartless whispers were barbs that pierced her heart. Shivers overtook Grace, and she pulled the blankets up to her chin, but she couldn't get warm. Would she die of fever? What about her baby? *Oh, Monty, where are you?*

She lay there, helpless, floundering in a sea of fever, drifting in and out of consciousness. She thought someone had come back in the room, heard more voices, felt a wonderfully cool hand on her forehead, then touching her belly. Someone put something to her lips and she drank. And then she fell into a slumber of death, unable to claw her way to the surface of her consciousness, where she searched futilely for Monty in her troubled dreams.

Three days later, Grace stood in front of the old scuffed desk in the sheriff's office in Fort Collins, waiting for Sheriff Mason to attend to her. Once her fever had broken and she was well enough, she bathed and dressed in the clothes Charity Franklin had dug out of an old trunk for her. The clothes were Quaker style—all gray dresses with little black buttons and collars riding up her neck. They fit her awkwardly, as they were not made for an expecting woman but rather were sized for a much larger one. The petticoats practically swept the floor. Although, the last thing Grace cared about right now was clothing. Grace assumed these were some of

Mrs. Franklin's discards, set aside to donate to someone less fortunate.

Well, she couldn't think of anyone less fortunate than herself. Even though her hosts had been kind and urged her to stay in bed longer, Grace could stand being shut inside not a moment longer. The Franklins had told her the sheriff didn't make house calls—even though his office was a mere five blocks from their modest home on Maple Avenue.

Grace frowned, but the tears had all but dried up. Now she was left with a gaping hole in her heart, fearing the worst. Surely if Monty had survived his ordeal in the river, he would have come straightaway to Fort Collins, looking for her. But the deputy she spoke with upon entering the office this bright, cold spring morning told her he'd heard no word of a man named Montgomery Cunningham, nor had anyone made mention of finding anyone dead on the banks of the Cache la Poudre.

A middle-aged man in a long woolen coat and brown canvas trousers sporting a cartridge belt around his hips tromped into the office from an adjacent room. Grace wrung her hands and fidgeted as he pushed aside a messy stack of papers on his desk and motioned for her to sit in the rickety wooden chair opposite his. When they were seated, he leaned his large head forward and put his elbows on the desk. His eyes were stern and small, and he had a trim thick dark beard on his narrow face.

Grace gulped, uneasy in his presence and still feeling weak and drained empty from days of crying.

"I'm Sheriff Mason, Miss . . . ?" His gruff voice was barely congenial. He raised his eyebrows, waiting for her to speak.

"*Mrs.* Cunningham. Grace Cunningham." He gestured for her to speak in a manner that said he'd heard it all and couldn't be bothered by the insignificant concerns of a pregnant woman. She noticed his gaze drop to her ring finger.

"I lost my wedding ring," she told him. "It was in my husband's bag—for safekeeping." Her hands had swelled with her pregnancy, and she'd hardly gotten the ring off after a long battle with a bar of hard soap. And now the ring was . . . where? Tumbling down the river? Lodged in mud at the bottom of the Poudre? Oh, her heart wouldn't stop aching. How she longed for Monty. For his arms around her. She glanced at the door, hoping against hope that he'd stride in, a relieved smile on his face, calling her name, his arms wide, eager to gather her up.

The pain of her loss crippled her, and she doubled over. The sheriff jumped up and fetched her a cup of hot coffee.

"Here, take a few sips to warm you. I understand you've been through a mighty ordeal."

She wondered what he'd heard. Had the Franklins spoken to him, after all? "My husband was swept away in the flood—just north of town. We . . . saw the bridge shake loose and fall into the river. And then the ground gave way . . ." Grace buried her hands in her head, reliving the moment she saw Monty slip from her sight, his stricken face looking at hers as she screamed.

"I'm sorry," she said, straightening and trying to compose herself. She pulled a handkerchief from her dress pocket and dabbed at her eyes. Her head still pounded—no doubt from all the weeping she'd done.

He waited until she sat still, then said, his voice brusque and all business, "Folks travel along the river and the roads north and east every day. If your husband"—he said the last word in a dubious tone, not unlike the one Mrs. Franklin had used—"or his . . . body washed ashore, we'd hear about it. I'll notify the Greeley sheriff of your concern. The Cache la Poudre joins the South Platte north of

Greeley, and the river there is shallow and wide—a veritable mud pit most of the year." He eyed her suspiciously. "You have nothing on your person—no papers or money, personal belongings?"

"They were all in our wagon. The horses were spooked by the lightning, so Monty unhitched them, and they ran off—"

"I see," he said with impatience, glancing over papers on his desk, drumming his fingers.

"I watched the wagon sink into the mud. Surely it must still be there . . . somewhere?"

She pleaded with her eyes for a response. He just studied her and said, "It just disappeared? Is that what you're saying?"

"Well, not *vanished*, as in a magic trick. Perhaps it washed downriver?"

He grunted in what Grace assumed was disbelief. She supposed if an entire wagon made its way downriver, someone would find that as well. Her heart and hopes sank as she realized he did not believe her, and had no plans to help her. She would hire someone to help her—but she had no money. She was at the mercy of the Franklins and their kindness. However, she knew she could not milk that kindness too long. She thought how she would have to find a job while pregnant, to support herself and her baby without Monty, make a life in this town. No. She couldn't do it. How could she?

Loneliness and fear assailed her as she numbly stood and politely took her leave of Sheriff Mason. On the way out of the office, she noticed a Wanted poster showing sketches of two men. The poster announced they were members of the Dutton Gang, at large and dangerous.

She huffed as she walked outside and into the spring morning. Standing on the wooden boardwalk, she took in the many stores with their false wooden fronts—the mercantile on the corner, a druggist's, a butcher shop, a large brick two-story building with the name "Metropolitan Hotel" over its doors. Most of the buildings on this very wide street were two-storied. This was the booming Western town she and Monty had talked about long hours into the night as they packed and prepared to move west.

But as sparkling and promising this town seemed from the outside, Grace already felt regret over being here. This wasn't her home—how could it ever be without Monty? But she had no home to return to, no one back in Illinois, now that her aunt was gone. And Monty had no family to speak of—he'd lost track of them years ago, and besides, they didn't sound like people Grace would want to know—or ask for help. No, she had to stay here. This is where Monty would come to find her.

She was on her own. Abandoned, pregnant, broke. Mr. Franklin had assured her she could stay until after the baby was born. Their children were all grown and back in Ohio, and they had recently moved out here to start a Quaker church, heeding God's calling to spread the gospel to "those unsaved in the unsavory West"—as Mrs. Franklin had worded it.

It didn't sit well with Grace to take charity from others. She had worked hard helping her aunt with the boardinghouse, and she'd been taught a skill. Her aunt wanted to make sure Grace would be able to support herself once she was on her own, so she spent years instructing her in sewing, and Grace had become a proficient seamstress. Surely in a town this size there would be a need for such a vocation. If she couldn't land a job in a shop, perhaps she could work piecemeal. But where would she get the money to buy a sewing machine? Her Wheeler & Wilson machine had been packed in a crate in the wagon . . .

Hopelessness threatened to engulf her as she stood gazing at the people walking through town, chatting merrily, wholly ignorant of her wretched plight. Carriages and wagons rolled down the wide dirt street, and neighbors shouted out greetings to one another.

She fingered the pendant around her neck. She would never forget the look in Monty's eyes the day he unclasped the chain from his neck and fastened it around her own, then dropped to one knee, taking her hands in his, and declaring his love. He had asked her—no, begged her—to marry him. Her aunt, sick as she was, rallied long enough to witness their vows—uttered before Grace's pastor at her aunt's bedside, a beatific and satisfied smile on her aunt's face as she listened, enrapt, to the pastor's words and the repeating of their vows. By morning her beloved aunt had passed on, but Grace was grateful Aunt Eloisa had seen the niece she'd raised married to such a fine, honorable man.

How Grace missed her aunt, and her warm and comfortable home in the town she'd spent her entire life in. She would have been content to stay there, but she knew how Monty loved the wilderness, felt more at home in mountains and under trees than confined by walls and the softness of down-filled mattresses and padded sofas. Insisting that Monty settle into such a mundane and predictable lifestyle would have been like caging a bear. He thrived on wide-open spaces. Running her aunt's boardinghouse would have smothered him.

Yet, as much as he liked the hard earth and toughness of the land, his heart had remained sensitive and tender. Grace he seen the way he was around children, and the kind way he treated all animals. She'd wanted nothing more than to see him hold his own child in his arms. To see all their children grow strong and brave and educated under his loving tutelage.

She stood unmoving, blinking back tears, wondering if one day her tears would dry up or if she would cry forever. The long winter was finally over, and only small patches of snow lay in the shadow of the newly built buildings. The young, new town was filled with people full of hope, looking forward to a bountiful summer, and next year would be the centennial for the nation. There was talk that Colorado would become the thirty-eighth state admitted to the union.

Hope rang out in the air all around her, but she was impervious to it. She felt nothing but loss. But for her baby's sake, she would hold on to hope. Hold on to it as if it were a lifeline—and never let go.

Chapter 6

Five months later
October 22, 1875

Malcolm Connors extended his arm as a cool breeze riffled through his hair and he took in the town. She gave him a smile as he wrapped the thick woolen shawl around her shoulders and stepped carefully down to the hard-packed dirt street. Stella surveyed with delight the many brightly lit shops in the waning evening light. Their two draft horses pawed the snow-dusted street in front of the wide wooden boardwalk fronting the business district of Fort Collins on College Avenue. The scent of pine and snow filled his nose as he looked around with curiosity at this place that would now be their home. As glad as he was to finally arrive, an sense of trepidation rumbled in his gut.

They had finally made the trip over from Greeley, and he looked forward with anticipation to picking out a parcel to homestead. He was glad to leave that tiny dilapidated cabin behind, and the thought of building a house stirred his excitement. Although, his lack of memories dampened the elation, creating an unease that simmered without letup underneath his feelings.

He watched his wife look into the windows of a dry goods store and sighed. These last few months would have been unbearable had it not been for his sweet Stella. She had painstakingly nursed him back to health when he'd been at death's door. With the patience of a saint, she had sat with him as week after week showed no sign of his memory returning. He hadn't missed the great sadness in her eyes as she recounted their prior years together in St. Louis, how they'd met on a paddle steamer on the Mississippi and fell in love—two young adventurers with the past left far behind them. How he wished he could remember!

His heart wrenched when she told him the horrifying story of the fire, and how her family had all perished when she was but a child. He learned his parents had succumbed to a virulent influenza that had spread like wildfire through the northern hills of Missouri, where he'd been born and grew up, only a year after he'd left home to work as a surveying apprentice in the city. He'd soaked up every tale she told, wishing he could remember something, anything. But the only images that came to him were in his restless dreams at night, where he rode down roaring rivers in canoes, and water tossed and tumbled him. No doubt these nightmares were due to his falling into the river and getting tangled in that tree.

"Darling, look," his wife said, pulling his attention to her. "There's a sweet little dress shop yonder."

She pointed down the long wooden boardwalk past a large white stucco building that looked like a mercantile, then turned to him and gave him that pouty look that made it hard for him to deny her. "I'm going to need *a lot* of dresses."

She eyed the women walking along the boardwalk, no doubt assessing their fashion sense. Malcolm smiled, glad to see her so happy and wanting to give her everything she desired. She looked so comely in her green silk dress, and he reminded himself what a lucky man he was. Stella had given up much to spend her days and nights in that unfurnished mildewed cabin, as he moaned and tossed and suffered through his recovery. She'd brought an Indian woman over—a local medicine woman named Sarah—who gave them herbs and poultices, which aided greatly in his physical recovery. But nothing could be done for his head injury, which had healed on the outside, the scar unnoticeable under his head of hair. He feared his memory would never return.

But he knew he shouldn't be disgruntled. He should be grateful for his blessings. He had his health back, and was married to a beautiful, devoted woman who looked after his every need, although her cooking left much to be desired. Good thing he knew his way around a stove, and cooked most of their meals, despite Stella's playful protestations. He often surprised himself with the tasty dishes he instinctively knew how to make. Must have been from living on his own those many years in St. Louis.

Malcolm gestured in the other direction. "The land office is over there. I'll probably be a while, so take your time—picking out patterns and fabric, or whatever it is you need to do to get yourself a passel of beautiful dresses."

She twirled around in her pretty green dress flouncing with petticoats, and tightened the bonnet strap under her chin. To his chagrin, she leaned over and planted a kiss on his lips and he blushed, aware of eyes upon them. Such a public display of intimacy unsettled him, and that was one thing about Stella that took getting used to.

"Now," she said with her cute little pout, "remember what I said. I want something far out of town, on a creek, with some pretty trees by the water." She put a finger on his lips. "I know you want to be close to town, but we spent years in a city—and although you don't recall that, *I do*. I want some privacy." She ran her other hand down from his chest to his belt buckle, then leaned close and whispered hotly in his ear. "And I don't want anyone to hear us when we're . . . well . . ."

Flustered, Malcolm pulled back, his face flushed. He dropped his gaze in embarrassment as a giggle carried to him on the air.

"Please," he whispered, "we've just arrived. I don't want to make a scene."

Her pout deepened into a frown of chastisement, and Malcolm felt a stab of irritation. Why did she do such things in public? She knew it made him uneasy. Sometimes she seemed downright oblivious to her brash behavior. He blew out a breath and rubbed his neck.

He watched her sashay down the boardwalk, admiring her figure but concerned over the way she brought attention to her femininity. Men on both sides of the street swiveled heads and watched his wife with appraising gazes. He thought about how uneasy he'd felt with her living with him in the cabin. But he'd needed care, and she refused to move into Greeley and find them separate accommodations. Although she made up a bed for herself, saying she respected his decision to wait until they married before they were intimate, he'd often had to struggle painfully to restrain himself. Having her in such close quarters—with her dressing and bathing, and often paying little mind as to whether he was awake or watching her—caused him great distress. He'd wanted to take more time to get to know her all over again, hoping his memory would start returning, but the agony of being with her day after day and not touching her was more than he could bear.

At times she'd lain next to him on the bed, stroked his chest, dropped tender kisses along his neck. Her passion simmered, but his boiled. Finally, he could stand it no longer. By the time he could walk without pain—three months after his injury—she ushered him to the Greeley Courthouse, where they were married without friends or fanfare. Finally, they could consummate their union without reserve, and oh, what a joyous feeling to be able to engage in such passionate embrace. But underneath all his joy lay an unsettling feeling. For every time he held Stella in his arms, something felt terribly wrong. He couldn't explain it, and he dared not say anything to her, for fear it would greatly upset her. All he could do was chalk it up to his memory loss and trust that, in time, the feeling would dissipate.

Truth was, he didn't really feel any love for her. He must have at some point in his life—for why would he have proposed to her, and traveled with her to start their married life together in the West? Even though he couldn't recall his own name, he knew he was a man of honor, and he had promised her he'd marry and provide for her. How could he renege on such a promise and break her heart? Still, he wished they had waited, and although he knew it was the proper thing to do, guilt and shame over his lack of self-control ate at him. But what man could resist such a woman?

He breathed out a long sigh. He was only human. And maybe in time, that love he once had—that Stella had recounted to him with such passion—would reawaken.

He walked over to the land office, nodding politely as curious townspeople greeted him with a smile or tip of their hat. With the railroad scheduled to come to Fort Collins inside of a year, the town was booming. He'd passed two large sawmills while riding into town, which sported lumberyards chockful of milled boards stacked in neat piles, and a two-story brick kiln and a flour mill. The population, now bursting out of the city boundaries, would require new streets and new homes—or so he'd read in the *Greeley Tribune*. He hoped he could get a job at the land office, or with the surveyor.

He'd read that they were short staffed, and the town, recently platted, would be expanding in all directions. Already a college had been built that would presently open its doors to students. An up-and-coming town, and Malcolm was glad to be a part of its infancy. No doubt it would grow to be an impressive county seat.

Although he had no memory telling him why he wanted to come to Fort Collins, of all towns in the West, his heart sang out in joy as he took in the sight of the majestic snow-packed Rockies, a picturesque backdrop to the town, with the vast open space of the Front Range spreading to the east. He drew in a deep breath, and a longing for mountains streamed through his veins like a river. His heart beat hard and powerful in his chest as he thought of climbing the peaks towering before him, exploring unchartered regions, and looking over vistas of flower-studded alpine valleys.

The images felt like memories, but he couldn't put names to the places he envisioned. Were they real? Had he been there? He couldn't see how, if he'd been living in a city all his life. He once suggested to Stella he try to get in touch with people he knew back in St. Louis. Maybe seeing other faces from his past would jar his memory, but Stella had been insistent he refrain. It would only add to his frustration to try to recapture the past, she'd told him. They had their whole lives ahead of them—a brand-new life and one they'd planned for so long. And now—here they were.

He frowned. Maybe she was right. Put the past in the past. With the money they had—money they'd both earned back in St. Louis and had been saving for their move—they could build a nice little house and maybe someday start a family.

The thought of having a child erupted a sudden ache in his heart. He stopped and caught his breath. How odd. He fought a need, a strong need, to go somewhere, find someone. But who? Where?

He clamped his eyes shut and willed the memories to come, but like a dream upon awakening, the urgency drifted out of reach, and he stood there, unblinking, feeling an uncanny sense of loss. For his parents? Had he lost a brother or sister? Stella said he was an only child. Then why did this feeling grip him so tenaciously?

Frustration mixed with sadness as he resolutely made his way to the land office, his excitement now strangely dampened. As if something in this town were affecting him, stirring his unease and creating a disquiet in his soul.

He shook his head to dispel the feeling, and turning his thoughts to acquiring his quarter section of land, he walked to the land office and opened the heavy oak door.

Grace pulled a straight pin from her mouth and poked it through the thick worsted wool. She eyed the line of the hem and made a slight adjustment, then stepped back and studied the finished dress with satisfaction. It felt good to be working again, doing something creative and taking her mind off her constant heartache. As much as she loved her precious son—Benjamin Montgomery Cunningham—seeing Monty's features in her baby's face only made her loneliness flare. Oh, how he looked just like his father. At three months, he had a boisterous laugh that made his eyes twinkle—just like Monty's. He looked at everything with riveted interest, his little head swiveling from side to side taking it all in. He loved it when Grace perched him next to the window, where he tried to stand on his wobbly legs and look out at his world. Grace would hold his chubby little hands while he balanced precariously on his tiptoes, his toothless smile showing his delight in life and his love for everyone. So like his father.

She took the dress off the mannequin and sat in the big stuffed chair to hand-stitch the hem for Mrs. Stroud. A warm winter dress this would be, and of the latest fashion. The back room where she worked, in the spacious dress shop inside the Old Grout building, was drafty and a bit chilly. In the front room a fire blazed, enticing ladies to come inside and get warm. Tildie Hortman, the owner of the shop, was an astute businesswoman with impeccable fashion sense, and she tolerated neither slacking nor sloppy work. But Grace paid little attention to her employer's complaints. She worked hard and produced quality work, and although Tildie doled out praise stingily as if it were diamonds, Grace knew she approved of her work.

Grace recalled how at one time she'd loved creating patterns to showcase the latest styles from back east. Her customers in St. Louis had money and taste, which made dressmaking enjoyable, for they would tell her to spare no expense to make them look beautiful. She thought of her own dresses, her favorites that she had brought on the wagon with her, now lost forever. During the summer months, she had made a few functional outfits—using the money the Franklins had collected from members of their small church to buy fabric. But they were simple and nothing as beautiful as the ones she had painstakingly created. Which now sat on the muddy bottom of the Poudre River.

But amid all the loss, she had Benjamin. Oh, how she loved him. Even working these few hours a day felt torturous, and when she finished her work, she'd hurry down the streets to gather him up in her arms. She loved cuddling him and smelling his wonderful baby smell. How grateful she was that he'd been born without incident, that her fever and grief had not harmed her little babe. The local doctor, out of kindness, delivered Benjamin without cost, and although the labor and birth had been horrific—made more so by

Monty's absence at this blessed occasion—she came through unscathed, and for that she was truly grateful.

Charity, glad to have a baby in her house once more—after having raised six children—was more than happy to care for Benjamin while she worked. Hopefully, when winter came—and the air hinted its close arrival—she could do piecework at home for Tildie. For now, the woman needed her in the shop for fittings and measurements, but Grace was told that during the winter they mostly kept the shop closed. In the spring, the ladies of town would emerge from their homes like bears from hibernation and descend with their appetites to buy more custom-made clothing.

She threaded her needle and got comfortable in the chair, with the bright kerosene lantern on the table beside her. Five months had passed since she lost Monty. She had spent those months inquiring of everyone she could think of—those in law enforcement, stage coach drivers, cattle ranchers, and any who may have traveled along the Poudre River in recent months. No one had seen sign of either Monty or their belongings. It was as if they had disappeared from the face of the world.

No doubt someone, at some point, would find a piece of her clothing or a water-logged book she'd once read by the hearth at her aunt's home washed up on some bank of weeds. How would she know? But surely, if her husband had washed up somewhere, there would be a notice in some paper—an obituary or news item. She had been checking the papers as often as she could, and although the sheriff deigned to listen to her unrelenting urgings to help her find Monty, he never had any news for her. Her most fearful thought was that Monty was at the bottom of the river, having been snagged by a submerged tree or pinned by a boulder.

The thought of his body decomposing in the frigid water, fish nibbling his flesh, made her tremble. Yet, she knew there was no other place he would rather be in death. He once told her if he ever died, he wanted her to send him down Yosemite Falls. She smiled despite her sadness. As if she could manage such a feat. But her smile quickly turned sour as she thought about spending the rest of her life alone, waiting. For she would wait—until the end of time, if that was required of her. If it meant waiting until they were reunited in heaven, she would do so. For she could never foster the thought of another man in her arms. Never. Those arms were meant for Monty and him alone.

Tildie's voice from the front of the shop shattered her thoughts.

"Grace," she called to her in her eloquent voice, poking her perfectly coiffed head into the back room and ushering in a wonderful blast of heat. "I have some items for you to wrap for a customer."

Grace set down her stitching and came to the front of the store, where Tildie motioned to a stack of clothing on the counter with a waggling finger. Tildie was a spinster, in her forties, and known to be the worst gossip in Fort Collins—as the gossip went. Grace hardly listened to anything the customers chatted about as she wrapped their packages or helped them find fabrics and dress patterns. Although, she always kept one ear turned to hear any news about her husband, as unlikely as that was.

Tildie, elegantly dressed, with every hair in place, was in animated discourse with Auntie Stone—an old but spry woman who was quite the entrepreneur. Auntie owned the brick house, which was a kiln that made bricks for the buildings in town, and she also owned the glamorous Metropolitan Hotel. Every time Auntie came in, she engaged Grace in friendly banter, and just spending a few minutes with the woman brightened Grace's day.

As Grace cut a long sheet of brown paper, the bell over the door jingled, and a woman in a very pretty forest-green silk dress came waltzing in, her lustrous black hair pinned up under a very stylish hat. Grace greeted her and asked, "May I help you with something?"

The young woman—perhaps a few years older than Grace but quite lovely and youthful, with a smooth and unblemished complexion—tipped her head as if looking down over spectacles at Grace. "Well . . . what a lovely little shop you have here," she drawled. "I've just arrived in town, and I'll be wanting to have some dresses made."

"Of course," Grace said, stepping back to let her peruse the bolts of fabric stacked on the shelves. The woman ran her finger along the rows of material, making little noises of approval or disapproval. She stopped at one section—the French laces—and pointed. "Nice. Imagine—a town in the middle of nowhere selling French lace. Isn't that something."

Grace stood patiently, trying to be gracious despite the woman's condescending tone. She glanced at the clock on the wall and realized it was almost time to quit for the day. And she was more than ready to go home, where she'd soak in a hot bath—after feeding and playing with Benjamin. The thought of his happy smile greeting him made her warm inside.

The woman stared at Grace, and with a brusque tone said, "I don't have time today, but I would like to come in at a later date and pick out some patterns."

Grace nodded, and Tildie, having finished exchanging pleasantries with Auntie Stone, came bustling over, her skirts and crisp petticoats rustling against the counters as she came to greet their new customer.

Grace said, "May I introduce Tildie Hortman, the owner of the dress shop."

Tildie smiled the way Grace imagined a shark would upon seeing a fat fish for the taking—if sharks could smile. She lifted her prominently pointy chin, exposing her long neck.

"Welcome. Are you new in town?"

"Yes," the woman replied, pulling off a glove and displaying a beautiful gold band inset with diamonds. She showed Tildie the ring, proffering her hand to the shop owner for examination and, no doubt, approval. "I've just gotten married, and . . . I must be the happiest bride in the world. My husband is over at the land office, purchasing some land for us to homestead. This seems like such a friendly little town."

Grace noticed the emphasis she gave to the word *little*.

"Oh, it is!" Tildie gushed. "All the modern conveniences and new stores popping up nearly every day. Why, an opera house is being built, and the railroad will be coming next year. Fort Collins is the gem of the West."

The woman gave a smile of approval, but Grace sensed coldness in her eyes. Arrogance seeped from her bearing.

"And your name?" Tildie asked sweetly.

"Stella. Stella Connors." She turned her head toward the window. "Oh," she breathed out in a kind of swooning ecstasy, "there's my loving husband. Mustn't keep him waiting. Ta-ta, I must be off." With a tiny wave of her hand, the woman spun around and waltzed out the door, as if skating on ice.

Grace heard Tildie sigh, and turned to look at her.

"New love. Is there anything more wonderful? More . . . romantic?"

A rock lodged in Grace's throat as she returned to wrapping the parcel in brown paper, unable to provide even a simple answer in agreement.

No, there was nothing more wonderful. She had experienced such love for too short a time, every minute precious and beautiful. But in a flash, she had lost it all, and now was left with a huge hole in her heart, as if someone had shot her but left her unable to die. Seeing that woman so radiant, with her whole life spread out before her—embracing her dream to homestead and raise a family and watch her children grow with her husband—made Grace's heart throb with pain. That had been Grace's dream, and it had been ripped from her.

All the bitterness and anger she had pushed down deep into her heart now erupted like a volcano. It wasn't fair. Why her? Why had she lost the man she loved so soon? He never got to hold his son, see his baby's beautiful smile—

Grace swallowed back the tears, not wanting Tildie to see her cry. She knew what Tildie thought of her story—what everyone in town thought—that she'd made it up. That she was a wanton woman who'd gotten herself pregnant, then took advantage of the kindness of strangers to take care of her and pay for her every need. She'd overheard Tildie whispering to customers about her, and Grace had seen the looks from many as she walked through the town, or pushed Benjamin in the perambulator that Charity bought for her.

Their cruel gossip hurt, but not as much as the truth of her loss. She'd hoped someday to find someone who believed her, someone who would be a friend, to be able to comfort her when she needed it. But so far she hadn't met anyone who seemed to care or want to get to know her. Adjusting to small-town life and gossip was hard, but she had to stay in Fort Collins. This is where Monty would come looking for her. If she left, he would never find her, and she would have to abandon all hope—and it was that hope alone that kept her going day after day.

She tied twine around the package and stared out the window at the front of the store. Without saying good-bye, Grace fetched her coat that was hanging in the back room and wrapped her scarf around her neck. Her head tucked down against the biting wind, she thought of what a long, lonely winter lay ahead of her. She wished she could hibernate like a bear, Benjamin sleeping soundly against her chest, the way he often did at night, his little breaths and sucking sounds a comfort to her soul. She could hide in the dark and dream sweet dreams of Monty, and lose herself in her memories. For that was all she had left of him, and it frightened her the way his features were starting to fade. Only when she looked in her son's face could she remember, amid the pain and sorrow.

Down the street a man was helping Stella Connors into a wagon. His back was to her, but he reminded her of Monty. Many men did. Anytime she saw someone of his stature and build she sucked in a breath, hoping against hope, knowing she was being foolish.

Unmoving, she watched, her heart aching, thinking of how that should have been her. Coming into town on their wagon, going to the land office and getting a quarter section to homestead. She and Monty by now would have built a little cabin, their first real home, and as winter blew in, they would sit by the big stone hearth Monty built, playing with Ben, with a fire crackling and fat flakes of pristine snow falling in quiet drifts, enveloping them in their joy.

Yes, she told herself bitterly, it should have been her.

Chapter 7

Seven months later
May 13, 1876

Warm, soothing spring sunlight streamed through the large pane glass of the front windows of Matilda Hortman's dress shop. Grace lifted her face to the radiating heat, so grateful the long, cold winter was over. Temperatures were now rising into the 70s midday, which afforded her jaunts outside with Ben in the afternoons, when she finished work. She had sewn dozens of dresses over the winter for Tilde, who had graciously allowed Grace to take the new Chadwick & Jones sewing machine home. The hours spent working—and sewing outfits for herself and her son—helped pass the endless days buried in snow and loneliness, as did little Ben and his antics.

As she reluctantly abandoned the warmth of the shop and returned to her chilly room in the back to cut fabric for her next order, she marveled at how much Ben had grown—and grown even more like his father. Every day saw a new skill Ben learned or a new tooth. He was now nine months old, and already trying to walk, grabbing on to furniture and toddling from room to room, eager to venture out into the world. He loved playing in the snow, and his face filled with wonder at all the new things he noticed as spring changed the landscape and flowers poked up from the drifts. So much like his father—having a zest for life and a cheerful countenance. He hardly ever fussed and loved to babble—although Grace could only guess what his long funny monologues meant.

She sighed and unrolled the bolt of chambray fabric, end over end, across the long wooden table. After evening out the edges, she began laying the pieces of paper patterns in a loose jigsaw puzzle arrangement, then pinned each piece in place.

She had to admit, she was happy enough. And Ben was the reason. Without him, she would have long ago dissolved in grief. She still held on to hope that Monty would one day walk into town. Throughout the winter she imagined every possible scenario that could reasonable explain his delay. Perhaps he'd been hurt, and was convalescing in a place where he was unable to get word to her. For, if he assumed she'd gone to Fort Collins, he would send her a letter by post, and the clerk in the post office in the Old Grout well knew she was awaiting correspondence, and had promised her that if a letter came, he would deliver it to her at the shop. So she concluded he was living in some remote place, and circumstances did not afford him the opportunity to either leave or contact her.

She knew how farfetched that seemed, but since his body had not been found, she had to hope he was still alive.

She had holed up in the Franklins' house all winter, rarely venturing outside and often getting cabin fever, so now her body ached to stretch and move, and she longed to ride a horse across the open range. She hoped once summer eased in she'd be able to take Ben up into the mountains. She longed to explore the Rockies and see the vistas of the Front Range from its heights. Growing up in flat Illinois deprived her of such exploration, and she'd never had much of a hankering to venture beyond the wilds of the local parks. But here—a world of mountains beckoned.

The bell over the door jingled, and Grace stopped what she was doing and went into the front room. Tildie had left her in charge while she went to Mrs. Tedmon's millinery and trimming store on Linden to pick up some notions. The front door opened and a woman came in, dressed in an elegant French toile jacket over a white silk button shirt with shirred cuffs and collar. Grace straightened, recognizing the woman who had walked through the door back in the fall—the one who had just married and was homesteading. A twinge of envy plucked her heart as she thought of this woman enjoying the warmth and comfort of her husband's arms through the long cold winter.

Grace pushed down the unwanted despair and pasted a smile on her face.

"Good day, madam. I'm glad you've returned. I trust you are well, and have settled into your new home?"

The woman gave her a small smile—one that seemed to cost her some effort. "Why, how good of you to remember. Yes, I am quite well, and we were so fortunate to take over a claim that had been abandoned—a few miles south of town, on a creek. With a sweet little house already built."

"Why, how nice," Grace said, walking to stand behind the counter so as not to block the door. "And would you like to look through patterns? Perhaps choose some fabrics for dresses?"

"I would." She loosed a sigh and patted her neatly pinned black hair that shone in the bright light filtering into the room. Grace admired the woman's figure and tiny waist, and wondered when—or if—she might ever regain her youthful shape after having a baby. She expected this woman would have been with child by now, but clearly she was not.

As Grace pulled out the large heavy pattern books, Tildie breezed into the shop, all afluster. "My," she said, breathless, "there's been a bank robbery over in Laporte." She cast a glance at the customer, who turned and looked at her curiously.

"Oh," Tildie said, waving her hand at her face as if the room were too warm. "Mrs. Connors. Have I remembered correctly?"

The customer raised her eyebrows. "Why yes, Stella Connors." She pushed a smile up her face. "Do tell," she said, clearly hiding her interest. Grace noted the woman had laid her hands on the edge of the table, as if anticipating bad news. "Laporte isn't all that far away, is it?" she asked.

"No," Tildie said, leaning close, her expression oozing concern. "Only a few miles."

"Did they catch the robbers?" Stella asked, her tone even, but her eyes betraying her. Grace could tell she was agitated. Why would a robbery in Laporte concern her?

"No, they didn't," Tildie said, her voice now a bit querulous. Then, in a whisper, she said with wide-open eyes, "They think it's the Dutton Gang. Or, what's left of the gang. The two men in the Wanted posters."

Grace recalled seeing the poster in the sheriff's office last fall. "So they haven't yet been caught, after all this time?" Grace asked.

Tildie shook her head spasmodically. "What if they come here next? Someone thought they recognized those men as they galloped out of town—and they were heading east!"

"When?" Stella asked, clearly worried. Perhaps she was afraid of outlaws. Although, why would that be so?

"Just this morning. Word came through the telegraph. I overheard men talking in the post office as I walked by. Oh my!"

Tildie waved her hand again and busied herself at the register—perhaps thinking about hiding her money from the robbers. Surely the sheriff had been alerted, and the banks would be watched and protected. There were only the two in town. Fort Collins saw little crime, considering the town was situated in the wild and untamed West.

Grace thought how not even ten years ago there had been unending Indian wars and skirmishes, with settlers attacked and killed. And now, towns were spreading across the plains accompanied by the railroad, which brought civilization and civility to the wilderness. She imagined in another ten years these small towns would resemble the larger cities back east. Progress, they called it.

Grace busied herself neatening up the fabric bolts on the shelves while out of the corner of her eye she watched as Stella, who sat in the big padded armchair near the window, thumbing thoughtfully through a pattern book. But upon closer scrutiny, Grace noticed Stella's hands trembling, and dots of perspiration covered her high forehead. Clearly something greatly disturbed the woman, but Grace said nothing, and left her to her perusals.

The front door opened, and the tinkling of the bell rang through the shop. A man, with his head down, stomped snow and mud off his boots, then wiped them on the mat just outside the door. He raised his head and stepped inside.

Grace gasped. All the blood drained from her face, and her knees buckled. Her breath snagged in her throat and she began to fall, grasping blindly for something to hold on to, unable to take her eyes off the man's face.

No. It couldn't be. But . . . there he was! Right in front of her . . .

She tried to say his name, but nothing would come out of her mouth. Her head spun wildly as she found her balance on trembling legs.

Monty! Monty! She froze in place, waiting for him to turn his head and see her. She made a mewling noise, a cry that erupted from her broken heart, bursting with love and longing and painful relief. *He's alive, alive! Oh, gracious God, thank you, thank you!*

Just as she found her feet and made to run to him with open arms, he saw her.

A puzzled look rose on his face, and he turned away.

He hadn't recognized her . . .

Grace stiffened. Horrified. As if a thousand lightning bolts had hit her, she sizzled in fear and confusion, unable to take another step. She forced the word out of her mouth on a tiny wisp of breath.

"Monty . . ."

But he didn't hear her. Grace watched in stunned agony as he walked over to Stella, a smile rising on his face.

Oh, that smile, his smile. Monty! Tears rushed to her eyes. She must be imagining this. It couldn't be real. So many times she'd pictured him walking through this door, crying her name, throwing his arms around her. But never had she envisioned this . . . this torture.

What cruel twist of fate had taken her husband from her? This was worse than death.

She stood frozen in place, her stomach churning violently in protest as she watched, as if from afar, as Monty—her husband!—helped Stella to her feet and spoke quiet, tender words into her ear. Stella grinned and met his eyes, oblivious to the maelstrom of anguish strangling Grace.

She forced herself to breathe, grasping the edges of the table, and turning so that no one could see her distress. But a moment later she felt a hand on her shoulder, and Grace spun to find Tildie at her side, her visage showing worry and concern.

"What is it, Grace? Are you ill?" Her employer studied her, then glanced back at Stella and Monty, who were both standing at the door.

Nausea rose into Grace's throat. "I think I'm going to be sick . . ."

She ran into the back room, hearing Tildie exchange polite good-byes with her customer as Grace threw open the heavy back door that led into the alley behind the building. There she heaved up the contents of her stomach as ripples of pain ran through her body and a sword pierced her heart.

No, no, no . . . she keep saying to herself. It couldn't be Monty. But it was. He could be no other. A year's absence—no, not even a hundred years'—could cause her to forget his face or his stature. He'd walked in with a bit of a limp, and a thin scar marred his right cheek, but she had not a speck of doubt this was her Monty.

She wiped her face and stumbled backward, finding the brick wall of the building and sliding down against it into a heap. She curled into a ball and wept, confused and hurting, as if someone had pummeled her with fists. How could he do this to her? Had he pretended he did not know her? Why would he have married another? It made no sense, none at all.

She poured out her heart in prayer, begging God to help her, to bring Monty back to her, into her arms. She lost track of time, and her legs grew numb. She lost all feeling in her fingers as she wept in the cold alley and clouds blew in to blot out the sun. What had promised to be a warm, hopeful day turned stormy and threatening.

She'd thought the long winter had ended, but now she realized it had truly just begun.

As Malcolm approached the door to the surveyor's office, he looked over at Stella, whose thoughts seemed miles away.

"Is something the matter?" he asked, stopping on the boardwalk and disengaging his arm from hers.

"Why, no," she said, surprised. "Why do you ask?"

"You seem bothered. Worried." He could tell she was doing her best to hide her consternation, and that troubled him.

She wave a hand in dismissal. "Oh, it's nothing. I was just . . . remembering how, a year ago, you had fallen into the river and I had to help pull you out." She shuddered. "The river was so cold, and you were so hurt. I-I thought I'd lost you."

A lone tear dribbled down her cheek, and Malcolm touched it with his finger. Once again, he was reminded of how indebted he was to her—not that she meant to make him feel that way. But he couldn't help it. He just wished he felt more than indebtedness toward her. He wished he . . . loved her.

Was something wrong with him? Just about any man would give his best horse for a woman as beautiful and devoted as she. But then he thought about the recent months they'd spent together in their modest little cabin along the South Platte. She'd grown sullen and restless, and he thought it was due to her wanting a baby—her maternal instincts acting up—but when he suggested that, she laughed—a sort of bitter, mean laugh. As if he was foolish to suggest that. He realized then that they had never spoken about having children. It appeared she didn't want any, although why she wasn't with child yet puzzled him. But he wanted children, very much so, and yet, when he thought about having children with her, his mind went blank and his longing faded.

He shook his head to clear out the cobwebs. He studied her distraught face. "But that's all in the past," he said, trying to lighten her mood. A year. Had it been that long ago? He breathed in a deep breath. And still—no memories. He had finally accepted the fact that he would probably never remember his past. But his dreams plagued him, and he had not said a word to Stella about them. Were they only dreams? He hated to think so.

"I'll be a while." He pointed to the hotel on the corner. "Would you prefer to wait in there, get yourself a cup of coffee?"

She patted his arm and smiled, but he could tell her thoughts were still troubled. "Yes, I'll wait for you there." She planted a kiss somewhere on the vicinity of his cheek and crossed the street with care, avoiding the deep mud puddles and horse droppings that hadn't been removed yet by the morning street cleaners.

He walked into the assessor's office—a spacious room with large windows and paneled in rich dark wood and smelling like cigars—and headed to the long front counter, where three men stood speaking animatedly. He immediately recognized the new sheriff with his broad-rimmed slouch hat and a shiny tin star pinned to his brown woolen vest. Malcolm had attended the town hall meeting in which the sheriff had spoken to the crowd after his appointment. The man seemed decent and upstanding, fastidiously dressed, and he had a bushy brown moustache that cast a shadow over his mouth and side whiskers that ran down his wide face. His eyes were big and gray, shrouded by thick brows, and they rested on Malcolm as he came up to him.

The court clerk was in his thirties and short, with a lean face and bony body. He seemed a bit nervous or shy, and wore thick spectacles that made his eyes look like a bug's. His light-brown hair was curly and unruly, and his clothing hung loosely on him, as if his mother had dressed him in a hurry and forgotten to comb his hair. But the man had a warm and friendly face, and Malcolm immediately liked him. Maybe he reminded of someone in Malcolm's forgotten past.

Malcolm tipped his head and touched the brim of his bowler hat. "Good day, gentlemen. I'm Malcolm Connors."

All three bid him a genial hello and introduced themselves.

"This here's the sheriff, Eph Love," an older silver-haired man with a clean-shaven face said. "I'm Fred Wallace, the city assessor, and this is Alan Patterson—the courthouse clerk."

"Pleased to make your acquaintance," Malcolm said. "I recently moved to Fort Collins, and I'm looking for gainful employment. I . . . have surveying experience. Back in St. Louis." It felt odd to say that, seeing as how he had no memory of doing actual surveying work, but when he'd looked at the surveying instruments Stella had shown him, with his initials scratched into them, a strong recognition came over him. He knew those instruments. When he picked them up and felt them in his hands, he had no doubt he could survey a piece of land—measure its size, use chain poles, and record the proper notations. Why would he remember this but not anything else—except, perhaps, how to cook and ride a horse?

"Well," the assessor said, his face brightening, "we could sure use your help. I was supposed to have a new man in here last spring, but he never showed, and I've been on the scout for more surveyors. The railroad's coming in later this year, and already folks are moving here in droves. I reckon I can give you as much work as you want, Mr. Connors."

"That's wonderful news, sir." Relief coursed through him, and he nodded as the other men said kind words of welcome. Malcolm thought about his recent arguments with Stella over his seeking employment. For some reason she didn't want him to take a job in town. Maybe she worried she'd be lonely being by herself out on the homestead, but he told her they were running out of money. She only huffed, but had no other suggestions for him. He was a surveyor. She had told him they'd planned to live in Fort Collins because that's where he'd find work. And now she was complaining about him doing that very thing.

He pushed down his mounting exasperation and smiled at the three men, whom he'd found himself taking an immediate liking to.

"So, how d'ya like our town?" Wallace asked him.

"I like it just fine. It has a lot of promise, and the location is beautiful."

"You been north of here yet—up on the Poudre River?" the sheriff asked. "There's some good fishin' up in the canyon."

Malcolm shook his head. "No. After we came out from St. Louis, I . . . had a mishap. Spent a few months near Greeley recovering."

"Oh, that's a shame," Love said, fixing his eyes on Malcolm and studying him. "But you seem all in one piece."

Malcolm joined the men in a friendly chuckle. "I'm ready and fit for work." He gave the assessor a smile. "Got a little tired of being trapped in my small house." He breathed in deeply. "I'm looking forward to getting outside and working in the fresh air."

The sheriff nodded. "The winters can be somethin' fierce out here on the Front Range—"

"And that's why we have so many saloons," Wallace added with a laugh. "Whiskey warms the ice out of the blood. It's what's kept me alive all these years."

Malcolm forced a chuckle. He didn't particularly like whiskey—or any spirits, from what he could tell. But he knew Stella did. He frowned thinking of the many times he watched her plow through half a bottle of whiskey in the cabin late at night. He'd told her he didn't think it was good for her health to drink, but she only laughed as if the notion was silly and childish. She told him he used to drink all the time with her, and frequented many a saloon in St.

Louis, but Malcolm couldn't see how he could have liked such a taste before his injury and then disliked it afterward.

"We used to have an ordinance of prohibition here, like they do over in Greeley," the sheriff told him. "But by popular demand, that law was rescinded last year—thanks to Marcus Coon, the fella that owns the Agricultural Hotel. Folks all seem a little happier these days." He gave a big grin, and Wallace bellowed in agreement.

The court clerk was quiet, saying nothing, just nodding his head. Then, he announced, "I'd best get back to work. But I wanted to hear the news." The clerk nodded a quick good-bye and hurried out the front door.

The sheriff turned to Malcolm. "Seems the Dutton Gang robbed a bank in Laporte." He shook his head morosely. "Those men have been hunted for a year now—ever since they broke out of jail in Denver City. Copeland Townsend, the territorial marshal, has tendered quite a large reward for their capture. You heard of 'em?"

Malcolm shook his head, although he imagined they'd wonder why he was so uninformed. He wouldn't lie, but he didn't want to tell them about his loss of memory. It might hinder their trust in his work, and he wanted to have the best chance to show his skill and earn their respect.

"Well, folks figured they'd left the country or fled to some other state. Or maybe got themselves killed somehow—no one's seen hide nor hair of them two hooligans. And now they pop up—like spring flowers—back at their crooked business."

"Maybe they ran out of money," Malcolm offered.

"More 'n likely," Wallace said, nodding. "But seems stupid to go back to what you got caught at in the first place." He looked at Love. "Well, I'm sure if they show their faces in Fort Collins, they'll end up in your jail. Those posters of their mugs are all over the town.

I know how keen you are to catch 'em." He gave Malcolm a smirk. "So, if you see the likes of 'em, be sure to let Eph know."

Malcolm smiled at their friendly banter. It felt good to stand around chatting with other men. A refreshing change from being stuck in the cabin with Stella.

A pang of guilt hit him as he berated his sour attitude toward his wife. What kind of man was he to so quickly forget what she'd done for him and how much he owed her? Yet, after he wished the men well, thanked the assessor for hiring him, and bounded out the front door of the building, he thought how being indebted to someone was another kind of jail. Maybe one without bars, but confining all the same.

He'd expected marriage to be freeing and joyous, but with each passing day he felt more and more trapped, and only now did he realize it—as feelings of regret bubbled up and his heart ached with a strange loneliness he could not understand.

Chapter 8

"GRACE, GRACE—WHATEVER IS THE matter?"

Grace heard Charity calling after her, but she couldn't bear to speak with her—with anyone. She hoisted Ben into her arms, hugging him tightly to her chest as she rushed out of the house, wishing she could run and run and keep running until she fell into some ocean at the edge of the continent.

Tears poured down her face, just as they had a year ago when she'd lost Monty. All this time she had waited for him or news of him—only to learn he was alive but married to another woman!

Her thoughts careened in her head, making no sense at all. What could she do? She had to do something.

She looked down at her precious son, whose little chubby arms held on to her shoulders, his cheek resting on the bodice of her dress. She pulled her coat around him to enclose him in her warmth, her shoal of safety for him. But was there any safe harbor for her? No. She had been cut loose, like a drifting boat on a wild river, and now she was crashing into rocks and tumbling down a treacherous waterfall to her demise.

There had to be some logical explanation. Monty would never do this. Something had happened, something horrible, but how could she find out? She didn't dare try to find him to speak to him. Her heart couldn't take that. And she certainly couldn't talk to his *wife.*

She could hardly form the word in her mind. Married. He was married to . . . that pompous, shallow, *beautiful* woman. Where on earth had he met her?

She fumed. Monty would never marry someone like her. Stella was the kind of woman he used to tell disapproving stories about when he lived in the boardinghouse. Women who chased after men and only cared about fancy clothes and money and making impressions on others—making other women jealous. Monty had told Grace he loved her because she was exactly the opposite. He loved her kind heart and gratitude for the blessings she had. He admired the way she had cared for her aunt, and how industrious she was, learning a vocation and not expecting a man to grovel at her feet.

The only conclusion she could make was that somehow Monty had forgotten her. He had lost his memories—but how many memories, and which ones? Did he remember some things? He clearly didn't remember his name, for he went by Connors, not Cunningham.

Breathless, she realized she had been running for blocks. She stopped at the corner of College and Maple, then hurried along Jefferson, finally ducking down the alley that ran behind the town livery stables. Ben squirmed, hot under the coat, and Grace realized her arms were aching from his weight. He was no longer the tiny baby she'd carried for hours during his first weeks of life, coaxing him back to sleep late in the night. He felt like a sack of potatoes in her sore arms.

The clouds overhead shredded into cotton wisps carried on an easterly wind, the cold mountain air pushing them out over the open range. The dry air made her skin feel raw, and her lips were chapped. That and the high altitude made Colorado so different from Illinois. Oh, if only she and Monty had stayed in Bloomington!

Grace smelled hay and heard horses snuffling and nickering. She'd never been to the livery in town, and Ben hadn't been up close to any horses, although he always squirmed in excitement watching riders trot them down the streets.

She wiped her face and pushed loose hair from her eyes, then stood her son on the ground. He was dressed in cute denim pants and a thick cotton nightshirt. Charity had bought him adorable leather moccasins, which he now wore on his feet. Sunlight splintered through the clouds and warmed the air, even though Grace felt chilled through and through from the damp perspiration cooling on her skin. Her stomach clenched in pain from the sorrow coursing through her body.

"Hey, baby," she cooed, "Mama's going to show you some horses. What's a horse say?"

Ben wiggled in place as she held his little hands and squatted in front of him. His eyes grew bright and he smiled—showing his four little teeth. "Naaaaaaaayyyyy," he said happily.

"That's right, sweetie. Let's see if we can get a horse to neigh for you."

She picked him up and carried him over to the open stable doors, pushing out every thought in her head so she wouldn't think about Monty. Her son needed her attention, and she needed the distraction.

She took a step into the darkened corridor that ran between rows of stalls. Horses pawed at the ground and munched on flakes of hay. The last time Grace had ridden a horse was back in Illinois, before she and Monty had married. More hurt welled up, pushing tears out of the corners of her eyes. She willed herself to stop thinking about him, but it was so hard.

"Here," she said, taking Ben's little hand and stretching it out before a curious bay horse who pressed its muzzle against the wood slat. The horse snuffed and Ben giggled. Grace couldn't help but smile when Ben shrieked in delight as the horse butted against Ben's hand, no doubt looking for a treat.

"I've a carrot he can give Apache," someone said.

Grace turned around. A young woman with bright red hair and an avalanche of freckles across her nose came over with a fat carrot in her hand.

"Hello," she said with a friendly smile, showing straight white teeth, although a tiny bit bucktoothed. She looked the same age as Grace, and was dressed like Calamity Jane—complete with a long Indian-style straight skirt—no petticoats underneath—and a fringed leather riding coat—the kind the cowboys here in the West wore. Grace hadn't seen many women dressed like that, and not around Fort Collins, but the young woman was very pretty, with a light complexion and sparkling eyes the color of emeralds.

"I'm Clare Ferne McKay, and who's this strappin' lad?" She tickled Ben under his chin, which caused an eruption of giggles from her son. "My, he's sociable."

Grace now noticed the heavy Irish brogue. "My name's Grace. Grace Cunningham. This is Benjamin."

Clare gave an exaggerated curtsey. "Please to meet ya." She handed Ben the carrot, and once he had it well in his grasp, Clare held his little hand and moved it to where the horse could reach it.

Grace watched as Apache took four bites, and when the carrot was down to a stub, Clare took the piece of carrot from Ben and laid it in the palm of her hand. "Now watch," she said to Ben, making sure he was paying attention. She put her hand under the horse's muzzle, and the horse picked up the carrot tenderly with his lips and chomped on it with strong teeth. Ben wiggled in excitement.

"Ma! Ma!" he cried out.

"That means more," Grace said to Clare.

Clare nodded. "I have six younger siblings—I've heard that plenty over the years." She turned to Ben. "You're a cute one. May I?" She looked to Grace, who understood she wanted to hold him. She handed Ben over.

Clare cooed and made funny faces and got Ben laughing riotously. Grace couldn't help but laugh as well, and the laughter eased the pain in her heart for the moment.

"Do you work here?" Grace asked, not imagining anyone hiring a woman as a stable hand.

"I punch leather, in a room over there."

"Punch leather?"

"Saddles, bridles, belts. Sometimes I do designs on saddlebags. I use leather punches. Come'ere, let me show ya." She led Grace to the room she had pointed to, still carrying Ben in her arms. Grace could tell Clare had carried a lot of small children over the years. Ben seemed very relaxed in Clare's arms, and she moved with ease, as if he were an appendage.

Across a long plywood table lay numerous leather goods. Closest to her was a Mexican saddle, and as she drew near, she saw intricate dark designs in the leather. Flowers cascaded over the cantle and skirt surrounding the seat, and the gullet in front had overlapping feathers. She was impressed by the fine detail and beautiful patterns. So much different from designing a dress.

"You do wonderful work. How did you learn this skill?" Grace asked.

Clare bounced Ben and answered, "I just moved here from Laporte. Next to my family's ranch lives an old Mexican who taught me what he'd learned in Sonora. I used to go sit next to him on a stump, watching him punch bridles and saddles for the local cowboys. He's well-known around these parts, and since I was such a curious lass, and would do anything to get out of the noisy house, he let me watch him. When I was about six, he gave me a strip of leather and showed me how to use the various punches." She deposited Ben into Grace's arms. She picked up a few tools that had wooden handles and different-sized metal tips. Then Clare reached for a bridle that sat nearby and demonstrated using a mallet to pound one of the tools into the leather.

Grace watched in fascination as Clare's fingers moved adeptly and a design emerged. "I'm impressed," she said. "Thank you for showing this to me."

They went back out to the horse stalls. Clare said, "I love horses. I spent more time on the back of a horse as a child than I did walkin', and although I'd rather be ridin', this is the next best thing." She walked down the corridor and stopped at a stall where a sturdy mustang nickered at her. She rubbed the horse's forehead and said, "This is my horse—Keeezheekoni. That's Cheyenne for *burning fire.*"

Ben reached out and petted the horse, and giggles erupted. Clare continued. "Well, I had named him Feisty, but Eli told me there's no word in Cheyenne for that, so he gave him that name. But he's Keezy for short."

Grace enjoyed Clare's exuberance, and her love for horses swam in her eyes as she rubbed the mustang's ears. "Who is Eli?"

"He's my sweetheart—over in Greeley. And we're to be married—although he doesn't know it yet." She wiggled her brows as if in conspiracy with Grace.

Grace laughed at her brashness and confidence. Clare wasn't all that unlike the way she herself had been, declaring a similar intention to an eighteen-year-old Monty when she'd been a mere ten. Recalling his humorous reaction to her innocent pronouncement sent another stab of grief to her heart, but she hid her feelings by looking away.

Clare tickled Ben under his chin. "I just turned eighteen, and couldn't get out of the house fast enough." She laughed. "Now it's Shannon's turn to be babysitter to the brood while our parents work the ranch. I took a room at the Agricultural Hotel, although I haven't brought over my things yet."

"I've recently moved here myself," Grace said, and then she felt the pang once more of her loss—living alone in someone else's spare room, instead of homesteading in a cabin with Monty.

"Is it just you and the wee one?" Clare asked kindly, not the way the prying gossipers might ask. She seemed to genuinely care.

Grace nodded, but before she could catch herself, she started crying. Oh, why couldn't she control her tears? She buried her head into Ben's soft hair and stood there, weeping and feeling foolish.

"Here." Clare led her over to a bench and sat her down, then swept Ben from her arms and eased down beside her. She pulled out a wrinkled handkerchief. When Grace looked at it, Clare said, "It's clean."

Grace shook her head. "I know. I-I'm sorry. I'm all alone. I lost my husband—"

Unabashed, Clare wrapped her arm around Grace and held her while she cried. When was the last time anyone had held her, comforted her? Too long ago. She had spent this last year trying to be brave and hopeful, but now all her walls protecting her heart crumbled to dust, leaving her with a sick, empty feeling.

When her tears were spent, she wiped her face with the cloth and looked at Clare, whose eyes showed a deep compassion. Grace imagined Clare had a lot of experience comforting her crying siblings over the years.

"How about we go get a soda?" Clare didn't wait for Grace to answer. She went into the back room and then returned with her straw hat—which was a cross between a sun bonnet and the kind of felt hat men wore—and walked toward the front entrance to the livery. Grace hardly noticed the men working with the carriages and wagons, hitching up horses and throwing saddles over horses' backs, or the strong stench of horse sweat and manure and damp hay.

After exiting onto the street, Clare said, "Where do you live? Do you need help with your precious babe here?"

Grace snuffled, so grateful for Clare's kindness. "Thank you so much. I'm sorry for crying. I don't even know you—"

Clare waved her away. "My mum always says 'Be kind to strangers and God will repay ya.' And then there's this proverb to cheer ya up"—Clare spouted something in another language—"It's Gaelic. 'There's nothing so bad that it couldn't be worse.'" She stopped and looked deep into Grace's eyes. "Life is hard, there's no denying, and surely you've been through hard times. But look." She smoothed out Ben's head as he nodded off in Grace's arms. "You've been blessed with this precious babe—and he's healthy and bright as a penny. He's who ya have to live for. The healing will come." She said something else in Gaelic, and then translated. "If God sends you down a stony path, may he give you strong shoes."

Grace smiled. "Maybe I need to shop for some."

Clare tipped her head toward the end of the street. "There's a cobbler's shop on the corner. Or maybe we can fit you with a set of iron horseshoes."

That made Grace laugh.

When they stopped in front of the green grocers, which had a soda fountain in the back, Clare said solemnly, "Anytime you need a listening ear, you know where to find me. Just neigh, and I'll come out of my stall." Clare giggled.

"Thank you, Clare. I've wanted to make a friend in Fort Collins, and it hasn't been easy. But I hope you'll be my first."

"I need a friend too. And as much as I'm glad to have peace and quiet away from my brothers and sisters, there's nothing so wonderful as holding a bawbeen—a baby."

Clare pulled open the door and ushered Grace inside. It felt good in the midst of her pain to talk to another woman close to her age, someone nice and nonjudgmental. Maybe Clare could help her unravel this mystery that had her husband entangled in another woman's arms. She couldn't bear thinking of Monty pouring out his love to someone else. Her heart had surely broken beyond mending. How could she go on, face tomorrow?

As they sat down at the fountain and waited to order, Grace looked down at Ben's head resting against her chest. He was deep in a peaceful, contented sleep.

Clare was right. She would have to go on for Ben.

Lord, you are going to have to give me those strong shoes—shoes of stone—if I'm going to walk this rocky road.

Chapter 9

LENORA DUTTON WASTED NO TIME easing up to the bar in the saloon next to the hotel and ordering a whiskey. Being that it was only ten in the morning, the barkeep eyed her strangely, but he said nothing. He slid her drink over to her and watched as she threw back her head and emptied the shot glass.

The whiskey went down smooth and she sighed, but although it warmed her innards and slaked her thirst, it did little to soothe her agitation. The idea that Clayton Wymore and Billy Hill Cloyd were still alive and maybe just a few miles away made her gut sour and her palms sweaty. If the news was true, it meant two things—two bad things. One, that those two men were still alive and hadn't gotten caught yet, and two, they hadn't found the gold. For if they had, they wouldn't very well be robbing banks, now, would they? Nosiree.

Lenora blew out a hard breath and ordered another whiskey. When the barkeep hesitated, Lenora said, "You deaf? I want another." She fidgeted on her stool, her corset pinching her waist.

She never did abide by those dang things, but she had to keep up the appearance of a somewhat refined woman. Once she was in San Francisco, she'd be wearing them all the time, so she lectured herself to buck up.

The barkeep jerked slightly and gazed around, as if looking for someone, then slid over another shot. No one else was in the dim bar with its dark wood paneling and shiny waxed counter. The large mirror behind the bar showed guests milling about in the foyer, near the registration desk. But Lenora didn't care who saw her drinking. She hardly knew anyone in this backwater excuse for a town—which was little more than an ill-arranged set of frame houses and shanties. So pretentious and shallow, all these women thinking they were something out here in the Wild West. Every one of them seemed so biggity and preoccupied with their silly little activities, so proper. And the men were so polite. Didn't anyone want to have a bit of fun in this town? Granted, at least there were saloons here. Lenora had ventured into Greeley weekly for food and supplies while she'd nursed Malcolm back to health, and it sorely vexed her that nary a pint of liquor could be procured in that "holy" town. For crying out loud, how in tarnation did those people get through the trials of living on the Front Range without a stiff drink or two?

Just her luck that the sucker who'd washed up on the riverbank was a teetotaler at heart. It sure would have made those long, cold winter nights more fun if Malcolm had joined her in a drink or two. Or three. She'd hoped that once they married, he'd loosen up a bit, be more fun. But he was a bore, and her patience was growing as thin as a thread living with this man while waiting for her chance to leave.

Lenora downed the second drink and winced. My, that was good whiskey. Her rattling nerves began to relax a bit as she sat on the stool and pondered her options. One stern look at the barkeep sent him scurrying off to wipe glasses at the other end of the bar. She didn't need him hovering. She needed to think, think.

So, if Clayton and Billy hadn't yet found the gold, and they were staying close to the cabin—or maybe they were on the dodge out there, which made a heap of sense—she figured they would keep hunting for the gold as the snow melted and afforded them the chance to examine the nearby woods for signs of the treasure. Lenora was certain they would never find the stash no matter how long they looked, for she had buried the box deep and covered it well, out in the meadow a ways from the cabin. Even shouldered a few big rocks to rest on the spot.

But as long as the gold was safe, she wasn't. She had to make sure those two ruffians never spotted her. They'd recognize her in a flash, no matter how well she tried to disguise herself. And that would mean she'd have to stay on the homestead, never venture out—which would make her go plumb crazy.

Her blood boiled. She felt like a trapped coon ready to bite at the slightest provocation. How long would she have to hide? Should she pretend to be with child, complain of the morning sickness, tell Malcolm she had to stay in bed? The thought of him fawning over her and worrying for her health made her wince. That was the last thing she wanted. She suspected Malcolm desired children; they hadn't talked about it, but she could tell. And he was the type to go all soft and mushy at the news of a pregnant wife. He would be intolerable in his ministrations to her.

No, she needed some other excuse to stay at home and not venture to town. Maybe something less complicated, like dysentery or malaria.

She shook her head, enjoying the wonderful woozy feeling the liquor gave her and wishing she could just drink away her problems. She had truly hoped Clayton and Billy had died. There'd been no news of them for a year, and she'd been fixing to sneak away to the cabin just as soon as the snow melted enough to allow her to trek up there. She figured maybe two weeks, if the weather held. She was so close to her goal—and now this!

She mumbled a string of curses under her breath. *Patience, patience. You've waited this long; you can wait a bit longer.* Besides, she told herself, there were some benefits to being married to such a hunk of a man.

A little smile inched up on her face as she thought about those warm strong arms and his firm body entwined with hers. Even though he was a bit too tender and sweet for her liking, he did provide pleasure on many a night, which was some consolation. But how much longer would she have to play this game? Malcolm was already showing signs that he was starting to remember something. Clearly, those dreams of his were memories bubbling to the surface of his mind. And like bubbles, she feared they would pop open, and then what?

In this gossipy town, she just knew her cover would be blown. Any man discovering such deception would be enraged. Maybe it was best if she left, just ran off and holed up somewhere else, until Clayton and Billy were either caught or killed. But making any move right now would be foolhardy and noticed. The last thing a hunted animal should do is bolt and run; that's when the predator would spot it. She couldn't know if Clayton was looking for her right now, here in Fort Collins. Chances were he could be. She shouldn't even be in town right now.

Just as she was about to signal the barkeep for another whiskey, she caught the reflection of a man entering the bar and marching her way. Her heart lurched into her throat, but then she sagged in relief. It was only her dutiful husband.

"Stella?" Malcolm strode up to her, his face etched with confusion and not a little irritation. "What are you doing in here? I've been looking for you everywhere." He cast a quick glance at her empty glass, then studied her face and frowned. "You've been drinking."

Well, wasn't that obvious? she wanted to say. But instead, she put on an apologetic face and ran a finger along his cheek. He flinched and pulled back. "I'm sorry, darling. I . . . I don't what came over me. I just felt so melancholy." She gave him her best pathetic weak-woman look. "Best I get home and to bed. I'm feeling right poorly." She plopped a few coins on the counter and gave him a sad smile.

She could tell from the way he was looking at her that, for the first time, he didn't seem to be swallowing her line. Maybe she'd need to bait the hook with some sugar. She leaned closer to him and ran her hand through his hair. He stiffened. Good, like hypnotizing quarry. She whispered, "And maybe you could join me in bed, for I'm so cold, and I know you could warm me up just so . . ."

He took her arm with a firm grasp and yanked her up from the barstool, throwing a quick look at the barkeep. Lenora could tell he was flummoxed and ashamed over her. Mercy, what a saphead this man was. Getting his dander up over a drink or two.

"Come on, let's go," he told her, not meeting her eyes. She couldn't afford to have him at odds with her right now. She needed him pliant, and since he didn't drink, the best way to do that was to coerce him into bed. So she went along meekly, her head hanging a bit in mock shame, and walked with him to the waiting wagon.

While he untied the reins from the hitching post, she glanced around under her lashes to look for any disturbance in the street. Nothing. A normal day in this boring town. As much as she'd like to think she'd be safe hiding out on the homestead, she knew better. If Clayton showed up in Fort Collins looking for her, with his sweet and wily ways, no doubt he'd suss out that she was here, and would eventually find her. Even though he didn't know the name she was using, he could probably describe her well enough for one of the old biddies in town to show a glimmer of recognition. And that's all it would take to have Clayton hot on her heels.

She let Malcolm assist her into the wagon, and moaned, feigning some unnamable pain. His face softened, as if he felt bad for doubting her. Good. She could count on his compassionate heart to cut her some slack. And she only needed a short length of it to play out until she could figure out what in tarnation she would do next in order to get the gold so she could catch a train to San Francisco.

Chapter 10

GRACE HAD NEVER BEEN INSIDE the courthouse before. She'd had no reason to before now. But she'd decided while tossing in her bed restlessly late last night it was time to do what she'd put off all year.

Her shoes clicked on the tiled floor as she crossed the high-ceilinged spacious room to the information desk. A short man with curly hair and a serious face stood behind the counter busily sorting papers and stamping them with an ink stamp. She noticed three high-society women in a close huddle over by the courtroom doors, whispering among themselves. When they saw her, they stopped speaking. Grace felt their attention rest heavily on her. She kept her eyes forward and walked up to the desk, then waited patiently for the man to finish his stamping and attend to her.

Tildie had given her the afternoon off, for, after seeing Monty walk into the shop yesterday, Grace couldn't concentrate on her work, and her head pounded mercilessly from crying. She had lain awake all night weeping, holding Ben close for comfort, and when the first streaks of dawn tickled the room, she rose and washed to get ready to go to work, exhausted and shaky. Her reflection in the mirror showed red swollen eyes and a wan complexion. It took every ounce of effort to brush out and pin up her hair and get dressed. She had no strength or courage to face the day, but neither did she want to cause any alarm or incite more gossip. Staying home would mean suffering Charity's probing questions, and she couldn't foster the thought of dodging such an interrogation. So she left Ben in her care with a cheerful smile and rushed out into the cold morning, a thin layer of ice crunching under her shoes as she walked, her mind numb and her heart aching.

The whole morning, Tildie had eyed her suspiciously but only shared the usual pleasantries. Grace feared the woman had seen the way she reacted when Monty came into the shop. No doubt she had. But what would she have thought? It was all Grace could do to pretend all was well with her world, when in reality it was shattered in a million pieces. With her employer's keen eye on her, she could not focus and declared her head was pounding. Tildie sent her off to City Drug to fetch some powders, even gave her a coin to cover the cost. Grace mumbled her thanks and hurried out, feeling as though she were fleeing a jail cell.

The man finally looked up and stared at her through thick spectacles. His eyes widened, and he got a bit flustered.

"Good day, miss. I'm the court clerk—name's Alan Patterson. How might I assist you?"

He smiled warmly at her and waited as she composed her thoughts. How much should she tell him? She laid her purse on the counter and said, "Thank you. I hope you can help me, but I'm not all that sure how to go about getting the papers I need."

His eyes urged her to continue. She noticed he seemed a bit nervous, or perhaps shy. She said, "I'd like to get a copy of my marriage certificate, which was recorded at the Bloomington Illinois courthouse on September 23, 1874."

His glance darted to her left hand, no doubt looking for a ring, but with her hands gloved, he might not be able to tell she wasn't wearing one. "I see," he said meekly. "Well, yes, I believe I can help you with that." He reached under the counter and fussed for a moment, then straightened and slid a piece of paper and a lead pencil over to her. "If you would kindly fill this out for me . . ." He gestured to the row of benches along the wall by the courtroom, indicating for her to sit there. "It may take some time to get the copy sent here, Mrs. . . . ?"

"Cunningham. Grace Cunningham."

The man's brows furrowed in thought. "Cunningham . . . that name sounds familiar." He paused. "What does your husband do for work, if you don't mind my asking?"

"He's . . ." Her throat choked up. How should she answer? Had this man not heard the gossip about her?

"I'm sorry, I can tell I've upset you," he said in a sincere tone. "I had no right to inquire. You don't have to answer that. It's not necessary for the paperwork." He nervously played with his hair, twirling it around his fingers.

Something about this man's kindness loosened her throat. "Please, don't feel bad." She breathed in deeply, then released a long shaky breath. "On our way to Fort Collins last May, we were overtaken by a storm, and while attempting to cross the Poudre, my husband was swept away in the river. I . . . I've apparently lost him." And so she had. The river hadn't killed him, but it had surely taken him from her just as cruelly, for he was still as far from her now as if dead.

"I'm so sorry," the clerk said. He added hesitantly, "May I ask, then, why you want a copy of your marriage certificate? For . . . sentimental reasons? If you don't mind my asking."

His sincere inquiry was another kindness. First Clare, now this man, Alan Patterson. How much she longed to pour out her soul to someone who would give credence to her story. But who in their right mind would believe her husband was living here in Fort Collins, married to another woman, and showed no indication he'd ever known her? Such a claim would only confirm the gossip that she was lying, fabricating fantastic stories to inspire charity and pity. Yet, keeping the truth bottled up was another agony she could hardly bear.

Monty had been her close companion and confidante, the one she could confide in no matter what the issue. He would listen to her with full attention, never disbelieving or belittling her. Oh, how she longed to talk to him and tell him everything she felt. What horrid fate had befallen her. Loneliness sought to swallow her up.

When her aunt Eloisa had lain dying of pneumonia and pleurisy, Grace feared for her own future, having no other family left in the world. Her parents and younger brother had died in 1860 from a cholera epidemic—when she was only six—leaving her in the comforting arms of her aunt. But in the fall of '74, Monty had walked through the front door to the boardinghouse—three years after she'd last seen him, that day he left to explore the wilds of the West. He found her frightened, alone, and lonely—and wasted no time telling her how all those months he'd thought only of her, anxious to get back to Bloomington, so he could marry the woman who had captured his heart. The spark of hope—for her future—had nearly been extinguished, but Monty rekindled it anew, promising her a secure future filled with love.

She hardly remembered her parents now. It had been her deepest wish and prayer that she and Monty would be blessed with many children, and would both live to see them grow up and become fine, upstanding adults. And now . . .

She realized the man was politely awaiting her answer. She said, "It's for my son. He's just a baby, but I want him to know who his father . . . was. So that he will know he was not illegitimate but the result of a marital union."

Alan nodded. "I'll do what I can to help, Mrs. Cunningham." He stopped short and cocked his head. "Cunningham. That name . . . Was your husband coming here for work?"

"Why, yes. He'd been offered a job with the land office. He . . . was a surveyor."

"Ah," Alan said. "That's where I saw his name. On some paper. The assessor is quite short-staffed. And you came from Bloomington, to settle here?"

"Yes," Grace said, suddenly feeling so weary she could hardly stand. "I suppose the assessor wondered why my husband never showed up . . ."

Alan must have noticed her face pale, for he hurried around the counter and took her elbow in a light, tentative grip. "Here, Mrs. Cunningham, come sit and fill out your paper. I'll go get you a glass of water." His eyes searched hers, perhaps watching to see if she might swoon.

"Thank you for your kindness," she said, taking the paper and pencil from his hand.

She did her best to fill out the certificate request through tear-filled eyes. It felt as though it had been only yesterday when she and Monty had exchanged vows at her aunt's bedside.

In the quiet of the room, she heard women's voices just around the corner. They drifted to her ears, and she caught snatches of conversation. She stiffened and stopped writing.

". . . has the gall to claim a married man is actually her husband! Sakes alive! Why, Charity told me . . ."

Grace gasped. *Charity*. Grace did not understand how such a devout religious woman could spread such gossip. Grace knew from the first morning of being in that house that Mrs. Franklin didn't believe her story. But she never imagined she would tell others.

Another woman's voice sounded excited. ". . . and showed up at Tildie's shop just yesterday. Tildie is sure that he's the one the poor girl imagines . . . must have suffered so from that fever . . . and her poor baby . . . should have put it up for adoption . . ."

". . . quite improper for her to raise the child without a father . . . has she no shame . . . ?"

" . . . says she is taking advantage of their kindness . . . a pretty sob story if you ask me . . ."

Grace's heart sputtered with indignation, listening to these woman deride her. She pressed her eyes closed, then startled at a touch to her shoulder.

Her eyes flew open, and she turned her head. Mr. Patterson was holding out a glass filled with dark liquid for her to take.

"I found some sweet tea. I thought, well, maybe, that would be better than water . . ." He shrugged and awaited her response, reminding Grace a little of a dog wanting to be petted with approval. He was awfully nice, and Grace smiled for him.

"Thank you," she said, taking a long refreshing sip. She finished filling out the paper, putting in the pertinent details of her former address, names and dates, and where the certificate should be mailed to. She was about to write in the Franklins' address, but then frowned. How could she continue to live with them, with Charity?

She knew now that she must find another place to live—and a new sitter for Ben. Oh, how would she manage that? She hardly made enough money to help pay for her food. She was tired of Charity's gossip and disapproving stares. Tired of *taking charity* from others. Perhaps Clare could help her—on both counts.

She hated to ask Clare's help, for she didn't want to appear to be asking yet another person for help. But she had a feeling Clare wouldn't see it the same way as these insensitive women. If they only knew the truth! How would they act then? Would it shame them at all?

She turned to Alan. "May I just have the certificate delivered here? I'm not altogether sure where I'll be living in the near future. How long do these things usually take?"

Alan shrugged again, and Grace thought the gesture innocent and a bit adorable. He did seem bashful, and it was endearing. "I'd guess about a month, maybe less."

"Well, I'm not in any hurry," she told him. "How much do I need to pay?"

"Oh, nothing, no charge," he hurried to say. Grace wondered if there was a charge and he was just being kind to her because of her circumstances.

"Thank you, Mr. Patterson—"

"Please." He faltered. "Call me Alan."

Grace nodded and stood, then handed him the empty glass. "I'm grateful for your help . . . Alan. I'll check back with you in a few weeks."

She made to turn around, but he cleared his throat. She looked inquisitively at him.

"If . . . if you need any assistance . . . with anything, Mrs. Cunningham, I . . . I, well, I'm here, Monday through Friday, all day. I know you work at the dress shop down the street . . ." His cheeks suddenly turned a bright shade of pink. "I don't mean . . . I mean . . ." He sucked in a deep breath and blew it out. "I walk past the shop every day, from my house. I've seen you there, through the window. You . . . um . . . make dresses?"

"Yes, I'm a seamstress."

"Well . . ."

He seemed to be at a loss as to what to say next, so Grace politely thanked him again and said good-bye. As she walked to the front doors of the courthouse, she caught a glimpse of the three elegantly dressed women who had been speaking about her. They glowered at her as she passed them. Grace gulped down her ire and stared straight ahead. She supposed they worked in the building somewhere, although at what, Grace had no idea. *If gossips were paid for their efforts, these women would have a thriving business venture.*

Holding her head up as high as she could, she headed toward her home, fighting the urge to pack a bag and leave with Ben on the next stage out of town. But more than a lack of money prevented her from leaving. Monty's presence was an anchor, an iron chain, fastening her to this town, and until she was certain there was no hope at all—hope that he'd remember her, for Ben's sake, so he could know his father—she was stuck here in Fort Collins.

Chapter 11

THE NERVE OF THAT WOMAN. Grace huffed as she puttered around her tiny room propelled by annoyance, making her bed and gathering warm wraps for herself and Ben. Wind whipped the trees outside the window, portending a miserable, cold spring day, but she could not bear to remain in this house a minute longer.

Charity's duplicitous conversation had set Grace's teeth on edge, with her forced smiles and words of endearment, all the while hardly masking her heartless and erroneous judgment of her houseguest. Grace could only conclude that Charity allowed her to live in her home to present the appearance to onlookers that she was the embodiment of her name's meaning, all to gain favor and to be regarded highly by the members of her church. That, as well as coveting her time with Ben, for it was clear she missed her children and grandchildren, and did not well hide her resentment for having had to move to Fort Collins at the command of her husband.

Well, as much as Grace greatly appreciated Charity watching Ben all these months while she worked at the dress shop, it was long past time to move out. If Clare couldn't watch Ben, she trusted she would find someone dependable. What choice did she have?

She had just returned from a lovely church service at the new Presbyterian church at the corner of Walnut and Linden, six blocks from the Franklins' house, and for the first time in days she felt a stirring of encouragement and hope. The pastor, Charles Bixler, gave a heartfelt sermon that Grace sensed had been somehow written just for her. It had centered on the passage in Hebrews that spoke of hope as an anchor for the soul. How odd that he chose that verse, and that the Scripture referred to an anchor, when she'd been thinking of that image for days. But instead of one that dragged and entrapped, this anchor spoken of in the Good Book was one that held fast one's faith to the secure rock, to God, who was the God of hope.

She needed that reminder that she was not ever alone, no matter how lonely she felt. The Lord heard her cries and supplications, and he was a God of comfort in hard times.

As she'd started to walk down the steps of the church to head home, with Ben in her arms, a sweet woman of middle age and austere comportment approached her and introduced herself as Elizabeth Stratton, the local schoolteacher. Grace was astonished to learn this woman had moved to Fort Collins a number of years back and, upon discovering the town had no school, she founded one, all on her own. And now the school was bursting its seams with all the children who now attended.

Mrs. Stratton, while speaking with Grace, asked where she was living, and whether it was God's intervention or the schoolteacher's astute powers of observation, the woman inquired if Grace was looking for other accommodations. Grace, stunned and flustered, admitted she was, and subsequently learned the Strattons had a room to let and were looking to fill it. She invited Grace to stop by her home on Locust Street at her earliest convenience, and Grace said she'd be delighted to.

She blew out an aggravated breath. She hoped Mrs. Stratton truly meant that, for Grace's earliest convenience was now.

She picked Ben up off the floor, where he was busily stacking wooden alphabet blocks, babbling in his usual serious manner, and dressed him warmly. She looked around the room and was struck by a pang of guilt. She did not want to be ungracious or unthankful for the kindness the Franklins had shown her—regardless of their reasons. They had given her much, and she would find some way to repay them. Later.

With her heavy dark wool coat buttoned to her neck, she carried Ben down the narrow hall and out the back door, to avoid encountering Charity. Upon pushing open the door, the brisk wind nearly knocked her down. She righted herself and wondered if it was wise for her to venture out. Clouds blotted out the sun, and the air was cold, but the sky did not threaten to pelt snow. So she tucked her head and walked around the house to the front porch, to fetch the perambulator, and after snuggling a very sleepy Ben down under blankets, she pushed her baby along Maple Street toward the center of town.

Few carriages and riders on horses traversed the road as wind whipped the remaining stubborn leaves off the big maples lining the street. Grace tightened her bonnet and held it with one hand for good measure as it tugged to fly from her head. The comforting smell of pine wood burning in a hearth swirled in the air with the leaves. Despite her inner protests, she let her thoughts drift to Monty, and her mind tormented her over and over with the expression on his face when he saw her in the shop—that look of utter puzzlement and lack of recognition.

She pressed forward against the wind, against the memories, battling her hurt and grief with every step. Each deliberate, determined step forward was a small victory, she told herself. She had to trust that somehow, some way, Monty would come back to her. Oh, the thought was ludicrous, but it would not leave her. In some way, it was another anchor for her soul. A reckless, outrageous hope, but she clung to it with all her might.

She pushed her baby along, passing no one on the streets as she walked briskly through the quaint neighborhood of pretty houses, whose formerly colorful flowerbeds were now barren and covered with clumps of snow. But soon, the sun would melt away the last vestiges of snow on the Front Range and summer would come—practically overnight—and the flowers would bloom and the trees would leaf out in vibrant green. Spring always symbolized hope to her, but what would this spring bring?

When she'd traveled a few blocks, she looked up at the street signs, getting her bearings. Locust was south along College five blocks down. She waited for a few wagons and carriages to pass before crossing. The block across the street displayed another small business district, but these buildings were one-story brick, without the false wooden fronts the downtown shops sported. She noted a small grocers, a tonsorial, and a harness shop on the corner. A few shoppers went in and out the doors and stepped lively along the sidewalk, buffeted by the relentless wind. Usually Sunday saw crowds of couples and families strolling the streets of town, but the inclement weather no doubt was keeping most people indoors by a warm cheering fire.

Her hands and feet were cold and becoming numb, reminding her of that awful afternoon when she'd lost Monty and lay in the mud, soaked through and nearly incoherent from shock and grief.

She shook off the memory and shivered. After peeking under the blankets to ensure Ben was sleeping, she checked the road and started across. The wind kicked up harder and blew dirt into her eyes and stung her face, the grit like pinpricks in her skin. She rubbed her eyes and hurried forward, trying to get across with the intention of popping into the grocers for a brief moment to thaw out before continuing the last blocks to the Strattons' house.

But in her rush, in the middle of the road, she tripped over a rock, and a pain shot through her ankle. The pram tilted, then threatened to fall over. She cried out in alarm.

Out of the corner of her eye, she saw a horse and wagon coming toward her at a fast clip. The horse pranced erratically, as if frightened by the assailing wind. The driver's hat was pulled down low over his eyes. Grace realized with horror that he didn't see her.

She grasped the sides of the pram and pulled it back toward her, trying to right it, but a wheel was lodged under the rock she'd tripped over. With her ankle throbbing in pain, she jiggled the pram, trying to loosen it, but to her dismay, the back wheel broke off and fell to the ground, causing the carriage to tip even further, threatening to dump Ben into the street.

Terror filled her and froze her in place. She couldn't move. Her feet wouldn't obey her silent commands. Ben started to wail. The sound of horse hooves grew louder, and she chanced glancing up. Her heart stuck in her throat.

The wagon was bearing down on her a mere ten feet away. Quickly she scooped Ben up, her son tangled in blankets and mewling, and pressed him to her chest. Abandoning the pram, she turned to run, but upon putting pressure on her injured foot, she fell forward and with her free hand cushioned her fall, her face inches from the dirt. Her wrist smarted from smacking the hard ground.

She had run out of time. The wagon would crush her and her son. She curled into a ball protectively, waiting in horrific anticipation for the impact, hoping her body could somehow shield Ben from being killed. She shook and clenched her teeth so hard, her jaw ached.

And then, arms wrapped around her and swooped her up from the ground. Strong arms that carried both her and her son. Whoever had her was running, pulling her tightly to a warm chest.

In a flurry of movement, Grace's head spun and Ben cried, but before she could even fathom she'd been rescued, she felt herself released—deposited on firm ground, clutching Ben with shaking arms. She let out a long pent-up breath and hung her head in shocked relief. Ben stared up at her wide-eyed, as if asking what happened, and tears of joy streamed down her face.

Oh, you're safe, you're safe, my precious baby. But who . . . ?

She looked to the street, where the wagon continued rattling along at a fast pace, the driver oblivious to the crushed perambulator lying like a dead animal in the middle of the street. Grace sucked in a breath and trembled at her close brush with death. Tears forced their way out her grit-encrusted eyes.

Then, she turned to see who had risked life and limb to save her. Her knees gave out when she looked in the man's worried face and saw who it was.

She cried out, but not from the stabbing pain in her ankle and wrist, then crumpled.

Monty caught her in his arms. Grace closed her eyes and remembered . . . Those arms that had held her so many times. She luxuriated in the comforting familiarity of his warm, assuring embrace, wanting never to let him go. Oh, how cruel was fate that it should land her here, in arms that now weren't hers, arms she could not linger in, not ever again . . .

But how was it that he was here, at this moment? That he—of all the men in town—had been the one to save her? Her heart hammered in her chest as she hung her head, afraid to look at him, knowing she would burst into tears. For there was no pain sweeter or more agonizing than this—being in his arms and Monty not knowing who she was.

"Miss, miss," he said, his words like warm water pouring over her.

That voice, his voice. A sigh shuddered in her chest. *Please, oh please, Lord. I can't bear this.*

"Are you all right?" he asked. And then, to Grace's horror—yet in answer to her secret yearning—he cupped her chin with his hand tenderly and lifted her face to meet his.

Her breath grew shallow, almost stilled completely. She looked into the eyes she had gazed so lovingly upon for so many years. Eyes that had brimmed with love for her, and that now only showed a stranger's alarm.

Her pulse racing at his touch, she allowed him to help her stand, but she could not put weight on her right foot. When she cried out in pain, he eased her over to the door of the harness shop, watching to see if she could manage the steps while holding Ben in her arms. His hands held tight her arm, as if he would never let her go, and Grace moaned, suffering his touch as if it burned her very soul. She cast a quick glance around for Stella but did not see her. She assumed Monty was alone, perhaps working, but where? Still, she could not believe he was here, holding her.

Monty swung open the squeaky wood door, and a blast of heat swept over her. In the middle of the shop festooned with all manner of horse and carriage harnesses and agricultural implements, a fire stacked high with burning logs raged in a stone hearth. The aroma of warm leather and dust hung in the air. Grace melted in the heat, uncaring of her pain or the destroyed perambulator. Her anger at Charity, her desire to see the Strattons' house—all her thoughts and intentions dissolved away in the heat of the room and from Monty's body close to hers. It took inhuman self-control to keep from throwing herself into Monty's arms and declaring her love. She prayed hard to resist, to hold back, even though her heart cried out to him in unbearable need.

Monty led her to a wide wooden bench just inside the door and helped her sit. Her body shook in shock from the near accident, compounded with the shock of finding herself in Monty's arms. She knew the right thing to do in this moment was to thank him and somehow get him to leave. She had to assure him she was fine even though she was utterly unhinged.

He knelt in front of her and searched her eyes. She couldn't help it then. Drowning in those eyes, the eyes of the man she loved so much, she started to cry.

"There, there, you've been through a shock. But you're safe. You'll be fine," he said.

If only that were true. If only . . .

She merely nodded in agreement. She caught him looking down at Ben, who was now squirming in her arms. He made whiny noises, indicating he was hungry, but this was no time or place to feed him. Could things get any worse? She thought of Clare's smiling face as she said to her, "Things can always get worse." Grace, in this moment, couldn't see how.

"I-I'm grateful to you . . . sir," she forced out. "But surely, you have somewhere to go."

"Do you live close by? I have a wagon around the corner. I can take—"

Grace willed her voice to sound calm, and with a forced smile said, "No, please, don't trouble yourself. You've already done more than enough, and I thank you. I'll . . . just rest a bit here and then head home. I only live a few blocks away."

His eyes showed he had no plans of leaving her. Monty, so honorable and helpful. This was one reason she loved him so much. He couldn't bear seeing anyone or any animal in pain. His compassion was boundless. She hoped that her nearness would make him remember her, but it was evident he did not—not at all. That look in his eyes radiated concern, not love—as unbearable as that was to admit to herself.

"You can't put any weight on that ankle; let me look at it." His eyes asked permission, and she wondered at his willingness to touch a woman so freely in public—a woman he did not know was his wife. But Monty was never one to care what anyone thought of his actions. He answered only to himself and God, and acted from altruistic motives.

Grace could only nod, bracing herself for his touch once more. She gritted her teeth as he tenderly moved her ankle in a small circle, then pressed his finger along her skin, assessing with the touch of a butterfly. Grace bit her lip and clenched her eyes shut, snuffing out the sudden passion that flared despite the pain. She looked with anguish upon the shiny gold ring on his finger. But it was not the ring she had put there when they wed. What had happened to that ring?

Monty's hand still rested on her ankle. "It's not broken. Only strained, thank God. You'll be all right, miss. You'll want to put some ice on it, then heat. Stay off it as best you can—if that's possible." He nodded at Ben—his baby, his child—with a dispassionate air of checking if he was hurt.

Oh how strange and awful this was, seeing Monty look over his son for the first time, wholly unaware that this was his child, the product of his love for her. This little boy with his father's eyes and smile. Could Monty see this resemblance? How could he? Why would he?

"I'm sorry about your baby carriage."

Grace struggled for words, not meeting his eyes. "You saved our lives. That's all that matters."

He smiled with genuine humility. "I'm just glad I was there to help."

"You risked your life. Not many men would do that."

He snorted. "I couldn't respect any man who wouldn't."

He was still kneeling before her, with her foot in his hand. She wondered why he hadn't moved. "Are you sure you don't want a lift?"

She swallowed and nodded. If he stayed much longer, she wouldn't be able to bear it.

Grace startled. The door to the harness shop flung open, and a swirl of freezing air blew in. A woman stormed inside, her pale organdy skirts rustling. *Stella!*

Stella stopped in her tracks upon seeing Monty. Her gaze jerked to look at Grace. Cold, angry eyes assessed the situation as she stood, unmoving, her pretty face turning blotchy red—whether from the heat of the room or from anger, Grace didn't know.

Grace's throat tightened, and she pulled her ankle from Monty's grasp. The chill wind of Stella's scrutiny cut through Grace's bones.

Yes, things could always get worse. They just had.

Malcolm stood—not in a rush, in the way a man might when caught in an indiscretion. Rather, he stood to face Stella the way someone might when sorely vexed, when his honor was questioned. For he could tell Stella had jumped to conclusions, and it irked him beyond tolerance. He waited for her to speak.

She hissed the words, "What do you think you are doing?" Her eyes darted around, aware others might be in the shop, listening.

Malcolm spoke quietly, evenly. "This woman fell and needed tending—"

Stella shook her head, clearly disapproving. "And why did you have to help?"

Before Malcolm could answer, aware of his anger rising to alarming levels, Stella straightened and eyed the woman and her baby.

"You . . . you're the seamstress—from the dress shop." Stella cocked her head, and Malcolm wondered what she was thinking. He so often saw her mind mulling things, but could never suss out what those things were. And she rarely revealed what was on her mind when Malcolm asked.

Her secretiveness was getting worse, he noted. And her drinking. After taking her home the other afternoon—after, to his horror, he'd found her drinking in that saloon—she went straight to bed, and Malcolm felt a bit bad about chastising her. But she had drunken whiskey in public, in the middle of the day. Didn't she realize what a small town this was? How something like that could affect his good standing in the community? Affect his new job? The last thing he needed was for gossip to spread about his lush of a wife. And when he'd tried to mention this to her in a kindly way, she became incensed, threw the covers off, and strode out of the cabin—and didn't return until long after dark, so soused he wondered how she'd managed to guide the horse and wagon back to the homestead.

Late that night, lying in bed unable to sleep, listening to Stella's drunken snores, something snapped inside him. All the misgivings and uncertainty and confusion that had been gnawing his gut since the day he'd had that accident gelled into a lump of understanding: he had made a grave mistake in marrying Stella Childs. How he had loved her and longed to marry her before his near-drowning in the Platte River, he had no clue. She was as unappealing and offensive and unpleasant a woman as he'd ever met—despite her outward beauty. And a curious thought had wormed its way into his mind that night—the possibility that somehow she had honey-fuggled him.

He hated to mistrust anyone, and felt guilty suspecting deceit from his own wife, for she had lovingly and dutifully nursed him for weeks untold, without complaint. It wasn't as if he was wealthy and she'd been after his money. He'd had nothing of value to offer her. So why would she fabricate such a ruse? Still, once the idea came to him, it caught hold, like a piece of dry tinder igniting from a tiny spark. And gradually that spark of suspicion was growing into a conflagration.

Malcolm struggled with what to do. He could hardly kick her out of the cabin, yet he couldn't bear being in the same room with her now. And he knew Stella sensed his unease, for he was never good at hiding his feelings; he'd never had good cause to.

Stella said to the woman sitting on the bench, who seemed utterly undone by Stella's harsh scrutiny, "That 'helpless woman' act won't work on my husband—"

"Stella!" Malcolm couldn't believe his ears. He grasped her arm tightly and pulled her away from the horrified woman, his jaw working. "We're leaving." As much as he wanted to stay and placate the woman on the bench, help her get home and make sure she and her baby were warm and safe, he had to do something before Stella made a scene. Already a few customers in the harness shop had turned and were gaping at them.

But Stella was unfazed by Malcolm's admonishment. A mean scowl rose on her face as she continued her attack, a finger waggling in front of the young mother's face. "Just because you don't have a husband, or a father for your brat, it doesn't mean you can steal one from another woman. Shame on you!"

The poor woman blanched and started crying anew, and her baby began wailing, as if in sympathy. Malcolm's heart went out to her, but he had no time to comfort her—and no intention of making excuses for his wife's vile behavior.

Malcolm yanked Stella toward the door, practically dragging her. He threw a glance in the woman's direction, apologizing with his eyes, horrified by Stella's deplorable behavior. He had never seen her like this. But then, most of his time spent with Stella had been in isolation, just the two of them—in the shack near Greeley and lately in their cabin outside of town. Malcolm realized he had rarely seen Stella in the company of other people.

Feeling the eyes of others upon him, boring into him like hot coals, Malcolm pushed Stella out the front door, and keeping the tight grip on her arm, marched her down the street and around the corner, to where their wagon was parked. Wind whipped around his head and lifted his hat.

"Get up there," he ordered, none too softly. He didn't reckon he could be more fed up or embarrassed. Stella, fuming and mumbling curses, climbed up and plopped on the bench seat. Malcolm reached down and picked his hat up from the dirt, brushed it off, and squashed it onto his head. Wind howled and moaned as its icy fingers raced down from the Rockies and poked through his clothes—the kind of wind that could blow the hair off a prairie dog. A chill rushed through him, but Malcolm knew it wasn't just the wind that made him shiver. It was regret that ran through his veins. Regret that he'd ever met Stella Childs. Regret that he'd married her.

But what could be done for it? Nothing. For he was a man of honor, a man of his word. He'd made a vow, and he intended to do his best to keep it, before the eyes of man and God. He would have to buck up, figure out a way to reach Stella. To love her. For he knew if he failed to do so, the remaining years of his life would be intolerable.

With his heart feeling as heavy as an anchor in his chest, he jumped up on the bench beside his now sullen, brooding wife and smacked the reins to get the horse to move.

Chapter 12

June 22, 1876

LENORA COMPOSED HERSELF AND DREW in a deep breath, then pushed open the door to the dress shop. The tinkling bell brought the store owner rushing from out behind the counter to greet her—Tildie Hortman, whose eyes swam with a lust for silver dollars. Lenora was not surprised the old biddy was a spinster. Who would marry such an ugly crow? Her nose was a birdlike beak, and her head rested on too long a neck. And her choice of clothing—so unflattering to her spindly figure.

Lenora was grateful for the ample curves she'd been born with, but she worked hard to stay beautiful—with her powders and creams, and by resisting sweets. Although, she wondered why she bothered these days to primp. Her husband hardly paid her any mind, but Lenora didn't care all that much. Once she got the gold and arrived in San Francisco, then . . .

Soon, she told herself. Another week with this warm weather, the trails up to the cabin would be manageable. In the last two weeks there had been no word of Clayton and Billy. The newspapers weren't even sure they'd been the ones to rob that bank in Laporte. So there was no way to know if they were around—or even alive. But one thing Lenora knew without a doubt—the longer she hung around in this poor excuse for a town, the more likely they'd find her. It was nearly time to skedaddle.

She considered slipping away without anyone the wiser, but where could she go? If she went to another nearby town, Monty could find her. Or he might put notices in the paper looking for her. Word—and her description—would get out. She'd hoped her "unladylike" behavior would push Monty to kick her out, but he was too honorable a man to do such a thing, she'd come to realize. No matter how much she grieved him, he always softened and tried to be forgiving and understanding, which made her want to gag. How'd she end up with such a sucker?

"Ah, Mrs. Connors, you're here. Your dresses are finished and ready for fitting." The woman's eyes brightened in curiosity. "And how are things on your homestead? I hear tell you took over the Hoskins's claim. Such a lovely spot on the creek, isn't it?"

The shopkeeper led Lenora over to an upholstered chair in the back of the room and sat her down. Clearly she didn't expect Lenora to answer her inquiries, for she continued rambling. "Now, just wait here, and I'll bring your dresses to you to try on. We have a nice private room over there where you can change, and I'll call Grace out here to help with the adjustments." Tildie flitted off to a back room behind a curtain, and Lenora heard muffled conversation.

Grace. That must be the young woman Lenora had seen in the harness shop a few days ago. She grunted, feeling the irritation rise in her chest. One look at that woman, sitting there on that bench, with her eyes pinned longingly upon Monty, and she knew just what that woman—

Lenora sucked in a breath and her eyebrows rose. Her jaw dropped. Yes, the woman had a look of utter longing on her face. Lenora knew the look well—she was a keen observer. One had to be to become a great actress. And the look on that young mother's face had been one of adoration. Lenora might even say the woman had the look of love on her features. The kind of love a woman felt only for a man she knew intimately . . .

Lenora's thoughts jerked to a halt before the glaring brick wall of truth.

Grace . . . that was the name on Montgomery Cunningham's marriage certificate—the name of his wife. Grace Wilcox. Lenora had memorized every little word of that little piece of paper.

She tapped her foot in a fast rhythm and fidgeted. Was this the same woman? Was this little mousy button-nosed nothing Monty's real wife? If she was . . . that meant the brat was his too.

A baby! Grace must have been pregnant when Monty fell into the river. The poor dear. Lenora sniggered. Alone, raising a child, and now—she learns her beloved husband has no idea who she is. And he has no idea that he is a father. Aw, what a sad story, one perfect for the penny dreadfuls.

Lenora was struck with equal parts amusement and worry. For if this woman was truly Monty's wife, her presence might jog his memories. And Lenora couldn't take the chance that Monty would start remembering—not as long as Lenora had to keep up this ruse and remain in Fort Collins. Nosiree. She had to be certain of her hunch.

The shopkeeper returned, with Grace following behind her, her arms overflowing with dresses. When Grace saw her, she stiffened. Lenora pasted on a smile. No doubt Grace did not relish the idea of another encounter with her. But Lenora would be on her best behavior and pretend nothing had happened at the harness shop.

"Now, let's have you try this one on," Tildie said, lifting up a pretty high-collared burgundy silk and handing it to her. Lenora had to admit—the dress was gorgeous. She gushed in delight, saying to Grace, "My, this is stunning. You do beautiful work." Tildie hovered, a wide smile creasing her severe face.

"Where did you learn to sew, if you don't mind my asking?" Lenora said to Grace as sweetly as possible. She noticed Grace's tight face loosen and her shoulders relax.

Grace spoke quietly as she pulled aside the curtain to the changing area and gestured Lenora inside. "I grew up in Bloomington, Illinois. My aunt was a seamstress, and she taught me all I know."

Aha, Lenora thought. *It's her—has to be. The marriage certificate was stamped in that city.* So, of all places, she had run into Monty's wife. But, why should she be surprised? No doubt Monty had fallen into the river close to Fort Collins. And, she reminded herself, Monty had a job offer—the very job he now had, with the land office. *Silly me. Of course she would be here. She would have come here in hopes her poor husband had somehow survived his ordeal.* But what a surprise the poor thing had! Lenora almost squirmed in delight, thinking how upset Grace must be knowing Lenora was married to *her* husband. She let out a little titter as she flounced into the changing area and disrobed.

The silk dress felt divine as she slipped it over her head and smoothed it over her corset and taffeta petticoats. Such a beautiful dress—one that would make Monty's heart beat a little fast. Knowing that Monty's wife was living here in Fort Collins and had seen him married to another woman was titillating. She pictured poor little Grace watching in horror as Lenora ran her hand through

Monty's hair. How agonizing it must be for her to know Monty slept in another's woman's arms. But what could the pathetic woman do? Surely she couldn't tell him the truth—he'd think she was mad. Would she dare tell him the brat was his? Had she told anyone else in this town?

Hmm, that could be a problem. Lenora stood there, thinking. What if Grace had told someone about seeing Monty in town? She wiggled her head and sniggered. Who would believe her? If she claimed she'd been married to him, but that he somehow forgot and married another, who would believe her? What proof did she have? None, nothing at all.

Lenora huffed and came out. The shopkeeper was busy at the counter. Grace had hung up the other dresses on a nearby rack and stood, waiting for Lenora.

Grace looked Lenora over, clearly avoiding meeting her eyes. "How does it fit? Does it need any adjustments?" Her voice was shaky and paper thin.

Lenora smiled. "You took careful measurements. It fits perfectly." She couldn't resist; she just had to stick a few barbs in. "So . . . what does your husband do?" she asked innocently.

Grace nearly choked. Her face turned red, and Lenora saw her swallow with difficulty. Lenora waited, her head cocked in polite curiosity.

"He . . . he . . ." Grace fumbled for words, much to Lenora's secret amusement. After composing herself, she said, "He was swept away in a river last year."

"Oh, I'm sooo sorry," Lenora said, shaking her head in commiseration. "And the poor baby. How hard it must be to raise him without a father. Oh, you must miss him so much." She turned and fastened her eyes on Grace, waiting to see her response.

Grace's face collapsed in pain. She jerked her head back and moaned, then ran from the room. The shopkeeper rushed over.

Tildie questioned Lenora with an intense look. She whispered, "Whatever is the matter with Grace?"

Lenora pasted on a puzzled expression. "I have no idea. I just asked her about her husband, what he does . . ." She let her voice trail off and looked toward the back room with grave concern. "Did I misspeak?"

"Oh, please, don't mind her," Tildie said, then lowered her voice even more. "She is a marvelous seamstress, but has some . . . emotional imbalances. Why . . . I believe she has it in her mind that your husband . . . well, it's not polite of me to make such assumptions—"

But that won't stop you from gossiping, now, nosiree. Lenora knew well her kind of woman. A spinster like her had nothing to live for *but* gossip. With bated breath, Lenora whispered back, her eyes wide. "Pray, do tell!"

"That day your husband came into the shop? Grace looked as if she'd seen a ghost—a ghost of her recently departed husband. She wants so very much for him to be alive, longing for him to walk in through the door . . . why, she just fixed it in her mind that he was her beloved. And she hasn't been the same ever since." The shopkeeper tittered like a chatty hen. "Can you imagine such a thing? I believe her misfortune has dismantled her mind, the poor dear. I've no doubt that soon she will think she sees her husband at every turn." She shook her head with sadness. "And the poor infant, having such a befuddled woman as a mother. How will he fare, with all the talk about town?"

No doubt much of that talk spread by you, Lenora concluded, nodding and commiserating along with the shopkeeper.

The woman laid a gentle hand on Lenora's shoulder. "I apologize for Grace's . . . unstable constitution. Here, let me help you with the other dresses. I'm sure you'll be pleased with them."

Tildie lifted the next dress from the hook on the wall and held it out to her. A lovely pale-green organdy dress, in the latest French style with buttons up the cuffs and lace around the collar.

"Ah, how lovely. Grace truly is a marvelous seamstress. And it's so kind of you to allow her to work for you . . . despite her . . . instability and . . . unpleasant circumstances."

Tildie glanced to the back of the room, as if expecting Grace to return.

"Yes, well, I do have a business to run," the woman told her.

"And you do a remarkable job. Not a finer dress shop have I ever seen—not even in Den—" She caught herself. "Not even in St. Louis, where I lived before I came here." Lenora smiled widely. "I'll try this on then."

She ducked back behind the curtain and carefully removed the silk dress. Well, her suspicions were confirmed. People in this town knew about Grace's unfortunate situation—and knew that she thought Monty was her husband. And even though Tildie imagined Grace saw her missing husband in the faces of other young men, Lenora did not rest easy. For Grace would not chase after any other man. In time, her belief that Monty—and he alone—was her missing husband would be voiced. And that meant Lenora would be in the limelight, which was the last place she wanted to be while in Fort Collins.

Something had to be done, and soon. Something drastic. For tongues wagged excitedly in this small town, and she didn't think Grace would be able to resist Monty. She would try to talk to him, to get him to remember. No doubt she would do anything in her power to win back her husband.

And Lenora couldn't let that happen. Hopefully the weather would cooperate, and she could leave town within the week. But if not . . . maybe, she thought with a sudden smile, there would just have to be another unfortunate accident.

Grace took her time walking down Jefferson Street, careful not to put too much pressure on her ankle. After soaking it in hot water and laying ice packs on it for a few days, it finally felt strong enough. How she'd managed to hobble home, carrying Ben after the accident with the wagon, was a blur in her mind. Seeing Monty so close, having him touch her, had been torturous. When she finally hobbled into the Franklins' house, she went to her room, bolted the door, and slept through most of the day and night—despite Charity's periodic knocking at her door—waking only to feed and change Ben, who seemed as exhausted by the traumatic ordeal as she.

She jostled the packages in her arms in the brisk clear morning as she approached the livery, feeling strangely empty, as if all the blood had drained out of her. She hadn't eaten much in days, and her small room had become so claustrophobic, she couldn't bear remaining in it a moment longer. Upon telling Charity the unavoidable news that the perambulator had been crushed by a horse and wagon, the woman threw her hands up in horror and poured sappy words of consolation upon Grace, praising the Lord for her safe deliverance from death, all the while prying Grace for the details—which Grace refrained from indulging.

Charity graciously offered to tell Tildie that her houseguest was feeling unwell and needed a few days to recover, but Grace had no doubt Charity's feet rushed to spread more gossip about her. And then, the day she went back to work, that *woman* came into the shop, as if sent by the Devil himself to sorely vex her even more. She rushed back home and locked herself in her room, then cried all afternoon. She yearned to quit her job, but it was her only means of support. With her meager earnings, she paid the Franklins for room and board, and bought necessities for herself and Ben.

Thankfully, as Grace entered the shop this morning, Tildie's eyes took on a glint of curiosity, but she merely exchanged the usual pleasantries. No mention was made of Grace's emotional outburst. Grace was grateful, when Tildie asked if she might deliver some dresses to an elderly customer and offer to check the fitting at the woman's home. Grace couldn't get out of the shop fast enough.

"Good mornin' to ya," a voice called out.

Grace looked up and saw Clare stepping out from the shadows of the livery. And with her stood an attractive young cowboy, dressed in brown wool pants with a pale shirt that had seen some years of wear. He tipped his wide-brimmed hat upon seeing Grace and gave a bright straight-toothed smile. Curly light-brown hair trickled down his ears and cascaded onto his shoulders. As Grace waved hello, she noticed his hand resting on Clare's back. This had to be her beau—Eli.

He stood a good foot taller than Grace and Clare, with a wide strong jaw, and prominent cheekbones that suggested he might have some Indian in him. Clare's face was a bit flushed, and she touched a hand to her throat. Grace wondered what they'd been doing in that back room, where Clare punched saddles and bridles. Grace smiled, for it was clear the two were in love, and she was happy for Clare.

"This is Eli Banks," Clare said, nudging her beau. "Eli, meet Grace. She's the gal I told ya about."

"Pleasure to meet you, miss," Eli said, nodding. He seemed all sweet and no-nonsense to Grace, with a voice as smooth as honey mixed with a little grit.

Grace replied, "Likewise, Mr. Banks."

Eli chortled and waved a hand. "Please, just call me Eli."

"All right . . . Eli," Grace said, not used to young men being so informal with strangers—and especially not women.

"How are ya farin'?" Clare asked sincerely.

Grace wished she could tell her the truth—that she was more than miserable—but she held back. When she didn't answer, Clare took the parcels from Grace's hands before Grace could utter a word of protest. "Eli and I were just talking about the upcoming centennial celebration—and the horse races." She led Grace to a bench inside the livery, out of the cold breeze. She sat down alongside Grace and set the parcels at her feet, but Eli stood facing Clare, his eyes swimming with love—which only made Grace's heart ache even more for Monty.

Clare continued. "We mean to take every ribbon this year." She threw Eli a sly look. "And we're going to enter as a team in the roping competition."

Grace was shocked. "You? You . . . rope . . . what? Horses? Cows?" Grace had never been to a rodeo or anything of the ilk. She had heard of such events, but had no idea women participated in them.

Clare and Eli burst out in laughter. He said, "We rope calves. It's a timed event. Two riders bolt out of the shoot when the gun goes off and—"

"One rider lassoes the calf's head," Clare interjected, "while the other snags a foot. Ya have to flip the calf on its back, tie up three legs, and let go."

Grace shook her head in amazement. "You know how to do this?" she asked Clare. She imagined Eli might have such skills if he worked on a ranch, but Clare?

Her friend laughed again—a warm, nonjudgmental manner that set Grace's heart at ease. "Sure, I've been on a ranch my whole life." She nudged Eli harder, playfully. "And I'm better with the lasso than this green cowboy."

"Hey," he said, grabbing her hands and pulling her close, his honey-brown eyes sparkling as he gazed into Clare's. "Who you callin' green—my little Irish lass from the Emerald Isle?"

Clare whacked him lightly upside the head and knocked his hat to the ground. Eli chuckled and picked up his hat, brushed it off, and stuffed it back in place. He narrowed his eyes at Clare. "Don't you be messin' with a man's hat. You should know better."

"Yessir," she said with the look of a misbehaving schoolgirl who'd just been chastised by her teacher—and didn't care a whit.

Clare shook her head and patted her hair, as if making sure it was all in place. She was wearing a gingham skirt and white tailored shirt. Even in such simple clothes, she looked beautiful. Clare had a natural beauty—of the spirit—that shone through, and Grace imagined that was what appealed to Eli. For he appeared wholly at ease with her confident manner and lack of concern for wearing fashionable clothes or putting on airs. They seemed a perfect match.

Again she realized how much she longed for a friend, someone to share her deepest joys and pains with—now that she no longer had Monty to confide in. His absence was an ache that hurt more than any illness, and she knew no way to heal it. Nothing but getting him back would cure her. But she had to stop thinking like that—it was only tormenting her.

"Grace, are you all right?" Clare moved closer and forced Grace to meet her eyes. Grace tried to smile, but once more the tears filled the wells of her eyes. "Tell us what's bothering you."

Grace looked at Clare, then Eli. These people were practically strangers, but she felt if she didn't tell someone her troubles, she would utterly fall apart. And she had to keep a right mind for Ben. She needed to move out, and worried the Strattons had already let out their spare room. What would happen if she told them the truth—all of it? Would they belittle her? Scoff at her story? Was it really proper for her to speak so freely to a man she didn't know?

She chortled bitterly. What did she have to lose? She doubted she could stain her reputation further.

"Do you really want to know?" she asked. "Aren't you supposed to be working on your saddles?"

Clare reached over and smoothed Grace's hair with the touch of a loving mother. Grace's heart melted at the tender gesture. A few tears worked down her cheeks, and she tried to suck the rest down her throat. Clare said quietly, "I have all the time in the world." She looked at Eli. "He's come over from Greeley to help me get my things moved into the hotel."

"How 'bout we head over to the café on Prospect? I heard a body c'n scare up a real breakfast there," Eli said, taking a look at the sky dotted with fat white clouds. "It's fixin' to snow this afternoon, but we have time for some vittles," he said matter-of-factly. "And I'm starvin'."

Grace studied the sky overhead, but saw nothing to indicate that snow was imminent. She glanced at Clare, who shrugged and said, "He's half Cheyenne. He can predict the weather."

Eli made a sour face. "Clare, that's hogwash. I don't predict the weather." He shook his head and rolled his eyes. "Any fool c'n see it's fixin' to snow."

"Well, I guess I'm a fool then, because I can never tell when the weather's gonna change. And you always know. It's a gift." She looked at Grace. "And he has a flawless sense of direction—never gets lost. Unlike me."

"Sugar, so long's you c'n find the right end of a lasso to throw and a gun to point, you'll do right fine," Eli said. "So, are we gonna stand around all day chattin' about the weather—or go eat?"

Grace's stomach rumbled, reminding her how starving she truly was. Good thing she had a few coins in her coat pocket. "I have to drop these parcels off." She supposed she could tell Mrs. St. Vrain she would return later in the day for a fitting.

"Just tell me where," Eli said, "and we'll stop on our way."

Clare took Grace's arm as they walked behind Eli to a wagon that had an empty flat bed in the back. A large chestnut draft horse stood hitched to it half asleep alongside the back wall of the livery. Clare lightly squeezed Grace's arm, making Grace turn to look at her.

"Ya like him?" she whispered to Grace.

Grace smiled and tried to think of something kind to say. "You roped in a good one, Clare."

Clare snickered and whispered, "Still don't have those legs tied . . . but I'm working on it."

"I don't think you have a thing to worry about," Grace said. "He's smitten."

Clare grunted. "And I aim to keep him that way." Her tone grew serious. "Listen, Grace. I want to know what's bothering ya. And you can trust Eli. He never talks to anyone about anythin' private. He's been raised right. And he has a smart sense for sussing out solutions to problems." Her eyes lit up. "And Eli's invited me to come to his ranch north of Greeley—to finally meet his mam! His da died when he was little, but she runs a horse ranch."

She gestured Grace to climb up to the bench. Eli held out his hand and took her parcels, then helped her up, and she was grateful because her ankle felt wobbly. She gathered in her skirts to make room for the others, then slid the parcels under the seat.

"See," Clare declared, "raised properly. Manners and all." She shot Eli a big smile. "What do ya think about my bringin' Grace over to your ranch this Sunday?" she asked him. Grace warmed at the invitation. It would do her good to get out of town a bit—away from Stella, and Monty. At least until she could get a grip on her feelings.

Eli nodded as he helped Clare up to sit beside Grace. "A fine idea. I don't want you ridin' there and back alone, 'specially not at night."

"Eli Banks—you don't think I can take care of myself? I'm a big girl."

"Yep—a big, beautiful girl that some rapscallions might be itchin' to git their hands on. All that Irish fire and a good trigger finger won't be enough to stop the likes of some."

"I don't think I'd be much protection," Grace said, now wondering just how dangerous the road to Greeley really was.

"You c'n shoot a gun?" he asked Grace. She nodded, thinking of the times Monty had made her practice, the memory stinging her heart.

Eli smirked and cocked his head. He said to Clare, "Well, then I reckon you'll be safe. No one'll mess with two armed women. They'd be a right fool to try."

Eli sat on the bench and wiggled close to Clare. He picked up the reins and got the horse trotting down the street.

"Don't you worry about travelin' to my ranch, miss," Eli said in a reassuring tone. "Folks travel it all the time. It's perfectly safe."

Clare nodded. "He was just messin' with us. That's his way." She elbowed him hard. He said "ouch" and pasted a fake scowl on his face.

"So, where's this place you need to stop?" he asked Grace.

She gave him directions, and after she dropped off the dresses with Mrs. St. Vrain with a promise to return later, they rode over to the café.

In a quiet corner of the eatery, with the morning light streaming in through mullioned windows, they ate a hearty breakfast. When they'd finished, Clare set her fork down and pushed her plate away. "All right, Grace, spill the beans. I can tell it's makin' you ill, keepin' all this worry bottled up inside. It is Ben? Is he ailin'?"

Grace drew in a long breath, then let it out, along with her reticence. She just had to tell someone before she burst apart. So, with her hands shaking, she told them everything—from the day she and Monty had set out from Cheyenne, to the flood that had swept Monty away, to being found by the old trader and taken to the Franklins, to the moment Monty walked into the dress shop. When she related how Monty had failed to recognize her, she choked up and shook her head, unable to say more.

"Oh, Grace," Clare said, her own eyes filling with tears. "How awful. How very awful!"

Eli had listened to her recount the entire story without so much as a word. But clearly he now had something to say. "You're a right brave woman, Grace. I woulda punched that woman's lights out."

Clare held his arm, keeping Eli in his seat. For he seemed so angry, he was ready to chase down Stella with the fork he was waving in the air. The image was so ridiculous that Grace almost laughed. Yet, the pain from telling her tale kept a frown on her face. She was moved by Eli's concern and Clare's compassion.

"I appreciate you listening to my woeful tale," Grace said. "I have no one to talk to . . ." Her words clogged her throat again.

Clare wrapped an arm around Grace's shoulders. "But who is she—this Stella? Who really? Ya said she claims to have met and married your Monty back in St. Louis."

"She's lyin'," Eli said evenly. "The question is why."

Clare nodded vigorously. "Grace, there's something very wrong here—"

"That's puttin' it mildly," Eli said. His face tightened, and he looked hard at Grace. "Stella . . . Stella . . . What's she look like?"

Grace described Stella, forcing words through her tight, aching throat. She drank some water, then added, "She goes by the name Connors. And he's called Malcolm. Malcolm Connors."

"It makes no sense at all," Clare said, shaking her head. "Why would she lie?"

"Because she's hidin' somethin'," Eli said with an emphatic tone. "I think I met this woman—last year, just south of Evans. The way you describe her makes me think it must be her. LeRoy and I fixed a wheel on her wagon." He narrowed his eyes and looked right at Grace. "But she was alone, and had come up from Denver City. She weren't with no man—if'n this is the same woman."

Grace grew quiet. Clare looked like a dog that had a tight grip on a bone and had no intention of parting with it. "So, this woman meets Monty somewhere. Grace—it's clear he's lost his memory. It must have happened when he was swept downriver. Hit his head on a rock or something."

Grace nodded, not caring that more tears were coursing down her cheeks. She looked across the table at Eli, who was chewing on his thoughts.

Clare continued. "So, she meets Monty, who is . . . somewhere. Maybe in Greeley? And he doesn't know who he is. Maybe someone found him near the river—like what happened to you—and they took him into town. Maybe he found some work, got a place to stay, all the while trying to figure out who he was—"

"And then Stella came along," Eli added with a scowl. "But why? Why set her hooks in him. Not like he had any money—"

"He's handsome. And kind. Most women would find him hard to resist," Grace mumbled, thinking of how handsome he'd looked the day he came back from his expeditions, intent on proposing to her. Her sorrow was a great big lake of tears that kept widening with each day. How could these friends help her? Was there any way to get Monty to remember her? Any way to get him back?

"Looks ain't enough," Eli said, shaking his head. "A woman like that—she'd want money and comforts."

"She doesn't love him," Grace blurted out. She wasn't sure how she knew that, but she knew. Eli and Clare were right. There had to be some other reason Stella married Monty. Did she know his real name? Or was that a name he thought up for himself, because he couldn't remember who he was? Oh, none of this made sense.

"What can I do? I can't tell Monty the truth. But I want him to know his son. He deserves to know Ben—and Ben has a right to know he's not illegitimate, that he has a father . . ." Grace buried her head in her hands.

"Maybe I could talk to your fella. Feel out what he knows, what he remembers. Find out where he met Stella, and how they ended up gettin' married," Eli said.

Grace looked at him, shaking her head. "Please, don't say anything. At least, not now. I . . . I keep hoping maybe his memory will return. Maybe in time—"

"But you might wait forever," Clare said. "Maybe if someone told him the truth, he would remember."

"I'm afraid I'd lose all chance of getting him back. Something like that might frighten him, and he'd think I was mad to make such a claim."

Silence filled the quiet corner where they sat. A few other patrons ate their breakfasts, unaware of the serious discussion taking place at the far table. Grace looked out the window and saw fat flakes of snow falling from a steel-gray sheet of clouds blanketing the sky. She said to Clare, "Maybe you should go fetch your things and get moved in. The snow's here."

Clare eyed Eli. "You said this afternoon."

He shrugged. "I was only off by a few hours. So shoot me."

She made a gun with her fingers and said, "Bang!"

Eli clutched his chest and groaned, his eyes swimming with mirth. "Ya got me."

"You bet, Cowboy. You're all mine." Clare smiled sweetly at Eli and took his arm. "Grace is right. Time to get packin'."

Eli palmed some coins on the table. When Grace pulled her money from her coat pocket, he stayed her hand. "My treat, Miss Cunningham."

She saw a deep compassion and kindness in those green eyes. "Thank you, Eli. I'm grateful." She looked at Clare. "For both of you. Thank you for listening, and for trying to help, but I fear there isn't—"

"Don't you fret, Grace," Clare said in a strong tone. "We'll get to the bottom of this . . . woman and her designs. And somehow, some way, Monty will be yours again. I just know it. I believe that with all my heart." She laid her hand on Grace's wrist. "What the Lord hath joined together, let no man—or scheming, lying woman—put apart. Keep praying, keep hopeful. God will champion your cause—you'll see."

Grace wiped her face and tucked a few loose strands back in their pins. "I do hope you're right. I truly do."

Eli stood and looked at her thoughtfully. "Nothin's hidden from the sight of the Lord. He brings all wickedness into the light of day sooner or later. Whatever this Stella is hidin', it won't be hid for long."

Grace nodded and followed Eli and Clare out of the café. *But that won't bring Monty back into my arms. And that's all I want, more than anything. Dear Lord, please, help Monty remember. Whatever it takes. I'll trust you and hold on to hope. Just give me the strength to face each day until my prayer is answered.*

Chapter 13

EPH LOVE REINED IN HIS Palomino mare, Destiny, and pushed his hat back to take a look-see of the foothills. Snowflakes drifted down from heaven dusting the green oceans of wheat growing alongside the narrow rut leading down from Trail Creek northwest of town. The Rockies rose up in all their glory as a backdrop to this pristine and peaceful scene, their peaks capped with glistening snow.

But Eph felt anything but serene and peaceful, and he trained his eyes on the clumps of brush and thickets to the west, watching for movement. When he'd been appointed as sheriff four months prior, it had been his lifelong dream come true. His fervent passion for the law and justice had been stoked his whole life by his father, who'd been a judge serving on the bench in three counties in Missouri and who'd retired just as the James-Younger Gang began their eight-year spree of robbing banks and trains—a goodly number of those robberies having taken place in his home state of Missouri. Eph had followed the news of the gang with unabating interest, year after year, reading everything he could of their exploits and crimes, growing more incensed with each new headline declaring another bank they'd robbed or another man they'd shot and killed.

Eph loathed men like Jesse James, and it infuriated him to read the blatant lies the outlaw would write to the newspapers, denying his participation in the purported crimes and decrying the evil committed by such reprehensible men. If there was one thing Eph hated more than men who broke the law it was men who lied about doing so. He reckoned the James's brothers' time was running out. Those Confederate bushwackers would be caught one of these days, but Eph reckoned it wouldn't be in Colorado Territory. How he'd love to bring those outlaws to justice, but it wasn't a portion allotted to him.

However, Jesse and Frank and those Younger brothers weren't the only outlaws needing to be rounded up. The Dutton Gang had robbed plenty, and killed many an innocent bystander as they rushed headlong to rob banks and stages. And this gang kept to Colorado Territory—Eph Love's domain. He'd thrilled reading the news of Hank Dutton's hanging last year, which had sent a shiver of satisfaction through his soul. All but the last two members of that gang were dead, but Eph would not rest easy until Billy Hill Cloyd and Clayton Wymore were dead as well. And Eph reckoned this was how he'd make his mark in law enforcement—maybe even earn him the job of state marshal someday, once Colorado became a state. Yes, he had high aspirations, always had. He saw his fierce determination for righteous justice a divine calling, and trusted the Good Lord to bless his efforts to catch the two outlaws and rid Colorado of their evil.

Which was why he was sitting his horse on the road down from Trail Creek. He'd gotten word early this morning from a wheat farmer who'd come into town to get parts for a broken plow that he'd spotted two men running through his field, crouched low and each pulling a horse along by the reins. Now, the old farmer had been quite a ways away and suffered from rheumy eyesight and couldn't vouchsafe the certainty of a proper description, but Eph reckoned it had to be Wymore and Hill. He just had a gut sense about the notion.

He'd been sitting awhile, letting the flurries settle on the shoulders of his linen duster, thinking on the Dutton Gang's past robberies and recollecting what he knew about the two wanted men. Ruthless and heartless is how Eph would describe Wymore—the meanest sort of outlaw. The older of the two wanted men kept a sharp nine-inch-long Bowie knife with a clip point tucked in a boot, and he'd used it in vicious ways on those who had stood atwixt him and his plunder. Billy Cloyd had a reputation as a sharpshooter but was known for having a weak stomach for violence, and from what Eph had gleaned from all the news reports had never killed a man. The youngest of the gang, he'd trailed along with Hank Dutton, who was some distant relation, because he had nowhere else to go—or so the *Rocky Mountain News* had stated in one of its editorials that ranted against the gang's travesties.

A rustle in a thicket of brush made Eph stiffen and swivel his head southward. Laying a hand on his Remington rifle, he craned his head, tense and watchful, then relaxed as three head of longhorn cattle emerged from the shadows just outside the fenced field. Eph's gaze traveled down into a draw, then up a far ravine where hundreds of cattle snuffled in the scraggly Junegrass and Buffalograss poking through the snow-crusted mounds.

A few birds trilled in the thickets, and the snow began to fall steady now, the air warming in the odd way it often did when it snowed. He'd already been halfway up the ridge and carefully explored the wheat fields, and located the spot where the men had trampled the vegetation. He'd followed their trail until it had come out to the road here, where he now sat. He'd knelt and studied the muddy ground but saw only fresh horse prints—some shooed and others not. No boot marks or anything to indicate anyone on foot—at least not here and not in the last few hours. Without knowing more about their horses, Eph couldn't come to any conclusions as to whether Wymore and Cloyd had come this way.

But he knew they had. He felt it in his gut, and his gut was never wrong.

Eph swallowed and rubbed his smoothly shaved jaw. He had a nose for evil and could tell when someone nearby planned to commit an injustice. And what his nose was telling him now was that the last two members of the Dutton Gang were somewhere close by, and probably fixing to rob one of the banks in Fort Collins. And he planned to stop them—whatever it took. Yes sir, there'd be hell to pay when those rascals showed their ugly faces in his town.

With a last glance around, satisfied his quarry was not on this hill, Eph Love swung Destiny back east and trotted toward town, watchful and alert, his left hand resting on his rifle, his fingers tapping the smooth wooden forestock. He pulled his hat down tighter on his head as snow fell around him, lighting on his horse's neck and melting faster than it could gather. Eph's stomach growled, making him itchy to get back to town and eat the sandwich his Sally had fixed for him.

The day felt heavy, ominous. Something was about to happen in Fort Collins. He didn't know when or exactly what. But he did know who. Of that he had no doubt.

"Guess we should pack it in," Bradford Bevington said, pulling up the long Jacob's staff and rolling in the chain. Bevington pulled his felt hat off, smacked the snow off it, and plopped it back on his thick head of russet hair. Snowflakes stuck to his beard and mustache, making it look as if he'd guzzled milk a little too hastily.

Malcolm nodded at the seasoned surveyor who had come to Colorado from England, wanting adventure, as the June snow fell around him and dusted his hat and coat. He thought Bevington perhaps had never seen snow until he came west. The man was like so many others Malcolm had met—tired of the rut their lives had fallen into and yearning for a change of scenery.

Malcolm raised his gaze to the imposing Rockies and whistled. He couldn't imagine a more beautiful sight, a more peaceful place to live and settle down in. Then he thought of Stella and the dissension between them, and his gut clenched. How could he truly find the joy and peace he desired on the Front Range with such contention in his life?

Malcolm turned to Bevington. "Looks like it's not going to let up. Maybe we can finish this quarter tomorrow." He began unscrewing his circumferentor from the flat plate while a chill breeze played at his hair.

He and Bevington had been surveying the land adjacent to the southern college boundary these last few days, and Malcolm had been glad to be buried in work, for it distracted his troubled mind and kept him out of his house—and away from his wife.

His mouth soured thinking about Stella. The last few days she'd been restless, irritable, cantankerous. He did what he could to stay out of her way, poring over maps and diagrams at his small desk, but their cabin was small, and her mood unavoidable. He wished he understood her, could find a way to help alleviate her unhappiness. For, he knew something was troubling her. And since he was stuck with her, he'd vowed he'd try harder. Do what he had to in order to make this marriage work, to make her happy. Surely this was a trial the Good Lord had given him to not only endure but to fortify him, improve his character. The Good Book said that God never put you through a trial without giving you the strength and wisdom to endure it, or without making the way out. But what way out?

He'd thought Stella was just beset by cabin fever, and figured once spring came and she could get outside and shop and socialize—do those things women did with their free time—her countenance would lift. But much the opposite had occurred. The more winter gave way to spring, the more unhappy and unpleasant Stella had become. And Malcolm was at a loss as to what else he could do.

He gathered his equipment and knelt to put everything into his pack. Bevington waved good-bye and swung up on his horse. Malcolm's bay gelding, Rambler, nickered at him from the tree where he was tied up, as if wondering what was taking him so long. The horse pawed the snow-encrusted ground, no doubt looking forward to a warm, dry stall and a flake of hay. Malcolm figured he'd head back to the office and neaten up his ledgers and notes, delaying his return home for a while.

He rubbed a hand across his forehead, feeling weary from the lack of sleep. All this week he'd been plagued by troublesome dreams—dreams filled with beautiful vistas and raging rivers. In his dreams he wrangled a canoe down wild cascades, aware of others in the boat with him. He stood on a promontory of flat rock overlooking an expansive valley in which steam and water geysers erupted from cracks in the hard rocky earth and shot high into the sky. He saw the faces of Indians, who were dressed in deerskin and had feathers in their braided black hair. And the most disturbing of all the images in his dreams were the ones of a woman—a faceless, nameless woman—with long golden locks and gentle hands. Hands that held his, and stroked his cheek, and rubbed the aching muscles in his back by the soft glow of candlelight.

In these dreams, he experienced an overwhelming desire to hold her, his love gushing from his heart like a mighty river tumbling down a canyon, seeking her, needing her. Often he bolted awake, drenched in sweat, his hands trembling. Overlaying the love was a smothering unnamable fear. Unable to drift back into sleep, most nights he would lie there in bed, wide awake, waiting for the pastel smear of dawn to creep in through his window.

He looked down at his surveying compass and ran a finger over the initials etched in the brass. He had a faint memory of pressing the point of a knife into the metal and making these marks. The images in his dreams felt like memories too, and the more he dreamed, the more real they seemed. But who was that woman?

Thinking of her brought a rush of sadness to his heart and a deep sense of loss. Was it his mother? His sister? No, he felt something deeper than familial love for this woman. The thought of her touch sent a shudder of need—strong, desirous need—through every pore in his body. He let loose a long sigh that sounded more like a groan of pain. Why couldn't he remember? He needed to remember! Not knowing his past or who he was tormented him. He had the terrible feeling he was forgetting something important, something of great value.

And yet, if what Stella had told him was true—about their lives together and why they had come west—these tenacious feelings were only the byproduct of meaningless dreams.

But what if her stories weren't true?

He stopped and straightened as the thought hit him as hard as a rock thrown in his face. He'd been skirting this possibility for weeks now, but had never fully faced his doubts—and fears. For, what if Stella had lied to him? About everything? What if he wasn't who she said he was—and what if she wasn't who she claimed to be? Was it possible?

His heart pained at the thought he'd been so deceived. He looked again at his initials staring back at him. *M. C.*

Malcolm Connors.

The name felt foreign to him, as if it was someone else's name. Surely his own name would *feel* like it fit, like he owned it.

A thought wormed into his mind. There had to be some record of his birth somewhere. Some proof of his former life back in St. Louis. He realized with chagrin that he didn't even know his age or what year he'd been born. Had he even been born in St. Louis? Without that information, he would not be able to get the proof he needed. Stella had told him he'd worked in St. Louis as a surveyor. Yet, when he'd asked her where, or suggested he contact former work associates in the hope that would help his memory return, she had dissuaded him from doing so. His jaw clenched as he thought of how she'd diverted him away from that idea on more than one occasion. She claimed it would only discourage him and keep him from getting on with his life.

Stella was hiding something. He now saw that. He'd noticed the tiny spark of alarm in her eyes when he made those suggestions, but had chalked it up to her worrying over him.

His gut twisted at the thought that he'd been lied to. He longed to know the truth, and he suspected Stella knew it—every bit of it. But she would not be forthcoming, no matter how Malcolm tried to wrest it from her. Why had she lied?

His mind jerked back to that afternoon when he'd opened his eyes on the bank of the Platte and saw her staring at him. How distressed and forlorn she'd been, gushing with love and relief that he was alive. How she'd helped him into the wagon and taken him to that ramshackle cabin, away from civilization, in order to nurse him back to health.

Why hadn't she taken him into Greeley? Why not rented rooms in town? Why keep him isolated? She'd claimed it was for his health and recovery—the solitude essential and healing. He never thought to question anything she did or said, for why would he have? He couldn't imagine any woman concocting such a detailed history of their lives, nor spending months nursing a stranger back to health without some personal recompense. If she had not been his fiancée, then who was she? And why the elaborate ruse? He was neither rich nor important—or so he assumed.

He shook his head in frustration and confusion. Maybe he was wrong—maybe she had told the truth. And maybe all his dreams were just dreams of no significance whatsoever.

He snorted and finished packing his things, then slung the pack onto his back and mounted Rambler. His horse's steps sounded muffled in the snow, and the dark clouds cast a shadow across the prairie, mirroring the shadow draped across his mind. He headed north, toward the center of town, longing for a hot meal to warm his stomach, but knew it would not chase the chill from his heart. A strange coldness had grown inside him, as if he were slowly freezing to death in the middle of a blizzard, with no one nearby to usher him to safety.

His thoughts drifted with the snow, and he found himself thinking about the woman he'd helped the other day. How frightened and vulnerable she'd been, and how sweet and brave. How unlike Stella in her manner and comportment. He cringed thinking of the poor woman, almost crushed by that horse and wagon. And her baby—he would have been killed as well.

A shudder danced across his neck thinking about the near calamity. He thanked God that he had been there, walking down the street at the moment of her crisis. He'd had his head turned, but her cry of alarm had alerted him.

As he trotted his gelding along the snow-blanketed road, the town barely visible through the flurries a mile up ahead, her lovely face fixed in his mind. Her skin was flawless and her cheeks rosy from the cold. Her eyes were a pale green, and he saw more than fear and shock in them. Something else swam in those troubled eyes . . .

A twinge of pain struck his heart as he thought about her, but he didn't know why. She seemed sad, lonely, as if bereft. He never thought to question if she was married. He'd assumed so, and that her husband was working that day. But now he wondered.

For some reason, his brief encounter with that woman unsettled him. Maybe it was because of the way Stella had attacked her, accusing her of trying to steal him away. Now he remembered—Stella said something about the woman not having a husband. And she had recognized her from the dress shop.

Malcolm flinched thinking of his wife's insensitivity and rudeness. It made him angry and even more regretful that he'd married her. His mind returned to his previous ruminations, and it verified his conviction all the more that Stella had lied to him about his past and his identity.

He knew if he confronted her that she'd be incensed and horrified and would deny his suspicions. But he could no longer suppress the growing unrest in his soul—he had to suss out the truth. He'd recently caught her lying about her drinking, and her face gave her away when she prevaricated in such a manner. He'd learned that if a person lied about one thing, it usually meant they lied about other things. If she denied the accusations, maybe he'd be able to see it in her face—whether or not she was deceitful. But then what? He couldn't force the truth out of her. Could he wheedle it out?

What if . . . no, that wouldn't be honorable to do. He pushed the thought away—of waiting until she'd had a lot to drink, then getting her to talk. But why not? He wasn't forcing her to get drunk. All he had to do was wait, and the opportunity would surely present itself. The thought, however encouraging, also greatly vexed him. How much more could he take? He didn't think he could bear much more unhappiness and this feeling of being trapped—and now feeling duped.

He kicked Rambler's flanks and got him trotting as he approached the outskirts of town. Wind blew snow in his face, and the world had gone white and silent around him. He'd thought spring was just around the corner, but now it looked as if winter had one last gasp to give. He knew how much Stella hated the snow and winter, and no doubt he'd find her back at the homestead, grumbling and miserable—and drinking.

Maybe before the day was over, he'd get the answers he needed. And as much as he wanted to learn the truth, the upshot was he feared it—feared what he'd lost. For something deep inside him told him that he'd lost something very precious to him.

No, not something. Some*one*.

Chapter 14

GRACE TUCKED HER BONNETED HEAD down as far as she could into her thick wool coat, but somehow tendrils of cold seeped down her neck and sent a chill through her. The snow that had been sliding down into her boots had soaked her stockings and now gathered in small puddles in which her feet sloshed around as she hurried along the wooden boardwalk on College Avenue. She should have had Eli and Clare drop her off at home instead of at Mrs. St. Vrain's. But Grace had promised to return and do the fitting for the old arthritic lady, and she'd had a nice visit by her crackling hearth, drinking hot tea and munching on delicious lemon cookies. Now, eight blocks from the Franklins', Grace trudged along, hoping Ben was warm and well fed, wishing she was back in her room, holding him in her arms. She so needed the comfort of human touch.

As much as it had helped to spill her heart out to Clare and Eli, and to be encouraged by them, recounting her story to them had reopened the deep wound in her soul. Although, she'd be a fool to think this wound could ever heal. *Keep hopeful,* she reminded herself. She had to trust and pray and believe—even when she didn't want to. She heard her aunt's words in her head: *"Faith cannot be your possession until it is truly and fully tested."*

Her aunt had raised her to believe in a just, loving God. And to be grateful for all the blessings bestowed upon her. Grace knew she had so much to be grateful for, and tried to think on those things rather than on all she had lost.

She warmed thinking of Clare and Eli, and looked forward to going with Clare on Sunday to Eli's ranch, where she'd meet his brother and his Cheyenne mother. She'd never met a pureblooded Indian before, although there were many in Illinois who had some Indian blood of one kind or another. Eli had said his grandmother had been a medicine woman of her tribe, and that his mother was a gifted healer and seer. Grace wasn't sure what a seer was, but maybe Sarah Banks could help her in some way. Help her see her way forward.

Grace heard the sound of horses and looked over at the street. An enclosed buggy pulled up to where she stood, and a small man got out and ran over to her, his head buried under a wide-brimmed hat. He wore a long dark woolen coat and nice leather shoes not meant for the snow. When he raised his face to hers, Grace recognized him—the clerk from the courthouse.

"Hello, Mrs. Cunningham," the man said, tipping his hat at her and wiping snow from his glasses with his other hand. "Alan Patterson—from the courthouse." He gave her a sweet smile that revealed a row of crooked teeth, and then quickly closed his mouth, as if embarrassed for her to see them.

"Yes, I remember you, Mr. Patterson." She tucked back against the Whedbee Mercantile's window, under the false front awning, hoping to get some relief from the deluge of snow, but the wind merely shifted and blew it into her face. She rubbed her arms with her gloved hands.

"This is no weather for you to be out in," he said. "May I give you a ride home?" He held out his hand.

Grace allowed him to take hold of her arm. "Thank you. I am grateful. I only live six blocks up Maple, but in this weather it seems more like six miles. Does it often snow in June here?"

"Sometimes in July and even August, Mrs. Cunningham. That's the Front Range for you."

Without further word or ado, he led her carefully off the boardwalk and into the buggy's interior, where she plopped down on the tan leather seat and gave a sigh. Although the buggy was cold, she was out of the snow and glad she did not have to walk the remaining blocks. The last thing she needed was to catch her death of cold from having wet feet.

"What address on Maple?" the clerk asked her, leaning in politely through the buggy's door, trying not to let any snow blow in.

"At the corner of Loomis. Do you know the Franklins—Jedidiah and Charity?"

He nodded, then gently clicked the door shut. Grace imagined that with his job, he knew where every person in the town lived.

Presently they were underway, the snow muffling the sounds of the horses and breeching and hooves trotting down the street. In no time at all they had arrived, and Grace felt it only polite to invite Mr. Patterson in—if Charity would allow it.

When she opened the door, she heard a gleeful shriek from Ben. He squirmed out of Charity's arms and crawled to her, and Grace gathered him up. She said to Charity, who stood eying her with what seemed disdain and judgment, "Mr. Patterson was kind to give me a ride home in this storm. I was at Mrs. St. Vrain's house, doing a fitting, and the snow caught me unawares."

Charity's face softened—whether due to her finding this an acceptable excuse for being in a man's company or because Mr. Patterson was standing in the doorway watching this exchange, Grace didn't know. But Charity became all smiles and welcomed him in, saying, "Oh yes, Mr. Patterson, from the courthouse—do come in," then hurried off to make tea and bring them something to eat.

With Ben in her arms, Grace gestured for the clerk to come inside, which he did a bit tentatively. Grace excused herself to get out of her wet shoes and stockings, and kissed and hugged Ben as she went to her room and changed into a dry skirt and sweater and soft fur-lined slippers. When she returned, feeling warm and flushed from the heated room, Charity breezed in with a tea service and biscuits. Mr. Patterson sat stiffly, a bit nervous, with his hat in his hand.

"Do make yourself at home, Mr. Patterson," she said. "I'll hang up your hat and coat by the door."

She held out her arms, and only then did Mr. Patterson realize he was dripping water from his coat onto the parquet floor.

"Oh, please forgive my lack of manners," he said, shrugging off his coat and handing it to her, along with his hat.

"Oh, do not concern yourself," Charity said, all smiles.

Grace was glad for her kind and gracious demeanor, but then, Charity prided herself in her hospitality. Grace glanced out the window at the endlessly falling snow. Would she ever find time to pay a call on the Strattons? She supposed she would speak to them on Sunday at church. And maybe if they were agreeable, she could go home with them after the service and see the room they offered to let out to her. She hoped they hadn't found another tenant.

Charity and Mr. Patterson exchanged pleasant conversation about this and that, but Grace did little other than smile and nod at times. She bounced Ben on her knee, but he crawled off to the pile of blocks in the corner and happily entertained himself. After they had drunk their tea and eaten the somewhat dry biscuits, Charity gathered the cups and plates and went into the kitchen.

Mr. Patterson watched her leave, and then leaned in and spoke in a subdued tone. "Mrs. Cunningham, I received a letter back from the courthouse in Bloomington." He glanced toward the kitchen, and Grace heard Charity bustling about, humming a little tune Grace had heard before.

Grace appreciated the clerk's discretion. She did not care for Charity to know any more of her personal business—which meant more for the woman to gossip about. Her pulse quickened as she waited for him to continue.

His face showed apology and kindness. "Apparently, there'd been a fire recently in the building in which all the records were kept. Firefighters had put out the fire in a timely manner, but many of the court documents had been burned. However, most were salvaged, but due to the water damage, it seems it will take some weeks to sort through the mess and put everything back in order. As it stands, no one has yet been able to find your marriage certificate."

Grace's heart sank at the news, but Mr. Patterson—seeing her dismay, no doubt—said reassuringly, "I'll inquire again in a few weeks. Perhaps by then they'll have all the papers back in order, and will locate your certificate." He added with a nervous expression, "I know how much this means to you, Mrs. Cunningham. I can only imagine how difficult your circumstances are . . . and living in a small town . . . well, people tend to talk . . ."

Grace had the feeling that this clerk had heard rumors about her—hence the reason for his nervous fidgeting.

"I thank you for your help in this matter. And your concern." He let out a long breath, and then rose to his feet. Grace stood as well, assuming he was ready to leave. She made to show him to the door, but he remained in place, his neat tweed suit rumpled and hanging loosely on his lean frame. His curly hair was a bit matted to his face, and he brushed it off his forehead and cleared his throat. He avoided meeting her eyes, and Grace wondered why he was nervous in her presence.

After another quick glance toward the kitchen, he said just above a whisper, "Would you . . . would you like to have dinner with me sometime? I know, I mean, I . . ." His words lodged in his throat, and he met her eyes. Grace startled at the unexpected invitation. Now she understood his unease. She was flattered by his interest, but the last thing she wanted right now was to fend off a man's affections. Yet, she could tell he was kindhearted and sensitive, and did not want to hurt his feelings.

"You are too kind, Mr. Patterson—"

"Please, call me Alan."

"I truly thank you for your generous offer, Alan. But . . . I am . . ." She paused, then continued. "I am not over the loss of my husband, and with a child to raise and my work responsibilities, I don't think I am ready for much . . . of a social life. But," she hurried to add, "it is good of you to care." She hoped he sensed her sincerity.

He looked a bit crestfallen, but nodded in understanding. "It may be that in time you will want to find someone . . . who can help you carry the burden you bear. I hope you will . . . consider me."

He said those words with such fear and trembling, Grace felt equal parts pity and humility. All she could say was, "Thank you, Alan. I will."

She retrieved his coat and hat and handed them to him. As he put them on, Charity came into the room, a dishtowel in her hand.

"So good of you to bring Grace home, Mr. Patterson. I hope the roads aren't too difficult for your horses to navigate."

He touched the brim of his hat. "They're plenty used to Colorado snow, although I'm certain they're as tired of it as I am. Good day, Mrs. Franklin." He nodded at Charity, then gave Grace a sweet but sad smile. His eyes burned with rejection, but Grace could think of nothing to say other than to thank him again and wish him well.

Charity mumbled something about needing to begin fixing dinner, and Grace offered to help. But, as usual, Charity declined Grace's offer in a brusque manner and bustled off in her busy manner. The exhaustion of the day pressed like a heavy weight on Grace's shoulders, and she longed for a hot bath. Seeing that Ben was still playing with his blocks, she headed to the bathing room to prepare a hot bath, hoping that when she went into the kitchen to heat water Charity would not ply her with questions or chastise her in any way.

She went into her room and stood by the window, watching the snow falling and piling in drifts in the yard. The white pickets of the short fence were nearly buried now, and the peaks of the houses down the street were capped in white as if wearing neat little caps. Clean white snow turned the town into a pristine winter marvel, reminding Grace of a snow globe her aunt had kept on the mantel in the boardinghouse sitting room. Inside the glass ball was an intricately crafted tiny European town, and when young, Grace had loved to shake the snow and watch it fall on the quaint cottages and shops.

Grace had longed to one day live in a small quaint town like that one, and when Monty had proposed to her, she envisioned the day when they'd move to Fort Collins and sit together by a warming fire, watching the snow blanket the world outside, enclosing them in their world of love—their own safe, pristine snow globe of wonder and joy.

But just as easily as glass shatters, her world had shattered. And now the snow fell upon the shards of her broken heart and broken life—cold, smothering, and stark. Somewhere, just a few miles away, her husband—the man she loved with all her heart—was in a house and in the arms of another woman, maybe sitting by a warm fire and looking out at the flakes swirling in the wind and feeling the joy and peace that she'd had stolen from her.

With a strangled cry, Grace fell to the floor and wept.

"What do you think you're doing?"

Malcolm spun around, startled, then pressed his back against her opened dresser drawer, closing it. He hadn't heard Stella come in, and there she stood, listing to one side, drunk, and waggling an accusing finger at him. But his surprise turned quickly to outrage.

"Just where have you been?" He gestured to the dark, foreboding evening sky out the window. "It's almost eight. You didn't leave a note."

She only shrugged and shifted her weight to the other side of the door frame.

He looked his wife over. She stood in the threshold of their tiny bedroom, her hands on her hips and her eyes glazed. Her clothes were in disarray, but not in the way a woman's might after riding a horse for miles on a cold day. Her blouse was missing two buttons at the collar, and her skirt looked as if it had been trampled by a herd of buffalo. A close look at her hair showed she'd stuffed her black tresses in sloppy fashion into their combs, implying she'd taken her hair down and then, without the aid of a mirror, attempted to neaten up. And her face showed smears of powder and rouge in the wrong places and in more quantity than she normally used.

He could almost feel his blood boil like a kettle on a hot iron stove. Was she so drunk that she thought he wouldn't notice these telltale signs of her infidelity? Did she think him such a sap that he wouldn't object to her outrageous conduct?

Bile rose up his throat in disgust. He slammed shut the other drawers he'd been rifling through—trying to find any clues that might tell him what he yearned to know about his past and his identity—and stormed out of the room, pushing past her and ignoring her whiny complaints.

He'd had it with her, and this latest humiliation—this betrayal—was unforgiveable.

He busied himself by washing his supper dishes, letting his rage propel him around the small kitchen. When he'd gotten home midday and found her and her horse gone, he figured she went to town for something. But when evening rolled in and she was still gone, Malcolm knew she was up to no good. He fixed a plate of cold hash and opened a jar of beans, then sat by the woodstove and fed it sticks of wood to rekindle the smoldering fire she'd left unstoked. After he'd gotten the chill out of the house, and she still hadn't returned, he went to task to find anything he could that might give him the answers he sought.

He knew now he shouldn't waste his time questioning her, for no matter what she told him, he would be hard pressed to believe her.

As he stood at the basin drying the fancy ceramic plates she'd ordered from Boston, he heard her stumble into the room. She knocked a chair over and righted it, emitting a little giggle, then sidled up behind him and stroked the back of his neck, trying to cajole him.

He bristled and set down the plate he was holding.

"Don't," was all he said, not turning. He didn't want to look in her face, see the mirth and inebriation on her features.

"Oh, my darlin' is upset. What's botherin' you, honey?"

He noticed her drawl got more pronounced the more she drank, and didn't know if it was an act or her actual voice coming out from underneath her disguise. She touched him again, and he swung around and pushed her hand away. She stepped back, incensed—although that too seemed an act. Was everything about her a falsehood?

His gut twisted as the truth sank in. She'd been with another man, and he knew that wasn't part of an act. This close, he smelled men's cheap cologne on her skin—wafting through the stench of whiskey on her breath. As much as he now detested her, he still felt hurt by her unfaithfulness. Why, after all this time of being loyal and devoted to him, had she abandoned him, uncaring of his feelings? Just what did she want? Someone to provide a roof over her head and food in the larder?

Stella dropped down into one of the kitchen chairs and propped her head up with her elbows on the table, pouting. "You haven't answered my question," she slurred.

"You haven't answered mine," he said tersely. "Who were you with?"

Her eyes widened, and then she closed them and chuckled. "Well, I guess yer a smart one. Can't pull any wool over yer eyes, now, can we?"

Malcolm, fed up, threw down the dishtowel and, reining in his anger as best he could, got up in her face, steeling his emotions. "I asked, who were you with? Where did you go?"

She huffed and leaned back, away from his imposing face. "Wouldn't you like to know?"

The urge to strike her flared in his chest, but he snuffed it out. He'd never hit a woman in his life, and he never would—no matter how much he felt they could use a licking. It wasn't his place to mete out justice; that was the Lord's. Malcolm wiped his hands, and noted the symbolism of his actions. He would wipe his hands of Stella as well. As much as he'd hoped to make things work between them, it was obvious now his hopes had been foolhardy.

He studied her puffy eyes and powder-smeared face, feeling only disgust for this woman he had previously valued. But she was like fool's gold—pretty and sparkling on the outside, but worthless and disappointing on the inside.

"I pity you," he said. Stella swiveled and narrowed her eyes at him.

"Oh, is that right?" she slurred, bobbling her head.

He put his hands on his hips and clucked his tongue on his teeth. "You're young and comely, and have a pretty smile. But you're empty inside. You don't care for others' feelings. You know nothing about loving someone proper. No man will ever truly love you—not the way you are—no matter how hard you try to win that love. You'll spend your life trying to find happiness, but it will always be just a finger's reach away. Men only want one thing from women like you—"

Stella's hand flew so fast, Malcolm felt the hot sting on his cheek before he realized she'd swatted him. Her cold, unloving eyes glowered at him, but he noticed her hands shook as she set them in her lap.

"How dare you . . ." She swung away from him and stared out the window, rigid in posture.

Malcolm regretted his outburst, but the God's honest truth was she needed to hear his words. His gut soured as if he'd eaten a rotten apple. He wanted to march out, right now. Leave and never return. But he knew deep in his heart that Stella was the only person who could tell him who he was and where he came from. Neither strangling her nor leaving would procure him the answers he sought, yet he knew now that sweet-talking or coaxing her wouldn't work either.

He stood, fuming, unblinking, unable to think, act, or decide on a course of action.

He looked over at his wife. She had fallen asleep at the table, her cheek pressed against the hard wood surface, her snores puncturing the silence in the small kitchen. Malcolm stared at her, befuddled and numb. How had his life taken such a turn? If only he could remember the past. Then, he would know what to do. He wouldn't need Stella or her secrets.

He resolved to ride this out—for what other choice did he have? Stay in Fort Collins, work, mind his own business. He hoped in time the truth would come out, or his memories would return. He knew his dreams were showing him bits and pieces of his past, of who he was. In time, he might have enough pieces to form a picture.

He looked at the bed in his bedroom with its neat patchwork counterpane draped over the goose-down mattress he had bought at Matson's Furniture Emporium in town. Stella had picked out the most expensive one in the store. She had spent all the money they'd brought with them to Fort Collins, which made him grateful he had a steady job. But no longer would he give Stella everything she wanted—or claimed she "absolutely must have." He didn't need much to live on, and since it appeared as if she'd found someone to share her affections with, if she needed money, why, she could just ask that scalawag for a few coins. Or maybe she was already wringing money from him—and who knew how many others.

Malcolm rubbed his face and blew out a long breath. He had hoped to make a good impression in this new town—his new home. But he now realized he'd probably have to leave sooner or later. How could he hold his head high once the rumors—no, the facts—of his wife's infidelity trailed after him like a hungry wolf? He couldn't bear the disgrace on his character.

He had hoped his integrity, honor, and upstanding comportment would be enough to earn the respect of those around him, but he didn't think those qualities could withstand the repercussions of Stella's wanton and churlish behavior.

He would just have to get to the bottom of her lies, he thought, looking around the house and trying to guess where she might have hidden something she wanted to keep secret from him.

He grunted and raked a hand through his hair. It was going to take a whole lot of digging to get to that rock bottom. But he had no other choice. And once he had his answers, he'd get shed of this town and go somewhere, far away, and start over.

Chapter 15

"THIS IS IT," CLARE SAID, pulling on the reins and steering the two draft horses to the right and along a wide, smooth dirt road bordered by splendid pines.

Grace was glad to have finally arrived at the Banks Ranch, having had to soothe Ben the whole way, who fussed in her arms impatiently, wanting to climb down and explore. He was so much like his father—already, Grace thought with a mixture of comfort and sorrow. Eager to discover new places.

She pulled Ben up to stand on her legs so he could look around, balancing him as he took in the sights with delight. He talked in his cute jumble of sounds, which made Clare laugh as she brought the horses to a stop and adjusted her bonnet.

At the end of the road sat a wood-planked ranch house flanked by three barns of various sizes. Pastures with pole fencing enclosed fields mostly buried in snowdrifts, which stretched out behind the simple house.

A dog with black and white splotches came running toward their wagon from behind the house, barking in piercing yips, but Grace could tell he was friendly. Clare tousled the dog's fur as she stepped down from the bench seat. "You're a cute one," she told the dog, then looked around the spread. Off in the distance, close to the farthest and newest barn, a dozen or more horses stood near a water trough.

Clare held out her arms for Ben, and Grace handed him down to her, then alighted from the wagon. She was grateful for a warm June day after the heavy snowfall days before. How quickly the weather changed in Colorado! Water dripped steadily from the pines lining the road and from the eaves of the house, and the air smelled wonderfully damp and invigorating. Grace gathered Ben into her arms, and he squirmed to get down.

"Do I look presentable?" Clare asked, her tone revealing how nervous she was. She smoothed out the pretty Irish plaid dress she was wearing, and Grace could tell Clare was not a bit comfortable in her petticoats. But Clare wanted to make a good impression on Sarah, Eli's mother. Grace chuckled recalling that Eli had sounded much more nervous than she about the meeting. But she couldn't imagine anyone not liking Clare.

Grace had dressed in a simple cotton skirt and blouse, and now, standing in the warmth of the late morning sun, she was glad she hadn't worn the heavy woolen traveling suit she'd first considered. The wind had made a bit of a mess with her hair, but she did her best to adjust the pins, which was awkward to do with a wiggling ten-month-old in her arms.

The door to the house flew open, and Eli strode out, walking toward them with a bright smile on his face. He was dressed in pressed brown trousers and a blue chambray shirt, and his wheat-straw hair was slicked back. His face was smooth, showing he'd just shaved, and he made a little clucking noise as he came up to Clare.

"Well, look at you," he said with a tease in his voice. "You look right pretty, Miss Clare Ferne McKay."

She punched his arm playfully and whispered, "You look like you're about to be hauled to church."

Eli chuckled and said hello to Grace, then tickled Ben under the chin. "Come on in," he said, looking at the horses, who stood sleepily in the driveway, no doubt enjoying their reprieve from both the recent winter weather and the trek over from Fort Collins on the slushy road.

"Let me get LeRoy out here to unhitch your horses, and then I'll bring you in for proper introductions." He gave Clare a wink and went back into the house.

Grace looked at her friend and saw the dreamy glow in her eyes. She smiled, glad for Clare's happiness, but her own misery assaulted her as she thought how she used to look at Monty like that. How that spark of new love had flared into a brighter, hotter fire once they married. How even now when she thought of him her pulse quickened and her body ached for his.

She pushed her painful thoughts aside and waited. Presently, Eli came out with another young man, one with darker hair and eyes, and clearly of Indian descent. Grace noted he walked with a slight swagger, and he stood a few inches taller than his fairer brother.

Eli said to her, "This here's LeRoy, Miss Cunningham." LeRoy gave her a friendly smile and nodded hello. It was clear he'd met Clare before, for he shot her a welcoming look that was a little less reserved.

"Please, just call me Grace," she told them both. It felt awkward to be called "miss" when she was truly a "missus," but she couldn't tell them that. No one in town deigned to refer to her as a married woman or even a widow. None except Alan. Patterson, the clerk. He at least seemed to believe her story.

The two men nodded, then LeRoy took the horses' reins and led them, still hitched to the wagon, in through the open carriage doors of the nearest barn.

"Ma's eager to meet you," Eli said, mostly to Clare. "I shouldn't have waited so long—she's been givin' me grief over it." He took Clare's hand and squeezed it, looking just as nervous as she. Clare drew in a long breath and straightened, then followed Eli into the house. Grace came in behind them, hoisting Ben in her arms. She hoped he didn't fuss too much or get into trouble, and she was thankful Eli's mother had allowed her to bring him.

A delicious aroma greeted her—baked bread and something savory, like stew. She took in the cozy kitchen with the yellow gingham curtains and the lacquered pine cabinets and plank flooring. A jar of perky yellow wildflowers sat on a big thick wood table, and Grace wondered where Eli's mother could have found such flowers in the midst of all the snow. The table was set with simple crockery and silverware, but everything was neat and clean, and showed thoughtful placement and a woman's touch.

Eli left Grace and Clare and went into the next room. Grace heard him calling, "Ma, Ma—where are you? Clare's here."

A back door slapped against wood, and presently Grace saw Eli come back into the kitchen with his mother.

Sarah Banks was a large woman with strong features, hers a round face with high cheekbones, her skin a gleaming brown. Dark hair fell back over her shoulders in two thick braids, and she wore a heavy brown linen skirt and something akin to a man's tailored plaid shirt, rolled up at the sleeves. Her fist clenched around a bundle of cooking herbs, from what Grace could gather. Eli went and stood by the big cast-iron stove, his head cocked, staring at Clare with adoration. He looked pleased to have brought Clare home to meet his mother, as if eager to show her off, although a bit worried if Sarah would approve.

Sarah greeted her and Clare warmly, and Grace immediately liked her and felt at ease. Without asking, Sarah scooped Ben into her arms and looked a long while into his eyes. Grace was surprised at how quiet and focused Ben got, staring into Sarah's face. Then Sarah laughed, and Ben joined her in his exuberant way, his eyes sparkling.

"He's a darlin', Grace. I bet he looks just like his pa." Sarah ran her fingers through Ben's wispy hair, and Grace thought with sadness—not for the first time—how much she wished her aunt was still alive so she could hold Ben in her arms. She had so loved children and had never had any of her own.

Grace's throat choked a bit as she nodded. Sarah studied her with compassion, which made Grace wonder how much Eli had told his mother about her.

Sarah gently squeezed Ben's cheeks, and he pulled on her hair. But instead of scolding him, she merely laughed and then set him down on the kitchen floor. He promptly headed over to a stack of pots and pans, but Sarah didn't seem to mind. Grace was glad she was comfortable having a baby crawling around her house.

"Now," Sarah said, turning to Clare and smiling approvingly. "I've been lookin' forward to meetin' you, Clare. Eli needs a woman that can keep him on the straight and narrow and outta trouble, and most of 'em he's courted have done nothin' but get him *into* trouble. You've made a new man of him, that's plain to see. Something a mother is glad for."

"Thank you for invitin' us," Clare said demurely, a blush on her cheeks. Grace hadn't seen Clare this shy. "I've been so lookin' forward to meetin' you, Mrs. Banks."

Sarah waved a dismissive hand in the air. "We don't cotton to formalities here. Just call me Sarah. Come, girls," she said, gesturing them to the table. "Sit here while I finish up preparin' lunch, and we can talk."

Clare threw Grace a nervous glance, but Grace shrugged and smiled. They both sat.

Sarah laughed. "Clare, Eli's told me so much about you, I feel as though I already know you plenty. But don't let that notion scare you—he only has nice things to say, and from the sound of it, you love horses almost as much as he does. And that's sayin' a lot." She turned and looked at Eli, whose smile took up most of his face.

"Wait till you see her handle a horse, Ma. She's the best roper I've ever seen."

Grace laughed behind her hand. It struck her funny that these seemed to be the highest compliments Eli could offer on Clare's behalf. But then, he and his mother and brother raised and trained horses. No doubt having some riding skills earned high marks with Sarah.

"I didn't tell you this," Eli said cautiously to his mother, "but Clare and I are gonna enter the team ropin' at the centennial race next month."

Sarah narrowed her eyes, then dunked the herbs into a tub of water that sat on the long wooden counter behind her. "Team ropin', huh?" She shook the water off the herbs and started chopping them on a wood block. "You think ropin' with a girl might raise a few eyebrows?" She turned and looked at Clare, assessing her. "Hmm. Maybe she'll show you up, make you look foolish."

Eli chuckled and waved a hand. "We've been practicin'. No one'll laugh when they watch us take the ribbon."

"You're awfully confident," she said, but she gave Clare a wink.

LeRoy came tromping in through the front door after wiping his feet on the rough doormat. "Hey, that smells great," he said, going over to the sink and washing up. "Lunch ready yet?"

Sarah tossed the seasonings into the big cast-iron pot simmering on the flat top of the stove. "Another ten minutes." She looked at Clare and Grace. "You girls want to freshen up after your ride? Eli, show them where the bathing room is." She looked down at Ben, who was banging on the iron pans with his hands. "I'll watch the little one."

"Thank you, Sarah," Clare said. "This is so nice of ya to have us over."

"About time Eli brought you home. I was beginning to think he made you up."

Clare laughed. "No, I'm real."

"I told ya, Ma." He chuckled, and then walked with them to a small room off the back of the house. "Privy's just out there, if'n you need it. There's a water pump just outside the door." He pointed through the window. "Glad you had a nice day to travel. Run into any scalawags along the way?"

"No," Clare said with a pout. "And I was itchin' for a fight too," she added in an exaggerated Western twang.

Eli snuck in a quick peck to her cheek, and his face flushed.

Clare smacked him on the head. "Eli!" she whispered harshly, "behave yourself. I'm trying to make a nice impression."

He laughed and swung her in close. She covered her mouth with her hand as a squeal eked out.

"Well, my ma's so keen to see me married and settled that I don't think you could do anythin' to spoil that good impression.

Less'n of course you say something unkind about her cooking. Or about her horses." He thought a moment. "Or start talkin' politics, or—"

Clare pressed her hand over his mouth. "Go," she said. "We ladies have to freshen up."

He smirked, gave an exaggerated bow, and spun around. Clare shook her head and said, "I really do love that man. He makes me laugh."

"You're well suited," Grace said. "And it sure looks like he plans to marry you."

Clare looked at herself in the mirror and fussed with her hair. Grace marveled at the rich red color that offset her shining green eyes. "You two will make some pretty babies."

"Oh!" Clare said, her eyes wide. "I'm not even hitched yet and yer already talking babies."

"Well, they usually follow . . . hitching." She laughed, and Clare joined her.

"Don't I know!" Clare said. "I've already spent most of my life changin' diapers and washin' clothes and chasin' toddlers around. Wouldn't be nothin' new."

Grace smiled. She was so glad to be away from Fort Collins, if even just for a day. Even though her problems would still be waiting for her when she returned, she vowed to push all her worries and heartache far from her mind and just enjoy the friendly company of people who didn't gossip or think badly of her. She imagined Monty here with her, and thought how much he'd fit in. He didn't abide pretentious people either, and liked nothing more than to sit around sharing adventure stories and learning where people came from and what they were interested in.

Monty. She let out a trembling sigh. She would never be able to stop thinking about him, stop hurting. He was such a part of her—how could she think she could push him out of her mind, even for a day?

She excused herself to go use the privy and went out back. When she finished, she washed up at the pump and smoothed her hair and clothing, then found Clare with Sarah and her family in the kitchen. Clare cuddled Ben on her lap. He had a slice of apple in his hand, and he used his four little teeth to scrape and eat the fruit, his face tight in concentration at the task. Grace noticed a big woven basket piled with clean white sheets next to the table.

Sarah took Ben from Clare and looked him over. His cheeks had bits of apple stuck to them. Sarah took a cloth from a drawer and wiped his face. "He's ready for a nap," she said. As if on cue, Ben yawned and fussed, making the mewling sounds that indicated he was tired.

"Too much excitement for the little one," Sarah said, and set him gently down in the basket. Ben nuzzled into the sheets and closed his eyes. Sarah adjusted Ben so that he was lying on his back, looking up at her. She said to him with a mock stern expression, "Time for sleep, little one." And then she said something else, in a language Grace didn't recognize. She assumed it was Cheyenne.

To her surprise, instead of crying—his usual response to being put down for a nap—Ben closed his eyes and promptly fell asleep. Grace's mouth dropped open.

"How did you do that?" she asked Sarah, who only gave her a shrug, her eyes twinkling in a mischievous way.

"She uses Indian magic," LeRoy said, standing by the stove and eyeing the large pot. "Is lunch ready now?"

Sarah rolled her eyes and went to the stove. "Yes, now." She looked at Clare pointedly. "These young, strong men—they eat a lot. Do you know how to cook?"

Clare was startled by Sarah's directness. "Oh, yes, I do—"

"She's a great cook, Ma," Eli said in her defense, and from Sarah's expression, Grace thought maybe she had said that to bait him.

Eli continued. "I told ya she helped raise six younger brothers and sisters."

Sarah nodded thoughtfully and hefted the large pot with two heavy towels. She set it on the table, on a wool pot warmer, and LeRoy pulled a tray of steaming bread rolls out of the oven. The yeasty aroma filled the kitchen, and Grace's mouth watered.

Sarah shook her head thoughtfully and said, "She can cook—and rope calves too. Imagine that."

"Ma!" Eli protested, "you're gonna scare her off."

Sarah shot Clare a smile. "Too late for that, I think." She laughed, then pointed at the ice box in the corner. "Eli, there's sweet tea in there."

He promptly fetched the tea and poured it into the glasses on the table. LeRoy sat down across from Grace and Eli across from Clare. Sarah brought over a bowl of applesauce and set that down too. Then she eased into her chair and nodded to LeRoy.

"Lord," he said, cuing them all to lower their heads. "We thank you for thy bounty and for thy grace this day. For friends and family and good health. Amen."

Grace said amen with the others and sighed. The comfort of this gathering soothed her heart, and a pervasive sense of peace seeped into her. At Eli's urging, she passed her plate, and he filled it with a dollop of the hearty stew of beef and vegetables Sarah had made. She chuckled watching Sarah's boys slather butter onto their rolls and trying hard to eat with table manners, saying please and thank you and chewing with their mouths closed. She got the impression this wasn't how they normally ate.

Little was said as they enjoyed the food, and Grace complimented Sarah on her cooking. This was the best meal she'd had all year. Charity's meals were simple and bland—she didn't believe in seasoning food, and had a tendency to overcook everything. But Grace had done a lot of cooking at the boardinghouse, and her aunt had been a wonderful cook. She'd taught Grace how to make a variety of dishes—from traditional to Cajun to French. She'd cooked for Monty when he stayed there, and after they were engaged, he "confessed" that he was only marrying her for her cooking. She'd laughed—because she knew how much he loved to eat, and he was a good cook too. Having lived on his own for years, and off on so many expeditions, cooking skills were a necessity—although many men were content to subsist on cans of beans and pemican. She and Monty had spent many fun and happy hours in the kitchen together, as improper or inappropriate as it may have seemed to some. But they hadn't cared. Grace missed that—the sharing and laughing and experimenting with ingredients.

Without realizing it, her eyes had filled with tears, and everyone around the table had grown quiet. Sarah was looking at her intently, studying her as if she were a strange animal she'd never seen before. Eli and LeRoy stopped eating.

Grace's face heated up in embarrassment. What was wrong? Had she done something to offend them?

"I'm . . . I'm sorry," she said, not sure what she was apologizing for. She suddenly felt self-conscious, and not wanting to spoil the light mood they'd been enjoying, pushed her chair back, about to excuse herself.

Sarah held out her palm. "No, stay, Grace. Sit."

Grace stopped. She felt all eyes on her and looked down at her empty plate, uneasy. Clare took her arm, and the touch comforted her.

Grace wanted to crawl under the table, but then she heard Sarah say, "It is a good thing to hope, no? Hope gives strength, fortitude." She got up and came over to Grace and knelt beside her. Then she touched the silver pendant on her neck.

"This is Cherokee," she said, studying it. "But the Cheyenne have a similar symbol for hope." She muttered a few words in her language with her eyes closed, and Grace saw from under her lashes that Eli and LeRoy were paying close attention to their mother. The room felt as still and solemn as a sanctuary.

"You fear all hope is lost," Sarah told her, stepping back and looking at her. Her voice was even and calm, but Grace had the sense that Sarah's mind was far away. "But it is not. You must not run away. You must not be fearful. The terrible thing that haunts you will lift you and carry you once more. Like a raging river, it will hurl you over the falls."

She stopped speaking and picked up Grace's hands in her own warm and weathered ones, and Grace's heart pounded in her chest as the memory of Monty being swept downstream played in her head, stabbing her with renewed pain, as if she'd torn a scab off a festering wound. A moan came from her throat, strangling her.

Sarah gave Grace's hands a gentle squeeze, and then she smiled at her with the tenderness of a loving mother. "Grace, you cannot see the end to your pain. But it rests at the bottom of the waterfall. The fall is terrifying, for with it all hope seems cast upon the water. But below the falls is the calm pool, where the water gathers and rests, then flows to the waiting sea." She touched Grace's pendant once more. "Hope is your lifeline. Cling to it. You will see. Let the river carry you, take you over the falls. For only then will you get to the quiet, clear pool where your pain will be washed out to sea along with the silt and mud."

Silence fell like the night—heavy, thick, and muffling Grace's thoughts. Gradually she groped through the pain to the other side of whatever spell Sarah had enwrapped her in so tightly, like a cocoon. But in moments the burden lifted from her, and she could breathe again. She'd felt as though she had fallen in the river with Monty—no, seeing through his eyes, feeling his terror.

Then, a strange calm lapped at her heart. She looked at Sarah, whose face was soft and unreadable. Then Sarah turned and looked at her sons.

"Do not sit easy, Eli. LeRoy. There is danger in this for you as well." She let her words hang in the air between them. *Danger?*

Grace, perplexed, noted a flash of alarm in the brothers' eyes, but they did not flinch. Sarah let out a sigh and glanced down at Ben, sleeping unperturbed atop the tangle of sheets. Eli and LeRoy, as one, exhaled, and their shoulders slumped.

"So, Ma, what is it? What danger?" LeRoy asked.

A songbird warbled outside the window. Grace looked out at the calm spring day, then turned to look at Clare. Her friend sat deep in thought, somber, respectful. Grace wondered what she might be thinking of all this. She herself didn't know what to make of it. Sarah's sons seemed to take stock in every word their mother had said. But what did her words mean? Her heart had clenched in fear and despair, and yet, Sarah had spoken of hope. That somehow, some way, maybe . . . Maybe Monty might come back to her.

Sarah's voice roped her attention in. "You still searching for that wild herd—the one with the appaloosa stallion?" she asked her sons. Eli nodded, but LeRoy only narrowed his eyes.

He said, "We've been following tracks for weeks. They're somewhere west of Fort Collins."

Sarah nodded. Her sons waited for more. Abruptly, she got up and started clearing the table, stacking plates and humming quietly.

When Eli and LeRoy made to get up and help, Sarah put out her hand to stop them. Grace felt she should help as well, but stayed seated, waiting. Sarah clattered around, putting dishes in the wash basin, collecting glasses and silverware. Then she stopped and looked at Eli.

"You heard about them bank robbers, over in Laporte?"

Eli frowned. "Some think they're those two outlaws from the Dutton Gang. The ones we went after last year. But that robbery was weeks ago. The trail went cold."

Sarah nodded at LeRoy. "You and your brother—you need to go look for those horses. And talk to the sheriff over in Fort Collins. He will need some good trackers. Some with good sense. Or good men will get killed." She looked over at Grace, and an icy cold chill raced up Grace's spine, as if someone had dumped snow down her neck.

"Blood will run," Sarah added without emotion. Then, with a smile that broke the thick tension around them, said, "I know you'll be careful. You always are. And heed what I always tell you—don't shoot unless you have to."

Eli and LeRoy nodded dutifully, then LeRoy pushed his chair back from the table. The noise woke Ben, who let out a little frightened wail. Grace leapt to her feet and cradled him to her chest. More chairs shuffled and shoes and boots stomped around her as the others cleaned up and put dishes away, washed pots and pans, and put things in the ice box. Sarah poured dark beans into a grinder box, and soon the delectable aroma of ground coffee beans filled the kitchen.

"Are you all right, Grace?" Clare came up to her and smoothed Ben's wayward tufts of hair. Grace nodded. Questions hung in the air between them, and Grace wondered what Clare thought about this Indian woman who might very well become her mother-in-law someday. Now Grace understood what Eli had meant about Sarah being a seer, but she wasn't sure how she felt about the things Sarah said to her. They sat as uneasy as a teetering rock on her heart, swaying her willy-nilly from fear to hope to worry.

Sarah came up to them and said, "We'll have some coffee and dessert—I made an apple pie just for the occasion." She gestured them into the small den, which had big overstuffed chairs and a ponderous sofa that looked inviting. Eli brought out two pieces of pie and set them on the low table in front of the sofa, and LeRoy followed with mugs of steaming coffee. All the food sitting in her stomach made Grace suddenly sleepy, and she nestled with Ben on the cushions, sipping her coffee and trying to get bites of pie into her mouth without Ben waylaying her fork. Sarah went into the kitchen and came back with a small wooden bowl of applesauce and a spoon.

"A snack for the little one," Sarah said, swooping Ben onto her lap and tucking a piece of towel under his chin. Grace watched, amused, as Sarah fed Ben. She imagined Sarah was more than ready to have a passel of grandchildren, and wondered if LeRoy was sweet on anyone. Eli hadn't made mention of anyone, but LeRoy was plenty handsome and had a kind disposition. He seemed thoughtful and gentle, soft-spoken—although Grace imagined he had no trouble speaking his mind. It was clear Sarah loved her boys. Which made Grace shiver at the thought of her sending them into danger. Just what did she think was about to happen, and why wouldn't she say, specifically? Did she even know, or was this just a feeling, like an intuition? Her sons, though, reacted as if whatever was about to happen was unavoidable.

While Clare and Eli bantered happily with Sarah and LeRoy about horses and roping and competing in the upcoming horse races, Grace mulled over the things Sarah had said to her. Why weren't they as worried and fearful as she? A sense of doom and danger simmered below the conversation—something to do with outlaws who had robbed a bank. Sarah had told Eli and LeRoy to help the sheriff—track those men? But what did that have to do with her? And what did Sarah mean about letting the river take her over the falls? Her relaxing visit had turned ominous, but she didn't want to be gloomy or give in to fear. Yet, Sarah had told her to hold on to hope and not let go. So that was what Grace would do—although she didn't see any other option.

Sarah finished feeding Ben and cleaned his face, then handed him back to Grace. To Grace's surprise, Sarah took her hand and patted it.

"Do not fret with worry, Grace. Wait and trust. Do not forget that calm pool that waits for you at the bottom of the falls. There is where you will recover what you lost."

Even though Grace didn't understand what Sarah implied, the words soothed her soul. She gulped back tears and nodded, and Sarah gave her a cheering smile and patted Ben on the head.

Not long after, she and Clare had said their good-byes and were seated on the wagon bench ready to head back to Fort Collins. Sarah and LeRoy left to tend to their horses, while Eli stood next to the wagon, holding Clare's hand.

"LeRoy and I'll be over in a few days," he said, his voice laden with seriousness. "We'll go talk to that sheriff, and see if there're signs of that herd in the vicinity." He scrunched up his face. "We almost caught those two outlaws last year. Followed them into the mountains west of Burlington, but somehow they plumb vanished, like some magical disappearin' act. If'n they're near Fort Collins, I want to help catch 'em. I won't rest easy while those killers are runnin' loose anywhere near you."

Clare clasped his hand tightly. "You just be careful, Eli. I know how reckless ya can be."

He cocked an eyebrow and shook his head. "You're starting to sound like Ma."

"Well, I don't want ta lose ya." She added with a sly smile, "A good ropin' partner is hard ta come by."

Eli chuckled and gave her a quick peck on the cheek. He looked at Grace. "Thanks for comin' with Clare. Ma doesn't often *see* somethin' portendin' for a stranger—or maybe she does but just doesn't say. I know her words kinda scared you, but if she says everythin' will work out in the end, it will. It may be a bumpy ride, but, well, what you're dealin' with ain't a bed of goose feathers. I side with Clare—like I said, the truth always comes out. I'm hopeful your man will get his memory back, and your family will be reunited. Like Ma said: wait and hope."

Grace tried to swallow past the rock in her throat. She hugged Ben close and said, "Thank you, Eli. I'm grateful for your kind words, and your mother's hospitality."

He nodded and looked at Clare with a cockeyed grim. "Be sure to miss me."

"Count on it, Cowboy," Clare replied. She shook the reins and led the horses around, then headed out the wide drive to the road leading north and west toward Fort Collins.

"Well," Clare said after they'd traveled a few minutes. "That went better than I'd expected."

"Sarah likes you," Grace said. "I don't think you have anything to worry about."

"Now, if I can just get Eli to propose. I already found a dress I like." She squirmed uncomfortably on the bench. "Ugh, I can't wait to get out of this corset and rid myself of these petticoats."

"It makes me wonder what kind of wedding dress you have in mind," Grace said with a bit of a laugh.

Clare laughed too. "I can bear wearing somethin' fancy for a few hours. I found a picture in a ladies' magazine of the prettiest dress . . . but my family has no money for such a purchase, and I'm sure it will cost a fortune. I'm hopin' to save some money from the punch work I'm doing, but I don't think it will be enough."

"Show me the picture, Clare. I'm sure I can make it for you—I've sewn plenty of wedding dresses."

Clare turned and looked at Grace in astonishment. "You have? I knew you worked at a dress shop, but I had no idea you could make a fancy dress just from an advertisement."

"I'd love to make your dress for you—you can just pay for the fabric, and I'll sew it for free. My wedding gift for you."

Clare erupted in giggles of glee. "Thank you! Well, now I just have to get Eli in the saddle. I'm thinking of a midsummer wedding."

"My, you aren't wasting any time. Maybe I should get started on that dress."

"Good thinking," Clare said, smiling wide and settling into the rhythm of the horses trotting along the road. "I'm glad we're friends, Grace. And I'm gonna help ya get your Monty back. I don't know how, but there has to be a way."

"Thank you, Clare. I'm grateful to you. And I'm looking forward to watching you and Eli tie the knot."

Grace sat with a sleeping Ben in her arms, the warm midday breeze caressing her face, listening to the soothing clopping of the horses' hooves and taking in the miles of farmland green with fields of wheat and hay and vegetable crops. Summer was coming, and all the snow that had dumped earlier that week had almost melted away.

Like the green vegetation around her, a sprout of hope grew in her heart. Would it thrive and come to fruition? Or would it wither and die? Only time would tell. She could do nothing but wait.

Chapter 16

MALCOLM RODE HIS CHESTNUT QUARTER horse along Linden Street, keeping his head tucked as a wild wind nipped at his ears and threw grit into his eyes. He'd decided to finish up working early, not liking the looks of the gathering thunderclouds ahead. Bevington was home nursing a stomach ailment—or so Fred Wallace had told him that morning as he came into the assessor's office to pick up some maps he needed for the sections he was laying out south of town. Few people were out on the streets this windy afternoon, the skies threatening to dump rain in buckets, from the looks of it.

He supposed he should go home, but that was the last place he wanted to be right now. When he was there, he hardly spoke to Stella, and she mostly ignored him. He'd made up a bed on the couch, and each night Stella would drink whiskey and stare out the windows and grumble about the snow. Then, she'd go into the bedroom and slam the door behind her. Night after night he lay on the couch, unable to sleep except in fits and starts, and when he did sleep, his disturbing dreams robbed him of much-needed rest. He was hard pressed to get through a full day of work without a weariness smothering him.

But a greater weariness weighed on his heart. And it was not due to Stella and her infidelity and lies. Nor was it because of his desperate need to know who he was and where he'd come from. No, this weariness grew out of the deep loneliness and emptiness he felt, and the uncanny sense of loss that plagued him daily. Since the day he'd ridden into Fort Collins, he'd become aware of it. And although he'd been able to ignore its proddings over the months, he could no longer do so now. The weariness had grown into a compulsion, a great need—one he could find no relief for. One that never let up, gave him reprieve. It had stolen away all his peace, and Malcolm knew no way to get that peace back.

He considered stopping and getting a bite to eat, but he had little appetite and instead chose to walk his horse along the streets of town in mindless abandon, hoping the brisk wind and new sights would distract his thoughts. Other than the main thoroughfares, Malcolm had seen little of the town, and as he took in the tidy, simple houses of the neighborhood, most of them small wood structures painted in subdued colors, he thought about all the sundry people that had come here from parts near and far, hoping to start a new life, like he had.

Were they happy? He imagined many had come with dreams that were never realized and after a time headed back to where they'd come from. As thriving as Fort Collins was, offering just about every shop and service a body could want, it was still primitive in many ways. The West seemed rough, untamed, dusty, harsh around the edges. He couldn't remember anything of where he'd lived prior—no images of St. Louis came to his mind or visited his dreams. But the way he felt about this Front Range town made Malcolm believe he'd lived in a big city at one point in his life. Maybe St. Louis. Or maybe not.

There had to be a way to find out where he'd lived before, where he worked. He'd tried asking Stella, but even when she was thoroughly soused, she wouldn't answer his questions, no matter how carefully or nicely he worded them. The more drunk she got, the less she said, and the more jumbled those words.

He grunted in frustration, then had an idea. How many surveyors could there be in St. Louis? They'd have a land office there. Maybe someone would know him. He rubbed his jaw and shook his head. If Malcolm Connors wasn't his real name—then no one would have heard of him. But if it was his name—if Stella hadn't lied about that—he might be able to learn something. And if he could find just one person, that's all he'd need. It would be a start.

With that encouraging thought, Malcolm urged Rambler around the next block and headed toward the courthouse, thinking the clerk there might be able to help him find a directory of surveyors in St. Louis. Malcolm could send a letter to the land office and inquire, although what would he tell them?

As he pondered this, he noticed a young woman in a dark-green woolen coat walking along the street in his direction, and she carried a big bundle in her arms, a gray wool shawl pulled tightly over her head as the wind tugged on it. Her head was down, but at the sound of his approach, she raised it and stopped suddenly and stared at him.

Malcolm recognized the woman as the one he'd rescued that day in front of the harness shop. A stricken expression lay across her face, which puzzled him. Her baby fussed in her arms, and he thought how heavy he must be, and that she no longer had a carriage to put him in.

For some reason, his pulse quickened as he looked at her, then realized he was staring. Her face, tinged pink from the abrasive wind, was like an angel's. Her pale-green eyes glistened as if filled with tears, and wayward strands of her golden hair tickled her cheeks. A rush of desire rose up his chest, and he chastised himself for the attraction he felt. He was married, he reminded himself, and no matter how lonely he was, he knew it was wrong to indulge in such feelings. But looking at her standing there with such a forlorn look on her face tugged every heartstring he had. He fought a powerful urge to pull her into his arms.

What was he thinking? He shook his head, trying to fling away his impure thoughts, and slipped down from his horse. He had to know if she was all right.

He walked up to her, holding his reins in one hand and tipping his hat with the other. The wind blew hard, pushing at them from the side. He reached for his hat before it flew off his head, and the woman pulled her coat tighter around her.

"Hello, miss," he said, "I hope you're well, and that you've recovered from your scare. I take it your ankle's mended?"

"Yes, thank you," she said, casting a quick glance at him from under her lashes. Her voice quavered when she spoke. He looked into her eyes and she met his gaze, then she turned her head and fussed with her baby. But in that brief moment, he saw a flare of pain or hurt streak those enticing eyes. An ache welled up in his heart, and he thought it strange.

"I don't believe we properly met," he said. "My name's Malcolm Connors."

She bit her lip and seemed to struggle with a reply. Maybe he was making her nervous. He stepped back.

"I'm Grace. Grace Cunningham." She said no more, but now regarded him steadily, as if waiting for him to speak. With the wind now whistling through the trees in a loud pitch, he had to raise his voice to be heard.

"Pleased to make your acquaintance, Mrs. Cunningham."

He thought she looked about to swoon. "Are you unwell?" he asked. "Can I help you somehow? Carry your baby for you? He looks heavy. How far are you going?" His questions gushed out before he could stop them. There was something about this pretty young woman that gave him pause. She seemed so familiar. Perhaps she reminded him of someone he'd known in his past. He couldn't take his eyes off her, and knew it was rude of him to stare. But the compulsion to hold her grew overwhelming.

"I'm just out for a walk," she said tentatively, but then a hint of a smile came up her face—and that simple shift in her countenance slid over him like warm honey. "But the weather's turned unpleasant. He's been so fussy lately—new teeth coming in . . ." Her voice trailed off, as if she suddenly remembered she was speaking to a stranger.

"May I . . . ?" He gestured at the baby. He had no recollection as to whether he'd ever held a child in his arms, but when she handed him over without reservation—the frowning, squirming bundle of blankets—a startling sensation struck him. He didn't understand what he was feeling, but it was profound and sobering. He sucked in a breath, and the woman—Grace—stared at him, her mouth dropped open.

The baby stopped fussing and stared into Malcolm's eyes, and then a big smile burst out on his face, revealing four tiny front teeth. Something about this baby also looked and felt familiar, but what was it—a memory? The baby didn't look much like its mother, from what Malcolm could tell, and now that he noticed, the baby had one eye that looked a little hazel, while the other was brown—just like his eyes. How unusual.

Maybe that was what lent a sense of familiarity, Malcolm thought. He tickled the baby's cheeks, and a little infectious giggle erupted. Malcolm laughed at his adorable antics.

"He's a sweet boy," he told Grace. "You must love him so."

She nodded briskly but said nothing. Still, her eyes looked filled with tears, and Malcolm sensed some great pain smoldering in them. "Can I . . . would you allow me to walk with you a while?" he asked, wanting to delve more into these odd feelings stirring in him. Maybe in talking with her some flashes of memory would come to him. He hadn't felt this before—this strong compulsion that had to be connected with his past.

"I'd . . . like that, Mr. . . . Connors," she said. "Are you all right holding him?"

More than all right, he thought. He wished he could understand the emotion coursing through him as he held this baby in his arms. He felt more than delight or amusement. He felt . . . sublimely content. With alarm, he wondered if perhaps he'd had a child sometime in his past. The pervasive feeling of loss rippled under the surface of his thoughts, which made him think this more a certainty than a possibility.

They walked side by side down the street, Malcolm leading his horse with one hand and holding the baby with the other. They lapsed into a silence that, to Malcolm, felt easy and relaxed, but his mind churned with thoughts. He turned his head to look at Grace. "What's his name?" he asked her.

She hesitated but kept walking, facing forward and watching her steps. "It's Benjamin Montgomery Cunningham," she said, sadness lodged in her words.

The wind kept up, dancing around them, throwing leaves and fluff from the blooming cottonwoods into the air and swirling them around. The smell of rain and wood smoke filled the warm street, and a few fat raindrops splattered them. They ambled down a pretty residential lane lined on both sides by bigleaf maples, but no one else was out walking, riding, or in carriages. Malcolm breathed in the baby's scent and nuzzled into his hair. Again, he felt that perplexing sensation of equal parts contentment and yearning.

"That's a good name," he said. "A strong one. Did you name him after someone?"

Grace hesitated a moment, then swallowed. "Benjamin was my brother's name. He died when he was two, of cholera." She paused, clutching her coat and not looking at him as they continued walking. "Montgomery . . . that was my husband's name . . ." The words sounded caught in her throat.

"I'm sorry," Malcolm said, "I didn't mean to stir up any painful feelings." From what Stella had said that day in the harness shop, Malcolm guessed Grace had lost her husband. It couldn't have been all that long ago, seeing that her baby looked hardly a year old. Her grief would still be fresh. He chided himself for being too forward.

Suddenly a loud rumble rolled over them, like a faraway train. Malcolm stopped short and swung around, looking to the southwest. The hair on the back of his neck stood on end.

"What is it?" Grace asked.

His horse neighed and pranced, then pulled on the reins. Malcolm calmed him with soothing words. Rain dumped suddenly on their heads, and Grace let out a small cry. Without thinking, Malcolm took her arm, then scrutinized the sky.

The swollen tin-colored clouds bunched and shredded overhead, and the wind grew into a squall that had him pulling his coat up over his head and yanking Grace in close. He saw fear and shock in her face, but he had no time to ponder whether she was alarmed by his touch or by the sudden turn in weather—or both.

He had to yell to be heard, even though she was inches away. The wind grabbed at his words, and it took all his strength to stand in place and keep Grace from blowing down the street.

"We better find shelter." He cast an anxious glance around, thinking they should run to the nearest house and get inside.

His horse then reared up, and Malcolm jerked back, protecting Ben, whom he'd practically buried inside his coat. The baby squirmed in his hot enclosure, but Malcolm worried the flying debris might hit him, and clutched him tightly to his chest.

Grace jumped at the sound of a large branch cracking overhead. Malcolm threw his head back and watched as a large maple limb snapped and lunged to the ground just feet from them.

Grace screamed and gripped his arm tighter. Malcolm started to run, jerking Rambler to follow. The baby was getting heavy in his arms, and his horse fought his lead. Just as he turned to try to calm his horse again, he heard Grace gasp. She froze beside him, and he felt her tremble through her coat.

He turned around and searched her face. She was looking across and up the street, her expression rigid in fright. He turned to see what she was staring at.

Malcolm's heart hammered in his chest. Not two blocks away, a massive funnel cloud opened like a drain, and a twister descended like God's wrath from the angry heavens.

For a moment, Malcolm's feet stuck to the road. He stared, horrified, at the gyrating black funnel of wind heading their way, ripping boards and siding off the houses on the next block, the roar growing, sounding like a train now upon them. Trees buckled and were snatched up into the air, like frantic birds flung every which way. The noise crushed his ears.

Grace screamed again, and Malcolm's feet became unglued. He pitched the reins, allowing the panicky horse to flee in a gallop in the opposite direction, then pulled Grace along.

"Run!" he yelled, hoping the twister would keep its straight course, but knowing how erratic they could be. He would just have to take a chance, and hope he'd make the right choice.

Grace kept up with him as he ran hard, away from the twister that was gaining on them and throwing the flotsam of the neighborhood at them. He dodged flying sticks and glass and pieces of roof, tucking Grace's head into his chest, ducking down and stumbling along. A boot skimmed his head, and a bucket clattered on the ground in front of them. From the corner of his eye he watched an entire row of fence pickets unzip from the ground and catapult through the air to spear a nearby house.

Through the attacking maelstrom he caught sight of an alleyway to his right and raced around the corner, nearly dragging Grace along, feeling her feet catch and trip up, and lifting her at times to keep her upright as he rushed headlong down the alley.

The wind clawed at him, pulling him backward the way water sucked down a drain. He fought the pull with all his strength, head craning forward, gaining one hard-won foot after another. His pulse thrashed in his ears, and his mouth and throat grew dry. His every thought centered on getting Grace and little Ben to safety, and he feared greatly for their lives, knowing he had to save them. He was their only hope.

Spurred by this conviction, he pushed harder, but could tell Grace was slowing, floundering. He had to get her and her baby sheltered out of the path of the dangerous wind.

He spotted a door fronting the alley. Without hesitation, he ran to it and with a furious blow smashed his foot into the wood, propelling all his strength forward. The door splintered, and the pieces smacked the floor. Malcolm hurled inside, pulling Grace with him. A second later what was left of the door was yanked out into the alley by the wind's invisible hands, and Malcolm heard it smash and clatter as it hit the side of the house they were in. The windows of the room he ran through exploded in profusions of glass, sounding like rapid-fire gunshot, and Malcolm buried Grace further under his chin, his arms clutched tightly around her and her baby.

He propelled them into a bedroom as a dark-stained armoire listed, then crashed to the floor. White bedsheets gyrated in the air like conjured ghosts. Malcolm took in the splattered glass littering the room and sparking like diamonds, searching for someplace safe as the wind bellowed in fury through the holes where the windows had once been.

A groan erupted from the ceiling. Malcolm's eyes locked on the stucco as it broke to bits, and holes appeared punched in the charcoal heavens beyond. The roof joists ripped from their nails and careened into the sky with a shriek.

Malcolm spun in place, frantic to spy a shoal of refuge. A door in the hallway beckoned, unmarred by the violent assault on the house. He ushered Grace back into the hall, praying the door led to more than a service closet. He threw open the door and, to his great relief, discovered a small storage room with ceiling intact.

With the twister screeching at his back, he lurched into the room and slammed the door shut behind them. He collapsed against the solid back wall and slid to the floor amid stacks of boxes, Grace still in his arms and clinging to him, whimpers coming from her throat.

Blood pounded his ears as he sat poised to flee, keenly listening to wind that scratched and kicked at the door like a petulant dog. The baby in his arms wailed, and Grace pulled back from Malcolm's tight embrace and took him. Malcolm's arms ached from clutching his charge so fiercely. As he rallied to catch his breath, he felt as if they were the last humans on Earth.

Gradually, his eyes adjusted to the darkness, and he noticed a sliver of light canting through the door, where something sharp must have pierced it. The room smelled of camphor and lilac, and dust danced thickly on the stream of light sliding in like a ray of hope. He blew out a long-held shaky breath and made out Grace's traumatized features as she ministered to her baby in comforting sounds, smoothing the child's hair and rocking him. The house continued to creak like a wagon barreling down a rutted road.

A great urge to comfort her welled in his heart. "Don't be afraid, Grace. We'll get through this. The Lord will make a way—He always does."

The moments those words left his lips, he shivered.

He had said those exact words before—sometime, somewhere.

Grace jerked her head to look at him, her eyes wide and her face blanched with surprise. Malcolm shook his head as fractured images railed at him. With a trembling hand on her arm, he heard a roar of water behind him. Mud encased his boots, and his wet clothes stuck to his skin. Rain beat down on his head as he looked in a woman's eyes—a woman like Grace.

He looked deep into her eyes, searching for something—some understanding, some key to this memory—for a lifeline. His legs gave way, and mud sucked him down into roiling water. His arms flailed, and he let out a moan. Gray-brown water spun and tumbled him, and he sucked in a breath, remembering.

Grace steadied him with her hands on his shoulders, and tears stung his eyes. A horrible fear overcame him. No, not fear. Worry. Something worried him terribly, but he couldn't figure what. But he knew what he saw was a memory of something that had happened. He'd nearly drowned.

Silence as thick as sorghum filled the room as Malcolm reeled with the images swatting him. The baby halted his mewling protestations, and Grace watched Malcolm without a word. He had another flash of memory—this one so different.

A balmy spring day, in a park with manicured beds of pink and yellow flowers lining a bridle path. Sitting on a spread-out patchwork blanket on an ocean of sparkling green lawn, horses snuffling nearby as they grazed, and a woman's light laughter tickling his ears. He saw a wicker basket and picnic fixings spread around him, and a woman in a lovely pale-yellow dress with ivory buttons, her skirts spread around her, the edges of her white crinoline petticoats peeking from underneath. His face cinched up as he worked the memory, coaxing the image clearer, but he still could not make out her features. He felt the warmth of her hand as she held his, and saw a gold band on her ring finger.

It had to be Stella he was remembering—but no. She wouldn't have had a ring on, and that wasn't her laugh. They'd only married just last summer. And the park—he'd been there many times throughout his life, he realized. St. Louis?

The fury outside the door lessened, as if the twister had given up its quarry and sought other homes to ravage. Malcolm shifted to ease pressure off a leg that was numb. He looked Grace over.

"Are you hurt? The baby?"

Grace swiped hair from her face as she shook her head in the negative. Long tangled locks of golden tresses tumbled down her shoulders. The glint of light from the crack in the door illuminated her face and showed tear streaks etched with dirt and grit.

Without thinking, he wiped her face with his sleeve, wondering why his heart was still thumping even though it was evident the danger had passed them by. More tears spilled down her face—

tears of relief, he figured—and she sobbed quietly, rocking her baby in her arms.

"You've saved me again," she said. "I . . . I don't know how to thank you—" Her body shook, and she buried her head into her child's neck and wept.

Pushing aside his chastising conscience that spewed out warnings against such improprieties, he gathered her into his arms and held her as the world fell away, leaving them unscathed and unnoticed. He sat there on the wood-plank floor in the near-dark, his skin tingling and every nerve jolted with electricity. He was surprised the woman didn't pull away, but he imagined her need for comfort snuffed out her concern over proper behavior. They had barely escaped death, and Malcolm sent up a heartfelt prayer to heaven, knowing that the hand of God had shown them mercy and sheltered them in the storm.

Grace felt so strangely wonderful in his arms. He allowed himself the indulgence of this moment, knowing it was wrong, so wrong, to revel being in another woman's arms. He was married, he lectured himself. Unhappily, yes, but he'd made a vow, and entertaining feelings for another woman was wrong. Yet, he couldn't let go of Grace. He didn't understand why. He just needed to hold her—more for his own comfort than for hers. And not just to satisfy a need to touch. There was something about Grace that triggered memories, that made him sense now more strongly than ever that the past Stella had recounted to him wasn't his. That he'd lived an entirely different life—full of picnics and geysers and raging rivers. A life of love and loss. Of a woman with golden hair . . .

He looked at Grace's face and studied her. She met his eyes, and he saw unmistakable yearning. Then he remembered what Stella had accused her of, and he grimaced at the thought. But Stella had been wrong. Malcolm saw only sweet sincerity and genuineness in Grace's eyes, which were completely without guile. The love he saw radiating from her for her son seemed to flow over him in a wash of comfort and need, and Malcolm's heart jittered.

Now, sitting this close to her and smelling her lilac-shampooed hair made him aware of that gaping maw of loneliness he had in his gut. He couldn't deny the intense attraction he felt for her, for she was beautiful and gracious, delicate yet strong of will and determination. He admired the way she cared for her son, and her voice oozed with kindness and intelligence and thoughtfulness. She was everything he respected and wanted in a woman. Even though he hardly knew her at all, he felt as if he'd known her for years. She felt right in his arms, as if she belonged there.

His thoughts tangled with his emotions as he realized he'd been smitten by her the moment he'd first saw her floundering in the middle of the street with the wagon barreling toward her. He'd smothered his feelings at the time, knowing they were wrong. But now, they hit him full force. A sweet pain spread through his chest knowing he had to abandon such reckless thoughts. Not only was it wrong for him to look at Grace that way, it was impolite of him to entertain such thoughts. He was a married man, and she was a widow raising a child alone. His reprehensible behavior could taint her reputation. He hadn't thought of her best interests or needs, and they mattered more than his own.

With a heavy heart, he got to his feet and offered Grace a hand to help her up.

As he pulled her to standing, she said, "Do you think it's safe to go out?"

Ben squirmed out of her arms and made impatient noises. Grace corralled him to her and shushed him. He imagined the distraught baby needed feeding and changing.

"I'll check. Stay put." He turned the knob and pushed gently, and upon feeling no resistance, he ventured out.

Breath hitched in his throat at the sight before him. The house was a jumble of rubbish—broken boards and huge chunks of stucco and bricks strewn over patches of jagged floor that exposed bare ground beneath. A glace upward showed a piece of precariously dangling roof that creaked and tottered in the backwash of breeze left in the wake of the twister—which was nowhere in sight. Clouds burdened with precipitation hung low in the sky, threatening to burst, but the air was eerily calm and portentous. Nary a sound could be heard from the street, and a weighty gloom blanketed the neighborhood as thick as the snow that had fallen the prior week.

Malcolm stepped gingerly over the debris, studying the remnants of the roof and marveling how the section above their closet was wholly intact. A cursory glance showed no signs that anyone had been in the house at the time of their intrusion, and he hoped no one had been hurt or killed by the twister. From what he could tell, only a few houses on two blocks had been destroyed, although the streets were a hodgepodge of downed trees and the offerings of house siding and roofing. A crushed wagon lay in pieces out the window, and white pickets from a fence speared the large maple out front that seemed unscathed by the mayhem.

As he surveyed the damage to the neighborhood, he whistled out in relief and gratitude for divine protection. People emerged from the more intact houses on the street and gathered on lawns and on the dirt. A siren wailed in the distance, and Malcolm smelled smoke.

A gentle warm breeze played with his hair as he navigated around the ruins of the house and opened the closet door. Grace emerged with Ben on her hip, and her stricken face took in her surroundings. She stood next to him, wide-eyed and unblinking.

"Mercy," she said quietly. "I pray no one was killed. It's a miracle we survived." She shook her head, her gaze riveted on the aftermath of the twister.

"I'll walk you home," he told her, reaching his arms out for Ben, who was now crying and gulping air. "Which way?"

Grace handed Ben to him and pointed. "Just a few blocks, on Maple."

Malcolm juggled the child in his arms as they walked across the street and down another that had merited the good fortune of remaining unscathed from the maelstrom. Ben settled down to the soothing rhythm of Malcolm's pace, and Grace walked at his side, no doubt in shock.

He turned to her and said, "I'm sure you'll want to feed and change him, and freshen up. I'd like to take you to coffee or lunch, but I need to find my horse. And I should go back and help, see if anyone's hurt. Maybe a couple more strong arms will be needed."

She smiled at him—a grateful, approving smile that made his heart soar. How close they'd come to dying, and how glad he was that he'd been there to help her and Ben—again. He had been in the right place at the right time once more—that couldn't have been a coincidence. He didn't believe in fate, yet, it sure seemed as if the Good Lord was using him to watch out for Grace and her baby. The thought both unsettled and encouraged him.

He realized, as Grace led him up the front steps to a simple white clapboard house, that he hadn't once worried about Stella and if she'd been harmed in the storm. A twinge of guilt stabbed his gut, but he pushed it aside. Of course he didn't want anything bad to happen to her, but he couldn't muster any warm sentiment for his wife. Not one tiny shred.

Grace stopped at the door and turned to him with outstretched arms. At first he thought she meant to embrace him. Then he realized he was holding her sleeping baby. Ben fit so naturally in his arms that Malcolm had forgotten he was carrying him. He almost hated to give him up.

Again, that disturbing feeling of loss swept over him as he settled the baby in Grace's arms. He looked at her, and his eyes dropped down to a silver pendant around her neck—a round disk with an eight-pointed star etched upon it.

Malcolm stiffened. "Where . . . where did you get that necklace?" he asked, then realized he was being forward to ask such a thing, since Grace seemed taken aback by his question.

However, her face softened and she answered, "My husband gave it to me . . . after returning from a trip. It's a symbol—"

"Of hope," he said, startling himself with his words. How had he known that?

Grace seemed startled as well. Her hand drifted to her neck, and she touched the silver disk. Her face clouded up like the sky above.

"I'm sorry," Malcolm said, "I've brought up difficult memories . . ."

She merely nodded, then said, "Does this . . . does this look familiar to you?" She unclasped the necklace with her free hand and presented it to him in the palm of her hand. He picked it up and dangled it in front of his face.

He shook his head, then answered the questions flickering in her eyes. "I . . had an accident and lost most of my memory." Frustration welled up as he rifled through his mind trying to pair the star with some moment in his past. He handed back the necklace.

Grace's face showed disappointment and compassion. "Maybe in time you'll remember." She added softly, "I hope you do . . . Mr. Connors—"

"Please—call me Malcolm." His words sounded like begging to his ears.

She nodded and smiled again, and that sweet smile made his heart like to break through his ribs. "I'll be home the rest of the day, should you still want to come by. I hope you find your horse."

"He's probably at the livery, since he spends a goodly amount of time there most of the week. He knows there's hay and a warm stall there for the taking."

Grace chuckled and Malcolm froze. Through a haze in his mind, he heard her say good day and saw her go into the house and close the door behind her. His feet remained glued to the boards.

That was the first time he'd heard her laugh, and it had jolted him with another shock of memory. A woman's laugh rang in his head, the faceless woman with the golden hair . . . He saw in his mind's eye the woman throwing back her head in laughter, amused at an anecdote he'd just told her, the sprawling verdant lawn of the park enclosing them. Her laugh sounded like Grace's. Could it be that she was the woman in his memory?

He chided himself with a snort. How could she be? She would have said something, surely. And the woman in his dreams and memories was . . . what?

He gulped. *She was my wife. And I lost her . . .*

This understanding hit him like a slap to the face. He grabbed the porch railing and steadied himself. Then he dropped to the steps of the porch and hung his head in his hands, trembling.

Chapter 17

WHAT WAS SHE THINKING? HOW could she have let herself suffer so?

Grace hurried down the street toward the center of town, grateful that Charity was home and willing to watch Ben while he napped. She had politely responded to Charity's alarmed questions about the twister, but Grace skirted the truth and said only that she'd witnessed the devastation after the fact. Her mind had churned with such troubled thoughts that she had to leave the house and calm her tumultuous feelings. She gave the excuse of needing to purchase some personals at the drugstore, and hurried out after feeding and changing Ben.

Her body shook as she relived the horror of the twister and how terrified she had been. But she trembled even harder at the thought of Monty's arms around her. Was it cruel fate or divine mercy that had sent Monty to save her once again? Despite her steely resolve, she had buckled under his touch. She ached for those muscular arms to enwrap her, and she'd come undone when he'd pressed against her, his warm body against her chest, where she could feel his heart beating as one with hers.

This was wrong, so wrong—but oh so right! He was hers, and he belonged with her, but he had no memory of her. He was married, and there was nothing she could do to make him remember or win his heart. After spending those agonizing moments with Monty in that small room, she knew she could not bear such torment ever again. Her heart had broken over and over as she held back her true feelings from him, longing to gush with the truth, tell him everything.

And the sight of Ben in his arms! Her deepest desire was for Monty to feel the bottomless joy that came with holding his own child. Yet, he'd had no recognition in his eyes. And she had given him the necklace to examine, and he'd failed to recognize that as well. It was hopeless. If her face and voice could not shake loose his memories, nothing ever would. He was lost to her, forever, and she had to accept that, once and for all—or she would go mad with grief.

She owed it to Ben to let go. Maybe one day, when he was grown, she would tell him the truth. How she'd fallen in love and married a kind, honorable man named Montgomery Cunningham, and had lost him. Maybe he would search and find his father and tell him the story he'd been told. Maybe Monty would believe him. Maybe not. She'd vowed she would tell her son the truth—someday. But for now, she had to put distance between her and Monty. She couldn't bear seeing him again. Seeing him with . . . his wife.

Tears flooded down her cheeks as the clouds broke apart overhead and the sun glared down on her in stark judgment. She longed to talk with Clare, but dared not chance going to the livery, where Monty might happen by. She could imagine what would happen when Monty came to the Franklins' later to call on her.

What would he say to Charity? Just his appearance at her door, asking about her, would set off a torrent of new gossip—gossip that could only hurt Monty in the long run.

Grace darted down a side street and came out on College Avenue near the south end of town. She'd seen no evidence of the twister tearing up this part of Fort Collins, but debris littered the streets, and men were working to clean up the branches and boards, loading up wagons and sweeping with brooms. The wooden boardwalk fronting the street on both sides revealed broken boards and cracked hitching posts, and some of the wood from the false storefronts had blown off, revealing stucco and brick underlayment. The town seemed aflurry with activity as shopkeepers and citizens worked to clear the mess and restore order.

Wanting to be alone, she rounded a corner and found a small corner park void of people. The park faced the back of the courthouse and other business offices, and no one was outside. She imagined many were busy at work, as of yet unaware of the twister that had torn up part of the town. Glad for a chance to catch her breath and collect her rampaging thoughts, she sat on one of the wooden benches, and knew she had to face her decision, as much as it pained her.

She had to leave Fort Collins—that was her only recourse. Maybe she would go back to Bloomington, where at least the neighbors and neighborhood were familiar to her. She'd attended church there, and her aunt had had many close friends. With her meager savings, she could possibly purchase a one-way train ticket to Illinois. Perhaps catch a coach to Denver, for she would not consider journeying north to Cheyenne to board another train. She never wanted to see the Cache la Poudre River again as long as she lived, and just the thought of the river sorely vexed her with uninvited memories.

As the tears dribbled down her face, her heart emptied out, the enormity of her decision like a coffin lid closing with a slap. She dried her eyes with a sleeve of her heavy woolen coat and thought about her months here in Fort Collins and how much she'd wished Monty would walk back into her life. Now she wished he hadn't come to Fort Collins. She could have more easily lived with not knowing his fate. Maybe even with learning he had drowned. For then she could have grieved the loss fully and found a way to move on, with her heart healing over time, even though she knew she would never—could never—love anyone the way she had loved him. Yes, staying here was worse than death—knowing he was within arm's reach, like the tempting fruit hanging from the forbidden tree.

She let her resolve build a thick stone wall around her heart—a fortress to keep out the pain and give her the courage to do what she must. It wouldn't take her long to pack. She wouldn't even tell the Franklins ahead of time, just leave a note with vague explanations and expressing her gratitude for their generosity. She needn't speak to Tilde at the shop. Charity would see to it that the gossip spread far and wide, and no doubt for weeks after Grace's departure, the rumors would pass from lip to lip. Well, at least she would be far away, where their hurtful words couldn't touch her ears—not any longer.

She tried to think of some other place she might want to raise Ben, but conceded it made the most sense to return to a place she was familiar with. She chortled bitterly thinking of how she'd resisted coming out west, and how much Monty longed to live on the Front Range, under the shadow of the majestic Rockies, close to the wild rivers and unspoiled wilderness he loved. And it wasn't even a wild river or dangerous Indians on a faraway expedition that had taken Monty from her, which had been her greatest fear.

Instead, a flood and an opportunistic woman had stolen him from her grasp.

She could get a room—maybe in her former home, if it was still being used as a boardinghouse. And perhaps she could get a job as a seamstress at the same shop she'd worked at for years. And she could go to the courthouse directly and request a copy of her marriage certificate, so she could one day give it to Ben. Yes, returning to Bloomington was the wisest choice. It was a wonderful town, a good place to raise her son. She would find a way to be happy—for Ben. And maybe in time the pain would ease.

She sighed resignedly. That was all she could hope for now. All hope of getting Monty back had been snatched from her and tossed into the river and swept away. She had tried to hold on to hope, to make it the anchor for her soul, but it was a fool's hope now.

As she sat there, with the warm sun baking her shoulders, she let her decision sink in. She needed to inquire about the coach to Denver, and look up the train schedules for Bloomington. There was no one else she needed to say good-bye to—except Clare.

She slumped, thinking how she'd promised Clare she'd make her wedding dress, and Grace would not go back on her word. Guilt prodded her to tell Clare she was leaving. But she could still make her dress. She only had to take Clare's measurements and get the design from her. Once in Illinois, Grace could sew it and then ship it to Clare when it was finished. As much as she'd love to attend Clare's wedding, Grace knew she could never risk returning to Colorado. Just being anywhere close to Monty would break her heart anew.

Against the warnings screaming in her mind, she pictured herself walking into town and seeing Monty holding another child in his arms, Stella at his side. The thought gnawed at her insides, and she squeezed her eyes shut. How could she even stay in touch with Clare now that her friend knew the truth about Monty and would no doubt write to tell her how he fared, even if Grace begged her not to?

Grace hung her head with this new predicament. She would just have to keep her destination a secret from Clare. That way Clare couldn't write her, and Grace wouldn't check the post each day hoping against hope for news. She would only continue to be tortured. Even though she suspected Clare would fume at Grace's decision, Grace hoped she'd understand and respect her.

Tomorrow, she would find Clare and tell her the news, and make her promise to never speak to Monty, or tell anyone the truth. She hoped Eli would keep his word and forget all she'd told him. She could leave inside of three or four days, she figured.

Grace lifted her head when she heard a man's voice.

"Mrs. Cunningham," a man called out to her from behind the courthouse. She recognized Alan Patterson walking toward her, the kindly clerk who had offered to help her. She straightened and drew in a deep breath, not wanting to be impolite or show that she'd been crying. She knew, though, that her eyes must be red and puffy and would give her away.

She stood and greeted him, and she noted his nervous hands fidgeting at his sides.

"Did you hear about the twister?" he asked her, sweat beading on his forehead. "I'm glad you weren't hurt."

"Thank you, Alan. I'm fine. I saw some of the damage from the storm. I trust the courthouse fared without incident?"

"Two windows blew out, but nothing irreparable." He removed the hat from his head and nervously twisted it in his hands. "I wanted to let you know that I have someone at the Bloomington courthouse working diligently to find your certificate." His face beamed with the look of a puppy seeking a pat on the head.

"That's kind of you," she said, feeling guilty that he was going to all that trouble for her. She almost told him she was leaving town, but caught herself.

An awkward silence ensured, and Grace was too exhausted to work at making polite conversation. "I need to get back to my son. He's being cared for, but he'll soon wake from his nap and want his mother." She gave the clerk a smile and hoped to leave his company without insult.

"I'd be glad to accompany you to your house."

"Thank you, but I cherish the time to think and walk without disruption. Being a mother of a toddler doesn't afford many opportunities to do so."

"I understand," he said, a bit too cheerily. She could tell he was disappointed. But she couldn't deal with one tiny bit more of any disappointment in her life at this moment—even if it wasn't her own.

She said good-bye and walked back toward her home—which would not be her home much longer. Her heart ached thinking once again of being ensconced in Monty's strong, warm arms, and the way he had spoken those words to her, telling her not to worry, that the Lord would make a way. She wished with all her soul that she could believe those words, but now they were only empty sentiments. There was only one way left to her—and that was to leave Monty behind.

Malcolm strode up to the desk and cleared his throat to get the clerk's attention. Every nerve in his body rattled, and his thoughts wouldn't give him rest. His miraculous survival in the path of a twister had left him humbled and shaky. He kept replaying the day's events in his mind, seeing the houses ripped apart, the pieces flung with fury every which way, the wind attacking like a savage beast.

But most of all, he kept reliving the way Grace had felt in his arms, how she'd sparked his memories into flames of visions, and how he knew without question that he'd been married before—to someone, somewhere—who looked and sounded like Grace Cunningham.

After he left her at her house, his restless, frustrated energy fueled him into a brisk walk to the livery, where he found his gelding tucking into a flake of hay that one of the stable hands had given him. Thankfully, Rambler had escaped from the twister with only a superficial gash on his rump that didn't need suturing. Other animals hadn't fared as well, he noted, as men tended to horses and mules that had been hurt and were making a racket in the stables.

Once he retrieved Rambler—who had managed to retain his saddle and headstall, despite the frantic run through town—Malcolm decided to stop wasting time and do what he could to recover his lost past. He'd been on his way to the courthouse when he'd seen Grace walking down the street before all hell had broken loose. He knew Grace was a key to his past, but maybe only because she reminded him of the lost wife he knew he'd left behind in the wake of those missing memories.

His gut clenched thinking he might be married to someone else—and maybe have a child—somewhere, and that he'd forgotten them. Maybe even Stella had no idea about his past. Had he fallen into the river and hit his head, and Stella had only happened to chance upon him? Over the last week that thought had drifted to him, but he'd discounted it. Now he wasn't so sure. His memory of that day was hazy, as were the weeks to follow. He hardly remembered what she said to him when he came to and saw her leaning over him. She had told him all those stories about how they'd met in St. Louis, but he still recalled nothing about that town. Not even perusing books he'd found on the Old Grout's public shelves could jiggle free a solitary image of the city.

He doubted he would be able to glean any helpful information by inquiring of surveyors in St. Louis, but he had to try. He hoped when he saw Grace later today more of his memories would come back. Although, he knew that wasn't why he wanted to see her again.

Besides being concerned about her and Ben after the traumatic fright of the twister, he had to admit he was falling for her, like a huge boulder rolling into an abyss. He knew in his mind it was wrong to allow any place in his heart for such feelings, but he couldn't stop them from seizing hold of his soul. His yearning for her was like a plant buried under snow that sensed the sun's warmth. He wanted to burst through that drift and lift his face to the warmth of Grace's presence. She was the sun in his otherwise gloomy, dark world. She gave him hope that he would recover those lost memories—no matter how painful they were. He needed her, and not just for help with his past.

Was he possibly falling in love with her? What else could these cantankerous feelings mean? But how could that be? He hardly knew her. Sometime in his past he had been in love—he was sure of it—if these twittery heart thumps were indication. His mind fixated on Grace's alluring smile and sweet temperament, and he pictured his arms around her delicate shoulders, pushing her golden tresses aside so he could kiss her neck and nuzzle her ear . . .

He mentally slapped himself out of his musings and answered the clerk, who had said something and was waiting for an answer, politely drumming his fingers on the polished counter. Malcolm let out a shaky breath and composed himself.

"I'm sorry, Mr. Patterson. What was that you said?"

The clerk smiled politely and adjusted the round spectacles on his nose. "I'm glad to see you again, Mr. Connors. I hear tell you've been surveying for the land office. How's that working out?"

"I'm pleased with it. It's nice to be out on the open range, in the fresh air—most of the time. Weather's been a bit erratic lately."

"That's the God's truth," Patterson said in firm declaration. "That twister made a mess of the east side of town. You heard about it?"

Malcolm merely nodded.

"I was working at a grocer's back in '64 when that big flood washed Fort Laramie away. They had to rebuild the fort on higher ground. That was when we still had Injun trouble." He clicked his teeth with his tongue. "And already in recent years we've had record snowfall and bad drought. It hasn't been an easy life out here, for most. Nature likes to have her way."

When Malcolm failed to reply, the clerk put fingers under his suspender straps. "So, how can I assist you today, Mr. Connors?"

"Well, I'm not sure you can, but I'd like to get some addresses in St. Louis. Could you help me with that?"

"Certainly." He picked up a lead pencil and slid a piece of paper in front of him. "Who d'ya need to find?"

"The address for the land office, for one. Then for all the surveyors, if you can find them. Would they work out of the city land office or the federal General Land Office?"

"Not sure." He narrowed his eyes in curiosity. "May I ask why you need the information? I might have to inquire of some folks at those offices. It would help to know what to tell them."

Malcolm swallowed, weighing what to say. He didn't think anyone knew about his memory loss, and wasn't sure it was a good idea to speak of it. But he reckoned Patterson could be taken into his confidence. He worked at the courthouse and had to keep certain records and knowledge confidential. It wouldn't befit him to talk about matters he'd be sworn to keep private.

Malcolm looked around the large open room, and upon seeing they were alone, he leaned over the counter and said, "I'm in a bit of a predicament, Mr. Patterson. Can I trust you not to speak to anyone regarding what I'm about to tell you?"

Patterson nodded emphatically. "You have my word. I'm not a gossiper, by any stretch. Don't believe I have the inclination to be such. I don't cotton to people who gossip about me, so I wouldn't do likewise to anyone else."

"I appreciate that." Malcolm rubbed his forehead as Grace's lovely face intruded. "A year ago or thereabouts I had an accident. Hit my head and lost most of my memories. Now, I . . . I remember plenty—how to survey and ride a horse and the like. But I don't recall people in my past. Or who I worked for back in St. Louis. I was hoping . . . if I could find some folks who'd known me, I could go see them and talk to them. Maybe help me get my memory back." Malcolm let out a breath. Patterson whistled low, his face showing astonishment.

With an empathetic frown, the clerk said, "I'm sorry to hear about that. Must be right difficult. Your wife can't help you? Doesn't she recall where you used to work? Folks you knew back there?"

Malcolm stiffened. Just how much did he want to tell this stranger? He shook his head. "She says she didn't know the men I worked with, never met them. She's not good with names." He shrugged.

Patterson thought for a moment. "'Member when we met, I told you we'd been expecting a fella to take the surveying job last spring—when did you come into Fort Collins?"

Malcolm considered what he was asking. "Last fall."

"And when did you have that accident?"

"I'm not sure. Sometime the spring prior."

The clerk pursed his lips, and Malcolm could tell he was chewing on something, but didn't think he should pry. Patterson then said, "And that fella never showed up, so you got his job, more or less."

"I recollect you telling me that."

The clerk nodded, then exhaled and rubbed his chin. "Well, let me do some research for you and see what I can come up with. I'm sure I can get you a list of surveyors who'd been working in the last couple of years in and around St. Louis." He lowered his voice as if someone might be listening. "Do you want me to mention your name, Mr. Connors? When I inquire?"

Malcolm wondered at the clerk's question. "I don't mind if you do."

Patterson nodded. "All right, then. It'll take some days, but check back with me, oh, end o' next week, and I'll let you know if I've learned anything."

Malcolm thanked the clerk and headed out the front door, feeling the clerk's eyes on him. What was the man poking about, asking questions about his accident and when had he come to town? Malcolm let the thought slip from his mind as the pretty face of Grace Cunningham intruded. It hadn't been all that long since he left her at her front door, but he was antsy to get back to her. Just thinking about her sweet smile and the soothing way her laugh had rolled over him made his steps quicken to match the pace of his heartbeat.

As he stepped outside, a squall of warm rain clattered to the boardwalk and drenched the streets. Fat drops deluged in sheets, quickly turning the dirt street into a sluice of scrambled streams and islands of mud. Riders and pedestrians hurried for shelter, their coats and shawls pulled up over their heads. Water snaked along the wood planks around his boots as he tucked his head into his collar and yanked on his horse's halter rope to unhitch him from the post. By the time he made the six blocks to Maple Street, he was soaked through, his clothes heavy and sticking to him like flypaper. The brim of his felt hat sagged, and a steady stream of water poured down his neck. One glance at his horse's petulant expression told Malcolm the gelding was as miserable as he was.

It wouldn't do to call on Grace now, looking like this. And he surely wouldn't dare try to take her out in this weather. He'd postpone his visit till the morrow.

He slumped down in the saddle and urged Rambler into a slow trot in the direction of his homestead, careful to avoid the puddles that were quickly becoming small lakes in the middle of the avenue. For some reason the rain made him edgy, and seeing the swollen dark clouds overhead gave him pause. Not that he thought another twister would burst forth from the mass dangling overhead. This wasn't twister weather. No, something else unsettled him, made him itching to push his horse into a run.

A finger of fear inched up his spine, and he gripped the reins tighter, having the inexplicable sense that he would be swept away somehow if he relaxed his guard even a mite.

He stared at his hands—they were shaking. He considered the nervousness might be just the aftermath of a close brush with death. But then the memory of an agitated river gripped him in its fist, and again he felt himself tumbled head over feet, sucking muddy water into his lungs and gasping for breath.

Malcolm heaved back in his saddle and brought the gelding to a sliding stop at the south end of town in front of The Forks Hotel. He worked to calm his breath and blew air out his nose like a winded racehorse. The horse pawed at the mud, digging a hole around his foot that filled with brown water. Rain kept pounding, as if trying to beat sense into Malcolm's head. He wished it would, for these visions were exhausting him.

But there was nothing for it, he reasoned. He would have to wait it out. Just like waiting for the rain to let up and the dark clouds to blow off. At some point the light of day would break through.

He looked at the flooded street and then out over the wide open range to the south—the empty prairieland smeared gray and colorless as the squall dumped hard sheets of water across the terrain. Last week's snow had disappeared as quickly as it had come. Still, it was hard to envision the warm summer days that lay ahead, even though Malcolm knew they were surely coming, just as the day followed the night. He only hoped his own bright day of understanding would dawn soon. His misery and desperate need was drowning him as surely as any river could, and he knew if he didn't find a way out soon, he'd end up going over the waiting falls and into a chasm, where all that awaited him at the bottom was a pile of jagged rocks.

Chapter 18

CLARE PLUNKED DOWN ON THE bench in front of the Chinese laundry shop and frowned at Grace.

"You mean to tell me that you're leavin'? Truly? After we just became friends?" Clare wrapped her arms around her waist and scowled, and Grace felt terrible. But nothing would soften her resolve, and this morning as she walked over to the livery, Grace had steeled herself for Clare's protestations. She would not change her mind about leaving, and although she would miss Clare, she didn't imagine she would miss living on the Front Range, and particularly in this small town, where her every movement was scrutinized, judged, and discussed.

Grace sighed and sat beside her friend, absentmindedly watching the wagons and riders splash through the puddles glistening in the street under the dazzling noonday sun. "I explained it to you—"

Clare waved her hand in the air and shook her head. "I know, I know. I just think it's wrong. What if after ya leave, Monty's memory comes back? Ya thought of that?"

Of course Grace had thought of that. And every other possible scenario. She felt a sudden weariness come over her. Clare had been trying to talk Grace out of leaving for the better part of an hour, and wouldn't let up. Grace smirked. Eli was right about her wild mustang spirit. She was like a horse that would chew through her rope to break free of her tether.

"Why are we sitting here?" Grace asked, hoping to sway the subject onto another track. "You said you'd go with me to the dress shop, to look at patterns and fabrics for your wedding dress."

Clare pouted. "You've spoiled my mood." Clare's face then lit up, her eyes sparking with excitement. "Hey!" she said. "Well, lookie who's come to town."

Grace turned to see Eli and LeRoy Banks trotting on pretty paint horses down the street toward them. The men had spotted Clare, and Eli's face showed a mix of pleasure and wariness. Grace immediately thought of Sarah's warning and admonition she'd given her sons Sunday last. They were here to scout out some wild horses, and to speak to the sheriff about something to do with tracking outlaws.

A shiver tickled the back of Grace's neck as she thought of violent men riding hard through town, firing pistols at innocent bystanders. She hoped Eli and LeRoy weren't about to get hurt, and by the look on Clare's face, Grace knew the sentiment was shared.

The two men pulled up to a steady, slow stop in front of the boardwalk, and Grace was glad they avoided splashing mud on her clean plaid linen skirt. Their tangled hair blew out behind their heads from under wide-brimmed hats, and their horses puffed from the exertion of the ride. Their cotton shirts were soaked with sweat, and Grace could tell they'd been on a hard ride.

Eli slid off the saddle, dropping his reins, and came around to hug Clare, slinging an arm around her waist and drawing her in for a quick kiss on the cheek. Clare blushed and pushed him away, but Eli only laughed, showing those bright straight teeth, his smile pushing dimples up his cheeks. Grace couldn't have asked for a better diversion to lighten Clare's mood and get her to lay off with her attempts at persuading Grace to stay in Fort Collins.

The men turned their attention to Grace and said their hellos. LeRoy continued to sit his horse, gazing out over the town and watching the goings-on—the local citizens shopping, tending shop, riding through town on some errand or other. His dark eyes took in the streets, which he assessed with the manner of a hawk circling the updraft waiting to pounce on a rabbit.

"Where did'ya go?" Clare asked Eli. "You look tuckered out, and I know that ride from Greeley ain't all that tirin'."

"Up Trail Creek, northwest of town. Then on into Laporte and back along the hogbacks." He tipped his head toward the foothills.

"We lost the trail for the horses up in a canyon just above the Poudre. The river's running way too high. We'll give it another go inside a week or two," LeRoy added.

"Are ya gonna go talk with the sheriff?" Clare asked them both.

"Yep, soon. He was out when we stopped in at his office," Eli said, chewing his lip and wiping his forehead with a cloth he'd pulled from his vest pocket. Grace noticed the pearl-handled revolver at his waist, under the front of his long duster. "No one's heard news of the Dutton Gang lately, from what we could gather."

LeRoy added nothing, just kept up his vigil, his face a strong Indian profile. The two brothers were markedly different, with Eli being the outspoken one, quick to japery. LeRoy spent more time in quiet contemplation, and didn't seem so easily riled. But the two appeared close, and Grace didn't doubt they'd have each other's back in any situation.

"So, are ya fixin' to stay a bit? Or head home?" Clare asked Eli.

"We're staying over," Eli said as a grin spread across his face. "I figured we'd take a room in that fancy-dancy hotel of yours. That way I can keep you in my sights."

Clare's eyebrows raised, and she gave Eli a mischievous smile. "You can draw a bead on me all ya like—until I lock my door for the night. Which is how it'll be until that time comes when you get the key." She dangled a pretend key in front of Eli's face.

He cocked an eyebrow and playfully snarled at her. "You don't have to remind me, Clare. You just love to torture a man, don't ya?"

"I want a proper weddin'—and Grace is gonna make my dress." She humphed and crossed her arms.

LeRoy whistled and repositioned his hat on his head. He said, "Now who's stuck in a box canyon, with no way out?" He shifted on his horse and added, "Not like you want out, Brother." His face showed no sign of amusement other than the mirth in his eyes.

"Ya already took me home to meet your ma, so what more are ya waiting for?" Clare sidled up close to Eli and caressed his cheek. "We gonna set a date or what?"

Eli threw back his head and laughed. "I never met a girl so forward as you, Clare McKay."

"And that's why ya love me so much," she finished, giving him a firm nod.

Eli offered his hands to her, palms up. "I reckon." He laughed heartily. "Yep, I reckon."

"So . . . ?" Clare asked, back to her persistence. Grace sat and watched this banter between them, thinking how she and Monty used to joke in like manner. Although, Grace was never so pushy about getting married. But she hadn't needed to be—Monty had proposed to her straight away after coming back from the Hayden Expedition.

Her sadness once more assaulted her, like a giant wave crashing on her head and snuffing out her good mood. Clare chatted to Eli beside her, but Grace's mind was miles away, back in Illinois, chasing after precious memories and clinging to them as if they were fragile soap bubbles that might pop if she squeezed them too hard.

"Hey," Eli said in a warning tone that shattered Grace's reverie.

She looked at him, and he jerked his head toward a horse and wagon rolling down the street.

Grace stiffened, and the hair on the nape of her neck prickled.

"I recognize her," he said quietly, then looked over at LeRoy, whose eyes narrowed into a questioning scowl.

LeRoy said, "That's the woman we helped last spring—with the broken linchpin. Outside of Evans."

Eli turned and threw Grace a penetrating look. "That her? Stella?"

LeRoy swiveled and studied Grace's face. "You know her," he said. It wasn't a question.

Grace could only nod. A rock lodged in her throat, and she slunk down into the bench. She felt she might be sick.

There Stella sat, up on the wagon bench, dressed in a bright burgundy velvet dress with a low bodice barely cinched with white laces, and an elegant matching sun bonnet atop her coifed hair. She held her head aloft and stared straight ahead, holding the reins in her hands that sported lace gloves that rode up past her elbows. She appeared more like a saloon dancer than a homesteader's wife.

Clare sucked in a breath beside her. "Well, I never . . ."

"Dressed a bit . . . odd for the middle of the day," LeRoy noted. "I don't s'pose she's fixin' to go shoppin'."

"Not likely," Eli said, craning his head to watch as the wagon rolled by.

"I wonder what she's doing here, in Fort Collins," LeRoy mumbled.

"She lives here," Eli told him. LeRoy raised his eyebrows but said nothing more.

Grace's heart railed in her chest. Seeing Stella detonated a profusion of emotions, and Grace floundered in a morass of anger, hurt, pain, and misery. She longed to run back to the Franklins' house, scoop Ben into her arms, and hurry to the coach station and board the next stage to Denver. At least Monty wasn't with Stella. That was a bit of mercy. He was probably at the homestead, seeing that it was Saturday and wouldn't be working.

Clare swiveled closer to Grace and looked at her with compassion. She said in a whisper, "I understand why ya want to leave." Her tone was conciliatory. "I guess I'd feel the same way, if I were in your shoes. If I saw Eli with another woman . . . why, I'd . . ." She scrunched up her face, and her cheeks turned apple red. "Well, I don't think I'd show the manners and restraint you show. I'd go plumb crazy." She took Grace's hand and squeezed it.

"You up for some lunch? I'm starvin'," Eli said, then pointed at a restaurant down the way.

Clare slugged him. "You're always hungry."

He exaggerated offense. "We just rode somethin' like a thousand miles this mornin'."

Clare chuckled and questioned Grace with her eyes.

Grace shook her head and got to her feet, watching the wagon turn the corner a half mile north of town. "Thank you, but I need to get back to Ben. I have some chores to do around the house." *Like packing to leave,* she thought with a sense of grim finality.

"All right," Clare said, fixing the strings of her ribbon-trimmed bonnet under her chin. "I'll come by in the morning, and we can go to church together."

Grace nodded, feeling grateful for Clare's friendship and already missing her. She hurried through her good-byes to the Banks brothers before the tears could leak out. With a tight throat and heavy heart, she watched the trio walk across the street, leading their horses, then turned and headed home, where she planned to rock Ben in her arms and cry herself to sleep.

Before the wagon had even rolled to a stop alongside the stucco wall of the saloon, Lenora slid down from the bench and pulled the long reins over to a corner post and tied up the horse. She needed a drink something fierce to slake her thirst, and had turned the house on end looking for that bottle of whiskey she was sure she'd hidden somewhere. One look at Malcolm's irate face told her he'd found the bottle and threw it out. That was last night—before he stormed out in the dark after the rain had stopped and the clouds moved east. She never heard him come back in, but he was asleep on the sofa when she stumbled out of the bedroom this morning. She'd given up trying to coax him to bed; he'd have none of it.

Ever since that night she'd come home late, Malcolm's words had haunted her. Like some evil witch's curse, she couldn't get them out of her head. How he'd said no man would ever love her, not truly. How she didn't know what love was.

She snorted, rage boiling inside like a whistling tea kettle. He was just like Hank—like most men she'd known. Two-faced, cruel. Treated her with contempt. Used her and lied to her. All she'd ever wanted her whole life was to be loved. Appreciated.

When she met Hank, he'd showered her with affection, bought her expensive perfume and pretty dresses. He promised he'd rescue her from a deplorable and dreary life as a saloon girl. She'd been impressed by the silver coins he tossed her way, implying there was more, much more, where those had come from. But what had he offered her? Not the life of adventure and glamour he'd promised her—that was for certain. Instead, most of the time she'd spent holed up in dumps, in close quarters with men who hadn't bathed in weeks or washed their clothes in months, places swarming with fleas and cockroaches and rats. Hideouts in the middle of nowhere, surrounded by cactus and coyotes and tumbleweed, with little more than a bottle of whiskey and a deck of cards to keep her entertained. Phooey!

She'd stuck by him, despite his mistreatment and infidelity. No matter how hard she'd tried to make him love her, she knew deep in her heart he hadn't.

And now this new husband of hers declared it was all her fault. That *she* was lacking. Undeserving of a man's love. How dare he? How dare he!

All week she thought of how she could repay him for his cruel words. She thought of slitting his throat while he slept, but what kind of revenge was that? No, she meant for him to suffer—the way she'd suffered. Pay him back with equal misery, so he'd never find that love and happiness he spoke of.

And then the answer had come to her, and it was a sweet taste in her mouth. She knew Montgomery Cunningham's memories were coming back, and it was only a matter of time before he'd recall his dear little wife. Lenora also knew that Grace had every intention of trying to get her husband back, and had no doubt she'd tell Monty the truth of who he was, and whose baby that was. And then the happy little family would be reunited and live happily ever after, like some pat and sappy fairy tale. The thought turned rancid in her gut.

So for the past few days she'd been toying with ways to get shed of Grace and her baby. She could just imagine that moment when Monty's memories all returned—only to realize it was too late. He'd search for Grace and she'd be gone. He would lose her again—but this time for good.

She hummed a little merry tune picturing Monty's horrified face at the news of his wife's death. So sad, so sad . . .

Warm sun baked her shoulders, and she smiled. She'd thought the snow would never melt, but finally, it had. And that was all she cared about. That, and getting properly soused—one last time—before she packed her bags and skedaddled. And, she figured, after all she'd been through, she deserved a little manly attention, and knew just the place to get it in this seedy part of town. Then she needed to purchase a few supplies and sundry personal items—enough to get her to California. Once she dug up the gold, she'd have to buy some traveling trunks—nice ones—to stash the gold in and transport it on the train. She didn't doubt she'd be able to find a buyer for all that gold in San Francisco—one who didn't ask questions.

She squirmed thinking of all the things she planned to buy with her money. She grunted as she looked down at her dress. This was about the nicest thing she could find in town—apart from those elegant dresses she'd had Grace Cunningham make for her. But they were too nice to suit her afternoon plans. She didn't want to chance dirtying them with a man's hands or a splash of liquor. Those dresses she would wear on the train and in San Francisco—to give the proper impression as she waltzed her way into high society.

Lenora chuckled with glee thinking about her months living here in this joke of a town, playing wife to that chucklehead who had no idea who he was. Too bad she wouldn't be here to see the sad story to its conclusion. But good riddance to Montgomery Cunningham and Fort Collins, Colorado.

Lenora pulled her purse out from under the bench seat, chuckling to herself, her palms itchy and sweaty as she thought about a glass of whiskey in her hand and a man's mouth trailing kisses down her neck. She had no doubt that Jacques—the French Canadian ranch hand with those broad shoulders and dreamy dark eyes—would be waiting for her at the bar.

"Well, if it ain't Lenora Dutton. Up to your ol' wily ways, I see."

Lenora froze, the voice sending a knife through her heart. Blood hammered in her ears as her head reeled in terror. She flinched, every nerve screaming to her to run, but her shoes were glued to the street.

Hands fell hard on her shoulders and spun her around. She gulped as her eyes looked up into the brooding, angry face of Clayton "the Blade" Wymore. He looked tickled pink at seeing her. How had he found her? Her mind raced, trying to figure how she'd been spotted, but it didn't matter, did it. He was here, and she knew there was no escaping his clutches.

She forced a smile up her face and dared raise a hand, thinking she'd run it through his hair and start working him, the way she used to those long, boring nights in one hideout or another, where the gang killed time between robberies. But Clayton stayed her hand, grasping it in a hurtful manner, which caused Lenora to yelp.

She eked out the words, "I thought you were dead. Oh, I'm so relieved. Oh, Clayton—"

"Quit with the act, Lenora." He took a harsher tone than he'd ever had with her, his face surly and disagreeable, and Lenora wilted. She put on her best acting face and hoped he would not hurt her. "We figured you'd be hidin' out someplace close to the gold."

He sneered and tightened his grip on her wrist. "And what with all that heavy snow, you wouldn'ta had time to fetch it yet."

"Why are you here, then? Why not just head up to the cabin and fetch it yerselves?" she asked, trying to look as surprised as possible. Out of the corner of her eye, she saw Billy Cloyd come around the corner toward them. His eyes betrayed the nervousness he felt, even though he walked with purpose, his lanky, tall body even thinner than she remembered. Clayton looked as if he'd dropped some pounds as well. She imagined being on the lam didn't afford many five-course meals.

Billy hung back and wouldn't meet her eyes. Lenora shuddered, guessing why. Once Clayton learned the location of the gold, he'd kill her. She had no doubt. Think, think! She had to come up with something.

"You know why we're here," he said, his voice hard and harsh. He grabbed her throat with one hand and squeezed, choking it closed. A sharp pain shot up her neck. Lenora slapped at him and tried to kick him, but he only laughed and backed up, dodging her pathetic attempts to break free.

He released her neck with a push, and she sucked in air, her throat burning. "We're takin' you to the cabin—so you can show us where the gold is hid."

"Surely you can find it without me," she offered, rubbing her throat and trying to put a few inches between her head and his hands.

"We already looked—last fall. Tore up the place. It's not in the house."

Lenora bristled as he grabbed the side of her head and pulled her close with a yank of her hair. He stared hard into her eyes and smirked. "You know where it is, and you're gonna show me."

"I'll just tell you—"

"Nice try," Clayton said. "And while we're off on a goose chase, you'll sic the sheriff on us. Nope, you'll come with us. Now."

Lenora pushed the rising panic down. She knew if she didn't cooperate, he'd use his knife on her. He'd escort her quietly out of town on his horse, the knife pressing against her back as she sat in front of him, through these back alleys and into the foothills, and if anyone saw them, they'd think nothing of it—except maybe wonder why a woman would be riding a horse in a dress like hers. Drat! If only she had left yesterday. She cursed at herself, but kept quiet while Clayton watched her, assessing her. He could read her every thought. *Think, think!*

"Listen, Clayton," she said, dropping the syrupy voice and trying to sound reasonable. "I have a good life here. I'm married to a fine man, and I'm happy—"

"Yeah, so why you over on this side of town—wearing that?" He'd cut right through her lie. "I don't reckon you're meetin' your fine husband for a drink, now? Not when he's s'posedly out surveyin' ten miles south o' here."

Drat! Clayton had been watching her—probably for days. He probably knew where she lived. Maybe even thought she had the gold. But he knew her well—knew she wouldn't stand for living in a backwater town like this—when she had done her share of bellyaching about Denver City and how uncouth and dirty it was. She cringed thinking how she'd once told him of her dream to act on the stage in California. There was no fooling the likes of Clayton Wymore.

And then it struck her—standing right before him was the answer to her pressing need. The perfect way to get shed of Grace Cunningham and her baby.

"All right. Here's the deal," she said. "Because I want to have my life back, and stop running. Hank's dead, and I deserve some happiness." She could tell he was listening. "I just have one itty bitty problem that's standing in my way to that road to happiness."

Clayton snorted and put his hands on his hips. Billy stood leaning against the side of the saloon, his wide-brimmed hat shading his face, keeping an eye out for anyone that might happen by. Lenora noted the way his fingers rested on the revolver at his hip. But no one was out this time of day in this neighborhood. The only folks around here were in the saloons, drinking and carousing—which is where she wished she was right now. She could sure use a drink, now more than ever.

"I'm listenin'," Clayton said, his expression wary but amused.

"My husband's prior wife is here in town—with her baby. And she wants him back. She's a thorn in my side." She paused and thought a moment. "I want you to kidnap 'em and take 'em up to the cabin, where I can watch you kill 'em. Then I'll show you where the gold is."

Clayton laughed and shook his head. "Now, why would I agree to do that?"

"Because I won't show you where the gold is otherwise." She hardened her face. He had to swallow her bait. Trying to flee to the cabin with a woman and baby would slow him down. Which would come to the attention of the sheriff, and he'd send a posse after them. Maybe she'd give a repeat performance and slip another little note under another sheriff's door. Then, after the posse headed out, she'd take a more convoluted route—the one Hank had led her on to ensure no one was following them—and hide out near the cabin and wait for the posse to catch them. If they got shot dead or were captured and hauled off, she could take off with the gold as soon as it was safe. Then maybe ride on up to Cheyenne to catch a train west.

She glanced over at Billy, who was still watching the street. He was a wild card. She knew he had a soft heart. He hated anyone killing anybody, and Lenora knew he wouldn't stand for Clayton killing Grace—and surely not a baby. He'd try to talk Clayton out of it—but she knew Clayton wouldn't listen to him. Not with the gold at stake. She wondered why the two were sticking together. But she supposed it was easier to rob banks if you had a sharpshooter to hold the gun while you stuffed money into sacks.

"How do I know that if I let you go right now you won't head straight to the sheriff?"

Lenora made a face. "And risk you slicing my head off with your Bowie knife?"

Clayton scowled. "Naw, I'm not fallin' fer it. You're comin' with us—right now."

Lenora scoffed. "Dressed like this? You think that won't attract some attention? 'Sides, I can't just disappear. My husband will be alarmed if I don't git home presently. And with the way he worries, he just might report my unexpected disappearance to the sheriff." She flounced her head as if he were a fool not to have thought of this. "Best you sneak out of town in the dark of night with the woman and her baby—I'll head out in the morning, after Malcolm's ridden off to work. Slip unnoticed out of town."

He chewed his lip. "You say a peep, and you're dead. You understand?"

She nodded. Clayton spit on the ground. "All right. I'll play it your way. But if you try one little thing, I'll be watchin'. I've given the law the slip for more'n a year—"

"I understand, Clay." She softened her voice and soaked it with allure. "I just want to be happy—and left alone. I don't need any gold. Look—I haven't taken it yet—and I coulda. It's only a half day's ride away." She noticed his tight face had loosened some. "It's been sittin' up there all this time, just waitin' for someone to claim it. May as well be you. It's the gang's gold anyways. If I got caught with it, I'd be hung as an accessory to all your thievery. You think I want that?"

Her words seemed to be making inroads. Clayton pondered awhile.

"D'ya know where this woman and her brat live?" he asked.

Lenora held back a grin and forced a straight face. He was falling right into her trap. He wanted that gold badly. She imagined all the cold, hungry nights he'd lain awake just thinking about getting his hands on that gold—his ticket to Mexico or South America. Freedom. Just like she'd been imagining for herself. She and Clayton—they weren't all that dissimilar, when it came down to it. They were both greedy and selfish, and liked to indulge in life's pleasures. She knew he'd keep his end of the bargain.

She described the house on Maple Street where Grace lived. She'd pried that information from the shopkeeper where Grace worked. Without another word, Clayton shot her a warning look that Lenora knew all too well—a look that made her tremble from head to toe.

"Do it tonight," she told him. "And then I'll meet you up at the cabin, as soon's I can slip out of town unnoticed."

Clayton merely grunted and pushed a swath of his black hair from off his forehead. She watched the two walk a block down the street, then veer into a narrow alley sided with tall bushes.

A long trembling sigh rattled her chest. Her hands shook as she steadied herself against the side of the building, willing her heart to stop thumping so hard. Her eye caught on the unmarked door at the end of the street—the side entrance to the saloon she liked to frequent. She knew she should head home and start packing to leave Fort Collins for good. But she couldn't do it without some whiskey in her gut, nosiree. She have a quick one, then take her time—do her shopping, act for all the world like nothing was the matter. Drat—now she'd probably have to leave all those pretty dresses behind. Such a waste.

Then, a tingle of excitement started in her toes and worked its way up to her head. She figured she was playing with fire, making this deal with Clayton—like dealing with the Devil. But come Monday, she'd have everything she wanted—the last of Hank Dutton's gang out of her life, Grace Cunningham six feet under dirt, and a sackful of gold coins and bars to finance her new life in San Francisco. Who needed love?

Alan H. Patterson stepped out into the street, exiting the rear door to Brett Hoskins's office, where he'd delivered some legal papers to the sawmill owner that pertained to an upcoming legal inquiry. He didn't like coming into this part of town, where drunks and loose women loitered, and who often called out to him and tried to part him from his money. He looked up and down the street before crossing to the other side, uneasy that not a body was outside in the middle of the day.

He hitched up his trousers and unbuttoned his overcoat, glad for the sudden change in weather, but regretting how overdressed he was in his three-piece tweed suit. After the recent snow, the twister, and the onslaught of rain, though, he wouldn't complain. It appeared summer had finally made a stop in Colorado, and the hot sun overhead was a welcome arrival.

As he peeled off his long coat and slung it over his arm, he caught movement out of the corner of his eye. The next block over, a woman stood at the corner, next to a rigged wagon, and she was dressed like a saloon girl. She was looking his way, but then he realized she was watching something in the alley across from him. Intently watching, with a serious look on her face. He thought he'd seen her around town, but wasn't sure who she was.

Alan craned his neck as he stood next to the two-story brick building, shading his eyes with a hand, and pushing his curly hair and his felt hat back off his forehead to get a better look. Two men walked close together, then stopped and turned to face each other. Alan didn't recognize the men, and from this distance, and due to the shadows of the buildings draping their features, he couldn't make out much. The taller gangly man slouched, listening to the shorter man, whose comportment and gestures spoke of authority. Why these men intrigued him, he couldn't say. But it seemed suspicious—their standing in an alley, sharing confidences in close proximity, as if up to no good. He had a hunch about them, but couldn't put his finger on why they seemed familiar to him.

Alan started walking, taking a slow pace, as he passed the alley on the opposite side of the street. He dared a quick glance at the men, hoping they wouldn't notice him. But they had.

Flustered, Alan thumbed his hat, jerkily acknowledging them. The two men glared at him, and tendrils of fear trickled along his spine. He hastened his step, eyes ahead, and kept walking. He felt like someone had traipsed on his grave—as the saying went. Sweat poured down his face and neck, soaking the tightly buttoned collar of his starched white shirt. The men's eyes bored holes into his back.

Alan gulped. He realized now why they looked so familiar. He'd seen their faces all over town on posters throughout the last year. Wanted posters. His hands started shaking.

He had no doubt he'd just seen Clayton Wymore and Billy Hill Cloyd—the outlaws that had broken out of the Denver City Jail and who'd robbed the bank in Laporte.

He'd better hurry and find Sheriff Love and tell him.

Chapter 19

GRACE AWOKE WITH A START, bolting upright in her bed in the dark. She'd been in a deep sleep, but a noise had jolted her—or so she'd thought. She threw the coverlet off of her and looked over at Ben, who was still asleep in his pine crib. A scant bit of moonlight seeped through the windowpane from outside, and then the sound of boots thumping floorboards gave her a start. She relaxed. It was probably just Jedidiah getting something out of the larder.

But then she heard what sounded like a scuffle, and an angry voice filtered through her door—a man's she didn't recognize.

Grace stiffened, and fear shot through her heart. She heard Charity cry out in alarm, then more heavy boots walking. Adding to her horror, Franklin yelled, his voice full of fear, and Grace heard something hard smack a wall, then fall to the ground.

In the few seconds of silence that ensued, panic enveloped Grace. She jumped out of bed, tripping over her long cotton nightdress, and grabbed her gray woolen shawl. Whoever was in this house had not left, and they were opening doors, talking in hushed tones, speaking words Grace could not make out. She no longer heard Charity's or Jedidiah's voice.

An icy coldness washed over her. She had to flee.

Stuffing her bare feet into slippers, she tripped her way over to her baby and collected him and his blankets into her arms, sending fervent prayers up to heaven while she fumbled with her armload. Her pulsed raced so hard she could barely breathe. Ben whimpered, "Mama, Mama," and Grace's heart lurched in worry. The only way out was the window.

She rushed over and worked the stubborn latch, trying to pry it up with trembling fingers. Just as she heard the click and pushed on the sash to raise the window, her bedroom door flew open. She screamed as a large man in dark clothes flew at her, and she clutched Ben to her chest.

A hand slapped over her mouth, smothering her scream. She smelled liquor and tobacco smoke and soot as the man's other hand wrapped around her waist and yanked her close to him. Rough leather scratched her face, and his fingers dug into her cheeks, hurting her.

"Get the brat," he said in a growl to a man who stood in the doorway, whose tall shape was a shadow cast into the unlit room. Grace squirmed and thrashed, screaming into her captor's hand, but the man was strong. She strained to see his face, but the room was as dark as pitch. That intruder jerked Ben out of her arms.

Horror coursed through her like blood. Why were they taking her baby? *No, God, please no!*

She kicked at her abductor's shins and fought him with all her strength, but he laughed, and the stark, cold sound of it tore her apart. Ben wailed into the night, and the man spit out, "Shut the brat up."

Graced lunged away from her captor, a futile effort, but she managed to pull from his hand enough to get the words out. "Please, don't hurt my baby!"

A backhanded slap knocked her half senseless, and she fell to the floor and moaned. Her throat choked close as tears gushed down her face and she reached her arms out blindly.

Ben, Ben! Oh, my baby. Please, God, don't let them hurt my baby.

Then, a damp rag was thrust over her face, and a sickening sweet and pungent odor wafted up her nose, making her gag and assailing her with dizziness. Bile rose up her throat, and the contents of her stomach roiled. The man hoisted her up from the floor, and the last thing she felt was her body being thrown over his shoulder as her flickering hope of escape was snuffed out.

Malcolm stood under a languishing weeping willow at the quiet residential corner as the Sunday dawn smeared rust all over the horizon. A cool wind tickled his neck, and he pulled his light leather coat tight, feeling conspicuous and as nervous as a youngster calling to court a girl. Despite his hammering guilt, his feet had slipped from the cool bedsheets while it was still dark, tired of agitating all night, Grace's face haunting him, almost pestering him, to the point of despair. With Stella none the wiser, her face smothered into a pillow and emitting loud drunken snores, Malcolm had snuck out and saddled his horse under a sliver of a moon.

How many nights had he lain alone in his bed, the moon tracing the curve of the sky and the stars shining without warmth on his predicament? Plenty. He'd sent a flood of prayers heavenward the previous weeks, but received back nothing but silence for his troubles. He kept telling himself it was wrong to think on another woman, and especially in the way Malcolm thought on Grace.

He'd pleaded with the Lord, arguing his case. He wasn't lusting for her, even though he would be lying like a blanket if he said he hadn't envisioned her in his arms. Hadn't imagined running his hands down her smooth skin, drawing her close and tasting her lips on his. How could he not relive the moments he'd held her, relishing how perfectly she fit into his arms? Into his heart? Why in all the world had he found Grace Cunningham now—when there wasn't a chance in hell she could be his?

And yet, he couldn't still his longing. His implacable desire. His unabating need for her. And not just for the comfort of her touch but for her very presence. For when she was near him, his careening world tilted back straight, and he no longer felt unhinged, dangling over the precipice of his lost memory. She was the calm in the middle of the storm—the eye of the twister. The place of refuge and peace he could run to for rest and consolation.

But she wasn't his, and should he leave his wife—which he knew he would have to do sooner or later, regardless of the ruin of his good name and reputation—he could never bring the shame of adultery upon Grace. No, he could not expect her to put her eternal soul in jeopardy by loving a man who was, in the eyes of God, bound in matrimony to another woman.

He stood quietly, listening to songbirds twittering in nearby trees and his horse snuffling softly at the post where he'd tied him. He smelled wet grass and wood smoke on the air, the scent of summer rich with the loam of the earth after the heavy rains. Like a hawk circling its prey in a far-off field, Malcolm eyed Grace's front door, waiting. At some point she would venture out, for she'd mentioned she attended church on Sunday mornings.

He thought about little Ben, and a smile creased his face. He had no memory of ever holding a baby in his arms before, but after holding Ben, he had no doubt he had. An instant affection and delight had bubbled up inside him as he looked into the eyes of that child and watched Ben's expressive face take in all around him. His heart clenched as the overbearing sensation of loss filled him, followed by the ever-present guilt. What was he doing here, waiting for a woman he could never have? He was only adding torment to his already miserable life. And what if he someday learned he'd had a wife and child before coming to Fort Collins? What if that wife was worrying over him somewhere, praying for his return?

Nothing you can do about that. It's a possible past you may never recover. He fisted his hands. *True, but you haven't even begun to search.* He answered back with anger stirring. *And where in tarnation would you begin looking for a lost wife? You don't even know where you really came from, or what your real name is. Your only hope is to wait for your memories to return.*

And that hope rested on Grace Cunningham, Malcolm conceded. For only around her did the images spark in his head, as if she were a piece of flint his thoughts struck against and ignited in an explosion of fragments that he knew were puzzle pieces to his past.

With a groan under the heavy weight of his heart, he once more faced the truth—regardless of the wife he now had and even the wife he may have had before Stella—he was falling in love with Grace Cunningham—as crazy as it seemed. Regardless of the fact he could never take her as a wife, he knew he could not deny the feelings he had for her. He could no sooner drown out the raging river of desire and need he felt coursing through his veins than turn the clock backward and erase all his regrettable decisions and careless actions that had led him to this dead-end canyon with no way out.

Still, it was wrong to indulge his feelings, wrong to stand here waiting for her like the fool he was. He could never tell her how he felt, though he ached to profess his affections. To fall to his knees before her and pour out his heart, his need. It would be more than an unkindness to her. He imagined it would greatly distress her, and would put her in an uncomfortable position that might lead to her pitying him, and more than likely losing all respect for him. For he knew she was a godly woman with high moral regard. Did he expect that she'd throw her faith and her morality to the wayside—just to assuage his needs?

There was nothing for him now but to leave. Not just leave the corner of this quiet street but leave Fort Collins. Where would he go? He had no idea, and no longing to be anywhere but here. If he left, would his memories return in time? Did it matter anymore? The question broke off and fell to the hard ground. *No, nothing matters to me but Grace. I want only her. But I can't have her. So I may as well close my eyes and head off in any random direction, start all over.*

The thought was akin to a death sentence, but it was the right decision. The only choice he could make, if he wanted to give Grace the chance at a happy life. In time, she'd no doubt meet a good man, someone who would love her and Ben, who would—

Malcolm's mind shut off as the door to Grace's house flew open and an old man with a gray beard and coat rushed down the front steps, shaking his head and waving his arms about as if swatting flies. From where Malcolm stood, he could detect the man's consternation as he hurried down Maple Street toward the center of town.

Something's happened. Something bad. Was Grace ill? Had she had an accident? What about Ben?

Before he could lecture himself anew, his legs carried him with all speed to the front door to her house. He grabbed the latch but the door was locked.

"Grace!" he yelled, running over to the window. He peered through the slit in the lace curtains, but the parlor was dark, and he saw no signs of movement inside.

He pounded on the door, calling Grace's name over and over. A strange panic churned in his gut. Something was very wrong—he just knew it. Then, he saw a shadow flit in the back of the house—someone moving about. He slapped the window to get the person's attention, calling out, "Please, come to the door. I need to talk to Grace." He supposed it was Mrs. Franklin, the woman Grace rented from, but why wasn't she answering? And why had her husband rushed off in such a panic?

Finally, after he resumed his pounding and pleadings for another few minutes, he heard a latch click on the door. He lowered his fist and stepped back, and the door swung open. A harried, distraught older woman with a Quaker head covering gaped at him through a small crack between the door and the frame. She trembled as she gripped the edge of the door and said, "Who . . . who are you and what do you want?"

"I'm Malcolm Connors, ma'am. I noticed your husband leaving in a huff. Is everything all right?" He pushed down his need to ask about Grace, but how would that look? No doubt the woman was already wondering why he'd been calling out Grace's name.

The flustered woman blurted out, "No, nothing's right." She moaned and clung to the barely open door, and Malcolm stepped back, not wanting to upset her further.

"Please," he implored, his heart about to burst out of his chest with worry, "tell me what happened."

Through her subsequent mutterings and fretting, Malcolm made out the gist of her words. They struck his gut with a sharp pain. His thoughts froze like ice in his head as he heard her say, "They took her. Took Grace. And the baby, the poor, poor baby. Oh, Ben . . ." She fell to weeping and collapsed to the floor.

Malcolm rushed to aid her, his limbs numb with shock but his heart racing with terror. "Who?" he asked, pressing her to answer, ignoring her hysteria. "Who took her?" Disbelief assaulted him. How could someone have taken Grace—and why? It made no sense.

"Robbers. Or brigands of a sort—two of them," she wailed. "They broke in last night and . . . and just took her!"

Malcolm stood, blinking back the terrifying pictures that played in his head of Grace being hauled off, screaming and kicking. Of Ben being stuffed under some ruffian's arm, his little cry piercing the quiet of night. Of mean, vicious, heartless men doing unspeakable things to Grace—to the woman he loved.

Fury filled him, and the rage seeped out his hot fingertips that yearned to strangle someone. He fought down the nausea and impotency and replaced it with determination. He had no clue who had Grace or where the men were taking her, but he would find her—come hell or high water—if it cost him his life.

Without uttering a good-bye, Malcolm ran down the steps, crossed the street, and swung up onto his horse. He kicked the gelding into a hard gallop down Loomis Street toward the south end of town. It wouldn't take him long to get to his homestead and grab his rifle. He figured by the time he got to the sheriff, Eph Love would have already heard the news. Malcolm hoped the sheriff would help him find Grace, but if he didn't . . . well, Malcolm would just have to find her himself. Some way, somehow. He couldn't bear the thought of her being violated. Or of Ben suffering abuse or neglect.

Oh, Lord, he prayed as wind whipped his cheeks raw, while his horse pounded hooves on the soft road, sending clods of dirt and splashes of muddy water into his face and over his duster, *protect Grace and keep her safe. And show me the way, Lord, so I can save her. Please, don't let any harm come to her or Ben. Have mercy, oh, Lord. Have mercy.*

Before Eph Love even stepped one foot through the front door to the sheriff's office, he heard someone calling his name. He spun around and saw, in the early morning glare, an old man with a ponderous gut and a long gray beard and black felt hat lumbering in an awkward run toward him, his dark-gray overcoat flapping against his sides. The man, in his haste, ignored the pervasive puddles that had made craters in the street and splashed through them as he came up to the boardwalk, breathless, his face paled in what Eph reckoned was pure fear. Before the man spoke a word, Eph knew the news the man brought to him had to do with Wymore and Cloyd.

"Sheriff—there's been a kidnapping!" The man clutched his stomach and practically doubled over from his exertion.

"A kidnapping?" Eph pushed his hat back on his head and rubbed his chin. Didn't sound like something the Dutton Gang would be mixed up in. "Who's been kidnapped?" After Alan Patterson had come to him yesterday afternoon, reporting a sighting of the outlaws, Eph had put his deputies on alert. He'd made his rounds to the local banks and spoken to the presidents, who agreed to posting armed guards in the shadows, just in case. Although he'd cautioned secrecy, not wanting to tip off the men to his knowledge of their general whereabouts, there was no keeping a secret in this town.

"A woman's been taken from our home, Sheriff—she and her baby live with us." He pulled a handkerchief from his coat pocket and dabbed his forehead and groaned. "My wife—Charity. They hit her on the head, knocked her out for a spell. And they tied me to a chair—I sat there all night until my wife came to and untied me—"

Eph held up a hand to slow the avalanche of words pouring out of the man's mouth. "When did this happen?"

"Last night, past midnight. I heard footsteps in the hallway, heavy ones. I knew they couldn't be Grace's—"

Eph's blood raced. A woman and her baby—kidnapped. Who would do such a thing, and why? The last thing he needed right now was something like this to distract him from his most pressing need—to protect this town by catching the outlaws. He blew out a frustrated breath as a pang gnawed at his insides.

"Do you have a notion who'd do such a thing?" he asked.

"No, Sheriff." The old man hung his head, and kept up his ministrations to his forehead with his handkerchief. "I've never been so frightened in my life. Gave my wife the most terrible scare. She's locked herself in our bedroom and won't come out. They pushed me against the wall. I-I couldn't stop them—"

"Did they rob you? Take anything of value?"

The old man shook his head dolefully.

Eph looked past the man and saw the street abuzz with people chattering, most of them church folks on their way to Sunday service. Their expressions showed the news had already spread like wildfire about the kidnapping. A block down the street, Eph made out Patterson skipping through the throng of citizens milling along the boardwalk and heading his way. His deputies, Colin O'Grady and Ezra Stapleton, were riding hard from the north end of town, and two other men on sturdy mustangs followed close behind them—one appeared to be an Indian. Within minutes, the street was a flurry of agitated voices clamoring to be heard.

"What's your name?" Eph asked the old man, who had taken off his hat and was kneading it in his hands.

"Franklin. Jedidiah Franklin. I live over on Maple."

"And the name of the woman who's been snatched?"

"Grace Cunningham." Franklin's eyes filled with tears. "Her baby isn't even a year old. Why, oh why, would someone do such a thing?"

Eph's forehead tightened as a face came to mind. Cunningham. That was the honey-haired woman who'd come on occasion into his office. Her husband had drowned, if he remembered rightly, in that terrible flood the prior spring. Patterson had once mentioned to him that the man had been offered a surveying job with the land office and that's why they'd attempted to cross the Poudre. Why would anyone want to kidnap her?

"Mr. Franklin, I need you to describe the kidnappers—"

"There were two men, but it was dark. I couldn't see a thing. Only one spoke, ordering the other to grab Grace's baby. He sounded maybe in his thirties. Gruff, and smelling of horse and tobacco."

Could be Wymore and Cloyd. But it still made not a lick of sense. Not likely they'd break into a house in the middle of the night just to take a hostage for a bank robbery. He gritted his teeth, knowing the outlaws had to be mixed up in this somehow.

Eph laid a hand on Franklin's shoulder. "Go tend to your wife. Git Doc Smith to take a look at her, maybe give her a restorative." Eph worried the man was so distraught, he might not find his way home.

Eph heard someone call his name. He turned and saw Marcus Coon, the owner of the Agricultural Hotel, rushing to his side like a lumbering bear. "Sheriff, one of my employees saw two riders gallop through the west side of town late last night." He raked a hand through his thick chestnut beard. "By the description, it sure sounds like them outlaws."

Eph stiffened. "I need to talk to your worker—"

"They had a woman with them. She was sittin' in front of one of the men on the horse. He couldn't see much, but could tell what kind of horses they rode."

Eph nodded and strode down the boardwalk, following Coon as he pushed through the din of noisy people congregating in front of the office and headed toward his hotel.

He trusted Coon—and the man was handy with a gun. Already Eph was forming a posse in his head. He had to act quickly and get on the scent of those outlaws. Thankfully, the storm front looked stuck on Longs Peak. And after the recent rains, those horses would leave clear tracks—at least so long as the renegades rode on soft ground. His deputies would be a help, but what he really could use was a good tracker. If those men rode west into the mountains and onto rock, he could lose their trail.

"Sheriff, wait!" a voice called out. Eph and Coon stopped and spun about. A man ran to him, waving a hand, his tan duster blowing behind him. The set of his mouth showed his consternation, and as he neared Eph recognized the tall, strong fella. He was the new surveyor Wallace had hired.

"Sheriff, a woman's been kidnap—"

"I know," Eph told him as the man nearly collided into him, his expression streaked with anger and fear. "Malcolm Connors—that right?"

The man clearly had no intention of wasting time to banter words. "Yes, Sheriff. Look, I'm going after those men who took her. They have her baby too—" Connors grabbed Eph's coat sleeve, and Eph wondered at the man's determination.

"Do you know the woman?" Eph asked. Coon stood silent beside him, waiting, glaring at the crowd and clucking his tongue. Eph caught a glance of his deputies sliding off their horses and tying them off at the railing. The two young men on the mustangs followed suit, and the four strode toward him, threading through the crowd.

"I do. Her name's Grace Cunningham. Sheriff, there's talk those outlaws may have taken her."

"Any reason you can figure?" Eph asked him. Connors fidgeted, his eyes darting through the throng of pressing people as if he was searching for someone.

"No. There's no rhyme or reason to it." His face knotted as he said, "Are you going after the kidnappers?"

"Soon's I can get riders—"

"I'm coming along."

"It's gonna be dangerous—"

"I don't care," Connors stated without hesitation.

He wondered at Connors's panicked manner. The man was married, from what he recalled. And this didn't seem like a simple case of citizen duty calling. But it mattered not the man's reasons—unless his feelings were to get in the way. He couldn't have anyone riding with him that would go off half-cocked and not follow his lead.

Coon said, "Lemme go git my gun and some supplies. Meet in front of your office?"

Eph nodded, and Coon rushed off toward the hotel. O'Grady and Stapleton came up to him, wiping their sweaty foreheads and looking for all the world like they'd just ridden to Texas and back.

"Where ya been?" he asked them.

O'Grady doffed his hat and smoothed back his thick red hair. "We saw their trail—they headed into the hogbacks. They're ridin' hard."

"We gotta hurry if we're gonna catch them," old Stapleton said in his growl of a voice. "They're three ways from Sunday by now." The lanky man had some years on Eph, but he could ride like the dickens, and he'd spent a brief spell as a Texas Ranger back in San Antone back in the day.

"We ran into these two boys," Stapleton added, nodding at the two young men who'd come up behind the deputies and waited quietly, listening with keen attention. "They were out lookin' for a herd of horses when they saw us. When we told 'em 'bout the Dutton Gang, they offered to help. They can track."

The boys stepped forward and introduced themselves as LeRoy and Eli Banks—brothers. Eph assessed them. It was clear they had Indian blood, and from what Eph noticed when they rode in, they were steady riders. Then he realized he knew who these boys were. These were John Banks's sons—they ran the horse ranch outside Greeley with their mother, a Cheyenne woman. Theirs was an honest trade, and their horses were the finest on the Front Range. What a stroke of good fortune it was, them showing up right when Eph could use their riding and tracking skills.

"We can find 'em for you, Sheriff," Eli, the lighter-skinned one, said. He looked early twenties, a mite younger than his darker brother. "We were on the posse last year out of Bloomington—with the territorial marshal, Copeland Townsend—looking for those scalawags. But the weather wreaked havoc with their trail, and they vanished up near Estes Park."

"We know the woman they took," LeRoy told him, his eyes seared with rage, but his face remained as calm as an undisturbed pool of water. "She's a friend of ours, and she has a baby."

Eph nodded, fingering the brim of his hat. "All right, let's git to it." He cocked his head toward his deputies, and they rushed to their horses. He said to the Indians, noting their cartridge belts peeking out from under their soft deerskin coats, "What sidearms you carrying?"

LeRoy replied with a level look that gave Eph pause—these young men were all business. "I have a Smith & Wesson, twelve inch, and a Henry strapped behind my saddle."

Eli pulled his coat back to reveal a nice pearl-handled Colt. "I got me a Winchester '73 and a Sharps carbine—an old '67 that I reworked. I keep a spare Peacemaker in my saddlebag."

Eph's eyebrows rose, and he tugged on his thick mustache. "Well, that'll do." *More than do, I reckon. Why'd they bring so many guns if they were just out chasin' horses?* He turned to Connors, who'd been listening to their discussion with a scowl on his face, clearly antsy to get a move on. "This is Malcolm Connors. He'll be riding with us."

Connors nodded a hello, but an unspoken thought passed between the two boys like a lightning flash. Their faces were hospitable as they returned Connors's greeting, but the surprise and recognition in their eyes were hard to miss. Eph said nothing though. They were burning daylight, and he was itching to catch Wymore and Cloyd.

"Get mounted and meet me in front of the office in ten," he instructed.

The men turned and left, and Eph marched down the street, making for the livery, to saddle up his mare. He'd pack his guns and ammunition upon returning to the office, grab some rope, his warm coat. They'd be up in elevation, possibly in deep snow. He thought who he'd put in charge while he was gone. He frowned and stroked his mustache. *Could be gone a long stretch.* He'd get that new fella—Fowler—to sit the desk. Eph doubted much trouble would foment in town while they were gone—so long as the outlaws didn't swing back around and snatch some other body.

His heart went out to the woman and her baby, for he feared there was little hope the posse would find the two captives alive when they caught up with the outlaws. What they meant to do to her, Eph couldn't fathom, and he didn't want to even consider. Why take a baby? Hostages would only slow them down. But maybe they'd come to town for that very purpose—to find and snatch the woman. Maybe they knew her. She'd only recently moved to Fort Collins. Maybe she had a history with the gang. *Didn't seem the type, though. Too sweet and innocent-like.* He shook his head and picked up his pace.

Clayton Wymore, you're in my sights now. And there'll be no escaping this time.

Chapter 20

WELL, THAT WAS CERTAINLY A surprise.

Lenora stood on the front stoop of the cabin and stared off toward the mountains, thinking of Malcolm's startling announcement. When he stormed into the house and demanded she tell him where his gun was, she'd sat up too quickly, her head pounding so hard she thought she'd upchuck her undigested dinner. It took her a moment to get a story out of him as he yanked open drawers and grabbed clothes, rushing around the house in a whirlwind.

And then it hit her. He was going after sweet li'l Grace, who'd been kidnapped in the middle of the night. With a hand over her mouth to suppress her glee, she'd pointed at the top of the wardrobe, where his Remington sat, then buried her head under the covers, listening to his rage spread through the house. And then she heard his boots tromp out the door, and the house fell quiet once more.

She couldn't have planned it better. Malcolm would go hunting for Grace, along with the posse she assumed the sheriff would organize, and when he found her, he'd find Clayton as well. She could just imagine what Clayton would do to him. Malcolm had no idea what danger he was walking into, nosiree. She hoped Clayton would get the chance to use his long, sharp knife on her hurtful, heartless husband before the sheriff killed or arrested him. However it played out would suit her just fine, though. One way or another, Malcolm would suffer. And the outlaws would be shot or hung. And she'd mosey off with bags of gold. Just dandy.

She turned from the door, reminding herself she had to get cracking, all the while wondering how Malcolm had learned about Grace's kidnapping. But that wasn't important. What mattered was that Clayton had done it—he'd taken the woman and her baby and was now riding to the cabin up in Coyote Gulch. The wheels of this locomotive were rolling full speed ahead, and would soon crush the last dregs of the Dutton Gang.

Lenora held a hand to her woozy head, regretting that extra bottle of whiskey she'd drunk before leaving the saloon yesterday evening. She'd had her fun and frolics—she'd needed some release after seeing Clayton in town. Thinking about him shook her to her boots, but she had no doubt Malcolm had gone straight to the sheriff, who would put together a search party. She knew the sheriff had no clue Clayton was the culprit, and she hoped he had the smarts to recognize the outlaws once he caught up with them. How could he not? Clayton's and Billy's mugs were plastered all over town, and a five-thousand-dollar reward was being offered for their capture. But if he didn't . . . well, she had to trust that the sheriff would presume the kidnappers were armed and dangerous, full of evil intent, and so would exercise caution. She'd heard this new sheriff was a deadly shot and had a hankering to round up outlaws.

The gossip about town said his sights were set on catching the last members of the gang. Well, now he'd get his chance, yesiree.

It was time to skedaddle. She stood in the middle of her small nothing of a cabin—her cage she'd been living in these last nine months. Good riddance! How had she borne it this long? But her waiting was paying off, finally. Thoughts of gold and all it could buy propelled her from room to room as she stuffed clothes and toiletries into the saddlebag she'd kept under the bed—just for this moment. When she'd gathered everything she needed—including her Colt .45 and her pouch of bullets—she headed for the back storeroom. She shouldered a stubborn closet door open, then tossed out the broom, cleaning rags, and mop bucket onto the floor.

In the tight dark space, she worked with a pocketknife on the back center panel, prying it up enough for her to slip three fingers underneath. With a hard wiggle, she loosened the panel and popped it out, and the nails she'd hammered it with clattered to the floor. With shaky hands she tugged on the strap of the satchel and pulled it out. She was glad Malcolm had never found her hidden cache—for if he had, her cover would have been blown. But he'd never had cause to examine the back of the mop closet, and that's why she'd stashed all the extra money and the things she'd found the day Montgomery Cunningham washed ashore. She'd hidden not just the bulk of his money but also his name and the keys to his past.

Lenora sniggered. All this time, and the answers he so desperately sought had been only inches away. Then she thought of him chasing after Grace and wondered if some of his memories had come back. Or if he'd been seeing Grace without Lenora knowing about it. She imagined that the day he saved her and the brat maybe something had clicked. If he fell in love with Grace before, it was likely he'd do so again. Maybe that was fate? Who knew? Who cared?

Lenora plopped down on the floor, and with legs spread under her calico skirts, she dumped the contents of the satchel in her lap. Five bundles of dollar bills tumbled out, followed by letters and sheets of paper that floated like feathers to lie on top of the money. She glanced briefly at the few bits and pieces of Montgomery Cunningham's life: the letter from the land office offering him employment, his letters of recommendation from various men back in Illinois, some of Grace's personal correspondence, the box with her wedding ring, and lastly, his marriage certificate to Grace Ann Wilcox, stamped by the Bloomington courthouse clerk.

Lenora had a mind to tear all the pages into little bits and leave them on the floor, but she chided herself. She was wasting time, and what if someone came looking for her? What if Malcolm came back for something he forgot? She needed to make herself scarce and quickly.

She jumped to her feet, spilling her treasures from her lap. After stuffing the bundles of cash into her saddlebag, she stuffed the papers and box back into the satchel, then worked the leather bag into the wall between the wood boards. Once she replaced the piece of paneling, she realized she had no way to keep it in place unless she dug out a hammer and nails from the tool shed out back. Drat. She didn't have time for this. She could take the satchel with her, maybe dump it somewhere along the way in some bushes.

But why bother? What did it matter anyway? She would be long gone, never to return to this backwash of a town. Using the mop bucket as a brace, she positioned the thin wood panel as best she could, then laid the mop and broom against it to hold it in place. One edge of the panel warped outward, but that was as good as it was going to get. The next time Malcolm took the bucket out, the panel would fall off the wall. But what did she care?

She pictured her poor husband stumbling back into his little house after losing Grace and finding his wife gone for good. He'd mope and fret even more than before, then, one day, he'd discover the loose panel and pull out the satchel. She imagined his surprise as he read through the papers and learned the truth—that he'd been married to Grace . . . but now she was dead.

Lenora did a happy little dance as she swung the saddlebag over one shoulder and skipped out the front door. The morning sun shone in all its beauty down on the spread of open prairie, causing the vegetation to glow like gold. To the west, the snow atop the Rockies sparkled like diamonds. But these treasures of the Front Range were worthless, like fool's gold. The allure of the Wild West was a mirage, a fake. She thought of all the people in this petty little town, seeking their fortunes, hoping to usher in a safe and prosperous future for its citizens.

Lenora snorted as she readied Nugget, her chestnut quarter horse, and threw the saddlebag behind the cantle. After tying the strings to secure it and adjusting the stirrups of her Mexican saddle, she took a last look at her homestead. One hundred and sixty acres of flat, boring land, with a pathetic little muddy creek wending through the acreage. Why anyone wanted to live on the Front Range befuddled her.

She worked the headstall onto her horse and threw the reins over his neck. Without a drop of regret, she mounted and kicked her gelding into a canter, leaving a trail of dust and the identity of Stella Childs Connors behind her.

Alan Patterson stood in front of Whedbee's Mercantile and watched the group of riders gallop out of town, the horses' hooves throwing mud and water into the air as they raced off to find the men who'd kidnapped Grace Cunningham. He pressed back against the store window alongside a dozen or so bystanders who watched, mouths open and hands clutching their hats as their sheriff led a posse west toward the foothills.

Pains assailed his chest and throat as he thought about lovely Grace, the woman he was so sweet on. For the life of him, he couldn't figure how or why anyone would have kidnapped her and her baby, and tried not to think of the horrible things that might happen to her. And he hated feeling so powerless! If only there was something he could do aside from praying.

Alan shook his head, trying to calm his frayed nerves. Ever since he saw those outlaws in the alley yesterday, he'd been a wreck. He couldn't stomach any food, and he hardly slept last night, picturing those killers sneaking into his bedroom to slit his throat. He was sure they saw his fear, sure they'd come after him. But when he woke this morning after finally falling into a hard, dreamless sleep, he realized he'd made it through the night without incident—only to come into town to attend church and learn that Grace had been kidnapped!

He hadn't had a chance to talk to the sheriff before Love rounded up able-bodied men for a posse and rode out of town. But what would Alan have told him anyway? It was clear the sheriff suspected the outlaws were involved. And he'd do everything he could to catch them and get Grace back, safe and sound. Alan knew of the sheriff's fervent love for justice and his just-as-fervent hatred of outlaws like Wymore and Cloyd.

Alan swallowed hard, forcing back tears. It irked him something fierce, thinking about evil men like that—men who'd steal an innocent, helpless baby.

He ambled aimlessly down the street, wending through the crowd that lingered and spoke in excited voices, their words falling incoherently upon his ears. He couldn't get Grace's kind, pretty face out of his head. Of all the women he'd met since moving to Fort Collins, none had caught his fancy the way she had. He often watched her from his office window, when she walked to and from work, or set out on an errand, and he longed to tell her how he felt. But he hadn't much to offer her. He'd always been weak and sickly, and he knew he cut less than a fine figure of a man. But he had a heart full of love, and he had been waiting a long time for just the right gal to walk into his life. He'd thought Grace Cunningham was that gal.

Then, after he spoke with her that day in the park a few weeks back, he started putting some puzzling pieces together. It was after Malcolm Connors had confided in him about his memory loss. And when Connors said he'd had an accident the spring prior—the same time Grace had arrived in town after the big spring flood, claiming her husband had been swept away—well, an idea had wiggled its way into his thoughts, the way ideas often did. And that little idea had grown into a startling realization. Malcolm Connors had to be Grace's husband. There was no dallying around the fact.

Connors had come into Fort Collins with a new wife—Alan had seen her with Malcolm on occasion through the courthouse window. It made sense that if Grace's husband had lost his memory, he'd think nothing of marrying another woman. But what Alan wondered more than anything was, had Grace seen him? For surely if she had, she would have run to him and claimed him . . . only to suffer the shock of his disregard.

At that thought he concluded she *had* encountered him, for her deep-seated sadness seemed ever fresh, as if paining her daily. He couldn't imagine the suffering it caused her. And now . . .

Alan rubbed his eyes and wallowed in his own pool of wretchedness. His thoughts drifted to Malcolm's anguished face, the day he came asking for help to find surveyors in St. Louis. Now Alan wondered why he said that's where he'd come from—when Grace had told him she had hailed from Illinois. Odd. Maybe that new wife of his was from St. Louis. But why would she tell her husband that's where he was from too—when he wasn't?

Alan stopped in the middle of the boardwalk, and his breath hitched. He tried to bring to mind Malcolm's wife. He recalled her name was Stella. She had raven-black hair and beguiling eyes. She carried herself with an air of wealth and sophistication . . .

He gulped past the rock in his throat and squinched his eyes in confusion. Another idea wiggled into his mind, but this one seemed preposterous. Yet, it had the undeniable smack of truth. That woman he had seen near the alley yesterday—that was Stella Connors. He was sure of it now. Same hair and face, same fancy clothing, same manner and comportment. Just what in the world would Malcolm's wife be doing in that disreputable, seedy part of town—and dressed like a floozy saloon girl?

He knew the answer but didn't want to believe what his own eyes had bore witness to. Stella Connors had been talking to Clayton Wymore and Billy Cloyd. He'd caught her watching them with the eye of someone who knew exactly who they were and what they were up to. She wasn't looking at two strangers in curiosity or wariness.

Stella Connors was not who people thought she was. Alan was certain she had lied to Malcolm about St. Louis. Malcolm Connors had come into Alan's office like a man at the end of his rope, desperate for the truth. What else had she lied about? He wondered.

This all pointed back to Grace somehow. He just had a hunch. Something very suspicious was going on. Grace had been kidnapped, and for some reason Malcolm had ridden off with the posse, leaving his wife behind. Alan had seen him on his horse, his face morose and worried. Why would a surveyor join a posse to go after deadly outlaws? Had Malcolm met Grace, talked to her? Had he suddenly remembered who she was?

None of Alan's musings was getting him anywhere, and his stomach ached thinking about poor Grace. He just couldn't spend his day walking in circles, worrying.

Presently, another idea came to him, although he wasn't sure how it would help Grace. He spun around and hurried back to the courthouse, which was closed today, but he had his key. It wouldn't take but a moment to look up the land claim Malcolm had filed—showing where his quarter section homestead was located. Maybe Stella Connors was home, waiting for her husband to come back. He doubted the likes of her would be at church this late Sunday morning.

Well, Alan would pay her a neighborly visit.

Chapter 21

GRACE'S HEAD JERKED FORWARD, AND her eyelids flew open. Nausea and dizziness assailed her as she strained to see her surroundings. An awful sour stench met her nose. Every muscle in her body throbbed in agony, and as she made to move her arms, panic struck her chest. She was tied with a thick hemp rope, trussed up like a holiday goose.

Instantly alert, her nerves jostled with fear as her hazy vision made out two arms in tawny leather coat sleeves encircling her waist and the pommel of a saddle in front of her lap. A horse's reins lay gripped in a gloved fist. She was on a lathering horse, which was clomping in a steady gait up a slope—with a man sitting behind her! He stank to high heavens of sweat, bitter tobacco, and putrid breath, which made her gag.

Ben! Where was her baby?

A scream erupted out of her mouth, but her captor slapped a hot gloved hand over her face. The air sweltered with heat.

"Hush, now. There's no one around for miles, anyways. No point in wastin' yer breath." His gruff voice, icy cold and heartless, made Grace shudder in terror.

With his smelly, dirty glove smashing her lips, she darted her head from side to side, taking in the steep mountain terrain, the pockmarked mounds of melting snow, the harsh glare of sunlight splintering through the boughs of pine trees and that stabbed her eyes. The scent of water saturated the air, and she heard a river tumbling over rocks to her right. She was in a narrow canyon with steep stony walls, and up ahead, half-hidden by the shade of thick branches, another man rode on a buckskin horse.

"You gonna cooperate?" the man said, relaxing the pressure on her mouth. She couldn't guess his age by his voice. Why in heaven he'd taken her and Ben? She nodded, frantic to know if her baby was safe.

The second his hand fell away, she whimpered, "Where's my baby? I swear if you hurt him—"

"Now, don't git your petticoats in a bunch," he scolded her from behind, returning his hand back to her waist, where he now fingered her nightdress. Oh horrors, she was wearing only her sleeping gown, and she could feel his fingers through the leather of his gloves playing with her skin!

"Please," she moaned, "stop . . ."

He laughed then—a cruel laugh that shot more panic through her heart.

She gulped, imagining the evil the man intended to inflict upon her. The realization that she—and Ben—were doomed to suffer and die at the hands of this despicable villain made her stomach lurch and blood rush to her head.

Underneath her terror, though, anger churned. She squirmed against her ropes and her captor's arms. "Where is my son? What have you done with him?"

"Stop caterwauling, for cryin' out loud—he's unharmed." The man raised a hand and pointed to the rider ahead. "Billy's got him." He then pressed his scratchy cheek against the side of her face and blew rancid hot breath into her ear as he whispered harshly, "And he'll stay that way so long's you cooperate, you understand?"

The man's touch made her sick, and she gagged, pushing down the contents of last night's dinner threatening to eject out of her mouth. Despair suffocated her, and all she could do was whimper in helplessness and give him a feeble nod. She swallowed as perspiration dripped down her back in the heat of the day. Memories of her abduction rushed to her thoughts—she'd heard the Franklins in the kitchen when the men invaded the house. Were they dead? She sorely hoped not. And hoped they'd run to the sheriff. Surely they would have. But would he do anything about it? Would anyone know where to look for her? Clearly they were miles from Fort Collins, somewhere to the west. Oh why had they taken her, and where were they headed? What did they want from her? She had nothing of value, if this vile man intended to demand some kind of ransom.

She strained to listen for Ben's cry, but she was too far away from the other rider to make out any sounds beyond the tromping of horse hooves and her captor's heavy breathing. She had to remain calm, to cooperate. Ben's life depended on it. She shuddered. She would do . . . anything. Whatever these men wanted—*anything, she instructed herself*—to ensure Ben's safety. Even forfeit her life.

Oh, Lord, please don't let it come to that!

Grace stiffened in agony as the man's leather-encased fingers explored her waist and stroked her thighs. She heard him moan behind her as he pressed his chest tighter against her back and lifted a hand to caress her cheek. She held her breath and gritted her teeth, squelching the terror as best she could, trying not to move, trying desperately to think how she could escape his lewd advances, but there was nothing for it. She was at his mercy—and she doubted this man had an ounce of it.

Oh, Monty, I need you. Where are you? She forced her mind to think of his kind, gentle face, his smile, his love for her that lay locked in his heart. Her captor said nothing more as the horse picked up a trot, the terrain canting more steeply now, and continued his violation of her body. He pulled off his gloves, and his rough, calloused hands prodded and squeezed her flesh in places no man but her husband should ever be free to touch.

She whimpered harder, knowing if she resisted or fought or screamed, Ben might be punished in payment, so she bore the probing and quelled her disgust and horror by keenly noting her surroundings. If by some chance she could escape, she needed to find her way back to the Front Range. The white pines grew thick in the narrow cut they were now traversing, with dwarfed twisted scrubby spruce poking from the rock walls on both sides. They appeared to be following a deer track up to the top of a ridge. Maybe once they crested the mountain, she'd be afforded a good look at the layout of the land, and get her bearings.

Her thoughts turned to Ben, knowing he must be hungry and wet. She was grateful he was so young. Although he might be unhappy, he didn't understand the peril he was in. Her arms ached to hold him, to comfort him. Being this close but unable to mother him was another torture.

The man put his lips on Grace's neck, and she cried out, tears exploding from her eyes. "I need . . . I need to feed my baby. He must be hungry. Please . . ."

"There'll be time fer that later," the man said as he slobbered her neck with his wet lips. "Much later . . . after we spend some time gittin' to know each other . . ." His hands suddenly grabbed her breasts hard, and Grace squealed in pain and thrashed about. "Ah, I like a gal that puts up a fight. You're a right purty gal, as fine as they come. And I have a burnin' need, one you kin satisfy fer me . . ."

Grace clenched her eyes and let hopelessness engulf her. So this was to be her fate. She'd suffered the loss of her husband and the ensuing grief, then the bitter agony of seeing Monty married to another woman . . . and now she would die, but not until after suffering violence at the hands of evil men. She had no doubt that once they were through with her, they would kill her and Ben.

But why had they taken her baby, if all they wanted was a woman to ravage? Then, she understood. They meant to sell him off to someone. She'd heard of men doing that—for money. As awful as it sounded, she clung to that hope, for it would at least ensure her baby—her precious baby—would live. And maybe someone would love him, care for him . . .

She could no longer hold back her flood of anguish. It broke through the dam of her weakened resolve and she wept in great sobbing heaves, barely aware of her captor's amused laugh and frolicking fingers on her body.

And then, after some time had elapsed—how much, she had no idea—the horse stopped. Grace lifted her weary, grief-laden head and saw they had arrived at a small clearing of sedge grass and melting snow mounds. The other rider was dismounting his horse—with a bundle in his arms. Ben!

And then her eye caught a glimpse of a structure through a copse of aspens. A cabin sided with weathered hewn wood sat nestled back against a sheer wall of rock that towered high above the trees. The horses snuffled at their bits in the midday sun that beat down on Grace's woozy head.

The man—her captor had called him Billy, she now recalled—strode toward them, and now in the quiet of the secluded surroundings, she heard Ben's pathetic mewling, and her heart raced. Still bound with rope—still held tightly by this vile man—she could do nothing about the yearning she had to run to her baby and yank him out of Billy's arms.

"He's hungry and wet, Clay," Billy said, a frown on his clean-shaven young face. Grace was startled—Billy looked younger than she, hardly a grown man. She caught what she hoped was a glimmer of compassion on his face.

"Let me feed him—" she begged.

A hand flew to her face. Her cheek erupted in heat as her captor backhanded her, knocking her head to the side. She screamed, uncaring if it angered the man. What did it matter? Her fate was sealed. He would have his way with her and kill her. Whether she cooperated and bore up under their torture or fought with all her might, she was dead. She may as well fight.

With her limbs tied, she did the only thing she could—she leaned forward, then thrust her head back as hard as she could and smacked the man in his face.

"Ow!" he yelled. His strong arms lifted her from the saddle and flung her to the hard dirt. He spat in her face. She groaned at the sudden stab of pain in her shoulder and rolled away from the horse's legs that pranced and stomped, startled by her fall. The back of her head—where it had met with the man's hard forehead—throbbed as well.

"Why'd ya have to do that, Clayton?" Billy asked, his face twisted in a scowl of disapproval.

Grace turned her head slowly, despite the shooting pain up her neck, and studied the young man that held her baby with tenderness. *Thank you, Lord, for this singular kindness.* At least Ben was uninjured. She was grateful Billy had been the one carrying her son—and not this . . . Clayton.

Clayton . . . Billy . . .

Her breath snagged in her throat. She dared glance up at the face that glowered at her from the horse's back. Her eyes widened in recognition as he cocked his head and spit off to the side. A new stab of pain streaked through her gut, and she shook all over, despite the heat of the midday sun.

Oh, Lord, no, please . . . But she knew now who her captives were. She'd seen their likenesses on the posters around town. Worse, she'd heard stories of Clayton Wymore's cruelty and lust for blood. How he liked to cut his victims with a knife, relishing the slow torture he inflicted upon them.

This was a fate worse than death, Grace now realized. She looked to Billy Cloyd, hoping against hope that maybe he'd help her. Have pity on her and her baby. By why would he? He'd helped kidnap her. He was a member of the notorious Dutton Gang. Yet, through her pain and terror, she sensed something awry. They were bank robbers—what were they doing kidnapping? Had they taken her just for a bit of entertainment? Diversion? Why travel this far up into the mountains for that? Surely if they wanted to have their way with a woman, they could have done so without so much arduous effort. No, there was something else, some other reason. But what?

Grace beseeched Billy with her eyes.

"Let her have her baby," Billy scolded Clayton. "We decided we'd wait for Lenora to get here anyways—"

Lenora? Who is Lenora?

"Hobble yer lip, Billy," Clayton warned him, then huffed. He dismounted and handed the reins to Billy, then set about untying the rough ropes chafing her wrists and ankles. She felt naked before these men as she stumbled to her feet and thrust out her arms for her baby, standing in the midst of the clearing in her thin, sheer nightdress.

Her body went limp with relief when Billy handed Ben to her, and sobs erupted in her throat as she looked into her baby's sad little face. She smoothed back his wisps of hair as her tears sprinkled his dirt-stained cheeks. His diaper was wet and heavy, and his sleeping gown was torn and damp from Billy's sweat. She held Ben against her heart, wondering if this would be the last time she would ever feel him in her arms. She winced from the agony of that thought.

"You gonna feed him?" Clayton asked, a twisted smile on his face as he leered at her. "Then go ahead."

Grace started to walk toward the cabin, but Clayton roughhandled her, grabbing her wrist and stopping her. "Do it here. So's I kin watch." His cruel laugh was a knife to her heart. "Nothin' so sweet and tender as a sucklin' babe at a breast." He laughed harder, but Grace noticed Billy continued to scowl—although the young man said nothing, clearly not wanting to rouse Clayton's ire. It was clear who was the boss.

"Nope, nothing like sucklin' on a creamy white breast." Clayton licked his lips and pointed to the ground in front of him. "So sit there and suckle." He added, "And I'll watch."

Grace hesitated, but Ben's renewed complaints won over her fury and embarrassment. Her son needed to nurse, and smothering her own misery and humiliation, she began unbuttoning the top of her nightdress, tears trickling down her cheeks and onto her baby's soft fine hair. She closed her eyes as she dropped to the dirt and prayed fervent prayers while she nursed him, pretending for this brief moment that she was in her safe, happy home, Monty snuggled up beside her, stroking her hair and gazing with love and adoration at his son, and all was right with the world. Even though nothing could be further from the truth.

"This way," LeRoy said, getting up from his crouched position and pointing over the scramble of broken rock at the base of a narrow cut in the cliffs.

Malcolm shifted his weight on his quarter horse, antsy to keep moving. The men had said little once they rode out of town, with the sheriff deferring to the two Indian trackers as to which direction to go. And so far the trail had been easy to spot with the soft ground. Malcolm worried the posse would be stymied upon reaching the base of the Rockies, but so far they'd made good progress, keeping up a breakneck speed.

The day was heating up, though, and the horses were lathering. They now stood snorting hard and pawing the hardscrabble ground. The riders had crossed miles of dry open range without seeing any sign of water, but Malcolm sensed a river was near. How he knew, he couldn't say. But it was as if he felt it in his blood.

LeRoy swung up onto his paint—a smallish horse with a white blaze down its face. Malcolm was impressed with the way the young men rode, and he was grateful they'd joined this posse—and he could tell Sheriff Love felt likewise. Malcolm looked over at the deputies, who chatted quietly with Marcus Coon. The older deputy, Stapleton, Malcolm had learned, had once upon a time been a Texas Ranger. And Coon had been in law enforcement in Indiana before moving to the Front Range. Malcolm felt confident they had enough experienced men to handle the firepower they jointly wielded. For if the sheriff's hunch was correct, and the men who'd kidnapped

Grace were indeed the wanted outlaws, they'd need every advantage possible.

Malcolm's heart wrenched in worry over Grace and little Ben. While they rode across the flat land, he'd let the pounding of hooves and the wind scratching his face sweep away his thoughts of her—and his fierce need for her—for he knew indulging in his fear would only hinder his concentration. He couldn't afford a misstep or accident, and although he knew his horse had sure footing, the Front Range was a mess of prairie dog holes and low, thick scrub brush and prickly pear cactus, which could trip up the most agile of mounts. Malcolm had forced himself to give close attendance to the buckle and swell of the terrain, and gave Rambler his head as they galloped as if the hounds of hell were nipping at their horses' tails.

"All right, let's keep going," Sheriff Love said with a stern expression, his jaw clenched, nodding at the trackers to start up the cut. His gaze shifted to the top of the mountain, and he narrowed his eyes.

The going was slower and arduous now, with the horses slipping and righting as they sought purchase for their feet, which set loose tumbles of boulders that ricocheted down the steep cliff. Just how far up the mountain had those outlaws taken Grace and the baby? Anguish bubbled up again. Why? Why would they take her?

He'd ask himself the same questions over and over, hoping an answer would come to him through sheer repetition. But, like the others riding alongside him, he could fathom no reason for two wanted bank robbers to kidnap a woman and her baby. It made not a lick of sense. It wasn't like they'd snatched her off the street or from a country road. They'd broken into a house, with clear deliberation. Which meant they knew Grace had been inside. So they either knew her or knew about her. What was her connection to outlaws?

Malcolm kept a loose rein on Rambler as he leaned forward on the ascent up the steep rocky escarpment. He couldn't see any trail, not even a deer track, through this jumble of dirt and rock. But the two Banks boys urged their horses on without hesitation, and then, when Malcolm crested the tight pass above him, he heard water.

They cantered across a fairly flat ledge that funneled into a dense forest. Close to the tree line, the spruce and pine had taken a beating from snow and wind, and they tangled together in squat bunches with down-hanging branches. Now Malcolm spotted the glint of a river to the north-northeast, a few hundred feet lower in elevation. Its murmur tickled his ears as it cascaded in wild abandon over boulders and waterfalled over cliffs. When they entered the woods, they slowed.

Eli and LeRoy conferred, then Eli swung his mustang around to face them and yelled over to the rest of the posse, "These prints are hardly an hour old. The must've rested their horses a spell." LeRoy had told them when they first set out that the outlaws had four to five hours on them.

The sheriff grinned. "They either aren't expecting to be followed or something's slowing them down." He smoothed his moustache and pushed his hat down on his head. "Keep alert. We might miss something. Or someone."

At his gesture, they pressed on, with Malcolm pulling up the rear, trotting where possible and walking their mounts when the trees and alpine sagebrush grew too thick. They stopped momentarily at a crawling creek to water their horses, but other than the brief reprieve, they worked their mounts hard in pursuit. Malcolm's shirt stuck to his back, and the cooler rarified mountain air that slithered down the Rockies into their glen refreshed him and cleared his head. He was thankful for the warm, clear day that allowed them to make fast progress up the mountain. At some point the trail would end—somewhere. It was clear these outlaws had a destination in mind, for their tracks had led straight up the side of the mountain into this wood tucked between towering cliffs. They'd have to have known this trail was here.

Suddenly the riders in front of him stopped. LeRoy raised his arm and waved them back. They fell quiet, not saying a word as the two brothers slipped soundlessly from their mounts and signaled the posse to wait. Malcolm caught Eli looking at him, hesitating, a strange expression on his face, as if he wanted to say something directly to him. Odd.

He'd noticed back in town the way the two brothers had studied him. As if they knew him, or knew about him. Their weighty consideration of him unsettled him, but he sensed no malice. Rather, they seemed curious about him, and from time to time as they'd ridden west, one or the other had glanced over at him. He'd heard they lived over by Greeley, but the months he'd spent in the cabin with Stella, he'd never encountered them—not on the road or in town the few times he'd gone there. Maybe they'd met Stella and she had talked about him.

LeRoy whispered something to his horse, and then he and Eli disappeared into the trees. Their mustangs stayed where they were left, not flinching a muscle, and the woods were thick with quiet, the only sounds the huffing of the horses and the squeak of leather as the riders shifted in their saddles. The men around him locked watchful, alert gazes in the direction the brothers had gone. Malcolm saw the sheriff fingering the gun at his side. Marcus Coon chewed his lip, and the two deputies sat as still as wolves eying a rabbit.

Sitting there, unmoving, the thoughts of Grace that he'd swept clean from his mind galloped back in like a herd of wild horses. With sweet pain he envisioned her pretty smile and gentle laugh, and anger swelled to bursting thinking those men might harm her and in what horrible ways they'd inflict pain upon her and the baby.

He seethed as he sat, his every nerve afire with the need to rescue her. It took all his resolve not to jump off his horse and rush through the trees yelling her name.

Movement caught his eye, and he sucked in a breath. But it was only the Indian trackers. The two slipped through trees in silence and came up to the sheriff's side. Malcolm couldn't hear what LeRoy whispered to Eph Love, but he didn't have to. He knew what the Indian was telling him. A shiver jolted across Malcolm's neck as his pent-up anger sprang a leak and filled his heart with rage.

They'd found the outlaws.

Lenora yanked on the reins, but Nugget refused to comply. Well, fine. She wasn't far from the cabin—maybe a mile at most. She'd run her horse hard, and he was played out. There was nothing for it but for her to leave him and hoof it over this last steep ridge.

After untying the saddlebag and stuffing the short-handled shovel inside it, she slid the headstall off her gelding. Without prompting, the frothing horse clambered back down the mountainside, toward the grassy gulch below. This high up snow still covered most of the ground, but it was melting fast, and rivulets of water poured in sluices down the rock wall of the canyon, emptying into the swollen noisy river below her. She'd ridden farther north than she'd done before, but she couldn't take a chance of running into Clayton. She knew he'd have taken the shortest, easiest way to the cabin, and she hoped the sheriff was hot on his tail.

When she raced off from the homestead, she'd given in to her burning curiosity and ridden to the center of town, only to discover the whole place aflurry with talk about the posse and the kidnapping. She didn't stay long enough to hear the Dutton Gang mentioned, but it didn't matter. If the posse was tracking her "pals," they'd find them at the cabin—where they were waiting for her. Unless they caught the pair on their way, slowed by the woman and her baby. Either way was fine by her, yesiree.

Taking care not to trip over the piles of rocks littering the trickling draw, she ambled her way up the outcropping, keeping her eyes fixed ahead, not daring to look down at the dizzying canyon a mile below. She breathed hard from exertion and elevation, and her hair matted to her head. Her stomach grumbled, and she chided herself for not eating something before she left. In her haste, she'd forgotten to pack any food, and her drinking bout the day prior had left her with an unabating headache. But she consoled herself. *There's only a half mile between you and that box of gold.* What did a little hunger or hangover matter?

Chapter 22

"I DON'T LIKE THIS, CLAY," Billy said, stepping in front of Grace, his legs widespread in a protective stance. "Just think it through."

Clayton's face twisted in anger. "I've thought it through. We need Lenora to tell us where the gold is, and she ain't gonna do it less'n we give her what she wants."

Another mention of that woman, Lenora. Who was she? Grace stood in the dank log cabin with her back pressed against the wall. She now understood why these outlaws had come to this abandoned cabin—for gold. No doubt bounty from the gang's many robberies over the years. She looked down at her baby sleeping in her arms. The ride up here, the thin air, and his stress from being wet and hungry had knocked him out. A mercy she was grateful for.

After she had fed Ben, Clayton had pushed her into the cabin with such roughness that she tripped and almost dropped her baby. He'd then made advances on her, grabbing the collar of her nightdress and ripping it open, while she tried to slap him, yelling at him to stop and shielding Ben from his clawing.

Just when she thought all hope was lost, Billy shouldered into the cabin and yelled at him to stop. An argument ensued, and Grace's heart thumped as she looked for any way to escape while they bickered. But she knew if she made a move toward the door, she'd face Clayton's wrath. She could do nothing but wait and watch as the tension built between the two men.

"You know as well as I do that she's set a trap," Clayton said, huffing, then reached over to the crate that served as a table and picked up a flint box and opened it. A scant stream of sunlight shone into the one-room shack, and Grace could barely make out the expression on his face. But she felt his rage.

"And I mean to set one fer her." He pointed an accusing finger at Grace and added, "And she'll only get in the way."

Billy set his face, his hands on his hips. "So we tie her up. You don't have to kill her."

"Lenora wants her dead. And I'm of the same mind. Last thing we need is a witness that might testify against us someday."

Dead? Grace swallowed hard. This must be a mistake. "I don't know anyone named Lenor—"

"Quit yer yammerin'," Clayton yelled at her.

Grace pressed her lips tight and shivered in fear even though the room was stiflingly warm. Why would some woman she didn't know want her dead? Why her? Was this a case of mistaken identity? If only these men would listen to her.

Clayton deftly struck the flint and sparked the wick in a kerosene lamp on the crate that illuminated two ratty, threadbare armchairs. The cabin was practically empty, and with the soft glow from the lantern, it was apparent that no one had been here in a long while. A coating of dust lay over the wide-plank floorboards and sparse furnishings, which consisted of a small tick mattress on a low cot and a warped wood slab dining table and two rickety wood chairs.

Billy took a step toward Clayton with his arms outstretched. "I'm jus' sayin'—"

Clayton spun around and stomped up to Billy's face. Grace gasped and inched away, steering clear of his swinging arm. She laid Ben on the cot with care, hoping he'd stay asleep. That somehow he'd be safe there for the moment.

Grace trembled as Clayton struck Billy in the shoulder with his fist, throwing him back against the wall. Billy put up his hands in defense.

"I don't want a fight," Billy ground out.

"Well, I'm itchin' fer one. Since you seem to wanna run this show."

"I don't. I . . . I just don't want you to hurt her."

Grace noted the determined look on the younger man's face, but it gave her little hope. She was certain Billy would not risk his own life to protect hers. And even if he tried, no doubt Clayton would win the contest of wills.

Clayton wagged his head slowly from side to side. "What's wrong with you? Here's a nice piece, all for the takin', and yer actin' all high and mighty all o' the sudden." He grabbed Billy by the arm and yanked him toward the door. "So's if you don't want any of this, then git out and stand watch for Lenora. And don't come in. I plan to take my sweet time with this purty thing . . ."

He handily threw Billy out the door, and turned his attention back to Grace. She gulped and shook anew as he marched over to her and grabbed her roughly. Before she could suck in a breath, his slobbery lips pressed against hers, and he thrust her tightly against his body. His rough trousers rubbed her legs raw through her thin gown as he twisted and clawed at her skin, his hands roaming freely, hurting her as he pinched and bit her mercilessly, like a man gone mad.

Grace screamed and thrashed, but he pinned her arms to her sides as he pushed her into a corner.

"Please, please . . ." she begged, knowing it was a futile attempt, and only seemed to flame the fire of his passion. He grabbed her by the throat to hold her in place, like a captive bird, and used his other hand to unbutton his trousers and drop his cartridge belt to the floor. Grace clenched her eyes shut as his pants slipped to the dust-choked floor, and let out a garbled scream as his hand crushed her windpipe.

A sharp creak made her open her eyes. The front door flew open. Billy strode in, and the flicker of the lamp's wick glinted on the gun he wielded.

Clayton's hand fell from Grace's throat. She coughed and clutched at her neck, stumbling away as Clayton let loose a string of curses at Billy. *Shoot him!* she begged Billy in her head, as she watched Clayton reach down for his revolver that lay at his feet.

"Why you lunkhead . . ." Clayton said, mean spite in his eyes. Instead of grabbing his gun, he jerked suddenly and lunged for Billy. He tumbled to the floor on top of him. Billy's gun flew out of his hand and skittered across the floor as he careened into the table, which splintered into pieces.

Now was her chance! Shaking hard, she fumbled along the floorboards and found Clayton's holster. The heavy revolver was jammed in tight, and Grace yanked with all her strength to get it free. But just as she had the heel of the gun in hand, Clayton swung around and whacked her head with his arm and sent her crashing to the floor, a shock of pain erasing her vision.

She held her reeling head and scurried backward across the room, away from his reach. She cowered in a corner as Billy jumped to his feet and barreled into Clayton.

Ben wailed from the cot, then clambered down on his little wobbly legs, his arms out, searching for her. She hugged the wall and worked her way to her baby, then scooped him up and retreated to the farthest corner, away from the men's swinging arms.

If only she could get a gun! She knew if she tried to escape, Clayton would shoot her.

She pulled Ben in tight and curled up in a ball, listening in horror to the blows the men landed on each other. With grunts and curses, they fought like two trapped wildcats, snarling and snapping, and tearing the cabin apart. She cried and ducked her head as a jagged piece of wood flew past her ear and ricocheted off the wall.

Ben cried in her arms, and Grace held her breath, hoping against hope that Billy would somehow best Clayton, or the two would just kill each other. But then, she heard Billy howl like a sick dog.

Clayton, snorting like a locomotive, stepped back from Billy as the younger man fell to the floor, clutching his gut and flailing about, trying to pull himself up alongside the crate in the center of the room. Grace's mouth dropped open in horror as her eyes caught the knife in Clayton's hand, which dripped blood in drops that looked like rubies in the lantern light.

"You had that comin' fer a long time," Clayton seethed, sheathing his knife down his boot, and spitting on the floor. "Good riddance." As if for good measure, he slammed his booted foot into Billy's bloody side.

Billy moaned and panted hard. The cabin fell quiet as Clayton turned and spotted Grace where she huddled. A smile twisted his face as he stared at her and wiped sweat from his forehead, the fire of lust rekindled in his eyes and his nostrils flaring.

Ben whimpered into Grace's chest, and her last tiny thread of hope snapped. She'd had her chance and lost it. Now she would suffer, and no doubt Ben would too. If she had the courage, she would suffocate her son and spare him the horrible torture she knew was about to come upon him. Grace had no doubt this monster would use his knife on Ben as a way to make her cooperate. Or just to make her suffer even more. *Oh, God. Give me the strength to do it. To end my precious baby's life.*

She hugged him tightly, her tears soaking his head, her heart broken beyond repair. With a moan of agony, she placed her shaky hands around Ben's neck, feeling his soft, tender skin around his throat, looking to heaven, praying God would take him quickly. For that was the only safe place now, for her precious baby—in God's loving arms. She did not doubt He would welcome Ben to heaven, although she knew she was doomed for eternity for what she was about to do. But she did not care about her immortal soul. She would not leave Ben's fate to the cruelties of this murderous villain, regardless of her fate.

Then, Clayton stopped and stiffened. Outside, the horses whinnied. Anger and fright seared Clayton's eyes for a brief second, and then he spun around and rushed to the door. With caution, he peeked out. Grace exhaled in reprieve and loosened her grip on Ben, who wriggled in her arms and protested by babbling at her. Her heart hammered in accusation, for what she had almost done. *Thank you, Lord, for staying my hand.*

"Shh," she whispered to her baby with trembling lips, stroking his head, relishing him alive in her arms. But what was transpiring? Had this Lenora arrived? Or was someone else there—maybe someone come to rescue her? Dared she hope?

Billy groaned again, and Grace turned to see him clawing at the crate. In her fright she'd forgotten him, thinking he was dead. Blood pooled all around him. Surely there was nothing she could do to help him. She had to flee—she'd been given another chance. Yet, how could she leave this man to suffer? He'd tried to save her life. The least she could do was help him somehow. But, how? She couldn't carry him. If the sheriff came, she could urge him to get Billy to a doctor.

If she managed to get away . . .

To her surprise, Clayton tore out of the cabin. Grace looked around, this time noting there was no other door leading outside. Her gaze strayed to the windows to her left. She looked at Billy, whose glassy pain-struck eyes encouraged her. With a barely perceptible nod toward the windows, he urged her to go, to leave him.

"Thank you," she said, a new flood of tears flowing down her face. "For saving us." She wanted to say so much more, but his head thumped to the floor and his eyes closed. He lay on his back with his hands trying to staunch his wound, but dark blood oozed out steadily between his fingers.

Then, to Grace's shock, his fingers clawed toward the lantern, and with a weak swipe of his hand, he knocked it to the floor. The glass shattered, and fire spread like liquid across the wood floor, licking at the legs of the chairs, the dry wood crackling into flames before her shocked eyes.

She hesitated in horror, then heard a noise out front. She could dally no longer. With a surge of resolve, she ran to the nearest window and pushed on it, trying to slide it open with one hand while clinging to Ben, but it wouldn't budge. A tin pail sat in the corner, with a broom alongside it. Grace set Ben on the floor away from the window, then grabbed the wooden handle and smashed it into the glass, which shattered in a thousand pieces.

Without waiting to see if Clayton heard the noise, she poked at the remaining shards still attached to the sash, then gingerly climbed out, shielding Ben with her arm and ducking her head as smoke and heat from the voracious flames swirled around her. Thankfully the window was fairly low to the ground, and when she tumbled out, neither was hurt.

She stared back into the cabin, aggrieved, overwhelmed with helplessness, but the thick smoke blocked out any view of Billy. How could she leave him to die like that?

Why had Billy started the fire? Surely he would burn to death. Then she guessed his reason—it might keep Clayton from coming back looking for her. With the cabin in flames, maybe Clayton would assume she had died, which was his intent. Her death for the gold. From someone named Lenora, who wanted her dead. What madness was this?

Her body ached from the hard, uncomfortable ride up the mountain and from Clayton's mean handling, but she was alive, and she could run. She listened for a moment, but couldn't hear Clayton on the other side of the cabin, or the horses. The day was draped in deathly silence, even as smoke billowed in great plumes out the open window. Any moment now the building would erupt in raging flames—and then the woods would be set afire. She dared not go back to the trail they'd followed—no doubt Clayton would spot her. Her only hope lay in finding another way down the steep ridge.

With a prayer of thanksgiving for her unexpected deliverance—and her heart heavy with grief and gratitude for the gift of salvation—she hurried downslope, clutching Ben—who seemed to get heavier by the minute—through thick brush that scratched and raked her skin, unmindful and uncaring where she was headed, so long as she put a distance between her and her captor. She knew he could find her, and that he would come after her once he noticed her gone. It was only a matter of time.

She chided herself for not taking Billy's gun, which had slid across the floor. Spurred on by a renewed surge of fear, she quickened her pace as the slope grew steeper and the ground slippery and wet from the melting patches of snow.

Suddenly, her feet gave out from under her, and she found herself sliding down a mud-slick ravine into a gaping dark chasm.

She screamed and clutched Ben hard, unable to grab at a bush or branch for fear of losing grip of her son. Together they fell, until Grace's back smacked hard ground. Pain shot through her back and legs, and her head was thrown back upon impact. Her neck spasmed, and she whimpered as Ben tumbled out of her arms onto a flat muddy ledge. A glance upward showed twenty feet of sheer cliff, with no vegetation clinging to the rock face. She crawled to the edge of the ledge, pushing Ben back with her feet and telling him, "No, Ben. Stay there. Stay."

Her throat choked anew at the sight. Below her, hundreds of feet straight down, a river raged, water spilling over its banks as it cascaded down treacherous drops through a narrow canyon. There was no way down, to any safe place. And no way back up the mountain. And one look at the ledge they were on showed it eroding and cracking from the sluices of water gouging into the side of the cliff and pouring down around her feet.

They were trapped.

She may as well have been killed by Clayton Wymore. It was only a matter of time before they would fall to their deaths, to the river below. There was only one thing she could do—two things—but she doubted either would help. Yet, she had no other recourse, so she prayed with all her soul that God would deliver her—and then she started screaming.

Chapter 23

MALCOLM RAN IN A CROUCH behind Stapleton to the next tree. He couldn't see past the deputy, but knew to follow his lead. Soundlessly the posse rushed through the woods, darting from tree to tree, and then Malcolm froze. He smelled smoke from a fire.

He and the deputy caught up with the sheriff, who stood stiff and still behind a large sugar pine, conferring with Coon, O'Grady, and the two trackers.

"Look." LeRoy pointed ahead. Malcolm now made out a dark structure set back against a sheer wall of rock. Smoke drifted from the side of what he guessed was a wood-sided cabin.

Eli ran toward the cabin, bent over, studying the ground.

Malcolm's gut knotted. Fear raced like blood through his veins. Grace! Was she in there? His legs screamed to run, but LeRoy stayed him with his hand, startling him. Malcolm looked into the tracker's eyes and saw a strange expression.

"Just wait," LeRoy told him firmly but kindly. "We'll find Grace. But no sense gettin' shot up in the attempt." He turned to his brother, who was now running back to them.

"One horse bolted." Eli pointed north of the cabin. "But someone's rode off, and they rode hard—thataway," indicating a rise to the south that led into a dark brushy thicket. He turned to the sheriff. "We'll go git him. You better check out the cabin—see who's inside—before it burns to the ground."

"Go," Sheriff Love instructed, gesturing to the two trackers and drawing his revolver from its holster. "We'll catch up with you." He added, "Be careful."

The brothers nodded and jumped up on their horses, breaking into a run before Malcolm could blow out a breath.

Throwing caution to the wind, the sheriff stormed to the cabin, his deputies on his heels, Malcolm and Coon right behind them. Wood crackled and tongues of flame now licked through cracks in the corrugated tin roof as they made it to the door.

Malcolm spun around, searching for any sign of Grace, of the outlaws, but he saw nothing other than muddy chaotic hoof prints and soft indentations from boots in the damp dirt. He dropped down and studied the ground, noting small footprints—from someone's bare feet. His heart caught in his throat. He had no doubt those were Grace's footprints.

He jumped up and pushed past Coon to get into the cabin. Sheriff Love flung open the door, and out exploded a cloud of dark smoke mingled with fingers of fire through the opening.

"Grace!" Malcolm yelled, his fear for her strangling him. He pulled his shirt up to cover his mouth and nose, and ducking low, ran under the ceiling of thick smoke that blanketed the rafters. Fire gobbled up furniture around them, crackling and snapping like a vicious dog.

Malcolm could barely make out the sheriff rushing ahead of him, then crouching close to the floor.

"Search the cabin," Love yelled, gesturing about wildly. "See if anyone else is in here!"

Malcolm exhaled hard in relief as he saw the sheriff kneeling beside a prone man. His eyes took in the pool of blood the man lay in, and the man's arms clutching his side. The man looked up at the sheriff and said, "Go . . . go . . . get . . . him . . ."

"O'Grady, help me." The sheriff grabbed the wounded man's arms, and the man cried out in pain. O'Grady took hold of the legs, and the two lawmen hefted him and hauled him clumsily toward the door. Malcolm's head pounded from the smoke as he raced around the dark, smoky room, feeling with his hands along the floors and walls and calling Grace's name.

Coon came rushing to his side just as Malcolm discovered glass all along the base of a large window. Smoke poured out the opening, where the window had been smashed.

"There's no one else in here," Coon told him. "Better get out now." He pointed out the window. Burning heat tickled Malcolm's back, and he felt the hair on his neck singe.

Without further hesitation, Malcolm dove out the window, with Coon right behind him.

Malcolm coughed and choked as he rose from the rocky ground and balanced on his hands and knees, trying to suck in clean air as the wind canted smoke into his face.

"Come on," Coon urged, yanking on his arm. "We need to get clear of the fire."

Malcolm stumbled alongside Coon into a stand of aspens. He wiped his soot-filled eyes and looked back. The cabin was now consumed in fire, and heat washed him in waves as he stood agape.

Where was Grace and the baby? He was sure they'd been here. Those had to have been her footprints. He fell to his knees and studied the ground. Had she escaped out that window? She had to be somewhere around. He thanked God he hadn't found her and Ben dead in the cabin. But . . . He swallowed hard. Chances were, whoever had ridden off had taken Grace and Ben with him. She was still in grave danger—especially if the outlaw knew he was being pursued. Would he kill Grace if she slowed him down?

"Let's go," Coon said, pointing at the wall of rock past the thick stand of trees, twenty feet south of the burning cabin. Malcolm made out the sheriff and O'Grady kneeling on the ground. He and Coon hurried over.

"What's he sayin'?" Coon asked Love, dropping to the ground alongside him.

Malcolm looked in the pained face of a young man—one who seemed too young to be a wanted outlaw. He then cringed and spun around as the front side of the cabin buckled and broke to pieces in a roar of flame. Fire licked at the nearby tree branches, and sparks and spatters of soot landed on their faces and shoulders.

"Can we move him?" Stapleton asked the sheriff, whose gaze upon the outlaw glared hard and merciless.

Love shook his head. "He's done for." He looked at Coon. "Said Wymore took off. Looking for some stash o' gold and someone named Lenora." He turned his attention back to the bleeding man, who lay panting in shallow gasps on the ground. Love leaned close to him. "Son, where's the woman you brought?"

Malcolm held his breath, churning with worry as the man closed his eyes and seemed to stop breathing.

"Son, tell us. Did Clayton take her?"

The outlaw said nothing. His head lolled to the side. Malcolm knew without being told that the man was dead. Fear struck him anew as he wondered where Clayton Wymore was taking Grace. If she was still alive.

He stood, recalling how her baby had felt in his arms. He pictured Ben's wispy hair and bright shiny eyes, full of excitement and wonder at the world. He then saw Grace look with such adoration upon her child, her face beaming with love—the kind of love he ached for—from her. How he longed for her, now, in this moment, his longing a sweet pain that tormented him, smothered by the unbearable worry he felt for her and Ben.

In a daze he watched the men around him hurry back to their horses, and heard the sheriff say something about coming back for Billy Cloyd's body. The men yelled to one another, to him, with urgency, but he stood unblinking, looking at the charred, smoldering cabin, tongues of fire hungrily eating up the remains, ashes flitting into his stinging eyes filling with tears.

He thought his heart would break—if it wasn't already broken.

But he couldn't give up hope. If Grace was still alive, she needed him. She needed his love and his clear head. Whatever it took, whatever price he'd have to pay, he would do all in his power to save her. Even face Clayton Wymore—if it came to that. He would gladly stand in the gap between that evil outlaw and the woman he cherished and sacrifice his life defending her. Of this he had no doubt.

His determination seemed to shake him out of his momentary stupor. The others in the posse had already mounted their horses, and Sheriff Love and his deputies galloped past him, weaving through brush and into the heavily timbered woods that sloped up the mountain toward what looked like a narrow pass between two towering walls of rock.

Coon sat his horse, gesturing Malcolm to hurry. He then kicked his horse's flanks and broke into a run, calling out to him as he approached. "Connors—rattle yer hooks—git a move on!"

Malcolm quickened his pace and came up to his horse. But just as he put his foot into the stirrup, he hesitated. Something . . . something felt wrong.

He stopped moving and listened. The sizzle and hiss of fire rent the air, but the woods around him were quiet in the heat of this early summer day except for the drowsy hum of insects. He didn't understand what he was listening for, but his gut told him to wait. His senses prickled, alert.

Then, he heard it. A faint noise coming from the east. He took a few steps toward the remains of the cabin, walking slowly, craning his neck and looking every which way. He paced eastward from where the broken window had been, which was now a pile of collapsed smoldering wood planks. The bunch grass had been trampled, but there was no telling what or who had run over it. His feet led him downslope, through patches of thick manzanita and aspen suckers. Without rhyme or reason, he kept walking, until his boots began to sink into mud.

He stopped and looked down. His chest fluttered as his eyes locked on to the small footprints that ran underfoot, and that smeared into a skid before him as the hillside tilted into a sharp, sudden decline.

Another sound drifted to his ears, this time closer. His blood froze.

It was a scream—a woman's scream. And it was coming from far below him.

He took careful steps in the skiddy mud, grasping branches and working his way, a foot at a time, down the treacherous side of the mountain. Snowmelt ran rivulets around his boots in the ochre mud.

His breath shallow, his heart smashing against his chest, Grace's repeated cries of fear directed his footing.

Finally he could go no further. He grabbed a twisted branch of manzanita and tugged it hard to make certain it was secure. Then he dared lean out over the edge of the cliff. Below him, a river cascaded through a narrow granite rock canyon, the gray rock laced with black basalt. Sweat streamed down the back of his neck, and his sweaty hands slipped along the slick bark of the branch.

"Grace!" he yelled over the pounding of his heart and the murmur of the river's rapids carrying upslope to his ears.

"I'm here! Down here!"

Malcolm's great relief turned to horror as his eyes found Grace. She was at least thirty feet below him, pressed up against the side of the mountain, huddled on a narrow ledge above the river, Ben tight in her arms. She looked up at him, but from this distance he couldn't make out the expression on her face. But he could tell by the fear in her voice that she knew the danger she was in.

Malcolm gulped, his mind racing. How could he reach her? He had no rope . . . but maybe the sheriff had some. He thought he'd seen some coiled on the side of Love's saddle. But did he dare race off to find the sheriff? Would he even be able to find him? How long could Grace last down there? Could she keep Ben from falling off the ledge? What could he do?

He closed his eyes and prayed as sweat trickled down behind his ears. *Lord, help me. Help me save Grace.*

"Hold on," he yelled down to her. "I'll be back."

He knew he didn't have time to get help. He'd have to think of something. Carefully he worked himself back uphill, inching along the slippery slope. He swiped a hand across his brow as he scanned the area. Then his eyes caught on a small structure yards north of the remains of the cabin. Through the tendrils of smoke rising from the charred piles of wood, he made out what looked to be a shed, and ran to it. The stubborn swelled door released after a few hard pulls, revealing the dark insides of a toolshed. A spark of hope ignited as he spotted some sort of metal implement that had a saw attached to a flat sheet of tin by a long length of thick rope.

His shaky fingers worked at the knots as he urged himself to hurry. Finally he extricated the rope from its strangled grasp of metal and looped it around his arm. He had twenty, maybe thirty, feet. His hope sputtered. It wasn't enough to reach Grace.

But it would be enough for him to reach her—if he slid down it and jumped to the ledge. What he would do once he got to her, he didn't know. But he'd tackle that when he made it to that ledge. He'd figure something out. What other choice did he have? None. No way would he abandon her—not now, when she needed him most.

He thanked God she was alive and unharmed. He thanked God for leading him to her, and for the rope. He wished he had ten feet more to reach her. But he knew whatever he lacked, God would make up the rest. All he needed was faith to bridge the distance. Faith and a determined heart. He lacked neither.

Monty . . .

Grace stared up at the top of the ridge as ash and soot sprinkled her face. Shock and relief coursed through her body. She shook in disbelief. How had Monty found her? Had he come after her alone? Or were there others? Surely he couldn't have followed the outlaws without help.

More importantly, why had he come? She imagined he had somehow heard about her abduction—no doubt the news had spread quickly through town. And he had left Stella to come find her. Oh, this could only be an answer to her prayers!

Hugging Ben tight as he wiggled to get free, she wondered if Monty was finally starting to remember her. His attraction to her was apparent, and despite the fact that he had married another woman, he was legally *her* husband. She had every right—under heaven and earth—to want him back, but she still feared telling him the truth. He had walked back into her life. She had to believe in time he would remember her. Remember everything.

"Mama," Ben cried, waving his arms around.

"No, Ben. Hush. Wait. It's not safe." She smiled at him and kissed his dirty cheek, and a few of her tears landed on his face. "Your papa is coming back." Ben looked at her, puzzled.

"Yes, that's your papa. And he loves you. He'll take care of us." She closed her eyes for a moment and soaked in the gratitude she felt. Every inch of her body hurt, but she knew no bones had been broken. Ben was unscathed, even from the long fall to the ledge. And of all people sent to rescue her, God had sent Monty. She believed in her heart of hearts that the great love Monty had for her and Ben was leading him to her, even without his knowing. Their hearts were entwined, like the strands of a tightly woven rope that could not easily unravel. And as her heart called out to his, he could do naught but respond.

Clayton's face, his bloody knife, Billy's moans, the fire and smoke licking her back as she smashed the window—the last hour replayed in her mind and set her trembling anew. She was so tired and sick and weary. How she longed to sleep in a soft feather bed . . . with Monty in her arms.

Grace sat on the wet ledge and shifted Ben in her arms so that he faced her. "Let's sing a little song, all right?" She had no idea where Monty went or when he'd return. She hoped the sheriff was with him, or some other strong men who could help. She didn't know how much strength she had left to corral her ever-curious son.

As she sang a nursery rhyme to Ben and he settled, for the moment, into her arms, she thought how she'd almost left Fort Collins, never to see Monty again. And she would have boarded the coach to Denver—if she hadn't been kidnapped.

The thought struck her—how this horrific ordeal was somehow a blessing in disguise. This had to be heaven's doing. And if that be truth, then she had to cling to the hope that Monty would someday be hers again. How, she had no idea. She just had to hold on tight and not let go. And trust that, as Monty always reminded her, "the Lord will make a way—He always does."

Chapter 24

LENORA PULLED OUT THE SHORT-handled shovel she'd tucked in her saddlebag. She walked to the middle of the clearing to the old twisted pine that stood as a lone sentinel in this high mountain canyon—a sentinel that had stood watch over the box of gold at its feet.

As she tromped back through the ankle-high alpine grass that spread like ratty green carpeting, she looked up the canyon beset with narrow slots and crevices to the snow-topped mountain peaks of the Rockies. The only way out of this boxed-in meadow was back down the way she'd come, which led to the Poudre River. She wished now that she'd tied Nugget up, so she could fetch him later. Her stomach grumbled at her for forgetting to bring food along. In her haste she'd done a lot of fool things. But she was determined to get out of the mountains in one piece, even if she had to crawl on all fours lugging the sack of gold behind her. Nothing and nobody would stop her now.

More than anything, she hoped Clayton had been captured by now. Or shot dead. There was no telling—not from here. She didn't dare sneak close to the trail, where the posse could spot her. And she couldn't take the chance of them seeing her footprints.

As much as she wanted to watch his demise, she couldn't take the chance.

The snap of a branch startled her, and she swiveled around, stiffening. She pushed back her sunbonnet to scan the far woods and fisted her hands. Was someone coming?

She pulled her pistol out and hefted it in her palm, eyeing her surroundings, keenly aware of her vulnerability in this exposed field. Hank had spent hours teaching her how to shoot—and shoot well. She could hit a bird between the eyes on a stump from fifty feet without a second's hesitation. Clayton wasn't all that great a shot, but she sure didn't intend to put his skill to the test, nosiree. And if that posse discovered her—well, why would they take umbrage with a woman traveling alone in the mountains? She'd read stories about that Englishwoman Isabella Bird. The fool woman spent years traipsing alone around the Rockies, fording dangerous rivers and waiting out blizzards holed up in some stranger's cabin.

A scent of smoke wafted up her nose. She looked to the north, where Hank's hideout was. A small dark cloud hovered above the tops of the pines, and flecks of ash rode on the soft breeze drifting down into the valley where she stood, wary, pondering.

Was the cabin on fire? Why? She hadn't heard any gunshots. Had the posse set it on fire to force Clayton to come outside and surrender? Wouldn't that be nice.

But she didn't have time to postulate on what might or might not have transpired. She was wasting time. The longer she tarried, the bigger the chance someone would spot her.

Lenora set her pistol beside her as she knelt at the base of the gnarled pine. With a grunt, she pushed aside the big stones she'd rolled onto the flat spot. Then she poked the shovel's tip into the ground until she hit the big flat rock she had laid atop the strongbox. In less than a minute she had the foot-long rock uncovered. She set down the shovel and with her gloved hands worked the rock free and lifted it out.

Her eyes widened as her pulse raced. The gray metal box sat undisturbed where she had left it the last time she'd been up here. A giggle burst out of her as she hurriedly wiped dirt clods off the top. It was hers! The gold—all of it. All she had to do was fill her saddlebag and—

"Well, fancy runnin' into you out here by yer lonesome."

Lenora gasped at the gruff voice and jumped up. Standing not ten feet from her was Clayton!

How had he snuck up on her like that, without her noticing? She had to think fast. It took all her resolve not to glance at her gun that lay inches from her boot. She knew if Clayton saw where she was looking, he'd shoot her without hesitation. Drat!

"Why, Clay," she said, pouring on the sugar and delicately wiping the dirt from her hands. She straightened and smoothed out her skirts. "We were s'posed to meet at the cabin. I was just gettin' your gold—"

Clayton stood erect, scrutinizing her. His hand dropped to the gun at his hip. Lenora gulped.

"Sure ya were," he said, a cynical chuckle following. "And I was jes makin' sure you were bringin' it."

"Where's Billy?" she asked innocently. But the icy rage searing his eyes told her the answer before he spoke. Billy Hill Cloyd was dead. Lenora guessed why—Clayton wanted the gold all for himself. She struggled to paste on a look of calm reserve, but her insides twisted with fear.

"He's . . . indisposed." He laughed. "An' I indisposed 'im."

Lenora took a step toward Clayton with her arms out and a big smile on her face, hoping the terror crawling over every inch of her skin was not telltale. "Oh, Clay, we can—"

"Jes hold it right there," he warned, pulling out his gun and fingering it by his side.

Lenora stopped, then took a step back, mindful of where her pistol lay. Fear filled every pore in her body. If Clayton had killed Billy for the gold, she was next. She had to think of something to distract him so she could shoot him first. *Think, think!* Where was her serendipity now, when she needed it most?

Her palms sweaty, she wiped her hands on her dress. The afternoon sun baked her head, and perspiration dotted her forehead. The smell of smoke was thicker now.

"What did'ya do? Set the cabin on fire?"

He humphed. "I reckon more'n likely 'twas that posse o' yours. Huh, don't look at me like that. You think I didn't figure on you alertin' the law? How stupid d'ya think I am?"

"I did no such thing," she protested. *Didn't need to, you lunkhead. You think the sheriff wouldn't've heard about the kidnapping?*

He pointed the gun at her. "Reach on down there and take that box out. Set it over there. Nice and easy and no funny stuff." He moved a few feet to her left, to get a clear shot of her without the tree in the way. She sidestepped enough to block his view of the gun, which was now hidden under her petticoats.

With his pistol aimed at her head, he watched her with a keen glare, never taking his eyes off her hand.

"For goodness' sake, Clay. Why are ya being like this? I'll give you the gold. I told ya I would. I don't need it."

"Sure ya don't," he said, his mouth in a twisted smile.

Lenora made herself breathe, but her corset suddenly squeezed the air out of her lungs. She knew she had to move slowly. One quick misstep and she'd find a hole in her heart.

"Hurry up!" he ordered, waving his gun.

For a brief instant, Clayton looked across the field. His eyes narrowed. He must have seen something. Or someone. Now was her chance.

With her head bowed, she pried the box up with one hand, while her right hand slid under her skirts, feeling around until she touched the warm metal barrel of her Colt. She inched the gun forward until she could get a good grip on the handle. Her hands shook, but she grasped it tightly.

Sucking in a breath, she pulled the edge of the box up, aware of Clayton's distracted eyes glancing at her hands as she peeked up at him from underneath her lashes. She pulled her other hand out from under her skirts, and as she got to her feet, she cocked the hammer back.

Clayton's eyes widened as she yanked the gun up and pointed it, straight-armed, right at his chest. "What are you—?"

She fired, the kick of the gun throwing her off balance. Clayton rolled to the ground as the bullet whizzed by his arm. Before she could get off another shot, he ran behind her.

She spun around—only to face him and his pistol head-on.

She threw her hands up, and a whimper escaped from her throat. "Please," she begged. "Don't shoot. I . . . I was afraid. I thought if you killed Billy, you'd kill me—"

Clayton smiled, but the mirth didn't reach his eyes. His hate and fury smoldered hotter than any fire. "Well, you thought rightly," he said, cocking back the hammer of his gun.

"Clayton, please—"

"Sorry, Lenora. You tricked me one time too many. Adios."

Clayton fired his gun. Lenora shrieked as the bullet sliced into her gut. A hot knife of pain seared her flesh and doubled her over. She heard the gun fire again. Another hot knife struck her shoulder. She screamed and toppled to the grass.

Her heart stuttered as her body convulsed. The hot sun burned her eyes, and she closed them. In her mind, she saw herself standing on a bright stage, in a fancy theatre house in San Francisco, spotlights baking her as she recited her lines—she was a star, and everyone applauded and threw bouquets of flowers at her as she took her many curtain calls.

She slipped along in her dreamy vision of her fame, gold coins raining down on her head and plunking on her shoulders. Gold, all that gold, all hers . . .

Tears welled up as her lifeblood seeped out, as the harsh pain careening through her body dulled to numbness. She tried to move her hands and her legs, but was unable to. She heard a voice. It sounded as if coming from miles away, the words drifting to her ears as inky blackness clouded her mind and she sucked in shallow breaths that couldn't fill her lungs.

"Good-bye Lenora. And good riddance."

Eph Love reined in his horse, skidding to a stop in the middle of the stand of aspens. Gunshots!

His deputies halted alongside him, alarm streaking their features. The shots were close—not even a mile away. He listened, then heard horses pounding soft earth. Eph drew his gun, then relaxed. Eli and LeRoy emerged from around a thicket on their mustangs. The two trackers trotted in quick step over to him.

"It's Wymore. He's in an open field over yonder," Eli said, animated and pointing in the direction from whence he and his brother had come. "He just shot a woman—she's got black hair. It's not Grace."

"Anyone else there with him?" Eph asked, smoothing his moustache, his pulse quickening. What in tarnation was a woman doing up here, dealing with the likes of Clayton Wymore?

The brothers shook their heads. Love looked behind him and took a head count.

"Where's Connors?" he asked Marcus Coon. Last Eph had seen, the surveyor had been riding alongside the hotel owner.

"Don't know. I told him to follow. Guess he had other intentions."

Eph pursed his lips. Maybe the sight of Cloyd dying scared him off. But they didn't have time to worry about Connors's whereabouts. He probably headed back to town, thinking he wasn't needed.

And he wasn't. Six against one made the odds look pretty bad for Clayton Wymore. Six men who were all pretty good shots too.

"Well, let's have at 'im," he told his posse. "Ezra—take Colin and try to find another way around, so we can surround him." He looked back at the trackers, questioning them with his eyes.

LeRoy nodded and said to Stapleton, "When we get beyond that narrow cut, where the trees thin out, you'll see a wider deer trail to the right. Just follow that for about a quarter mile, then swing sharp toward the mountain. You'll circle the meadow and come out on the north side of the ridge."

"Okay," Eph said. "Good." He shifted in his saddle and sidestepped his horse to face the five men. "Men, I don't have to tell you Clayton Wymore's wily and dangerous. He's a murderer. Don't hesitate to kill him. He'll hear us coming, and he'll find some cover, no doubt. So keep your wits about you."

Eph checked his pistols and nodded at his deputies to follow. He gestured at the brothers to lead the way. As they trotted across stony ground up through a narrowing pass, Eph smiled, the eager anticipation of this moment building like a ball of snow growing in size as it tumbled down a hill. Billy Cloyd was dead. There was one remaining member of the notorious Dutton Gang on the loose—but not for long.

Eph had no intention of capturing Clayton Wymore alive—knowing the outlaw's propensity to escape every trap that had ever been set or sprung on him. Eph would not take that chance. He had not a lick of mercy in his heart for this thieving, murdering piece of work that had no resemblance to a man made in God's image. No, Wymore would breathe his last upon God's good earth at the top of this mountain, and then Eph and his men would haul the body back to Fort Collins, where his death would be welcomed and broadcast across the thirty-seven united states. Eph could hear it now—the applause, the praise, the acclaim. He would go down in history as the man that put an end to the trail of victims that suffered at this monster's hands. His appointment to the office of state marshal was a done deal.

Suddenly, the Indian brothers reined to a quick stop in front of him. They had arrived at the top of the draw, and Eph noted it opened out onto an alpine meadow dotted with wildflowers, clover, and patches of snow. His gaze snagged on the woman's body lying prone in the tuft grass.

"There's the varmint," LeRoy said, pointing across the wide expanse. "Gettin' on his horse."

Eli's mustang pranced in place. He gazed off toward the mountain peaks. "LeRoy," he said, his voice arresting.

"What?" LeRoy asked him.

Eli only stared hard, facing west, at the towering western wall of the Rockies.

"Well, I'll be . . ." LeRoy said.

"What is it? What do you see?" Stapleton asked, riding up to them, craning his neck to look off in the distance.

Eph saw only something that looked like a haze of dust. Buffalo? Not this high up.

"Horses," Eli told Stapleton, then looked over at Eph, his face shining with excitement. "That's the herd we've been tracking."

"For two years now," LeRoy answered wryly. Eph noted a wistfulness in his gaze.

"You boys want to go after them, go ahead," Eph told them. "We can handle Wymore."

"No," LeRoy said firmly. "We'll see this through. Won't be hard to pick up that herd's trail from here."

Eli nodded and looked to Eph for instructions.

"All right then. Let's get Wymore . . . and then we have to find the woman and her baby."

O'Grady nodded. "She couldn't have gone far. Maybe Connors found her."

"One thing at a time," Eph said. "Least it's warm and sunny. Not a cloud in sight. She'll fare all right until she's found."

He hoped Wymore hadn't done anything to that woman before he fled. He couldn't imagine the fright he'd have if someone stole away his Sally. He'd spit nails chasin' down the scalawag, and he'd show no mercy. But this woman—she had no one. No one but him and his men. He'd find her and take her safely back to town. But not until Wymore got his comeuppance.

He wished Cloyd hadn't died on him. He wanted the kid to explain why they'd taken Grace Cunningham and her baby. And tell him who this woman was. Although, now it appeared the woman was dead. If they killed Wymore, then all his unanswered questions would be buried six feet under. Would he ever uncover the truth behind this puzzling mystery?

He spurred Destiny into a run, his posse right behind him. Across the meadow, Wymore stopped and turned at their approach. In a flash, he mounted his horse and raced away to the southwest, as if the Devil were hot on his heels.

He is, Eph thought, giving his mare her head and galloping after the outlaw. *And I'm right behind him.*

Chapter 25

MALCOLM SLITHERED DOWN THE ROPE with care, one gloved hand over another, the roar of the river floating up to him like the rumble of a oncoming train. Sweat poured down the back of his shirt as he swiveled from side to side, keeping an eye on Grace, who stood pressed against the back of the mountain wall, hugging Ben and watching his progress.

When he reached the end of his rope, he smiled wryly. For, in a whole lot of ways he was at the end of his rope. Here he was, dangling over a river canyon, with no idea how to get Grace and Ben off this ledge to safety, but all he could think about was how relieved and happy he was. Grace was alive and unharmed. His heart ached for her, yet he was married to a woman he detested. He'd left Stella, knowing he would never return to her. Yet, Grace was a moral and upstanding Christian woman, with a child to rear and bring up in the faith. There were no two ways about it—he could not corrupt her morals or tempt her by proclaiming the feelings he held for her. He was not free to marry her, and no amount of rationalizing—with himself or God—would change the sad fact of the matter.

Malcolm flung his thoughts aside and gauged the distance to the ledge, then let loose his grip and tumbled the eight or so remaining feet onto the soft mud, rolling into the wall.

"Oh, thank God," Grace said, rushing to him and placing a hand on his shoulder. "Are you all right?"

Malcolm did his best to brush off his clothes, but they were damp and smeared with dirt. More than anything, he wanted to throw his arms around her, longed to pull her to his chest and kiss her sweet, lush lips. Desire flared in a hot flash of need, but he squelched it as he looked her and the baby over. She was in a thin white nightdress, ripped at the collar and caked with muck He forced his eyes from her shapely curves that left little to his imagination, seeing that the fabric was sheer and clung to her damp body. He unbuttoned his long-sleeved chambray shirt, which left him bare-chested, but there was nothing for it. Better that Grace was modestly covered. How embarrassed and exposed she must have felt in such a state of undress around those two outlaws. He shuddered thinking of them taking advantage of her.

Malcolm wrapped his shirt around her shoulders. "Here. You can put this on over your nightgown."

"Thank you," she said, her cheeks reddening.

"Did . . . Wymore hurt you?" He hated to hear the answer, but he had to ask. Rage simmered under the heat of his desire, and he prayed that the sheriff had caught—and killed—Clayton Wymore.

Grace hesitated, and her face paled. "He meant to," she finally said, "but Billy stopped him." Her words choked in her throat. "He died saving me . . ."

Malcolm nodded, and gratitude surged for the young outlaw and his unexpected sacrifice. He felt sad for Billy Cloyd—for getting tangled with the likes of Wymore. Seemed a fool thing to do. "The sheriff got him out of the cabin, before the fire reached him. If that's any consolation."

Her light-green eyes searched his, as if looking way down into his soul, and his passion stirred anew.

"So . . . he's dead then?" she asked.

He nodded again, then stroked the baby's head. A quiet snore wheezed through Ben's nose.

"Is Ben . . . ?"

"Just tuckered out." And then she smiled, and he thought her smile was the prettiest sight he'd ever seen—even despite her filthy clothes and dirt-streaked cheeks.

He tore his gaze from her face before his hands got the better of him. This close, it took all his willpower not to kiss her and run his fingers and lips over every inch of her body. He had to get these lustful thoughts from his mind!

"Don't move," he told her, huffing out a breath that carried upon it all his fervent desire for her. He walked the perimeter of the ledge—fifteen or so feet—peering over the crumbling edge to the steep jumble of sagebrush and rock cascading to the river below. Water moved swiftly through the canyon, but a wide beach of sand and tufts of grass leveled out on a riverbank that ran for a hundred or so yards below them. If he could just get Grace and Ben to that flat spot, they could follow the river down the mountain until it came out to civilization.

He'd seen and studied maps of the Cache la Poudre River in the assessor's office. It tumbled and turned from its headwaters high up in the Rockies, but emptied out on the Front Range, into the South Platte—the place where he'd woken without a memory to see

Stella's face. That was miles from here, but he knew that much at least—at some point they'd get down to the open range and eventually find a road.

After studying the slope leading to the riverbank, he devised a plan. He'd set Grace and Ben on his lap and slide down the mountain. If he dug his boot heels hard into the ground, he could control their speed. Little by little they could work their way to the bottom. His body might acquire some bruising along the way, but if that was the price he had to pay for a safe deliverance, so be it.

He didn't dare waste daylight hoping the posse would come back looking for him or Grace. They probably figured he'd found her and took her back to town. Unless they found his horse wandering where he left it. He imagined Rambler was doing what he loved most—snuffling the brush for grass to eat. What would the sheriff think when he found the horse? Would he spend the time looking for him? Not likely—not if he had Wymore in tow. No, Malcolm didn't dare take the chance of waiting. Who knew how far he and Grace would get before darkness—and a freezing cold night—descended upon them?

"I'm going to get you out of here, Grace Cunningham," he told her. "Come'ere." He gestured her to his side at the lip of the ledge. "I'm going put you and Ben on my lap, and we're going to scootch our way down, nice and easy."

She nodded, but her face was etched with fear. He couldn't bear it a moment longer; he had to touch her, to reassure her. He walked to her and stroked her cheek and met her eyes. Tears filled hers, and she choked back a sob. To his surprise, she covered his hand with her own, holding his palm against her chin.

"You've been through a lot—more than a woman could possibly bear. You're brave and strong. You did what you had to, to save Ben. Don't for a minute think you've done anything wrong."

She nodded as the tears spilled down her face. Her forlorn expression tugged his heartstrings so hard, he thought they would snap. He gently wiped her tears with the back of his hand, and she squeezed her eyes shut and whimpered, and the sound of it hurt his chest.

"Thank you . . . Malcolm. You didn't have to come for me. With the posse. Why . . . why did you? You risked your life for me . . . again." She lowered her eyes and bit her lip, and Malcolm saw her restraint. She meant to say more, but stopped herself.

Oh, how he ached to tell her he loved her. Tell her how much he needed her, admired her. She was unlike any woman he'd ever met—at least, the ones he could recall meeting. She was not only kind and honorable. She was courageous and resourceful. She'd escaped from one of the most dangerous outlaws in the West. That took hard resolve, determination, a fierce desire to live. And yet, she was soft and tender and vulnerable. He wanted nothing more in this moment than to protect her and love her and make sure no one ever harmed her again.

"Here," he said, sitting on the ground and dangling his legs over the ledge. He held out his arm, ushering her toward him.

He whispered, "Don't be afraid, Grace. We'll get through this. The Lord will make a way—he always does."

She stopped suddenly. "You said that to me . . . before. When the tornado . . ."

"I know," he said. "And we got through that ordeal—you and me, and Ben—without a hitch. I'll have you back to town in no time." He gave her a grin and patted his lap. She carefully sat down, and Malcolm wrapped his arms around her, reveling in her warmth and the feel of her skin against his bare chest. He forced his thoughts to the task at hand, away from his passionate stirrings for her.

"Ready?" he asked. She shifted Ben in her arms, then nodded. Malcolm inched his way off the ledge and onto the slippery slope. Mist from the river wafted into his face as he repositioned his feet, working his way down the cliff side. Thankfully, his boots dug into hard dirt and rock as he slid a few inches at a time, craning to see ahead of him and keeping Grace in his tight embrace.

He thanked God again for the sunny, clear day. He reminded himself that the danger was over. Grace was safe. She'd escaped unharmed. He might never know the reason Clayton Wymore kidnapped her, but it didn't matter. Not now. He would get her and Ben safely back to town, and then . . . then . . . ? He had no idea. But he knew after today, he wouldn't be able to push Grace from his heart. She had lodged tight in there, like a heavy rock stuck in a riverbed. No amount of prying would ever dislodge it. Was he destined to suffer the rest of his life, loving a woman he could never have?

Malcolm eased down the steep slope. His mud-caked clothes stuck to his skin by the time he'd made it fifty feet. Another fifty and they'd be at the bottom. Grace leaned back against him, and Malcolm felt tension ease from his neck and shoulders, even as sharp rocks gouged into his back. Just a little bit farther . . .

A noise above him made him dig in his heels and turn his head.

"What is that?" Grace asked, her voice wavering.

Malcolm swallowed as the noise grew into a loud rumble. The ground shook under him, and small rocks clattered down the hill from high up the mountain.

Then, his entire body shook, dislodging him from his precarious perch. Grace yelped, and Malcolm crammed his boots into the hillside, cradling her and Ben tighter as larger rocks from above whacked his head and shoulders.

A giant boulder, as large as a horse, crashed down the slope only feet from them, bouncing in great leaps, careening and crushing rocks and plants until tumbling into the river.

Grace screamed. Malcolm huddled over her and yanked his feet out of the ground, hastening their slide down the mountain. It was his only recourse. He lay back to keep from toppling forward head over heels, covering Grace's face with his arms, rocks now spilling down the cliff in great numbers, and smacking him in the head.

He glanced back, then wished he hadn't. The entire side of the mountain groaned and broke off like jagged teeth, sliding down in massive avalanches into the river. Unable to get purchase for his feet, Malcolm slid down the slick shaking mountainside, out of control, holding on to Grace and Ben with all his might.

And then, a surge of earth lifted and carried them the last twenty feet, as rocks and debris rained on them, battering and bruising them, until they hit the sandy bank now buried under muddy sludge and rock.

The impact jolted Malcolm forward, and Grace flew from his arms, landing facefirst on wet sand inches from the roiling water. The river churned in a deafening clamor as Malcolm finally stopped moving and wiped the grit from his eyes, and the sight of it suddenly made his stomach sick. Memories of floundering in thick violent water assailed him once more. His head pounded from the assault of both memory and rock, and blood trickled down from his head into his left eye.

Then, the mountain behind him quieted as the avalanche settled around them, a few rocks still trickling downhill. His pulse throbbed in his ears as he stared at Grace lying prone on the riverbank, the water splashing up onto her head. His breath caught in his throat at the sight of her.

To his relief, Grace lifted herself shakily to her hands and knees. But then she screamed. And screamed again.

Malcolm jumped and stumbled to her. She fastened startled eyes on him, then pointed at the river—at the powerful current and choppy waves crashing into rocks and overflowing the eroding banks.

His gaze fell upon Ben's small body—bobbing in a slipstream not three feet from them, his little face etched in shock. Before Malcolm could suck in a breath, the current snagged the baby and yanked him into the swift-moving current.

Without hesitation, Malcolm dove into the river.

Chapter 26

CLAYTON WYMORE, YOU MAY HAVE a fast horse, but you've got nowhere to go.

Eph Love led the pursuit after the outlaw, their horses stomping through the wet tufted hairgrass and alpine sage as they forced their quarry toward the towering rock cirque backing the thin strip of meadow. Wymore took potshots over his shoulder at them, the bullets chipping tree branches and ricocheting off rocks. Stapleton and O'Grady fired back, forcing Wymore to pick up speed. *At some point, you'll have to dismount and run for cover.*

Eph signaled his deputies and Marcus Coon to break rank, and they rode wide, casting a net to the north. Wymore, in response, swung west toward the rock wall, where patches of brush and small dwarfed pines lined a shallow wash. The outlaw's horse kicked up water as he galloped at breakneck speed, distancing himself from Eph and the Banks brothers. But he was heading right to where Eph intended him—backed up against a steep ravine that cornered an outcropping of rock and disappeared from view. A jumble of boulders littered the ravine, which would make it difficult—if not treacherous—riding. Once they had Wymore afoot, he was a dead man.

Eli and LeRoy rode alongside Eph, matching his speed and shooting their pistols. Eph admired the way the Indians rode, smooth on their mustangs as if they'd been born on them. He loved his mare, but she was getting up in years and soon wouldn't be able to tolerate this kind of strain. He imagined these young men could fix him up with a good horse that would handle any sort of danger on the Front Range.

Eph noted his deputies slowing down as they got within target range of the outlaw. He reined Destiny in as the Indians veered off to his right, just enough to make it clear to Wymore that he had nowhere to go. *Now whatcha gonna do?*

Stapleton and O'Grady slipped off their horses and made for a stand of aspens pressed against the cliff. They dropped behind a jumble of rock and positioned their rifles, then fired off a volley of shots. Coon jimmied himself between two fat trees and aimed his Winchester at Wymore.

Wymore urged his horse to the edge of the ravine as bullets streaked over his head. Water splayed down the cut in the mountain in a three-foot-wide stream emptying into the lazy creek hugging the cirque. As Eph brought Destiny to a halt, Wymore dismounted, grabbed his gun, and hopped over the creek to get behind a crag of limestone and volcanic rock.

Now it begins . . .

Shots blasted again from Wymore's gun, this time in Eph's direction. Eph heard the bullets whine in the air, but he knew Wymore's rifle didn't have the range to reach him. At least not yet.

Eli and LeRoy trotted back to his side.

"What's the plan, Sheriff?" LeRoy asked, keeping his eye on the ravine.

"I'm thinking we'd be in good position over there." He pointed at a half-dozen tall white pines nestled up to the rock wall, on the other side of the crystal brook that meandered through the meadow.

The brothers nodded, and together they trotted over to the trees and led their horses to a safe distance and dismounted. Eph swung off Destiny and ran in a crouch to the tree on the far left. A grassy swale ran up the hillside and flanked the mountain, and Eph noticed the grass was heavily trampled. He turned to Eli, who had come up to squat behind the tree next to him, his Henry balanced on his knee as he took Wymore's position in his sights.

"What do you make of that?" he asked Eli, nodding at the grass.

LeRoy scurried to Eli's side, his rifle tucked under his right arm and a revolver in the other.

"Elk?" Eph suggested.

Eli's eyes narrowed. He cast a quick glance toward the ravine, then crouched over to inspect the grass, running his hand along the ground, studying it.

As Eli hurried back, three more shots punctured the air. Eph heard his deputies fire off a couple of rounds. He looked around the tree and saw Wymore tuck his head back as chips of rock flew around him.

"If'n he's thinking of waitin' for us to leave or run out of bullets, he's gonna have a long wait," LeRoy said, shaking his head.

"I'll wait until hell freezes over, if I have to," Eph told him. "But I'd like to find that woman and her baby. So let's get this over with."

"LeRoy," Eli said, running up to his brother, "it's the herd."

LeRoy cocked his head. "Here?" He took in the meadow. "So, where'd they go? That's a dead end." He nudged his head to the south, beyond their stand of trees. Then LeRoy's eyes widened.

Eli smiled and nodded. "Must be another pasture up there." His face suddenly darkened. "Feel that?"

Eph regarded him questioningly. "Feel what?" But Eli's eyes were locked on his brother's.

LeRoy dropped to his knees and laid both palms on the ground. He nodded, then let out a soft whistle.

Eli scanned the mountain. "There's no other way out."

Eph was about to interrupt, but Eli swung around and looked him in the eye. "Sheriff, we gotta go. Now."

"What—?"

LeRoy took him arm and pulled him along, toward the horses. He stopped and said, "Feel the ground."

Eph pulled off a glove and flattened his palm to the dirt. The ground shook. Elk couldn't be causing that.

As if reading his mind, Eli said, while swinging up on his horse, "It's that herd. Sheriff, it's a big one—a hundred head at least."

"Well, where are they?" Eph scanned the meadow.

LeRoy mounted his horse and spun around to face Eph. He smiled and tipped his head toward the ravine.

"Up there?" Eph scratched his chin, then smoothed out his moustache.

"Yep," Eli said as Eph mounted Destiny. "And they're coming this way."

"You sure?" Eph said, hearing and seeing nothing. How could those Indians know which way a herd of horses was running?

Eli gave him a look as if he were a three-year-old asking if the sun was going to come up in the morning.

"What about Stapleton, Coon, and O'Grady?" Eph asked, shifting uneasily in his saddle and sensing Destiny's growing agitation. She tossed her head and chomped her bit.

"If they stay where they are, I'm thinkin' they should be safe."

"And Wymore?"

LeRoy smirked and wagged his head. He said nothing. Eph clicked his tongue against his teeth.

"Won't he run—when he hears them coming?"

"Probably be too late," LeRoy replied. "So long as we keep distractin' him a bit. Although, we better not dally too long. That meadow narrows yonder, and there's only room for maybe three abreast a good ways down. Which means—"

"Means we need to git movin'." Eli took the cue and kicked his horse into a canter and rode back north, out in the open and facing the ravine head-on. He kept back just far enough that Wymore's bullets couldn't reach him. But his presence there detonated another series of shots.

Eph and LeRoy came alongside him. Eph fired a few rounds. The bullets dinged off the rocks along the creek and ricocheted into the sides of the ravine, and the smoke from his gun twirled lazily into the air.

Eph's mare pranced in place. She wasn't one to flinch at gunshot, so he knew it was the proximity of the wild horses that had set her feet dancing. He suspected that he and the Indians were playing a dangerous game, but if they fled now, Wymore just might get away.

"How long we wait?" he asked LeRoy, whose mustang seemed unperturbed by the danger.

LeRoy looked to Eli, who scrunched up his face and stared up the mountain.

Eph followed his gaze and then noticed a dusty haze drifting down the draw. He spotted Wymore's dark horse pressed against the side of the mountain. Suddenly it whinnied, then bolted to the north, passing the deputies and disappearing into trees that hugged the cliff.

"We're done waitin'," Eli said, pushing his wide-brimmed hat down on his head.

Eph took a long look at Wymore as he backed up, one step after another. Eli and LeRoy swung their mounts and galloped east, away from the mountain and down the grassy swale behind Eph.

Destiny reared up. Wymore came out from behind his rock. Eph could barely make out the outlaw's words as Wymore yelled and waved his arms at them.

"Yeah, run! You'll never git me. A bunch of yellow-bellied cow—"

Eph didn't wait to hear the rest. As much as he longed to see Wymore's demise, he couldn't risk it. No sense losing his life over the sight. A quick glance told him his deputies were holding tight. No doubt they'd heard the horses—for Eph could hear them now. Sounded like a buffalo stampede. He wondered if their gunfire had set off a panic.

He yanked Destiny around and kicked her flanks. She tore off, following after the Indians, who were a hundred yards downslope. The thunder of hooves rode on the air and soon engulfed him in a deafening smother and cloud of dust. But he didn't look back. He pictured Wymore under all those hooves, hundreds of pounds of horseflesh squashing his body into the soft wet grass, rocks and boulders tumbling down on him and burying him in a shallow grave.

Destiny spurred faster as the herd came up close behind Eph. He could almost feel the heat from their bodies as their heavy panting and snorting reached his ears. Eph hunkered down and rode like the wind, then veered sharply to the north after the Indians. At the turn, the swale opened into a wide sloping mesa of sage and small spruce, and a hefty wind blew at him as the horses galloped by and spread out, slowing as the open space afforded them room to collect and calm.

LeRoy's horse reared and danced among a stand of pines, and the Indian on his back whooped and hollered. His brother's grimy face gleamed with sheer excitement.

"Woo! Wasn't that some ride!" Eli yelled. "You all right, Sheriff?"

Eph nodded. He soothed Destiny as she high-stepped in place and presently settled, her ears pricked back, listening to the wild horses trek down the mountain. The dust-choked air settled over them as the men sat their horses and chuckled. Eph doffed his hat and smoothed down his sweaty head, then his moustache.

Eli trotted back out to the swale, then returned as the sound of hooves softened to quiet.

"S'pose we should see what's left of Wymore," LeRoy suggested.

Eli chortled and shook his head. "Fool way to die."

Eph trotted back the way they'd momentarily come, the soft ground now chewed up into a mess of clods and trampled grass. The Indians followed behind. As soon as he caught sight of the ravine, he spotted his deputies cantering toward him. A blanket of rocks and dirt and torn-up brush littered the base of the ravine the horses had run down. There was no sign of Clayton Wymore.

When O'Grady reined in his horse a few steps ahead, he said, "He tried to clamber up the side of the mountain . . ."

Stapleton trotted up to Eph and the Indians, relief written all over his face. "Sheriff, I thought you were a goner. Them horses were chomping at Destiny's tail."

Eph chuckled and patted his mare's neck. "She wasn't gonna let that happen. She's fond of her tail."

They all laughed, and Eph felt the knot of tension loosen in his gut. "Well, I reckon that's the end of the trail for the Dutton Gang."

The men sat in a somber silence for a moment, and Eph thought about all that had transpired in the last twenty-four hours. It had taken a while, but justice, in the end, had prevailed. A warm feeling of satisfaction filled his chest. He'd done it—Wymore and Cloyd were dead. He'd remember this day, years from now, as one of his best days. But they weren't through yet, and there was still the woman and her baby.

"Colin, Ezra—go see what you can find of Wymore's body. Haul it back to the cabin. We need to get that woman's body too—the one Wymore shot back in the meadow. Coon—go with them. Can you manage that?"

The deputies nodded. Coon said, "And there's Cloyd as well. Three bodies we have to carry back to Fort Collins."

"We might be able to fetch Cloyd's horse," Eli said. "That woman musta had one too. I reckon it's somewheres around."

"That would help," O'Grady said, raking fingers through his thick red beard.

Eph nodded, hoping that was the sum total dead for the day. It bothered him that Connors had disappeared. He knew there weren't any other outlaws up to mischief in these parts, but the mountain had other dangers. Not so bad for an able-bodied man with a gun or two, and a surefooted horse. But the woman and her baby could be wandering lost, with no water or food, and only the clothes on their backs.

He glanced up at the sky. There were maybe two hours of strong daylight left. Once the sun sank behind the mountain, their missing persons would have a hard time of it.

He turned to Eli and LeRoy. "Good work back there. I'm grateful." He had no doubt he'd have failed to find those scalawags without them.

The Indians only nodded, as if it was all in a day's work. They certainly were a godsend.

"We still need your trackin' skills," Eph told them.

"Let's go find Grace and her baby," Eli said. "If'n we don't, Clare will kill me." LeRoy nodded.

Eph didn't have a chance to ask Eli who Clare was—for the trackers had galloped off before he could even open his mouth. Eph took his leave of Coon and the deputies, then coaxed Destiny into a run, following the two Indians as they backtracked toward the burnt cabin.

Chapter 27

"MONTY! MONTY!" GRACE SCREAMED, HARDLY hearing herself over the roar of the river. She ran on her mutilated bare feet over sharp rocks, tripping and smacking her hands as she fell over and over, trying to navigate the riverbank. Pain shot through every muscle and bone, and she cried out, tears streaming down her face.

"No, no, no!" She pinned her eyes on the glimpse of blue cloth that bobbed up and down in the tumbling current. Seconds felt like hours as she watched her baby—her precious baby—sink under the water, then pop up again. The river rumbled and churned, and Grace waved her arms wildly, overwrought with helplessness. He was only yards away, but Grace couldn't reach him.

This was her worst nightmare—doubled. Monty's head emerged from under the muddy brown swirls as he was swept along, careening into large boulders and cascading down steep drops as the river rushed down the canyon. With strong strokes, he swam toward Ben, but her baby whisked downriver just out of his grasp time and again.

Grace ran and ran, trying to catch up, praying she wouldn't lose Ben, her sweet baby. Oh Ben!

And Monty . . . had she just found him, only to lose him again? Would this river—this same river, she realized with a shock—take her beloved husband from her yet again? *No, please, don't do this to me!*

Her heart felt like a hard rock in her chest. She sucked in quick shallow breaths but her throat had clamped shut, as if she were drowning. And she was—drowning in misery and grief and despair.

She hurried as fast as she could, jumping over rocks and gritting her teeth as her feet were sliced over and over. The river began to widen and slow, but Ben was sucked down a narrow channel between two boulders, and she lost sight of him.

"Monty!" she yelled. He submerged once more, then bounced back up. He swiveled his head, frantic fear in his face as he searched the surface of the water for Ben.

"There, there!" she screamed, pointing at the sluice her baby had been sucked through.

Oh, God, please have mercy. I can't bear this. Not again. Please . . .

She kept up her litany as Monty catapulted his body through the narrow channel. Grace stumbled along a sandy bank thick with sedge, grateful for the tiny reprieve from the sharp rocks underfoot. She ran past a jumble of giant rocks, but when she came around the other side, she saw neither Monty nor Ben.

Where were they? Her eyes roved across the river as her heart hammered her chest. She held her breath, about to swoon. *Where, Lord, where?* Seconds dragged like hours as her blood throbbed in her ears and she craned to see under the cloudy water, but to no avail. There was no sign of her husband or her baby. They were gone.

A horrible dread gripped her. Her hope snapped. She'd lost them both. Ben. Monty.

Drowned. Dead.

She fell to the sand and rocked back and forth, wailing and sobbing, her heart shattered.

After the first freezing shock of water hit him, Malcolm sucked in a breath and swam. The river carried him, lifting him and banging him into rocks, but, strangely, he wasn't afraid. An unexpected calm washed over him as he scanned the roiling water and spotted Ben only a few feet downstream.

He prayed with fervor, *God, help me. Help me save Ben. Don't let him die.* He had to reach Ben before it was too late.

He heard Grace yelling, but couldn't take his eyes off Ben. Out of the corner of his eye, he saw her running and tripping along the bank, following him downstream. Then a wave engulfed him and tumbled him underwater. He spun and twirled, unsure which way was up, snuffing water up his nose and choking. His teeth chattered from the snowmelt, and his chest felt like a block of ice. Cold needles pricked his fingers and toes. Then, a voice in his head told him to relax and lie back, to let his legs lead.

He rolled onto his back and popped up to the surface. He looked around him as the current swept him along. Where was Ben? He couldn't see him.

"Monty!"

Grace yelled at him. She called again. "Monty!" Then pointed.

He didn't understand why she called him by that name, but he looked to where she pointed—over at a narrow channel between two huge rocks.

Malcolm turned on his side and kicked over to the channel, then let the water drag him through the passage that was barely wide enough for his body. The force of the suction swung him over. He smacked his forehead on a rock. Then the water tossed him as if he were a rag doll, smacking him into the opposite rocks. He hit his head again, and pain stabbed behind his eyes. Suddenly he lost his bearings and began to sink. Water filled his mouth as his mind numbed.

All he could hear was the loud bubbling of water as he fought unconsciousness and thrashed his arms futilely.

Ben! I have to save Ben!

With a burst of panic, he jolted upward and broke the surface again, finding himself in a wide, calmer stretch of water. He swiveled around in fear. Grace was nowhere in sight. Neither was Ben.

Malcolm's heart thumped against his ribs. He gritted his teeth as blood trickled into his eyes. He swam hard, swinging his arms with broad strokes to first one bank, then the next, diving again and again underwater and straining through the hazy silt-laden river to spot any glimpse of clothing.

Oh please, Lord, show me where he is! Let me save him.

Nothing. Ben was gone.

He paddled in circles, feeling around with his hands, diving under the water, his tears merging with the river. Black speckles dotted his vision, and his head throbbed as if knives were stabbing him. His mind began to drift downstream with the water. *No, no . . .*

The river lifted him and sped him down more rapids. Malcolm fought the current with his exhausted heavy arms, checking the little inlets and eddies, hoping Ben had somehow been washed to the shore.

And then—he saw a flash of blue.

Malcolm craned his neck and narrowed his eyes. Downriver a dozen yards, a toppled tree lay partially submerged, creating a strainer in the river. In the wavering branches, a piece of clothing snagged.

With his last ounce of strength, Malcolm dove underwater and swam with all his might, the current bulleting him straight to the strainer. In a quick flip, he lay back and bent his knees, instinctively positioning himself.

His water-filled boots hit the thick branches with a jolt. Malcolm fought against tumbling forward, which would cause his head to get trapped in the strainer underwater. He would not drown!

Sharp pricks of wood poked his arms and chest as he threaded one hand through the maze of branches and long brushes of pine needles bobbing in the surge. With his other hand he braced himself to keep from being swept away.

He prodded around, unable to see anything but tree. Then, his fingers met wet cloth.

But he couldn't do a thing from his precarious position in the river. He had to get to the downriver side of the strainer.

Grasping tightly to a sturdy branch, he slowly extricated his feet from their wooden perch. The moment he swung out away from the tree, the current snatched him up and tried to yank him away, tugging on his legs with all its might, but Malcolm held fast with his numb grip. He had lost all feeling in his hands but he held on, his fingers curled in a death grip, as his body flattened out across the top of the water and bobbed away from the tree.

Now he could see Ben clearly. He gulped. The small bundle of clothing was snagged in the branches, but at least Ben was up out of the water. But could he still be alive? After minutes of submersion in the freezing water, if Ben hadn't drowned, he'd likely be dead from hypothermia.

He sent another desperate prayer to heaven as he fumbled with his useless hands to work his way over to Ben. It seemed to take forever, but eventually he pulled himself out of the current and over to the downriver side of the tree. Here the river eddied around him in slow swirls as the water behind him slapped and splashed in its race down the mountain.

Suddenly, he heard a sound seep out under the cacophony of the river. A tiny little mewing sound, like that of a kitten.

Ben! He was alive!

Malcolm gulped back tears as he worked frantically at the tangled clothing. Carefully he wrapped his hands around Ben's cold, lifeless body and jimmied him out an inch at a time. Malcolm, numb from the waist down, rocked in the water as he pried Ben's little arms from bunches of pine needles.

Finally, the baby's little body slipped out of its sheath of wet clothes, and Malcolm delivered him, as naked as a newborn, into his own waiting cold arms. Ben's wide eyes stared into his, and Malcolm shook with wonder as his legs trembled from exhaustion and relief.

He wept as he stood there, clutching Ben to his chest, one icy body against another. But soon they both began to warm in the weak sunlight of the June afternoon, and Malcolm dared not pull him back to check him over. Not yet. He only needed to feel the tiny fluttering heart beating against his chest to know that Ben was alive. He prayed the baby would not die or suffer from exposure or bruising. But he couldn't worry about that right now.

Exhaustion crushed Malcolm's shoulders as he salvaged the torn blue blanket from the thicket of branches, then trudged out of the water and collapsed with care onto the sandy riverbank, blood dripping into his eyes. He clutched Ben in a loving, tender embrace as he eased onto his back, the sun tingling his chest and face, warming the baby's tiny body, bringing a pink color to his blue-tinged skin.

Malcolm's energy was spent. He knew he should yell for Grace, but he couldn't form words in his numb throat. His head throbbed in an agonizing cadence. He was oh so tired . . .

As he lay there, images of the river assaulted him. Waves tumbled and tossed him as he crashed against rocks, but all the while he heard Grace calling for him. He could see her, sitting on the mud in the pouring rain, in a brown dress, a gray shawl over her shoulders. He sucked in a breath as he studied her fearful face close up, then glanced down to her mounded waist . . . and spotted a large wagon beside her, half sunk into the mud . . .

What was he seeing? It was Grace, but she was pregnant and wet, and lightning ripped the sky. Thunder exploded, and two horses ran off, their reins trailing the ground. He was standing next to the wagon, watching them, a scowl of frustration on his face. He heard his own voice say, "Don't be afraid, Grace. We'll get through this. The Lord will make a way—He always does."

He must be losing his mind from the cold and trauma, Malcolm told himself as his thoughts shredded apart and a black cloud blocked out his sight and snuffed out the images.

Grace . . . Grace . . . where are you?

Grace lifted her heavy head and listened. She thought she heard something over the river's din. It sounded like a voice, a cry. Her breath quickened.

She leapt to her feet on the warm sand. Needles of pain shot up her heels, but she ignored them. Where had the sound come from? She searched the far shore, then upstream.

Then she heard it again. A tiny sound. Her body shook all over. Could it be . . . ?

She dared not hope—not again. Grief swallowed her up; she could barely walk, but she forced herself to take a step, then another. She ran pell-mell, looking behind rocks and in clumps of shiny thick grasses that grew along the riverbank.

There—again! Her eyes grew wide. She blurted out a cry. Ben! It had to be Ben!

She ran hard, stumbling and tripping as she followed the river along its bank, down one drop after another until she burst out onto a long sandy beach.

Ten feet away, next to the river, lay Monty, stretched out on his back. And a naked Ben was in his arms, wiggling and crying. She threw a hand to her chest and uttered a strangled cry.

Ben, oh, Ben!

"You're alive. Oh my God, thank you, thank you, Lord!" Her throat ached as she cried out her words and ran with renewed vigor.

Grace sprinted to Monty and dropped to his side. She pulled Ben into her arms, surprised at how hot he was, and cradled him to her chest. Her poor baby was feverish! She rocked him and caressed him, splashing kisses all over his head and face, and he made little noises that kindled her joy. From what she could tell, he was unhurt. But the sudden fever sparked more worry in her heart.

She leaned over and nudged Monty. He didn't respond.

Monty . . .

Oh no!

He lay unmoving, but Grace saw his chest rise and fall. A deep gash angled across his forehead, and his bare chest was abraded with raw welts and dozens of deep scratches that bled. Blood trickled down his chest and sides and face, and his trousers were ripped into shreds. His handsome, strong, beautiful body had been pummeled and pierced—all in an effort to save Ben. His son.

Grace threw a hand over her mouth and cried, shaking her head in amazement at this man she loved so much. How could she ever have thought to leave him, to give him up? To let Ben grow up without knowing his brave, selfless father? She could not. She would not.

She would tell Monty the truth and trust that he would believe her. And if he didn't? Well, she would worry about that later.

Right now, she needed to get him conscious. But what if she couldn't? Her flame of joy sputtered out as she studied his impassive features.

She glanced up at the sky. There were only a few hours of daylight left, if that. At this elevation, nightfall would drop below freezing. They would all die without warm shelter. No way would she leave Monty. Yet . . . could she risk Ben's life by staying? Oh, what should she do?

Grace's head reeled thinking of all that had happened this day. She had been kidnapped, dragged up a mountain by outlaws, mishandled and terrified. She'd escape the outlaws and a fire, slid down a mountain, was nearly buried in an avalanche, and watched her husband and baby get swept down a raging river. How much more could she take?

She leaned over, and with the torn hem of her filthy nightdress wiped the blood from Monty's face, tenderly cleaning his eyes. Upon closer inspection, she determined that none of his wounds were very deep, and soon the trickle of blood stopped.

"Monty. Monty, please, wake up. Open your eyes." She fingered the gash on his head and felt the swelling. He'd hit his head hard. *Just like before. He must have hit his head when I lost him the first time.* Grace shivered. Would he forget her again? Would he wake up and not even remember her name? What a cruel turn of fate that would be.

Noting Ben had fallen asleep in the warm sun, she laid him on his belly against Monty's big, broad chest, and Ben's little fingers tangled up in his father's chest hair. Grace couldn't help but smile at the peaceful, sweet sight of her son lying on his papa—a sight she had envisioned dozens of times. If only . . .

She brushed the tears off her cheeks and went over to the river's edge. After ripping off two long strips of cotton cloth from the bottom of her nightdress, she dipped them in the water and wrung them out. Then she spotted Ben's torn blanket on the sand and picked it up. She hobbled back to the two people she loved most in the world, ignoring all the aches and pains that screamed for her attention, and sat down next to Monty. She slid his head into her lap and cradled it, gently wiping away the dirt and blood and sand that had caked in his cuts and crevices. His rugged, handsome face so close set her heart racing. With his eyes closed, he seemed in a peaceful sleep.

Oh, he had to wake up—he just had to! But she didn't know what else she could do.

"Monty," she said softly. "Monty . . ." She studied his face—his strong jaw and straight nose. His tender lips she had kissed so many times, so many nights while in his arms in their bed. A whimper seeped out of her mouth as tears rushed to her eyes.

And then she could resist no longer. She leaned down and touched her lips to his. They rested there, and she reveled in the soft warmth of his skin.

She closed her eyes and remembered.

Chapter 28

"ELI, SEE IF YOU C'N figure out which way Grace went," Eph told the tracker. Eli left his side and ambled, hunched over, around what used to be the east side of the cabin, studying the ground. LeRoy had ridden off to see if he could find any sign of Connors or his horse.

Eph stood before the smoldering remains of the cabin, hands on his hips, listening to the quiet hissing of the timbers and siding, the coals crackling as the heat chewed at what was left of Clayton Wymore's hideout. A sense of satisfaction simmered in Eph's chest as he smoothed out his moustache and considered the day's successes. Colorado Territory was now rid of the Dutton Gang. No longer would the banks and stages and trains be bothered by any of their ilk. He was proud of his posse—they'd done good. But they weren't done just yet.

Eph turned and saw Eli Banks pushing through the thick brush to the east, down a steadily dropping slope. Then Eph spun around at the sound of horses trotting through the pines pressed against the mountain wall. Coon, Stapleton, and O'Grady came out of the shadows on their horses, and ponying behind them were two other saddled mounts—quarter horses. A bay, and a chestnut with a blaze on his forehead. The dark horse sported a Texas-style saddle, upon which lay the bodily remains of Clayton Wymore.

Stapleton trotted over to him, leading the bay gelding. "Here's Wymore. We got the woman and her horse too."

Eph looked over at O'Grady, who held a lead rope in his hand that led to the chestnut horse's halter.

"Found this one wandering around a glade with no bridle. Just saddled," O'Grady said. "I figure the woman cut him loose when coming up the rock fall."

Across the saddle lay the dead woman, her head buried in the gelding's mane, and her raven-colored hair splayed out over the horse's neck. Lenora somebody. Clearly she'd known Wymore. Maybe he'd had a wife Eph didn't know about. Nothing he'd ever read in the papers mentioned anything about a woman tied to the gang. But he'd have time later to figure out who she was.

Eph walked over and looked at Wymore's body draped sideways and facedown over the seat of the dark horse. His body was a bloody mess, the clothes drenched red in blood with bits of mutilated flesh clinging to fabric. Eph circled the horse, who didn't look all that happy having the body roped to the saddle, and lifted what was left of Wymore's crushed head. The face was barely recognizable, but Eph figured there wouldn't be cause for doubt over who they'd brought back to town. Plenty of people would be able to attest to the identity of the outlaw once the undertaker cleaned it up some and got the body on ice. He knew Wymore had certain identifiable scars and birthmarks.

He patted the horse's neck and gave it soothing words of encouragement. The horse nickered in appreciation for the kind attention, and Eph got the impression the horse had not been kindly treated. Eph snorted. He'd find a new owner for this creature—someone who'd give him a good home. The horse deserved at least that much.

Stapleton, still holding the reins of the bay horse, said with a gleaming smile, "Sheriff, take a look at what's in them saddlebags."

Eph raised his eyebrows at Stapleton's tone and expression. He glanced over at Coon, who nodded with a smile set to break his face. O'Grady chuckled.

The gold! Had to be. Billy Cloyd had said something about Wymore going after the gold—and probably why he killed that woman. Nothing like a little gold to get people killing one another.

Sure enough, his quick inspection into the darkness of the leather bag showed the glint of gold bars. He whistled. That was an unexpected piece of pudding. Who knew how much this was all worth. Or which banks it rightly belonged to. Well, the Pinkerton Detective Agency would know. And probably the territorial marshal.

"We found a hole dug under that gnarled pine in the middle of the meadow. And an empty metal box," O'Grady said, his bright-green Irish eyes dancing. He put a water skin up to his lips and drank.

"You know there's a reward for the return of that gold," Coon told Eph.

"And for the capture of the last two members of the Dutton Gang," O'Grady added, chuckling.

Eph clicked his teeth. "I figure you men will be collecting that reward soon enough."

His deputies laughed merrily, no doubt already spending their fortune in their head. But a reward was the last thing on Eph's mind. The deaths of those outlaws was its own sweet reward—all that Eph had ever wanted. He'd dreamed of such a day as this all his life, from back when he was a boy reading Beadle's Dime Novels of the Wild West. Long before the James's brothers joined up with the Youngers.

"You want us to look around for Connors and the woman?" Coon called over from his horse.

"I think it best we let the Indians do the tracking. We might muddy up the tracks—"

"Sheriff!"

Eph spun about and saw Eli hauling toward him.

"Connors and Grace went this way." He looked at the other men sitting their horses, then his eyes rested a moment on the two bodies draped across the saddles of their mounts. He turned his attention back to Eph.

"I need to show you somethin'," Eli told him in all earnestness. Eph did not like the flare of worry he saw in the Indian's eyes.

"Stay here," he told the others, although he needn't have said the words. They would wait for his instructions.

Eph fingered the collar of his shirt as the warm midday sun overhead caused sweat to dribble down his neck. He pushed aside the thick scratchy branches as he stepped carefully through the brush, following Eli's lead. Soon the ground's slope canted sharply, and he couldn't help but notice the broken vegetation, indicating someone had run through this thicket, heedless of the danger. His boots slipped along the soggy ground, and Eli slowed, taking cautious steps until he came to a stop.

"Careful, Sheriff," Eli told him, nodding for him to take a look-see ahead of him.

To Eph's surprise, the Indian took hold of his left arm and steadied him. Eph inched forward and craned his neck. The slope broke off into a sharp vertical descent. His gaze followed the drop down to a small ledge perched above the swollen, noisy river hundreds of feet below. He swallowed back his fear that he'd see a body or two lying on the ledge, wondering why Eli had brought him here. Then he noticed the way the ground below him had crisscrossing indentations.

Footprints. Even from this high up, he could see both footprints and boot marks. Two sets of feet.

Connors. And the woman.

They'd fallen off the cliff? Eph whistled low. Well, if they had, they'd survived the fall. It was clear they'd walked around on the broken ledge. But then where'd they go? The precipitous mountainside was a jumble of mud and rock, indicating a recent avalanche. He shook his head and gulped. It wasn't much of a leap to assume Connors and the woman—and her baby—were buried somewhere under the slide. His hope at finding them plummeted down the mountain.

"Here," Eli said, fingering a line of thick old gray rope. He handed it to Eph. "It was tied off over yonder"—he tipped his head indicating the trunk of a small twisted spruce—"Connors used it to git down to Grace."

Eli stared at the water. "There's a lot of mud and rock on the riverbank. I can't see prints from this far up." He looked at Eph, his face stricken with worry. "There's no way to tell if they made it down safely. And I don't see any clear way down for us without riskin' settin' off another avalanche. This hillside is precarious."

Eph nodded. "They either made it out or they didn't." He let the words hang between them. There was nothing for it; they had to get back to town before dark. He hoped Connors was taking the woman and her baby to safety. They would no doubt follow the river down to the Front Range. Eph pictured a map of the Poudre canyon in his head. From where the timber drivers worked the Poudre further up, where they sent thousands of saw logs downriver during winter—logs that floated the miles to the railroad in Greeley, where they were milled into boards. How far were they from the northern road? Ten miles, at most? They'd either come upon Whitcomb's ranch at Boxelder Creek or bisect the northern road. But it wouldn't be easy going—not with a barefooted woman and a baby. Assuming they were alive and unhurt.

"You don't see anyone down there?" Eph asked Eli, trusting the Indian's keen sight over his own weak eyes. Anything beyond fifty feet started looking blurry around the edges for him. From up here, all he could make out were sandy banks of the river splattered with shadows cast by the large rocks. Shadows that, for all he knew, could be bodies.

"Nope," Eli replied. "But it's hard to see past the bend in the river. Could be they're there." He paused. "Could be they're under three foot of mud on the mountain." His voice was low, quiet, thoughtful.

Eph turned away from the edge and looked at Eli. "You said you knew Grace."

Eli nodded. "She's my gal's friend. A right nice woman." He chewed his lip. "Sure makes no sense that those outlaws woulda taken her. I can't figure it."

"Neither can I. But I intend to get to the bottom of this mystery."

Eli rubbed his jaw. "Well, s'pose we best head back. Nothin' more we can do here."

Eph nodded at him to lead the way. When they got back to the cabin site, O'Grady was tying Billy Cloyd's body onto his own horse. LeRoy had returned and was sitting his little mustang, his eyes narrowed in expectation. The men all looked to Eph, questions on their faces.

Eph shook his head. "All we know's they fell down the cliff to a ledge and survived that. Saw footprints, but there's been a recent slide."

He faced LeRoy. "No sign of Connors's horse?"

"Looks like it hoofed it down the mountain. Might be because of the wild bunch."

"I wonder why the horse'd take off," Coon said. "Makes more sense he'd stay here, with these others."

Eph nodded. But horses often had a sense about things. Maybe Connors's horse knew his owner was gone. Maybe even knew he was in danger. Some horses picked up on such things.

"Well, if we're done here, let's get back to town." Eph swung up on Destiny and clucked at her to get moving. His posse followed, with Coon walking alongside his red saddlebred burdened with Billy Cloyd's body, lead in hand. They couldn't go at too fast a pace, what with three bulky bodies tied to unhappy horses that had to navigate down tricky patches of rock fall. But once they got to the Front Range, he'd have Eli and LeRoy gallop ahead and grab a horse from the livery to take back to Coon so the hotel owner didn't have to walk all the way to Fort Collins. Even at this slow gait, they'd all trot in before dark, now that summer was easing in and the daylight lingered longer in the evenings. What a surprise they'd give the folks in town.

As much as he wanted to soak in the anticipation of such a glorious and welcoming homecoming, he couldn't help thinking about Grace Cunningham and her baby. He hoped Connors was getting them to safety. If there was no word of them once he got back to town, he'd have to round up a search party first thing in the morning. No chance anyone would be able to scour the river canyon in the dark of night, seeing that the new moon was already arcing across the sky, fixing to set. But he could send word to E. W. Whitcomb to be on the scout, to go send some of his ranch hands up into the canyon at first light.

Whitcomb was the fella that had that huge cattle ranch north of the Poudre. He was known for his wild parties and free-flowing whiskey, and although Eph had been invited on occasion to attend by some of the town's friendly revelers, Eph always declined. He and Sally preferred quiets nights rocking on the porch and looking out at the stars as they twinkled over the open range. He and Sally were of a mind—they preferred the kind of solitude that allowed a man—or woman—to think over their life and dwell on all the things they were grateful for. And Eph had plenty to be grateful for—especially after today.

"Sheriff," LeRoy yelled over as they came to that steep last draw they'd climbed before coming upon the cabin. LeRoy had trotted over to a promontory that looked over the long dusty trail they'd crested up into the mountain.

Eph looked over at him, shaken from his weary musings, the warm afternoon sun making him drowsy and stirring the longing to lay on the soft grassy bank by the creek out behind his house. His stomach grumbled loud enough to make Destiny's ears twitch back. It had been too many hours since he'd eaten a thing—last night, he now reckoned—and he was starving. He usually kept some dried fruit or hard tack in his saddlebags, but today they were filled with guns and cartridges.

"What is it?" Eph called back to him. Eli, at LeRoy's signal, had joined his brother, and the two Indians stared down in the direction of the open range.

"The horses them boys want," Stapleton said, chewing on a wad of tobacco.

Eph saw the brothers fist their reins, and their mustangs now danced in place, as if they'd spotted some of their distant relations in that herd below.

"Go on," Eph told them, trotting over to them and seeing at least a hundred head of horses cantering across the wide open plain a half mile east and north. At the head was an appy stallion, kicking up his legs and snorting. Eph figured he had once been someone's prized horse brought out to the Front Range and who'd gotten tired of a cramped stall and three squares of hay a day. Some stallions, however well trained, could not risk that call of the wild. Eph believed deep in every horse's heart was the yearning to run free. Not unlike a whole lot of men he knew. That's why so many came west, and left comfortable lives behind. It was a siren's song, and one Eph knew well. Out here in the West, horse and man heeded the same song—one that stirred the blood and sent a body's feet running for adventure.

"You sure, Sheriff?" Eli asked, his horse prancing in place, the rider's mind already halfway down the mountain after the herd.

"I'm sure."

LeRoy said, "Soon's we're done, we'll meet you back in Fort Collins. If Grace and Connors ain't back by then, we'll need to go find them." His expression was somber. Eph wondered if he and Eli thought there was much hope their missing persons were still alive. "We won't be gone long," he added. Then, without further ado, the Indians kicked their mustangs and trotted down the draw.

Eph smiled as he watched the pair break out into a run upon touching flat ground, thinking of how it would feel racing along the Front Range on the back of a wild mustang, chasing a herd of wild horses. There were plenty of pockets of herds all around the open range, but most were scraggly, runty specimens, hardly fit for ranch work or pulling a wagon. But Eph could see why these young men had set their sights on this bunch of horses. They were sure a fine brood of strong-legged creatures, running smooth, like water, over the land. Eph imagined the Indians could make a fortune from these horses—although after cashing in on the reward money for "capturing" Wymore and Cloyd, and returning the gold to the Pinkerton Detective Agency, that, under the auspices of the Department of Justice, doled out such rewards—it might cause that fortune to look pretty meager. But Eph reckoned they didn't round up and break wild horses for the money. It was in their blood, and something they loved to do.

With a nod to Coon and his two deputies, Eph swung Destiny around and headed back to town, a few tiny bits of ash floating in the breeze and entangling in his mare's mane.

Chapter 29

As if coming from a deep, dark well, a sweet voice tickled Malcolm's ears. In the forlorn blackness he wallowed in, he grasped the sound, groping at it, as if for a lifeline, and let it bring him to the surface of his consciousness.

A woman's voice. The soft tone soothed the searing pain in his head, and he forced heavy eyelids open. The glare of bright sunlight blinded him momentarily, but a shape hovering over him shifted and blotted out the light.

Where was he? He moved his fingers and touched warm sand. Then he brought a hand to his forehead and winced with a sharp intake of breath.

"Oh, thank God, you're awake," the voice said, filled with relief and agitation.

He knew that voice, but he couldn't place it, couldn't think clearly . . .

"Shh," she said, her face coming into focus in front of his.

"Grace . . ."

Images assaulted his mind, bringing back to him the past hours. He struggled to sit up. "Ben. Where's Ben?" he asked, his throat hoarse and dry. He tried to swallow.

"He's safe," Grace said, resting a warm hand on his cheek. "You saved his life."

Only now he could make her out clearly, her wheat-colored hair waterfalling down her shoulders in disarray, her nightdress torn and caked with sand. Her pale-green eyes glistened with tears, and her face bore scratches from their tumble down the mountain. Even so, she was the most beautiful thing he'd ever seen in his life. Ben lay curled in her lap, sleeping in his ripped blue blanket. He touched the baby's soft hair and smiled, grateful and amazed.

"Oh, Grace . . ." He searched deeply into her teary eyes, and grasped both her hands. "How long have I been unconscious?"

"An hour, maybe two."

He fingered a bandage of cloth tied around his head.

She reached over and adjusted it. "The bleeding's stopped. Monty, we have to—"

He straightened and stayed her hand. Her scent drifted to him—of river water and warm feminine skin. His heartbeat quickened. "You called me that before. I remember . . ."

Her face blanched. Malcolm studied her. She looked stricken with fear.

"What is it, Grace?" He stood and reached for her. She laid her baby down gently on a patch of short grass, then stood and faced him. "What's wrong?" In his head, he heard her calling him by that name, and suddenly remembered what he had seen in his mind's eye before he passed out.

"I have this strange memory," he told her, placing his hands on her quivering shoulders. "At least it feels like a memory. Of you—pregnant."

Grace choked back a sob. Malcolm kept talking. "You were sitting on the ground—in the rain. And . . . next to you was a wagon that was sinking in mud. There were two horses, but they ran off. I can see it so clearly now." He winced and looked out over the river. "And a . . . bridge. A heavy wooden one. The river rose, engulfed it. Flipped it over, and it broke the bank . . ."

He stopped speaking. Grace stared at him, her jaw dropped. He looked at her lips, so tender, so inviting. Her eyes simmered with love. Love for him. He could not mistake what he saw there. For his heart pounded with the same passion. He swallowed and stared at her, unblinking.

A surge of need brought a moan to his own lips, and he could not hold back. He squelched the tiny voice of warning, uncaring of the consequences of his actions. There was only his need, and hers, and this moment—far from any watching eyes, except those of heaven. And if heaven wrought judgment upon him for the fervent love he felt for Grace Cunningham, then so be it. He would willingly be damned for eternity in exchange for this one kiss . . .

He pulled Grace into his arms, and with his love pouring out of his heart like an overflowing fountain, his mouth found hers, and they joined, her lips as eager and needy as his. As they stood on the sand, a soft wind blowing down the river canyon, Malcolm no longer heard the tumble of the rapids behind them. He blotted out the world and the broken pieces of his past. He blotted out everything and every thought and kissed Grace with such a passion, he thought he would collapse.

She pressed her warm, soft body against his bare chest, the swell of her breasts so voluptuous through her thin nightgown. His hands roamed her body, as if exploring an exciting unchartered wilderness, yet every place his fingers lit upon felt so familiar to his touch. As if they belonged there. As if she had always belonged to him.

A shudder ran through Grace as he pushed aside her hair and kissed her neck. His mouth moved hot against her skin, and he whispered her name in her ear.

Grace groaned with desire, and cradled his chin in her hands. She sought his mouth with fervent desire, and Malcolm's head spun. Oh, how she made him feel. His every nerve tingled. His skin felt on fire. His heart melted in the warmth of her love. He longed to join his body with hers, here and now. It took inhuman strength to keep from pulling off her threadbare gown and losing himself inside her. He longed for nothing more in this moment than to immerse her in this river of love and together be swept away in the floodwaters.

Oh, sweet agony. He forced himself to pull back, and lifted her chin so she would look into his eyes. She stroked his cheek as she gulped and drew in a breath, as if she had been submerged underwater too long.

His gaze dropped to the necklace around her neck. He outlined the silver circle with his finger, and then froze. He saw his hands fastening the chain around her neck, heard her lighthearted laughter as he kissed her playfully, as she blushed demurely, a bright-blue bonnet on her head, her hair swept up in the latest style, tucked tightly to her head and adorned with beaded combs.

He took a step back and sucked in a breath. How could he have such a memory? Yet, it was a memory—he was sure of it.

"Monty, what is it?" Grace asked.

Monty. That was his name. Monty . . .

How did she know? This woman he had chanced upon in the streets of Fort Collins. He had so many questions, but they only seemed to lead to more questions. A shadow fell across his face. He looked up at the sky. The westering sun slipped behind the jagged ridge of the Rocky Mountains.

His questions would have to wait. There would be plenty of time for his questions—*if* they made it out of the canyon alive. Already, with the sun sinking behind the Rockies, the air had cooled. Grace shivered as she studied him pensively.

He drew her to him, and once more the warmth of her skin set him on fire. He kissed her and cupped her face in his hands.

Grace lingered in Monty's muscular arms, feeling so safe, so right. How she had longed for this—for his kiss. She missed the taste of his mouth and the feel of his gentle lips. Every inch of her skin burned with pent-up desire for him. She didn't care what he thought of her compliance. How wanton she must seem, giving in so readily to his amorous advances. But what did it matter? All that mattered was that Monty loved her. Even if he didn't remember her, she knew he loved her with all his being.

And she was heartened by the evidence that his memory was truly returning. If he now recalled the day she'd lost him, maybe all those other lost days would come tumbling back into his mind and heart. Her hope had been sparked anew, and a hot flame of desire and passion raged inside her.

She had to tell him the truth. She'd forgotten and said his name, and now she knew it was time. No more pretending. No more holding back. Perhaps by confessing, the rest of his memories would flood back. Like breaking the wall of a dam. Or tossing one rock down a mountain and creating an avalanche.

Her body throbbed with need. The need to feel him close. To feel his body joined with hers again. These months of separation had been unbearable, but even more unbearable was the thought that she'd almost lost him again. That she still might lose him. She must tell him—everything. And then what? Would he leave Stella?

Oh, if only she had proof of their marriage. If she could get that copy of their marriage certificate, it would prove to Monty that he was married to her. That he'd been hers long before Stella sank her hooks in him. He was lawfully *her* husband, not Stella's. She had to get that proof. And then they could be together again. Monty might never get all his memories back, but that didn't matter so long as he loved her.

Monty pulled back, breathing hard, sweat beading on his forehead. He looked tenderly in her eyes and caressed her cheek. Everything she had suffered this day blew apart in the sweet breeze playing in her hair. It seemed as if all the forces of the world had sought to tear them apart, but somehow their ordeal had finally brought them together.

Malcolm sighed, the taste of Grace's lips lingering on his mouth. "Grace, I won't apologize for my behavior. For I love you, with all my heart. I know it's wrong. I'm married. But—"

"I love you too," she said with firm conviction. "I . . . I . . ." A flustered look came over her, and he knew she had so much she wanted to say to him.

He stared at her in stunned silence. Her words were a balm to his soul. How had she come to love him? She hardly knew him. But maybe she'd felt the same uncanny attraction to him that he had for her the first day they'd met. He had no idea she felt this way about him. But he was glad. Oh so glad! He couldn't bear to think otherwise. But she knew he was married, and surely she knew the sin they were indulging in. How could God think their love was wrong when it was so very right?

"We have to hurry, or we'll never make it out of the river canyon," he told her. His words sobered her, and her face grew instantly serious. She reached down and scooped Ben up into her arms. The baby protested in whiny cries, and Malcolm guessed he was hungry.

"Do you need to feed him?" he asked.

She nodded. "But if we start walking, I might be able to distract him awhile." She shot him a look that froze him on the spot. "He's got a fever." She gulped, and Malcolm could tell she was fighting back tears.

"Mama, Mama," Ben said, waving his little hands weakly in the air, his face flushed and twisted in discomfort.

Grace kissed the top of his head. "Come, sweetie. Let's take a walk and look at all the pretty birds and flowers."

Malcolm longed to take her hand. Even only three feet apart, he felt torn asunder. He ached to touch her. He needed to hold her. The urgency of his need astonished him. He'd never felt anything like this with Stella. His chest tightened, and he took shaky breaths as he led her at a fast pace along the riverbank. Cool air chilled his bare chest, and water squished in his boots. Every bone and muscle hurt. A tingle of panic ebbed at his mind. It was getting late, and he'd stalled too long. His indulgence just might cost them their lives.

But her kisses and proclamation of love gave him the strength and determination to keep going, despite his bruises and pains and cuts. And then he realized Grace was barefoot, noticed her feet cut up and swollen. How far could they get? He waited for her to catch up and saw her wince with every step. If only he had the strength to carry her and Ben. But he knew he couldn't. They would go too slowly, and with his head injury, he was unsteady on his feet. No, their only hope was to hurry, despite their many pains.

"Can you manage?" he asked her as she hobbled to him. "Here, let me carry Ben."

"No," she said kindly. "You've suffered a terrible blow to your head. I'm used to carrying him."

He leaned over and rested his lips on her forehead and stroked her tangled hair. "You're a brave woman, Grace Cunningham. I'll get you and Ben home, whatever it takes."

At that, Grace chuckled. "I think we've been through hell and high water already. It's all downhill from here."

He shook his head in amazement at her. "All right," he said, his heart soaring with love. He kissed her sweetly once more on her lips, then trudged through the rocks and bunchgrass, seeking out the easiest path for Grace's tender feet.

Chapter 30

"HELLO? ANYBODY HOME?" ALAN SWUNG down off his horse and stomped the dirt off his feet, looking around the homestead. He hadn't ever been out here, south of town, where remote cabins dotted the range amid the mats of cactus and arid range. Malcolm Cunningham's parcel, though, sported a friendly little creek out back, although he wondered at the lack of womanly touch on the property. No vegetable or flower garden skirted the house, as was the case with most of the homesteads. No cheery curtains bordered the windows. Alan had read in the files that a Matthew Hoskins had up and left this parcel three years in. Alan couldn't place the man's face, and had no idea why he left. But he'd build a sturdy little house with pine siding and a shake roof that seemed to handle the Front Range wind and snowstorms.

"Hello," he called again, noting the front door cracked open. His breath caught in his throat, and he chided himself for not carrying a gun. He hated guns, and he kept a pistol out of necessity, but truth be told, he'd never fired it—not once in his life. He grimaced at the thought of that round bit of lead piercing flesh of any kind.

He threw Rattler's reins over the post out front and climbed the two steps to the porch. He craned his neck and peeked through the crack. Afternoon light splashed across a dusty wood floor, and from what he could see, someone had ransacked the place—or had left in a hurry. He imagined Malcolm had rushed out upon learning Grace had been abducted, but where had Stella gone? Surely Malcolm wouldn't have left his house in such disarray. Or maybe he had, in his hurry to go save Grace.

Steeling his nerve, he pushed the door open, guilt berating him for trespassing. But he reminded himself he was doing this for Grace, to find something that might help get her back. That might help lead to the truth about Stella Connors, Malcolm's wife.

He walked to the center of the living room, noting the furniture at haphazard placement, cupboards all swung open, dishes littering the counter. He tiptoed around the room, although he knew it was silly to do so. He worried at any moment someone—particularly Stella—might walk in on him and question his presence in the house. And if Stella was somehow tied up with the Dutton Gang . . .

Alan gulped down the fear and quickened his step. Methodically he looked through closets and rifled through drawers, pulling out what scant papers he could find. After about twenty minutes of careful searching, the last being the most embarrassing for him—going through Stella's closet and armoire full of clothing and ladies' undergarments—he'd found nothing incriminating. His face still felt hot from blushing at the . . . personal attire his fingers had touched. He had no idea women wore such things.

He blew hair out of his eyes and wiped his sweaty forehead. He removed his spectacles and cleaned them on the sleeve of his starched white tailored shirt. As he walked toward the door, frustrated and defeated, scrubbing a speck of mud off his spectacles, he slammed into a low table he'd forgotten was there. A large vase of wilted daisies crashed to the floor, water and shattered glass splattering the wood planks.

Alan sighed and stared at the mess. He couldn't leave without cleaning this up. As messy as the house was, Stella might return and know someone had trespassed. He tried to think up some excuse to give her should she walk in on him, but his mind went blank. No idea of any sort wiggled into his head.

He stood and fretted, then recalled seeing rags and a sweep broom in the back closet down the hall. As he hurried to fetch them, he thought about poor Grace, and fear once more bubbled up in his chest. Why had those men taken her? What did they want with her? Had they hurt her? Oh, he felt so helpless. How long would it be before the sheriff and posse returned? Every minute that passed felt like a week to him. He knew he'd never be able to sleep tonight. He would just plan to sit in his chair in his office and stare out the window for any sign of the sheriff's return.

He swung open the utility closet door and reached for the broom and a rag from the bucket sitting against the back. The broom was wedged between the bucket and the wall, so Alan yanked hard and pulled it free, nearly tumbling backward from the effort. He straightened his crooked spectacles on his nose, then peered into the dimly illuminated closet.

Odd. The back panel hung out from the wall at the top. Upon closer inspection, he noted that the nails had been pulled from their holes and still clung to the thin wooden paneling.

"What's this?" He tugged on the board and pried it free. He jostled it out of the cramped space and set it flat on the hall floor. Then he leaned into the closet and gaped at the dark space he'd uncovered.

A tan leather satchel lay on the floor, its flap open with a few papers spilling out of the top. What a peculiar place to store papers. Alan grinned. But exactly the type of place if you didn't want anyone to find them. Alan just knew the satchel belonged to Stella, and his palms grew itchy thinking about what he'd find inside.

A noise made him spin around. He clutched a hand to his thumping chest at the sight of a mouse scurrying across the floor just outside the closet. His feet were itching to run. He dared not dally any longer.

He grabbed the satchel, fastened the top, then slung it over his shoulder. For good measure, he placed the length of paneling back in place, and secured it once more with the broom and bucket. On his way out of the house, he frowned at the mess he'd made, but he just had to leave it. Every minute he tarried, the more anxious he felt. He was all alone out here on this homestead, miles away from the next neighbor—away from anyone who might hear him cry or come to his rescue should Stella or those outlaws come to find him here.

He mounted Rattler and kicked him into a gallop. Only when he reached the southern outskirts of town did he slow to a walk. His eyes darting from side to side, scanning the streets and casting quick glances behind him, told him no one was watching or following him. Fear crawled along his spine, but he kept Rattler walking at an unhurried pace, and he pasted a look on his face that said he was merely out for a peaceful afternoon ride through town—although the satchel was burning a hole in his back.

When he arrived at the livery, he put Rattler in his stall, then hurried to the courthouse, hoping no one would recognize him and engage him in friendly discourse. Without further ado, he slipped his key in the lock, turned the bolt, then locked the door behind him.

He blew out a breath and rushed into his office, then locked that door as well. After calming his heart, he dumped out the contents of the satchel on his immaculately clean desk, and papers fell out before him in a cloud of dust and dirt.

He picked up the papers and studied them. His eyes widened at letters written by and to Grace Cunningham. What in the world were her letters doing in Stella Connors's house? That pricked his curiosity. But not as sharply as did the next papers he perused: letters of recommendation for a position of surveyor from various educators and officials *in Illinois* . . . for *Montgomery Cunningham*. Not Malcolm Connors.

Alan jumped up from his chair. He was right! Malcolm *was* Montgomery Cunningham—Grace's husband, whom she'd thought had drowned. He knew it! Which meant Stella Connors had hidden that satchel and its contents from her husband.

Alan quickly read through the offer of employment Fred Wallace had mailed to Cunningham more than a year ago—to an address in Bloomington, Illinois, where Grace was from. And from where, no doubt, Monty aka Malcolm hailed.

Then he picked up another sheet of paper. His breath hitched. He held it aloft and stared at it. A marriage certificate. This was what Grace had asked him to request a copy of. Recorded at the Bloomington, Illinois, courthouse on September 23, 1874, it named Grace Ann Wilcox and Montgomery Cunningham. Married.

He felt around inside the satchel. At the bottom his fingers chanced upon a small box. He pulled it out and opened it. A small, simple gold band sat on a bed of burgundy velvet. This had to be Grace's wedding ring. But why would it be in here, instead of on her finger? Maybe Grace had kept it in the satchel for safekeeping while she and Monty traveled.

Although Alan's hopes for a chance with Grace sank like lead, he was glad he'd found the proof she wanted. He truly wanted her to be happy, and even though he knew she would never be his, he'd be doing right by her and her baby—Montgomery's son—to give her this very good news. Whether her husband would be happy to hear this news was another story. Which brought him back to why he'd gone out to pay Stella Connors a visit in the first place—to discover her secret.

There had to be something in the satchel that would give him a clue to her identity . . .

But after scouring every inch and seam of the satchel, he could find nothing more. Not one tiny clue that might shed some light on Stella Connors.

Alan sank down into his large padded leather chair and thought. First thing in the morning, he'd send a telegraph message to his pal who was a reporter at the *Rocky Mountain News* in Denver City. If anyone could find out Stella's true identity, Chuck Smithers could. Chuck knew everything there was to know about the Dutton Gang. He'd once witnessed the gang robbing a bank—from right across the street. The last time Alan had visited Chuck, his pal had shown him the very spot he'd stood on while watching the robbery four years ago.

With that decided, Alan stuffed the papers back in the satchel and stared at it, his thoughts returning to Grace's plight. It would be night soon. He may as well make himself a strong pot of coffee, seeing as he planned to stay up and worry. All this fretting and sneaking about had exhausted him. Maybe he'd allow himself a nap—just a little one, so he'd be fresh in the morning to set about his business bright and early.

As he lay back in his chair and closed his eyes, he let his thoughts drift to Grace's gentle face. He said a prayer for her safe return, but his grief and worry rekindled in double measure. Would anyone come back alive after chasing down Wymore and Cloyd? He feared the worst. And what a sad tale it would be if Montgomery Cunningham lost his life at the hands of a killer without learning the truth about his real wife, and his baby. Yep, that would be the worst tragedy of all.

Their horses' hooves sounded a somber knell on the hard-pack dirt as Eph Love shambled into town with his posse late that night. What with the Indian brothers off after their wild horse herd, Eph figured it a better plan if their small band stayed together—rather than have him or another run back to Fort Collins and fetch a mount for Coon. So, they'd alternated riding and walking, leading Coon's saddlebred topped with Cloyd's body, until, after long, uneventful hours navigating down the canyon and crossing the open range, they forded the Poudre at the intersection of the northern road to Cheyenne under a dusky sky and headed into town—hungry and weary but none the worse for wear. All they'd had to eat was dry tack and jerky that Coon had thought to bring, which rumbled like stones in Eph's cavernous stomach.

After the sun dropped behind the peaks halfway to town, the temperature plummeted, which swayed Eph's thoughts of accomplishment to ones of grave concern over Connors and the woman. He sure hoped they'd made it out alive, but he knew it was a fool's hope. That rockslide looked something fierce. But he'd know more on the morrow.

He wanted nothing more at this moment than to ride swiftly home to Sally and a hot meal, but first they had to get these bodies put in cool storage. Their horses, too, were hungry and weary, and they needed tending to. O'Grady's roan, Firebrand, had thrown a shoe and hobbled the last couple of miles. Eph hated to bother the undertaker on a late Sunday night, but there was nothing for it.

They came to a halt in front of the shuttered windows of the sheriff's office. The street was shrouded in darkness, and all the closed-up shops' windows looked like gloomy lidless eyes watching them in silence. Not the exuberant reception Eph had hoped for—no triumphant procession trotting into town with their prizes. But there would be plenty of time for celebration. He smiled thinking of that telegram he'd send to the Denver City sheriff's department first thing in the morning. And the one to the Pinkerton Agency—to claim that reward for his men.

"Help me lay out these bodies on the boardwalk," Eph told the men. "Then you can all git home and eat supper, and git a good night's sleep."

Stapleton slid off his horse and began untying the woman's body from the chestnut gelding. "You sure, Sheriff? You'll need some help gettin' these moved."

Eph noted the old Ranger's careworn face and shaky hands. "Nope. I'll see to it. Come on round in the morning. There'll be paperwork and statements to record."

The men, laden with exhaustion, acquiesced, and Coon and O'Grady set to work loosening knots. Once the horses were unburdened of the bodies, Stapleton set off down the street, leading the weary mounts to the livery to rub them down and situate them in stalls. Eph would speak with Joe Mason tomorrow and see about finding proper homes for them.

Soon he and Coon and O'Grady had the three bodies laid out on the wooden planks of the boardwalk. They were not a pretty sight, neither did any sport the peaceful look that death sometimes afforded. Mangled, shot up, bloody, caked with dirt—just the way Eph figured such outlaws would look in the end. Yet, the young woman was a cipher. She had a pretty-enough face, comely features. He wondered where she was from. Probably Denver City—if she had something to do with the Dutton Gang. Well, he'd get those telegrams sent at daylight.

"G'night, Sheriff," Coon said, rubbing a fatigued hand across his eyes. His deputies brushed their hands on their trouser legs. O'Grady looked over his roan's sore foot and rubbed the horse's ankle.

"He all right?" Eph asked.

"Yeah. I'll soak it some when I get him home."

Eph nodded. "You all did good today." He smiled, and the men stood next to their horses with thoughtful faces, looking at the bodies lying on the boardwalk, the outlaws' tale over and done. Cloyd and Wymore wouldn't cause anyone any trouble anymore.

Eph felt a heavy sense of finality with the blanket of night lying over them and the quiet, cool summer night punctuated with the drowsy chirp of crickets. A peaceful feeling seeped into his heart. The niggling threat that had been hanging over him for months—knowing these men were loose and up to more trouble, fearing they'd come into his town and wreak havoc—was gone. A great burden had lifted from his shoulders.

He blew out a long breath, then bid the men good-bye. He watched them until they turned down side streets and vanished from his sight. Then, his thoughts weighed by worry over Connors and the woman and her baby, he strode down Jefferson Street heading to the undertaker's house on Oak, the crickets serenading his quiet footfalls.

Grace wrapped her arms around her chest as she huddled on the cold rock under a murky night sky, her teeth chattering and her bones aching from injury and the freezing temperatures. She could hardly feel her cold bloodied feet, and her hands were so stiff, she thought they'd break if she hit them.

How many hours had passed since they started their trek downriver, Grace had no idea. But it felt as if they'd been walking for years. She was so cold, but refused to give up hope. She would not lose Monty—not now, after all they'd been through. Her mind, although a boggy mash of wandering thoughts, latched on to this one resolve—to not lose hope. It truly was a tenuous anchor to which she clung with her last ounce of strength.

"It can't be much further now; we're practically down to the Front Range," Monty told her, hugging Ben to his chest and keeping him warm. He cast concerned eyes upon her and drew close. As soon as it got dark—when Grace had stumbled and nearly thrown Ben from her arms—Monty had taken the baby from her, brooking no argument.

Stroking her head, he said, "I promised I'd get you and Ben to safety. If I have to carry you both, I will." He gave her an encouraging smile, and Grace tried to smile back, but she couldn't muster it. He kissed her forehead and added, "Come. Just one little step at a time. You can tell the air's a little warmer now that we're almost down the mountain. Wait here—I need to scout ahead again, see which way to go."

He looked up at the star-studded sky. "I'm sure we're heading in the right direction. The river hugs the mountain along the range not that far north of Fort Collins."

Grace closed her eyes, wishing she could chase away the fear that gripped her. She could tell Monty was doing all he could to cheer her up. But he was hurt, and each step for him was a struggle—holding on to Ben and finding his footing with his head pounding. Twice Monty nearly passed out, and she'd had to wait anxiously for his fuzzy vision to clear before they could set out again. His voice was full of courage and hope, but she imagined he was just as frightened as she.

She watched him stumble off in the dark, and her stomach clenched with fear. How could he see anything? At least the murmur of the river and their steady descent assured her they had to come out on the open range at some point. But when? She couldn't make it another mile.

Exhaustion lay heavy on her, pushing her to the ground, and every step she took was a monumental effort. They were weak from hunger, but it was the cold that was their undoing. Cold clenched her in a tight fist, and the black bowl of twinkling stars overhead mocked her with their weak sparkles of light. Under other circumstances she might have looked upon this river canyon as stunning wild scenery, with the snow-drenched Rockies as a picturesque backdrop. Tonight, it was the harbinger of her death, sucking the life from her—and from Monty and Ben—without remorse, without noticing.

The shushing of water rippled over her. She closed her eyes and slipped off the rock to the sandy hard ground. Memories of the day Monty had been swept downstream haunted her. She recalled the way the water had churned with its splashing brown waves, the tumbling logs careening off its overflowing banks. She could hear the clamor of the river's rage, and the loud squeal and crash of the bridge as ground gave way beneath it and it heaved into the maelstrom of water.

Monty had loved rivers. He lived to explore them. Wild water ran in his blood. Yet, this river—the Cache la Poudre—had been her nemesis from the first day she set eyes upon it. It was a demon, a beast that strove to rip from her hands everything she loved. It had taken her husband—twice—and her child. It had taken her wagon with all her belongings. Of all the trials she'd thought she would encounter in the Wild West, she never imagined her greatest foe would be a river. Wild Indians, disease, blizzards, drought and dust—she'd anticipated those, and they had been the stuff of her nightmares in the weeks preceding their departure for Colorado Territory.

She let her mind drift off and felt a stupor of calm envelop her. Soon, the last vestiges of pain dissipated from her body, and her teeth stopped chattering. She hardly felt the cold now. So tired, so tired. All she needed was sleep, sweet sleep . . .

"Grace. Grace!"

She felt someone shaking her, but she couldn't open her eyes. Where was she? She had been floating, floating. Drifting along on slow-moving water, warm and peaceful. *Leave me alone,* she wanted to say. So peaceful, so quiet . . .

"Grace!"

Malcolm shook her shoulder, at first gently, but then with more urgency. Ben slept hard in his arms, his body radiating feverish heat, and Malcolm jostled him as he dropped to his knees on the sand beside Grace.

Fear gripped his chest. She had slipped unconscious. What was he to do?

He peered into the darkness at the river valley they'd entered. Only small shrubs and grass grew amid the strewn rocks. There were no trees other than spindly aspens and cottonwoods. Nothing he could use to make a shelter.

"Oh, Grace, please. You must wake up." He ran his hands over her arms. She was freezing, and her breathing was shallow and thready. *Please,* he begged, *don't die on me!*

Fighting down the panic fomenting in his gut, he strained to think of some way to save her. His head felt like a box of lead; thinking took more effort and strength than he could muster. He cursed his uselessness, his lack of a rope, of supplies, extra clothing, a blanket.

But he could not afford to sit there cursing his bad luck. He would not give up, or give in to the hopelessness strangling him. Like a noose, he felt it tightening around his neck. He knew the only way they would all survive was if he carried them both. Yet, he hardly had the strength to carry Ben much further. How could he carry Grace?

But he had to. He had no other options. He could not leave her here. Neither could he abandon Ben to carry Grace to safety. He refused to choose between the two.

"I will not play God!" he yelled into the night. "Don't make me choose!"

He felt his mind unhinging. He heard laughter and spun around, but no one was there. Cold coated his skin; he felt encased in ice. It was so tempting to curl up on the ground next to Grace and close his eyes too. Sleep beckoned like a temptress, casting alluring glances at him and gesturing him to her side. His eyelids, so heavy, began to close, his thoughts wandering off to the memory of that woman he had picnicked with, in the sunny warm park, surrounded by pink and yellow flowers next to a bridle path—

Malcolm's eyes opened wide. He now saw the woman's face. She was the same woman he'd kept seeing, the one who flitted in and out of his dreams. She was Grace, and he remembered that day in the park. He saw the place clearly in his mind, as if it were yesterday.

He looked down at her as she lay there unmoving, barely breathing. She had maybe minutes left before she would succumb to the cold. All the answers to his past lay with her. And all the hope for his future. He could not let her die. He loved her. He had always loved her. Heaven had somehow returned her to him. And if that was true, then God could not intend for him to lose her now.

With a prayer on his lips, he felt a burst of energy infuse his limbs. *Lord, you are able to provide abundantly more than anything I could ever ask or imagine. Please, give me the strength I need. Show me the way to your safe place of refuge.*

He gently lay Ben down, then with a sharp intake of breath, he reached for Grace and hefted her over his shoulder. Oddly, she felt as light as a feather. The determination coursing through his blood pushed the fog from his mind, and his thoughts were sharp and clear.

Carefully squatting, he reached over with his free right arm and lifted Ben to his chest, the sick infant's breath wheezing against his shoulder. Then, he stood, getting his balance with this bulky weight in his arms. His legs newly invigorated, he took a hesitant step, then another.

As he walked he felt the warmth of his body, heated by the exertion of movement, seep into Grace's chilled skin. He fought off his trepidation with faith—the only weapon he had left in his arsenal. He had been stripped of everything, even of hope. But now he realized the reason, for it was faith alone that would see him through.

When all else failed, faith remained. That, and love.

With those two powerful divine gifts clutched in his heart, Malcolm marched resolutely down the gently sloping hillside, feeling renewed strength in his thighs and back. Soon sand and rock turned to grassy swales that rolled into pastureland. And under the canopy of a million winking stars, Malcolm came to a promontory that overlooked a wide lush valley filled with thousands of dark shifting shapes he guessed were cattle. His gaze swept the prairieland until it settled on the faint outlines of buildings.

A ranch lay below him, and a few tiny lights glowed in soft amber through windows.

Encouraged by the sight, Malcolm quickened his step, hugging Grace and Ben tightly against his chest, Grace's head hanging over his shoulder and her hair tickling his neck. Her skin was warm now against his body, and Ben's little snores were the sweetest music to his ears. As he stumbled his way down a deer track leading toward the ranch, he heard the soft sound of cattle lowing, and the nicker of horses.

Through the haze of his exhaustion, as he kept his eyes riveted to the ground, careful not to trip and fall as his last reserve of strength petered out, he heard men's voices. Shouts of alarm. Excited conversation. He swore he even heard the voices of the trackers—Eli and LeRoy Banks.

I must be delirious. Malcolm struggled to keep his eyes open, then felt his knees begin to buckle.

Flashes of bright light flickered through the brush ahead. He stopped, unable to take another step, and dropped to the ground. But as he fell, the dizziness consuming him, strong arms grasped his. Arms hefted him, took Ben and Grace from his deathlike clutch, led him in slow steps.

His arms felt empty and cold without Grace and Ben to hold against his bare chest. His head hung lifeless. He couldn't raise it to look at the men who supported his weight in their arms, helping him stumble along, the rough cloth and leather of their coats and sleeves abrading his raw, bruised body. He wanted to say something, to thank them, to ask them where he was, to tell them Grace was hurt and Ben was feverish and needed tending . . .

"Shh," someone with a deep, soothing voice said. "You're safe now. We've been looking for you . . ."

Malcolm heard no more. A sigh rattled his chest—a sigh of relief and exhaustion and utter joy. A blast of heat met his face as he heard a door swing open. His rescuers lowered him down onto a soft cushion. Tears wet his cheeks as his thoughts drifted off.

He could sleep now. Now that they were safe.

Safe. Grace and Ben are safe. Thank you, Lord. Thank you, thank you . . .

Chapter 31

THE PHOTOGRAPHER'S FLASH MOMENTARILY BLINDED Eph as he stood at the back of the large room in the courthouse that was serving as a makeshift viewing arena for the three bodies he and his men had brought back to town. The room was a flurry of agitation and wonder, filled with town officials talking in excited voices. Soon the photographs of the wanted men would be plastered on the front page of every newspaper west of the Mississippi.

The undertaker had stayed up with Eph long into the night, preparing the bodies. Making Clayton Wymore presentable had been a challenge, and since most of his face had been crushed, they mutually agreed, for the sake of those with weak stomachs, that a shroud should be placed over the outlaw's head. Eph had already wired the Denver City sheriff's office, as well as numerous county agencies. Soon, news reporters from every town in the territory would descend upon Fort Collins, eager to catch a glimpse of the bodies of the last of the Dutton Gang.

Wrought with sleeplessness, Eph had gathered his deputies at the onset of dawn and gave them the task of keeping order while he sent off the many telegrams. He'd told Jenkins in the telegraph office he'd be expecting replies, and to watch in particular for one from the Denver City sheriff. Eph sent a query with a brief description of the dead woman, but he doubted he'd learn anything. He knew as much about the Dutton Gang as most anyone, and although the outlaws had engaged plenty with women—mostly of the unsavory type—he'd not heard of any so close to the gang that she'd be privy to the location of the stash of gold. But they'd spent months in hiding, and there was no telling who Hank Dutton had brought into his confidences.

Tired of the sweaty, sweltering room full of gawkers—and soon to get even more packed and claustrophobic—Eph squeezed through the crush of onlookers to get a breath of fresh morning air. He worked his way past jubilant townsfolk who showered praise and gratitude on him as he walked the narrow hall and exited onto the boardwalk. A crowd had gathered at the corner in front of the Old Grout, and upon seeing him emerge from the courthouse door, they cheered in an uproarious manner.

Eph tipped his hat at the smiling faces, but his joy was still dampened by the lack of word about his missing persons. He'd sent Coon out early, before dawn—after finding the hotel owner sitting in his lobby with a shot glass of whiskey in his hand. Coon made no apology for his premature imbibing. Only raised the glass at Eph in a celebratory salute. Eph figured Coon was still making up for all the years of prohibition that he'd had to endure until recently. Coon, though, comfortably situated in a large leather chair, was quick to his feet at Eph's request to ride up to Whitcomb's ranch and see if the cattle rancher would spare some of his men to search the river canyon for signs of Connors and the woman.

Now all Eph could do was wait. He had to stay in town and field the questions and respond to the telegrams. He doubted Fort Collins had had this much excitement in many a year.

Just as he was about to duck into the telegraph office, he spotted Alan Patterson, the courthouse clerk, rushing toward him. The small bespectacled man waved his arm and called to him.

"Sheriff, Sheriff!"

He came pounding to a halt in front of Eph, his face flushed and his curly hair flying out from under his hat. Eph smoothed his moustache and waited for the serious-faced clerk to catch his breath.

"Where's the fire, Patterson?" he asked with a chuckle. Surely there'd be no more kidnappings today.

Patterson glanced left, then right, as if on the scout for another member of the Dutton Gang. "I have something I need to show you," he said. Then his face soured. "Has anyone seen Malcolm Connors yet?"

Eph could tell by the clerk's expression that he'd already heard the entire tale of their pursuit and return of the prior day. He gestured Patterson to follow him, and they walked down the boardwalk and turned in at the alley behind the courthouse, where ears would have trouble listening in on their conversation.

"Nope," Eph told him. "And to be frank, I hold little hope he's alive. He and the woman were caught in an avalanche—"

"Grace. Grace Cunningham," Patterson said, his face chalky and perspiring in the cool morning breeze. "And Connors—that's not his real name. He's Montgomery Cunningham. Grace's husband."

Eph's eyes widened. "What are you talking about?" While Patterson slipped a satchel from his shoulder and opened the ties, Eph chewed on Patterson's words. He recalled Connors coming into the assessor's office that day, inquiring about employment. He seemed to remember the fella was married too. But not to Grace Cunningham. Odd.

Patterson pulled out some sheaves of paper. "Here. Look. This here's his offer of employment. And this here's his marriage certificate, showing he and Grace were married in Bloomington, Illinois, back in 1874. And this here's her ring." He handed Eph a small wooden box.

"I don't understand," Eph said. "Why are you telling me this?"

"Connors—I mean, Montgomery Cunningham—was swept away in that flood last year—when that bridge R. V. Cloud built over the Poudre was washed out, remember? He lost his memory, and somehow he ended up married to a woman named Stella. They purchased a homestead south of town last fall."

"And?" Eph wondered where Patterson was going with this line of talking, and he couldn't spend all day standing in an alley. He had important things to do.

"Sheriff—that woman you have dead and lying in the courthouse? That was Connors's wife."

"His wife—?"

"And not just his wife. Her real name is Lenora." He lowered his voice to a trembling whisper. "*Lenora Dutton.*"

Eph jolted back and studied Patterson's face. Dutton? "Hank Dutton's sister?"

"No, his wife."

"Dutton was married?" Eph narrowed his eyes. "How'd you know that?"

"From a pal in Denver City. But look—that's who you got lying in that room—the outlaw's wife. She knew where the gold was, and she rode out to meet up with Clyde Wymore. 'Member I said I'd seen 'em in town, in that alley? She was there too. Only, at the time I didn't recognize her. But then, after you all had rode off to go after them outlaws, I recollected I had seen her before. I'd seen her with Connors—I mean Cunningham."

"Where'd you git those papers?" Eph asked, his mind reeling with this astonishing information.

"I . . . uh . . . went out to his homestead, to see if I could get some information pried out of her. But she had gone, and the house was in shambles, as if someone had been in a hurry to leave. I . . . I found the satchel there, and . . . looked through it," he said sheepishly.

Eph laid a hand on the shaky man's shoulder. "Well . . . this brings a whole lot of dark secrets into the light." Dutton's wife, hiding out in his town, pretending to be married to some other fella. Or maybe not pretending. Eph wondered how this Lenora had gotten Connors to marry her. It made sense she'd want to disappear under another name and in a small town close to the stash of gold. Eph reckoned she'd been biding her time after her husband had gotten hanged, just waiting for the chance to fetch the gold belonging to the gang.

"If . . . if Cunningham comes back . . . alive . . ." Patterson stuffed the papers and the ring box back into the satchel and handed it to Eph. "I hope he does, and you can tell him." His face turned thoughtful. "I can't picture how he'll react to all this news. What with him being legally married to Grace, and his other wife lying dead over yonder." He tipped his head toward the courthouse door.

Before Eph could say another word, Patterson hurried off, flustered and emotional. Eph scratched his head at the clerk's odd manner.

Well, that sure was some hair in the butter. Which made him wonder if this Montgomery Cunningham had somehow regained his memory. For why else would he have been so adamant about joining the posse? And risked his life sliding down a rope to save Grace—

his wife? Eph shook his head. This surely was a story for some penny dreadful, that was certain.

Lenora Dutton—posing as Connors's wife. She must have been the reason Wymore kidnapped Grace. No other possible explanation made sense. Woman's jealousy? Maybe she did love Connors and he'd realized he was married to someone else. He had a hunch Lenora put Wymore up to the kidnapping. But now, he'd never really know, would he? All parties involved in the kidnapping were dead. It sure was a strange turn of events though. And one he had little time to ponder at the moment.

He slipped the satchel over his shoulder and strode to the telegraph office. As soon as he rounded the corner, grateful citizens of Fort Collins hounded him with praise and questions. He smiled and answered them in polite but terse phrases, pushing his way inside. *Lenora Dutton. Who would have figured?* Well, that was one piece of the puzzle put in place. He'd best send another telegram to the Denver City sheriff and to Governor Routt's office. Likely there'd be someone who'd recognize the woman's face and could confirm Patterson's claim.

Grace walked unsteadily in the too-large ankle boots Mr. Whitcomb had given her, but those were the only shoes he could find that were close to her size. Every step made her wince in pain, but she knew those wounds would heal. Whitcomb had instructed his Mexican cook to find her suitable attire from a closet full of clothing that Whitcomb said various and sundry guests had left behind after attending parties at his ranch. In a loose-fitting white button blouse and pretty olive-green skirt, Grace made her way out to the wagon awaiting her out the front door of the spacious log home. How wonderful it felt to be washed and wearing clean clothes. To have a full stomach and be alive to live another day.

Gratitude spilled from her heart as she saw Monty standing by the wagon hitched up to a team of black mules, Ben in his arms, wearing a brown work shirt, brown trousers, and some old scuffed boots Whitcomb had given him. They'd all had hot baths and a hot meal late in the night, once their wounds had been tended to by the ranch's vet. Grace barely remembered anything besides the delightful soothing feel of the hot water on her skin, and she'd been allowed to bathe an hour in a private room in an oversized tub—a luxury for her scratches and scrapes and bruises that stung and throbbed. She'd given Ben a lukewarm bath and nursed him, and after a long, hard sleep in a marvelously comfortable bed, she'd awakened to his smiling face and chubby fingers patting her cheek, his fever gone and his light-pink color restored to his face. The vet said he'd been dehydrated, and his exposure to the cold had brought on the fever. They'd all had a dangerous brush with death, but by the grace of God—and Monty's unwavering determination—they'd survived.

Monty's eyes brightened with love upon seeing her. He came over and took her hand and led her to the wagon. Presently Eli and LeRoy came out of the log home, the smiles wide across their faces as they chatted genially with Whitcomb on the wide porch. She'd been stunned to learn, later that night, they were here, at this ranch. And that they'd joined the posse to come rescue her. At breakfast, sitting at a long heavy oak table with the Whitcombs and Monty, the two brothers related the entire story of their coming to her rescue, and Grace had been shocked to hear how Clayton Wymore had died. She could tell they were holding something back, for they glanced at her from time to time, worry searing their eyes.

"You ready to head back?" Monty asked her. Ben reached out his arms for her and she took him, inhaling the fresh lavender scent of his hair, and planting kisses on his cheeks. How good it felt to hold him in her arms, to know he was out of danger.

She looked at Monty, who couldn't seem to take his eyes off her. But what would happen now? She thought about Stella and wondered what she was doing in this moment. Was she worrying over Monty? What would Monty say and do upon returning to Fort Collins? Through their ordeal, she hadn't allowed herself to think ahead, not knowing if they would survive. But now . . .

She wanted nothing more than for Monty to wrap his arms around her, and ride off with her, far away from Fort Collins. But she could only meet his eyes with polite aplomb in the presence of all these men. Whitcomb's ranch hands were busy in the front yard with daily chores, hauling hand wagons loaded with hay and pumping water into troughs. Off in the grassy fields grazed hundreds of longhorn cattle, red and black, and the air was redolent of moist grass and hay and cow. From where she stood she could neither see nor hear the river, and for that she was glad. She'd had enough water and rivers for a lifetime. A few clouds floated lazily across the sky, and the mountains glistened in the morning summer sun. It was a glorious morning, and she was glad to be alive to breathe it all in.

She calmed her anxious heart. *Somehow, some way, she would get her Monty back.* She'd had no time alone with him since they'd arrived at the ranch. But she would have to speak to him soon and tell him the truth—hopefully before he set eyes on Stella.

Just thinking about her made Grace's pulse race. Just what was Stella up to? What did she want with Monty? Well, Grace planned to find out. She knew Eli and LeRoy would help her, as would Clare. Maybe if she could expose Stella's secrets, Monty would leave her and not look back.

Monty took her hand and helped her up to the wagon's bench seat. His gentle touch sent a shock of warmth tingling across her skin. Eli and LeRoy came trotting over.

"Let's git goin'," Eli said, hopping into the back of the wagon that was littered with scraps of hay. "Clare's gonna kill me if I don't git you two back to town quick as a wink. I'm sure she's sick with worry over you, Grace."

Monty had been surprised to learn that Grace knew the brothers, and she'd explained to him at breakfast how she'd met Clare. Grace was glad that Eli and LeRoy hadn't said a word to Monty about what she'd divulged in secret—about Monty's true identity and his past. About her being married to him. They acted as if they hadn't an inkling at all, and for that she was grateful. Though, she saw the questions in their eyes and knew they wondered just how much she'd told Monty during their ordeal.

Mr. Whitcomb came over and shook the brothers' hands. "Well, I have to hand it to you boys—ya done good bringin' in that herd. And I thank you for givin' me the pick of the mares."

He gestured over to a ranch hand who was walking toward them, leading a saddled quarter horse. "This fella yours?" he asked Monty.

Monty swiveled to look at the horse being led. "Hey, it's Rambler." He rushed over to the gelding and threw an arm over its neck, patting it and beaming in affection. "Where'd ya go, fella?"

"I reckon he got tired of waitin' for you up on the mountain. He ran in with the herd," Whitcomb said. "But he sure seems happy to see you now."

Monty chuckled. "And I'm happy to see him." He took the lead rope from the rancher and tied the end of it to the side of the buckboard. He said to his horse, "Well, pal, you had your fun, but it's time to head home."

Whitcomb turned to Grace and patted her hand in a fatherly manner, and smiled at Ben, who reached out to grab the man's thick beard. "I'm glad you an' the young'un are all right. You take care now, and may the good Lord take a likin' to ya."

Grace thanked him with a heart full of gratitude, and after shaking Monty's hand, the rancher ambled over to the bunkhouse and went inside.

Monty climbed into the back beside Eli as LeRoy took a seat next to Grace and picked up the reins to the two large mules that stood half asleep in their harness. LeRoy's face was exuberant as he gazed out over the wild horses in the pasture.

LeRoy had recounted at breakfast how he and Eli had chased the herd down the mountain to Whitcomb's ranch. The horses had made so much noise that a mile before they came upon the ranch, the hands were ready for them. With the help of all Whitcomb's men, they funneled the herd into fenced pastures, where they now grazed, no longer free to roam the open range.

LeRoy said to Monty, "Glad you got your horse back."

"Wait till Clare hears about the herd," Eli said, fidgeting with excitement behind her on the flat bed. "She's gonna fall on her face."

LeRoy laughed and slapped his brother on the shoulder. "She didn't figure on us ever catchin' that stallion. They'll sure bring us a passel of money." He nudged Eli. "Now you can marry Clare proper—give her that fancy wedding she wants."

Eli merely chuckled and stared out at the mountains.

"You picked a ring out yet?" LeRoy asked in a prodding tone.

Grace listened to their playful banter as LeRoy drove the wagon down the long flat dirt road. After a mile or so, they emerged out from under the arch that Grace had seen all those months ago on that stormy day—the name "Whitcomb" carved in wood overhead. How long ago that seemed. She had been so happy, so innocent. They'd just come from Illinois to Cheyenne, ready to begin their exciting new life in the West. They'd hardly been in Colorado Territory a day before tragedy struck.

Grace shivered as they turned down the well-packed road south heading toward Fort Collins. She'd heard a new bridge had been built in the place of the former one—the one she'd watched tumble into the muddy waves of the angry river. Trepidation and fear clutched at her throat as they approached the crossing, and she shut her eyes, not wanting to look at either the water or Monty. Would he recognize this place, now that he'd remembered that horrible day?

As the mules' hooves clomped on the bridge's wood planks, she felt a hand light on her shoulder. Then, Monty's words came softly to her ears.

"I told you I'd get you home safely, Grace Cunningham. There's never a need to worry. The Lord always makes a way."

Chapter 32

MALCOLM WAS ASTONISHED AT THE crowds filling the streets of town, cheering as they rode down College Avenue and stopping in front of the courthouse as they arrived midmorning. Everyone in Fort Collins seemed to have heard about the posse killing the outlaws, and about Grace's kidnapping and rescue. The attention was a little unsettling, for all Malcolm wanted right now was to be alone with Grace, to hold and kiss her, to wrap her in his arms and never let her go.

His heart ached as he got out of the wagon, feeling confused and flustered now that they were back. His head throbbed with a pain that speared his eyes. He scanned the street, looking for Stella and hoping she wasn't there. The last thing he wanted at this moment was to see or talk to her. Maybe she was at the homestead. He pictured her pacing and cursing, furious that he'd joined the posse and gone after Grace. But he didn't care what she thought. Yet, he was stymied over what to do now. He had confessed his love to Grace. Would she leave town with him? Would she give up her life here? He couldn't imagine she'd sin against God and take up with a married man. And even if he divorced Stella, her joining him would still be a sin in God's eyes.

He'd been over and over this in his mind, and he couldn't see a way out. He couldn't bear the thought of walking away from her—especially after what they'd been through. And she loved him; she told him so. And he believed it with all of his heart. Were they destined to keep at arm's length, never be free to love? Would he never be able to consummate the fiery passion he felt for her?

Oh, Lord, what do I do? How could I bear such torment?

"Grace! Eli!"

Malcolm turned at the cry. A pretty young woman with red hair was waving, pushing through the crowd, her face exuberant. Malcolm guessed this was Clare, Eli's sweetheart. Malcolm's heart sank at the sight of Eli leaping from the wagon and sweeping her up into his arms and kissing her. And here he was, inches from Grace, and he couldn't touch her. The closeness was agonizing.

"Clare!" Grace yelled, climbing down from the wagon and running to her. Malcolm jumped to the ground and stood and watched, an outsider, a bystander. He felt suddenly alone and terribly lonely. His arms ached for Grace, for Ben. For a family with them. Nothing would make him happier.

"Mr. Connors," a man said behind him.

Startled out of his musings, he spun around and faced Sheriff Love.

"We thought we'd lost you," the sheriff said, a big smile lifting the corners of his thick peppered moustache. "We knew you'd gone down that hill . . ." He glanced over at the wagon, where LeRoy still sat up on the seat. Marcus Coon, who had met them halfway to town, sat his horse next to the wagon and was engaged in discussion with LeRoy. The sheriff gave a puzzled smirk. "The Indians brought you back?"

Malcolm nodded. "They drove that herd into Whitcomb's ranch. We managed to get down to his place around dark. Eli and LeRoy had alerted Whitcomb that we were missing, so he sent his men into the hills looking for us. The found us—just in time too."

The sheriff looked him over. "Well, I'm pleased to see you're in one piece." He looked over at Grace. "And the woman and the baby. They seem unharmed. You did a good job."

Malcolm let out a long breath, feeling the ordeal of the last couple of days weighing heavily on him. "Thank you, Sheriff, for getting a posse after her so fast. If you hadn't . . ." He let the words trail off, his throat cinching tight at the thought of Clayton Wymore's hands on Grace.

"Come into my office for a minute, will ya, Connors? I've got somethin' I want to show ya."

Malcolm chewed his lip as he studied the sheriff's face. The man's visage was calm and unruffled, but his eyes danced mischievously. What could he possibly want to show him?

He followed the sheriff through the front door and down the hall. When they got to the sheriff's large desk, Love motioned for him to sit. The office was empty and quiet, a contrast to the ruckus outside.

"I s'pose I've got some good news and some bad news," Sheriff Love said as doffed his slouch hat and set it on the desk. He motioned to Malcolm to take a seat, then he sat in the one behind the desk. "Though, the bad might not be so bad. Hard to say." The sheriff played with his moustache and leaned back in his chair.

Malcolm wondered at the sheriff's cryptic explanation. His palms got sweaty, and he swallowed. The last thing he wanted was more bad news. He'd had more than enough in the last two days.

"It's like this," Love continued, reaching down to the floor and coming back up with a tan leather pouch. "I've come into possession of some interesting documents."

He pushed the pouch across the desk to Malcolm, then rocked back in his wooden chair.

Malcolm hesitated and stared at the offering. He'd never seen it before. Was there something inside that would shed light on his past? Had to be. Malcolm's pulse quickened.

"What is it?" he asked, stalling. For some reason, a prickle of fear poked at his nerve.

Love indicated the bag with his head. "Just take a look-see."

The ticking of a grandfather clock sounded loud in his ears as he pulled a handful of papers out of the bag. He noticed letters addressed to Grace Cunningham and froze. Letters to Grace? Why was the sheriff showing these to him? He turned and looked at Love, who nodded at him to go on.

Malcolm set the dozen or so envelopes aside and opened a folded piece of paper. He perused the creased and wrinkled sheaf—a letter stating an offer of employment . . . to Montgomery Cunningham.

Malcolm's head throbbed anew. "I don't understand . . ." he mumbled, mostly to himself. Letters to Grace. A job offering to Montgomery—

Monty. That's what Grace had called me. My name. This is mine . . .

Malcolm's head reeled, and the room tilted. He put a hand to his forehead.

"This belongs to me," he said, aware of the sheriff's quiet, keen gaze resting upon him. Malcolm picked up another piece of paper. A letter written by the famous explorer John Wesley Powell, written on a letterhead indicating Wesleyan University, Bloomington, Illinois.

Suddenly a face came to mind. A big man with a large square head, sporting a huge moustache and beard, his face both stern and jovial. Powell. His instructor at college.

Malcolm gripped the edge of the desk. He saw the classrooms, the campus, the buildings. He heard Powell's voice as he lectured about geology from the dais at the front of the wood-paneled classroom.

Malcolm picked up the next piece of paper and read another letter of recommendation, from a man named Albert Peale, a mineralogist. Then another, from a surveyor in Bloomington. Their faces were as sharp and clear in his mind's eye as if the men were sitting in the sheriff's office with him.

The sheriff waited while Malcolm's thoughts whirled. *I'm not Malcolm Connors. I'm Montgomery Cunningham.* He sucked in a breath. *Which means . . .*

The sheriff slid another paper over to him—a small yellowed square sheet that sported an official stamp in the bottom corner. Malcolm lifted it with a shaky hand and read it.

He stared slack-jawed at the marriage certificate. His eyes caught on his name—Montgomery Cunningham—and the woman's name: Grace Ann Wilcox.

Suddenly he saw Grace in her beautiful sweeping white wedding dress, her hair up in pearls and lace, her face shining with joy. And then he saw the room in the Bloomington Courthouse, where he'd married her that spring day, and heard him speaking his vow to her. *I promise to love you and to cherish you, through sickness and in health, till death us do part . . .*

A cry blurted from his mouth as he set down the certificate. He stared at the sheriff, but no words came out.

"So . . . I reckon I should be calling you Montgomery," Love said matter-of-factly. "And I reckon this here's her ring," he added, sliding a small dark-wood box over to him. Malcolm opened the box and looked at the slender gold band sitting inside. That was the ring he'd put on her finger. Which she'd given to him before they left

Illinois, to keep in his leather bag for safekeeping when her fingers swelled from her pregnancy.

I'm married to Grace. She's my wife. My true wife. He looked at the date on the certificate. September 23, 1874. Nearly two years ago . . .

Monty. My name is Montgomery Cunningham . . .

Monty squeezed his eyes shut as the memories flooded into his mind like a raging river. Sweet memories of his life with Grace, back in Illinois, in her aunt's boardinghouse. But unlike the wild river that had wrested his past from him, he welcomed this assault to his senses, and reveled in all the memories of the passionate nights he had lain with Grace and showered his love upon her. He could feel her in his arms, and recalled the softness of her skin in all her wonderful hidden places. Memories of their long shared kisses sparked his passion and stirred his body with a fire that made him leap to his feet.

"I . . . I don't know what to say," he told the sheriff, eager to run to Grace, to take her in his arms, to shout to the world his great joy. Never in a hundred years would he have imagined such an answer to his desperate prayer. He no longer had to bear this horrible pain of loss, of confusion, of loneliness. He didn't have to run off with Grace or tempt her to sin. She was already his.

His wife. They were married.

Monty grabbed the desk to steady himself as the truth slapped him. Grace knew. She'd known all this time. Of course. From the moment he walked into town, when he stepped foot in the dress shop where she worked . . . Oh, poor Grace. She had borne this terrible secret and never said a word to him. But how could she have said a thing? He'd married another woman. He'd forgotten her. What pain he'd caused her!

"I see this is quite the shock," the sheriff said, his words startling him. Monty had forgotten the sheriff was in the room with him.

Monty looked at him. "I'm starting to remember." He held his head and gulped. "This is . . . unbelievable. But it's true—all of it. I am Montgomery Cunningham. I grew up in Chicago. Then I went to college to study geology in Illinois with John Powell. I was on the geological survey of Yellowstone with Ferdinand Hayden."

Monty shook his head, the memories now washing over him, one after another, like rapids in a river, but these waves caressed and soothed him as each memory fell into its rightful place. "I need to go—" He couldn't wait to tell Grace! And Ben . . .

Tears squeezed out of his eyes as he realized Ben was his precious son—the one he and Grace had made together in love and whose arrival into this world he had eagerly awaited. No wonder Ben had felt so wonderful in his arms. Ben was his baby! He had a son—a son! His heart soared with boundless elation. He made for the door.

The sheriff stood and stayed him with his hand. "I told you I had some bad news."

Monty stopped and turned around. His stomach flip-flopped What could possibly be bad? Grace and Ben were safe, back in town. They were his, and no one could ever come between him and his family again.

In silence, the sheriff led him out of the room and in through another door off the hallway. The came out into the large anteroom of the courthouse, where a dozen or so people milled around talking in excited, hushed voices.

Sheriff Love yelled above the chatter. "Please, everyone leave the room."

The townspeople looked at the sheriff, then exited out the double doors that fronted the street. As they filed out, Monty noticed three bodies laid out on tables—or more like coffins. Upon closer inspection he saw they were on blocks of ice. On the closest table lay the body of Billy Cloyd—the man the sheriff and O'Grady had dragged out of the burning cabin. The body next to Billy's was a man's, but the face was covered with a burlap sack. And then Monty's eyes snagged on the last body, set a few feet away from the other two.

The afternoon sunlight streaked in through the bank of windows, casting a soft yellow glow on Stella's face. Stella? Half a minute passed before Monty realized he was holding his breath. His mouth went dry. Stella—dead. He shook his head. She looked peaceful, as if sleeping.

"What . . . what happened? Why is she here—with these outlaws?" Maybe she'd had an accident while he was gone. But if that were the case, she wouldn't be here, on public display.

Quiet enveloped the room as the shock of seeing her here sank in. He tried to muster some sadness for her demise, but he felt nothing. "I don't understand . . ."

"Her real name's Lenora."

The sheriff let that hang in the air a few moments before he continued. "Lenora Dutton. She was Hank Dutton's wife."

Lenora. Lenora Dutton? This was . . . Stella? His Stella? Monty shook his head. How was this possible? He sifted through what he knew about her, the days and nights he'd spent with her in that ramshackle cabin near Greeley. All those lies she'd told him—about their past life in St. Louis, how they'd been engaged . . .

Anger rose up his chest and slung a noose around his neck. Why? Why had she done this to him? He knew she'd lied to him and kept his true past hidden from him.

He wrenched his gaze from her body and turned to the sheriff. "Did she have that pouch on her—when you found her?"

Love shook his head. "The clerk, Patterson, went over to your house after we'd headed up into the mountains. He'd had a hunch. Said he saw your . . . Lenora talkin' to Wymore in town jus' before they snatched Grace. He recognized her as your wife and so decided to go talk to her, see what she knew about the outlaws. He found that pouch at your homestead."

Monty stared, unblinking, as this bit of information sank in. All this time—the key to his past had been under his very nose. Hidden by his lying cheat of a wife. Stella—*Lenora*—had been responsible for Grace's kidnapping. Now he understood. He rubbed a hand across his forehead. How had he been so gullible? So stupid?

Yet, if he hadn't married Stella, he'd never have come to Fort Collins and found Grace. He might even have died along the banks of the Platte.

He closed his eyes and prayed. *Lord, you sure work in mysterious ways. But you answered my prayers—every last one of them. And for that, I'm eternally grateful.*

"What we figure is that Dutton's widow left Denver City last year—May sixteenth is when Hank Dutton was hanged. She headed north, to fetch that gold her husband had stashed up in the mountains, at that cabin. And on her way, she chanced upon you—"

"I had an accident."

"That's what Patterson told me. Grace had told him you'd been swept down the Poudre. You probably hit yer head on somethin'."

Monty nodded. "When I awoke, Stella was at my side. She told me I slipped and fell. That we were engaged to be married. I was badly hurt, and she nursed me back to health. She told me we'd come from St. Louis and intended to marry and settle in Fort Collins."

"No doubt she planned to bide her time, hidin' out, waitin' for Wymore and Cloyd to git caught or killed, then figured she'd get the gold and take off somewhere. She was jus' usin' you for a cover." The sheriff then went on to detail everything that happened at the cabin after Monty had left to rescue Grace on the mountain, including how Wymore had shot Stella—*Lenora*—when she was digging up the gold. When Eli and LeRoy had told their tale at the breakfast table this morning, they'd left out a lot.

"She told me my name was Malcolm Connors." His gaze drifted back to her body as he thought about his initials etched on his surveying instruments. She'd used those to give weight to her lies. He shook his head, dizzy from the realizations that assailed him.

He blew out a long shaky breath. "Well, Sheriff, this all comes as quite a shock. An outlaw's wife . . ."

"There's no way you'd have known. I didn't even know Dutton had been married until this morning." He nodded at the body. "But I s'pose this takes care of one big problem—you now only have one wife, not two. I imagine Grace will be happy to get you back." He gave Monty a big grin. "That's a lot of secret for a woman to keep. She never told you?"

Monty shook his head, suddenly remembering all the times Grace had seemed about to confess something important to him. "No, she never did. But I know why."

Sheriff Love merely nodded. "My wife told me some of the gossip going around about Grace. Folks claimed she'd made up the story about a husband who'd been carried off in a flood, hoping to inspire pity from charitable folks. Meant to cover the shame of her bein' pregnant with an illegitimate child—"

"He's not illegitimate," Monty retorted. "He's mine. My son."

Monty froze. Ben was his son, *his* baby. Grace had given birth to him while her husband lay in the arms of an outlaw's wife. He groaned at the thought of Grace going through her difficult ordeal all by herself, without him there by her side to help her through it. To be there to welcome Ben into the world.

More tears filled his eyes. He recalled asking her the baby's name the day of the tornado. She'd told him she'd named him after her brother, Benjamin. Back at the boardinghouse, Grace had told him the story of how her parents and her little two-year-old brother had died of cholera, and how her aunt had then raised her—oh, how the sad story had rent his heart. Monty remembered assuring her the day her aunt Eloisa lay dying, when he'd returned from his latest expedition intent on marrying her, that she'd never be alone again. How he'd take care of her from now on, forever. And then he'd broken that promise—granted, by no fault of his own. Yet guilt still chewed at his gut for having abandoned her. And she had come here, to Fort Collins, and waited for him to walk into town. She had never given up hope. Even when she saw he'd forgotten her . . .

He let the tears fall down his face, not bothering to swipe them away. The sheriff stood in respectful silence a moment, then patted him twice on the shoulder, gave him an understanding smile, then left the room, allowing Monty time to sort through his warring emotions.

When his tears were spent and those emotions settled into their places of rest, a calm also settled in—like fog spilling down over the Rockies onto the wide-open Front Range. It coated his heart with a warm blanket of peace, for it was time.

Time to reclaim both his past and his loving, ever-hopeful wife.

He strode to the double doors of the courthouse and pushed them open, the warmth of a genial summer breeze brushing his face. Rarified mountain air fragranced with wildflowers and cut grass filled his nostrils. He stopped for a moment on the planked boardwalk and searched the elated crowd for Grace, then spotted her sitting on a bench, Ben—*his son*—standing and bouncing on her lap as she talked animatedly to her friend Clare.

With a smile so wide he thought it might crack his face, he bounded down to the street, eager to fill his aching, empty arms.

Chapter 33

"I'M SO RELIEVED YOU'RE ALL right," Clare said, taking Ben from Grace and cradling him in her arms. Ben sang and blabbered in her ear, and Grace laughed. Oh, how freeing it felt to laugh when she'd thought she never would again.

Ben pushed back with his hands and with a serious look on his cute round face said to Clare, "Mama, mama, mama."

Clare chuckled and tickled his cheeks. "I'm not your mama. I'm Clare. Say 'Clare.'"

"Mama, mama, mama!"

Clare ruffled Ben's hair. "I guess that's the only word he's learned so far."

Grace shrugged. "I can't get him to say anything else." She kissed Ben's cheek, and he squirmed in delight.

"Someday he won't like those kisses," Clare said, tickling Ben under the arms.

Grace sighed and took in the sight of her precious healthy baby boy. "I'll rue that day. I hope he'll always want kisses from his mama."

Clare's expression turned serious. "I know you probably don't want to talk about what happened. When I heard you'd been kidnapped—" She paused and pinched her lips together. "I'm just glad they found you in time."

Grace nodded. She would tell Clare the whole dreadful tale someday. But right now, she just wanted to feel the warm sun on her shoulders and revel in her freedom. But where was Monty? She'd caught a glimpse of him entering the sheriff's office. Maybe the sheriff needed him to make a statement.

She kept trying to think of how she would tell him all the things she wanted to say to him. And everything she came up with led her back to the same questions: What would he do? Would he believe her?

What if she could never prove they'd been married? Then Monty would never leave Stella, for he was an honorable, God-fearing man. Even though he'd kissed her, she could never expect him to sin against God. And it would be wrong for her to press him. What would happen if she told him about their marriage—and that Ben was his baby—and he thought she was lying?

Yet, anyone could see Ben's resemblance to his father. He had his father's chin and jaw. Even the one hazel eye. How could Monty look at his son and not see she was telling the truth?

Grace's gut soured with worry. Had he only declared his love to her up in the mountains in a moment of passion and relief in the aftermath of his near-death ordeal? Or did he truly love her? Did he love Stella more? If he did, why had he risked his life and joined the posse?

She should just go home, back to the Franklins'. She wondered if they were all right; she didn't spot them here in the crowd. If Monty wanted to see her, she supposed he knew where to find her. Maybe after he'd had some time to recover from his new head injury, she would find the nerve to talk to him. If she could get him away from Stella. Oh, this was all so complicated and disheartening.

She stood and reached for Ben.

"Where are ya goin'?" Clare asked, still cuddling Ben. "You're not still thinkin' of leavin' town now, are ya?" Clare narrowed her eyes at Grace in a playful way. "Ya still have to make my weddin' dress—or have ya forgotten?"

Grace smiled, but her heart felt heavy and her limbs weak. "I've not forgotten," she said. "Maybe tomorrow we can—"

Her words stuck in her throat as she caught sight of Monty hurrying down the street toward her, his face lit up like a Christmas tree.

"Monty!" Grace called out. Clare looked at her in surprise when she said his name.

He descended upon her in a whirlwind of joy, causing the breath to whoosh from her lungs. He swung her up into the air with his strong arms, then pulled her into his chest. She sucked in a shocked breath as he searched her eyes, as if looking long and hard for something he had lost.

"Grace, oh, Grace," he murmured, drinking her in. Grace's blood ignited with desire as he stroked her cheeks, which had flushed in embarrassment at all the eyes turned toward them.

"Monty, I . . . I . . ."

Before she could finish her sentence, he smothered her words with his mouth, and kissed her deeply and passionately, pressing her close and wrapping his arms around her. Grace heard shocked gasps and whispers erupt around her, but she didn't care. All she wanted was to feel Monty's lips on hers, the heat of his skin, his hands claiming her as his own.

After his long amorous kiss, he pulled back and smiled at her—with the same smile that had won her heart so many years ago. It was a smile full of unbridled love, running free and wild, like an untamed river. Like a herd of wild horses running roughshod over her heart.

"Grace," he said breathless, in a whisper, his eyes wide with astonishment. "I remember."

She stepped back, trembling. "What? Monty, what do you remember?" The question hung pregnant in the air between them, and her pulse throbbed in her throat.

He laid a hand on her cheek and said, "Everything, Grace. I remember *everything* . . ."

"Oh, Monty!" Grace threw herself back into his arms and sobbed into his chest. She heard Clare's voice. Then Eli's, and even Tilde's. The voices blended together into a murmuring river that flowed past her ears and left her untouched. For she stood upon a rock above the noise and roar of the crowd, in this sacred place of refuge, in her husband's arms, and nothing now could hurt her ever again.

He released her and reached into his trousers pocket, then pulled out a folded piece of paper.

"Here," he said, handing it to her.

Grace questioned him with her eyes, but he merely nodded for her to read it.

She gasped. It was their marriage certificate. She looked closer and ran her finger across her partially smeared name.

"This . . . this is our marriage certificate. The *original.*" How could it be? "Monty, this was in your satchel—the one you were wearing when you fell into the river."

He nodded. "Stella had it—hidden in the house. With a stack of your letters." He paused, then added, "And this . . ."

He reached again into his pocket, and then opened his hand to show her.

Her wedding band lay in his palm.

As the tears poured down her cheeks, her heart bursting with joy, Monty slipped the ring on her finger—back where it belonged. She held up her hand and stared at it, incredulous. She never thought she see her ring again—and not on her finger.

"I love you, Grace Cunningham. I always have, and I always will." He cupped her head in his gentle hands. Then he turned to Clare, who Grace only now noticed was crying and sobbing in joy, standing beside her, with Eli next to her, a simpering grin pasted on his face, his arm entwined in hers.

From the corner of her eye, she spotted Tildie and Charity, staring in shock at the spectacle unfolding before them. Grace smiled, imagining what they must be thinking, seeing her in Monty's arms. No longer would anyone in town claim she had made up the story about her lost husband—or call Ben an illegitimate child.

Monty held out his arms, and Clare deposited Ben into them. Ben flung himself at his father and grabbed Monty's face with his little hands.

Grace cried at the sight of Ben laughing and pinching Monty's cheeks. Oh, it was too wonderful, the sight of father and son laughing together—only hours after they'd both nearly drowned.

"That's your papa," Clare told Ben. The baby turned and looked at her, attentive and curious. "Say, 'papa,'" Clare instructed.

Ben gave a big toothy smile and turned to Monty. "Papa!" he shouted. "Papa, papa, papa!"

Grace gasped in delight, and Clare swiveled to her. "See," she told Grace. "He was just waiting for the right time to say his next word."

Grace looked at Monty, whose face radiated with rapturous joy and delight in his son. Monty said, his eyes riveted on his baby, "That's the sweetest word I've ever heard."

"Eli," LeRoy yelled over the crowd from the direction of the courthouse. Grace turned with the others as LeRoy ran over to them, holding on to the wide brim of his black hat, his eyes excited in a way Grace had never seen before.

"You're not gonna believe this," he said, then looked at Monty and shut right up.

"What?" Clare asked, as Eli narrowed his eyes at him.

LeRoy glanced at the expectant faces, then cleared his throat and said to Monty, "It's about . . . Lenora."

"Lenora?" Clare asked. "Who's she?"

Grace waited for LeRoy to explain, but he only shared an unspoken thought with Monty. Odd.

"I already know," Monty told LeRoy, his face shifting into a somber expression. "But Grace doesn't."

"Know what?" Grace asked, her heart racing. Something bad had happened, but what could it be?

"Grace," Monty said quietly, Ben hoisted in his arms, "let's walk."

Monty nodded at LeRoy, and as soon as she and Monty were out of earshot, walking down College Avenue toward Maple and the Franklins' house, she glanced back and saw her friends talking in a close huddle in all seriousness.

As they walked, Monty had his arm wrapped around her but said nothing, his thoughts seeming far away, and she recalled the day the tornado had swooped down on them—not all that long ago.

Although, it seemed years ago. So much had happened in the last week, her head reeled trying to sort it out. Even though she'd slept the sleep of the dead last night at Whitcomb's ranch, overcome by exhaustion and relief, she could now hardly keep her eyes open. Yet she couldn't bear the thought of returning to her little room in the Franklins' house and closing the door behind her, leaving Monty to go home to Stella.

He wouldn't now, though, would he? No, of course not. But what would Stella do when she discovered Monty had learned the truth about her deceit? When she learned his memory had returned? Would she retaliate? Grace wouldn't put it past Stella to do something awful.

Then, Grace stopped suddenly her heart pounding. She looked at Monty. "It's about Stella, isn't it? She had something to do with my kidnapping." Grace's mind raced. Was it possible? Did Stella hire the outlaws to kidnap her—just to get rid of her and Ben? But why would she do that? Then she remembered Billy and Clayton arguing about a woman named Lenora, and how Lenora wanted Grace dead.

"Lenora is Stella . . ." Grace muttered, more to herself than to Monty.

She looked into his face, and his eyebrows raised. "Yes, she is. Or . . . was."

Grace's hand flew to her throat. "Was?"

Monty's face clouded over. "She's dead. She came to the cabin to get the gold, hoping the posse would kill Wymore and Cloyd first, getting them out of her way. But Wymore shot her—after he ran out of the cabin. After he stabbed Cloyd." He fell silent, letting her think on his words.

Grace was speechless. Stella was dead.

"Lenora's surname was Dutton. She was married to Hank Dutton, the leader of the gang. He was hanged last year in Denver City. Then she rode north and found me unconscious on the bank of the river. She told me she was my fiancée and that we'd come from St. Louis." Monty looked apologetic. "She told me my name was Malcolm Connors."

Grace nodded and swallowed past the lump in her throat. "And you had no reason to disbelieve her."

He took her hands in his and faced her. "If she hadn't found me, Grace, I never would have found you," he said, then stroked her cheek. "Likely I would have died, or else ended up wandering off somewhere, picking a name for myself, settling into a town and working at some odd job or other."

When she didn't say anything, he touched the pendant hanging from her neck and looked at it. "I remember telling you not to lose hope, when I left you by the river that day—when you lost me. And you held on to hope and didn't let go. I'm grateful for that, Grace." He leaned in and kissed her long and passionately, then Ben grabbed her hair and pulled.

"Papa! Papa! Papa!"

Monty laughed as Grace untethered Ben's little hand from her hair. "He sure is a happy baby," he said.

"He's just glad to finally have his pa." She put a finger on Monty's lips, and he kissed it. "And I am too."

"And I also told you not to worry—that the Lord would make a way. And even though it seems an odd sort of way of bringing us back together, well, here we are," he said, the love burning like a hot fire in his eyes.

Grace looked up the street at the house she'd been living in for more than a year. It had never felt like home—no place ever would without Monty. She then recalled what Sarah Banks had told her—

about how she'd have to go over the falls to get to the calm, quiet pool, where everything would be restored to her. And where all her pain and suffering would flow out to the sea. Grace luxuriated in the calm place of restoration, feeling renewed, reborn. Washed clean of her pain and grief.

"Let's go talk to the Franklins—tell them the news," Monty suggested. He pulled her in close again, and she wondered at the sparkle in his eyes. "You know that man Marcus Coon—who rode partway into town with us—the one who rode with the posse to save you? He has a fine hotel in Fort Collins. How 'bout we have dinner in his restaurant and stay in his finest suite? Leave Ben with Clare for the night. Have ourselves something like a second honeymoon—since our first got a bit waylaid." He gently cupped her cheek, then let his hand wander down her neck. Grace shuddered at his sensual feathery touch, so full of promise.

"Whatcha think about that, Mrs. Cunningham?"

Grace's pulse raced, imagining the long-awaited night of passion ahead of her. The love inside her swelled and overflowed the banks of her heart, and she joyfully let it sweep her away.

"I like it just fine, Mr. Cunningham," she said. "It's all I could ever hope for."

Chapter 34

Two months later
August 2, 1876

THE GRANDSTANDS AT PROSPECT PARK were packed with gaily dressed townsfolk and visitors from parts far and wide—a jubilant crowd whose loud discourse made it hard for Grace to hear what Clare was saying to her.

"Let's get closer," Clare said, tugging on Grace's arm and jostling her parasol that blocked out the hot summer sun. "I want to hear the mayor's speech."

Grace turned and shrugged at Monty, who wove through the pressing crowd behind her, Ben in his arms, working to keep up with the ladies. Eli and LeRoy marched behind him, dressed in new dark trousers and starched white tailored shirts, chatting about horses, from what Grace could tell.

How handsome Monty looked in his three-piece tan linen suit, the first time she'd seen him dressed up since they'd been reunited.

But everyone in the crowd wore their finest, and she loved the feel of the taffeta petticoats lifting her soft pale-green silk skirts as she swished ahead of Monty. Clare wore a lovely indigo-blue dress with pearl buttons that Grace had made for her, and light sparkled on the diamond engagement ring on Clare's finger.

She thought about Clare's upcoming fall wedding and was glad she would be here to celebrate with her friend. Since she'd quit her job at the dress shop, Grace had had plenty of time to work on Clare's wedding dress, as well as make Monty and Ben new clothes. She was amazed at how quickly Ben was growing—tall and strong, just like his father.

"Here's a good spot," Clare declared, stopping a dozen feet behind the raised dais upon which a large contingent of colorfully dressed musicians played brightly sounding brass instruments and booming drums, announcing the mayor's arrival upon the larger stage to the right. Mayor Ben Whedbee walked to the front of the stage and waved his arms to quiet the crowd.

Monty came alongside Grace and wrapped his arm around shoulder, careful to keep Ben's wiggly fingers out of her perfectly coiffed hair that she'd spent an hour working into pins and combs and that now sat under her feathered green felt bonnet. She looked into Monty's eyes, so grateful he'd been returned to her—along with all the precious memories they'd shared. Although, she knew that even if Monty hadn't recalled them all, he'd have never lost the deep love he held for her that was trapped in his heart. And as sad as she might have been if Monty lost those special times they'd shared, they had their whole future ahead of them to create new memories. All that mattered was that they were together again, finally. She'd held on to hope, and the Lord had made a way.

"Ladies and gentlemen. Visitors to Fort Collins, I welcome you on this very grand and special day for the great state of Colorado!"

The mayor raised his arms as deafening cheers erupted from the hundreds of onlookers. Grace looked at the radiant faces around her, and felt the hope and pride surge in ripples across the crowd. Eli stood with his arm entwined with Clare's, LeRoy next to him, and they all listened in rapt attention as the mayor recounted a brief history of Colorado Territory and its entrance into the union the day prior—as the thirty-eighth state.

"We stand upon the threshold of a new era," the mayor yelled out to the crowd in the sweltering heat of the summer morning, his voice amplified by the large megaphone stationed before him. "This new great state of Colorado with its 150,000 citizens has a prosperous future ahead. Gone are the days of war, of perilous danger on the Front Range. With the advent of the railway, thousands more are flocking to Colorado—and to our quiet little town of Fort Collins—seeking a new life, new hope. And here they will find it . . ."

As the mayor spoke under a clear blue sky, cheers erupted amid blasts of triumphant music from the band.

Grace caught a glimpse of Monty from the corner of her eye. He was smiling broadly and listening, nodding his head. Grace thought about the ordeal they'd been through over the last year, and already the pain and heartache was fading into the past. Their love had been challenged by every possible tragedy and danger, yet it had not only survived but thrived.

She rested a hand on her flat stomach and smiled, knowing soon she wouldn't be able to fit in any of her dresses or skirts—presently her little secret. She would have to get back to her sewing, even though she'd been too busy decorating their new brick house in town, which they'd purchased partly from the money Monty had saved from working, with the rest coming from the unexpected boon of nearly two thousand dollars given them as part of the reward for the capture of the last two members of the Dutton Gang. Another five hundred had been found in Stella's—*Lenora Dutton's,* she corrected—bags that had been tied to her horse's saddle the day she'd ridden off to meet with the outlaws. *The day she'd planned to have me and Ben murdered,* Grace reminded herself with a twinge of ire.

But she harbored no ill feelings for Lenora, for, as Monty said, if it hadn't been for her actions, Grace would never have seen Monty ever again. She wondered what kind of childhood had made Lenora turn out so selfish and greedy, which made Grace grateful that her loving aunt had raised her and given her a home after her parents died. She was blessed to have had such an upbringing. And now, she could give Ben the very best. Not just a comfortable pretty house in a sweet Western town with a brand-new schoolhouse. More than that—more than anything the town had to offer—Ben had his father to raise him and teach him how to be honorable, kindhearted, and faithful. And with Monty as a father, she knew Ben would grow to be an upstanding man of God. She was so glad she wouldn't have to raise her boy to bear the hurtful gossip and mean names he might have been called had she raised him alone.

Grace smiled as she recalled Charity's shocked face when she heard the story Monty told her that morning they'd come into town after their ordeal. The Franklins had listened in horror as Monty recounted the perils they'd endured in the mountains, and how the outlaws had been killed. Grace had chuckled thinking of all the grist for the gossip mill Monty was giving Charity Franklin. But she didn't care. Charity and Tildie and all the busybodies of Fort Collins could gossip all they liked. Their words would just slide over her head, like the waves of a river over smooth rocks.

Eli wormed his way over to Grace's side while the mayor continued his speech. He had to practically yell to be heard.

"Ma wants us all to come over for supper after the celebration. She's fixin' her special prairie stew." He wiggled his eyebrows. "And she wants to see that baby of yours again, Grace." He made a funny face that she couldn't quite interpret. And then he added, "She's been remindin' me how long she's been waitin' for some grandbabies. Maybe if she sees yours more often, she'll lay off houndin' me."

Monty chuckled and Grace said, "She's not the only one who'll be hounding you for babies. You know Clare wants a passel of them."

Eli threw back his head and groaned. "Well, so long as she takes care of all the laundry and feedin', I'm fine with it. It'll be fun teachin' those rascals how to ride and rope."

"If they turn out anything like *Clare*, they'll be fine riders," Monty said evenly, not a hint of mirth on his face.

Eli gave Monty a playful slug. "Thanks a lot, pal."

Monty laughed. He and Grace had watched the team roping at the Greeley One Hundred Grand centennial celebration last month, and they had been astonished at Clare's riding ability. But who wouldn't be? She beat out all the competitors for every blue ribbon, wearing her "Calamity Jane" leather jacket and fringed skirt. The cowboys were none too pleased either, but Clare didn't care, and Eli gloated over her like he'd won the best prize of all. And he had. He'd won Clare's heart.

"I brought the big wagon to town—so's we kin all ride together back to the ranch after this here mayor finishes speakin'," Eli said. "How's that sound?"

Monty questioned Grace with a look. She nodded, thinking back to Sarah's disturbing pronouncements. How she'd told Grace not to give up hope, and then told her sons to go find the Fort Collins sheriff and offer their help. She warned them there'd be danger, and how right she was. Yet, they hadn't hesitated to risk their life to save her—a woman they hardly knew.

Grace looked over at Eli and LeRoy, and another surge of gratitude filled the well of her heart. Not many would risk their lives to save someone they loved, and even fewer for someone they barely knew. Sarah's sons were men of great integrity, courage, and honor.

She glanced at Monty, who caught her gaze and squeezed her closer. *But no man has greater courage and honor than this one—my sweet, dear Monty.* She recalled how he'd dived into the river without a second of hesitation upon seeing Ben floundering. He'd had no thought for his own safety. This was the Monty she'd fallen in love with, and even though he'd forgotten his past, the tragedy that had erased his memories had not erased the man and all he was. Another thing to thank the good Lord for.

She sent up yet another prayer of thanks to heaven, picturing it floating skyward on the light breeze that drifted across the wide-open rangeland. From where she stood, she saw the miles and miles of prairie with its prickly pear cactus and dry, untamed land that herds of wild horses and miles of wild rivers crossed unhindered. She pictured the thousands of people who would pour into Fort Collins in upcoming years on shiny new locomotives, smokestacks puffing steam into the bright Colorado air with the majestic snow-capped Rocky Mountains glistening in the distance.

She hadn't wanted to come west, she recalled. Monty had spent weeks convincing her a wonderful new life awaited them on the Front Range. If they'd stayed back in Illinois, none of the tragic things they'd endured would have befallen them.

Yet, if they hadn't come out west, they wouldn't be standing here now, their love so greatly deepened, their ordeals having entwined their hearts even tighter together—such that Grace couldn't imagine anything in heaven or on earth that could ever tear them asunder. And she never would have met Clare and Eli and LeRoy. Or Marcus Coon and Sheriff Love and his deputies, who had risked their lives to save her.

She'd worried that the West was full of dangerous, hurtful characters—and it was. She'd found Fort Collins to be a town full of small-minded, insensitive gossipers. But it was also a place filled with unselfish people who wanted nothing more than to live in peace with their neighbors and treat them with kindness and respect. She was proud to be a citizen of the burgeoning new town of Fort Collins. She looked forward to raising her children here, knowing the West had more to offer than tornados, outlaws, avalanches, and floods.

For it offered hope. And when you held on to hope, nothing and no one could wrest it from your grasp. It anchored you against all the raging elements that sought to sweep you away.

The band suddenly struck up a loud Sousa march, and the hundreds of citizens in the crowd let out loud cheers, the men throwing their hats in the air and the children dancing around in joy.

A man pushed through the crowd toward her, and Grace recognized Alan Patterson, the shy courthouse clerk. A week or so after Grace and Monty had reunited, Sheriff Love had told them how Mr. Patterson had found the satchel that contained their papers and Grace's wedding ring. Through his caring effort, they'd learned Stella's true identity. Grace had gone over to the courthouse and thanked the clerk for his kindness, and he'd flustered at her gratitude. He was yet another kind neighbor she'd come to value.
"Mr. Patterson," Grace said warmly, "so good to see you." Monty shook the clerk's hand, and the two men exchanged pleasantries.

"A momentous occasion, isn't it?" Alan said to them, gesturing to the stage, where the band played one lively march after another. Some of the townsfolk now headed back to their wagons and horses, men chatting together in amiable conversation and women with colorful bonnets and parasols tending to their children and babies. Others congregated around the long tables full of platters of food behind the stage. Grace caught sight of Charity speaking to Tildie, the women's eyes riveted on Monty as he hoisted Ben up on his shoulders. When they spotted her staring at them, they pasted on neighborly smiles and stopped speaking. Grace chuckled and turned her attention back to Alan.

"It is quite the historic moment," Grace answered. "Now that Colorado is a state in the union, it doesn't feel all that wild anymore."

"Oh no?" Monty asked, his eyebrows raised, as if he meant to remind her of all they'd been through in the last year. Ben bounced excitedly on his father's shoulders, and Grace was grateful her baby hadn't suffered from the trauma of kidnapping and near drowning and deadly exposure up in the mountains. She sighed. She had so much to be grateful for.

"Huh," Grace said in a tease. "It feels downright civilized to me." She turned to the clerk. "What do you think, Mr. Patterson? Has the wild gone out of the West in Colorado?"

"Not by a long chalk, Mrs. Cunningham." He added, "But it's a start. Once the railroad comes into town, I reckon Fort Collins will become the gem of the West. Not a whole lot o' places prettier than this spot on God's green earth."

His gaze shifted to the pristine white-topped mountains west of the park that ran north and south as far as Grace could see, fronted by amber fields of undulating wheat. It truly was a breathtaking sight—one she would have never witnessed had she remained in flat Illinois. Although, after her horrific ordeal, she'd content herself with staying on the Front Range and gazing at the beautiful Rockies from afar.

"It's a new beginning for this territory," Alan said. Then he gave Grace a sweet knowing look. "And new beginnings are full of hope."

A pretty pert young woman in a bright yellow-and-brown calico dress walked up and stood beside Mr. Patterson, holding two tall glasses of lemonade in her hand. She offered one to him and said in a Southern drawl, "Alan, here you are. I wondered where you'd gone off to." She entwined her arm around his, her action causing the clerk's cheeks to instantly redden.

"Thank you, Marylu." His voice faltered as he made introductions, and perspiration dribbled down the sides of his face.

"Alan, I've fixed you a plate of food," Marylu said, tugging gently on his arm. "Nice meetin' y'all."

Alan gave Grace an embarrassed smirk and tipped his hat at her. "I wish you all the happiness in the world." He looked over at Monty and nodded, and Grace could tell he was sincere. She chuckled as Marylu practically dragged the clerk toward the food tables, yet she could tell Alan was sweet on the girl. She was happy for him.

Clare came over and took Ben from Monty's arms, then swirled him around. Ben squealed in delight under a beautiful, shimmering blue sky. Monty then pulled Grace in close and planted a long, sweet kiss on her lips. He leaned back and looked into her eyes, snagging her heart.

"I'm glad we moved into town," he said. "I've had enough rivers to last a lifetime."

Grace chuckled. "You've lost your thrill for adventure?" She couldn't picture Monty content to sit around town and not go off exploring the wilds of the West.

"Are you kidding? Life with you is the greatest adventure I could ever have." He added under his breath, "And I mean to live it to the full."

Grace pulled him in close and smelled a whiff of his cologne as he pressed his clean-shaven cheek against her neck and sprinkled her skin with hot kisses. Her heart skipped at the touch of his lips.

"I certainly hope so," she whispered back, holding him tightly and reveling in his strong, muscular arms encircling her. "I expect nothing less."

ACKNOWLEDGMENTS

I AM GRATEFUL FOR THE support and encouragement from so many. A heartfelt thanks to Marylu Tyndall for reading and instructing me in this genre that she knows so well. As always, her insights and edits were tremendously helpful. Thanks also to Pamela Walls, whose loving and supportive spirit got me through many difficult days.

A special thanks to my cover designer, Ellie Searl, of Publishista.com, for her great help and patience in creating the beautiful look of this book, inside and out.

I appreciate the assistance from Deni La Rue, Larimer County community information manager, and Lesley Drayton, archivist and director of the local history archive at the Fort Collins Museum of Discovery. Their resources and research helped me infuse my novel with authentic details.

Having lived in Greeley, Fort Collins, and other places along the Front Range for years, delving into the historical aspects of the region was enlightening and entertaining. My husband is to be thanked for many of the great plot ideas and his support and patience as I wrote long hours into the night. All those Westerns he made me watch with him over the years sparked my love for this genre (and gave us endless hours of entertainment).

NOTE FROM THE AUTHOR

IN MY DESIRE TO BRING the Western town of Fort Collins to life, I took many liberties in creating my characters. A goodly number of them are real historical people—such as Sheriff Eph Love and A. H. Patterson, Larimer County Clerk—and the historical data on them is practically nonexistent. I spent a lot of time researching the lives of these colorful characters who were foundational in the establishment of Fort Collins as a booming Western town.

I also attempted accuracy in the description of this town and region where I'd live for a number of years and which I enjoyed immensely. I chose this decade (1870s) to write about because it was a pivotal time for Colorado—a time when this wild and untamed territory was ushered into the "modern" era with the coming of the railroad and with achieving statehood in the year of the centennial (hence, why Colorado is called the Centennial State). In *Colorado Promise,* I wanted to note the plight of the Indians, who had been whisked off to other states, onto reservations, to make way for white settlers to take hold of the land. By the mid-1870s, most of the native tribes, as well as the herds of buffalo, were gone from Colorado Territory. A rich piece of this county's history was fading away, and I wanted to capture it at a time before it vanished altogether.

Often in romance novels, historical accuracy is sacrificed on the altar of telling a love story. But I believe most readers appreciate attention to detail and want to get a sense for a place and what it was like long ago. I am greatly inspired by the prolific writer Zane Grey, whose sweet novels (especially *Riders of the Purple Sage*) showcased not only beautiful descriptions of the lands his characters roamed but showed me the heart of romance stories—which are filled with tenderness and inner conflict without needing to cross the line into excessive physical detail.

I hope you enjoyed this foray into Fort Collins's past, and will watch for the next full-length novel in the series, *Colorado Dream.* I also plan to release a novella—*Wild Horses, Wild Hearts*—which will share the story of how Eli and Clare met. Following that will be the next trilogy in the Front Range series, set in Wyoming.

Be sure to read *Colorado Promise*—you can buy it on all online venues as an ebook or on Amazon in print.

~ Charlene Whitman

About the Author

Charlene Whitman spent many years living on Colorado's Front Range. She grew up riding and raising horses, and loves to read, write, and hike the mountains. She attended Colorado State University in Fort Collins as an English major. She has two daughters and is married to George "Dix" Whitman, her love of thirty years. *Colorado Hope* is her second Historical Western Romance novel. If you missed the first best-selling novel in the series, *Colorado Promise,* you can purchase it online at any online venue.

If you enjoyed this book . . . One of the nicest ways to say "thank you" to an author is to leave a favorable review on Amazon! I would be appreciative if you would take a moment to do so! Thanks so much!

Comments? Questions? I love hearing from my readers, so feel free to contact me via my Facebook page: Charlene Whitman, Author, or e-mail me at charlwhitman@gmail.com.

Made in United States
Troutdale, OR
11/28/2023